Heat of the Fire

Heat of the Fire

Where Heroism, Love, Deceit and Affluence are all consuming

Alan Lazzari

Library of Congress Control Number:		2007908264
ISBN:	Hardcover	978-1-4257-6839-3
	Softcover	978-1-4257-6824-9

This book was printed in the United States of America.

To order additional copies of this book, contact:
Xlibris Corporation
1-888-795-4274
www.Xlibris.com
Orders@Xlibris.com
40170

HEAT OF THE FIRE is dedicated to every emergency worker who, for the good of others, is not afraid to put themselves in harm's way no matter where he or she has chosen their honorable profession. Let the men and woman of FDNY represent the true commitment of how all emergency workers need to respond.

On September 11, 2001, firefighters, with bravery and valor, ascended the stairs of the Twin Towers, knowing they were walking straight up the stairways of hell. They knew this was far more than just a "job"—you could see it in their eyes; it was etched on their faces. These extraordinary people knew, yet they did their job because that's what they signed up to do.

This was a true act of bravery performed by real firefighters under extraordinary conditions. May their spirits live on and their commitment long overshadow the cowardice of some who still serve in the fire departments today.

ACKNOWLEDGEMENTS

Though an author's name appears as a lone signature to one's work, there are many others to thank in appreciation for helping to make a project successful.

I'd like to thank Joel Hochman, Joe Pawlikowski and Kerry Zukus for making this book possible. Kerry, I could not have done this without you. Thank you very much for your effort.

Mr. Robert Walker was an inspiring English teacher and superb coach for 45 years. Thank you for your dedicated service and longtime friendship, Bob. Your consultation and pre-copyediting has been invaluable.

For all the phone calls and emails they persevered, I'd like to thank my sisters, Carol and Susan for your reading and rereading chapter after chapter. You too play an important role in the success of this book.

Ellen, you played an important early roll in my original cover concept. Thank you for your concern and your professionalism.

Dawn, you've been a good friend for 12 years whom I could always count on. Thank you for your candid honesty and your never wavering support.

Xlibris Corporation, Philadelphia, Pa. is one of the cornerstones of Heat Of The Fire. Thank you, Jhoanna Mack and Rhea Villacarlos for your professional guidance. Shawna Solano and Sherwin Soy, you did an excellent job with cover design. Last but not least, Kathrina Garcia you did an outstanding job with final copyediting of the manuscript. Thank you all very much for bring this project to fruition.

Linda, thank you for your support.

Thank you to my children, you've always been my strength and I shall always love you. Thank you for staying so strong and being who you are today!

PROLOGUE

The deep blue autumn sky stood testament to the splendor of this third weekend in October. Not a cloud could be seen as the vibrant hues of red, yellow, and orange leaves glistened brilliantly in the rays of sunlight, then softly fell to the ground from the tree-lined streets of affluent Coventry. Mother Nature's own version of one final, but glorious, breath of life as trees fall dormant to the cold New England winters. A few hours earlier, the sidewalks along the town common had been busy with families dressed in their Sunday best as they sauntered from their respective places of worship. Among them a woeful woman who had cleansed her soul in purity while asking for forgiveness; surely no one suspects her licentious ways. Men repented their unscrupulous deeds of the past week while asking for absolution, now absolved for another week of work at the firm. Free of guilt, at least until tomorrow, they could enjoy their young children innocently running ahead of them to catch the falling leaves as if treasures from the sky. With Coventry's gourmet coffee shop serving freshly baked muffins and hot bagels to accompany their triple lattés and Nantucket Nectars, the short stroll down the main street was a Sunday tradition for all to enjoy.

Two hours having passed since the last church service, Coventry center was now quiet as a mouse; its only activity was that of a dozen high school kids playing their weekly Sunday afternoon game of Frisbee on the common and a few remaining cars parked outside the market just across the street from the fire department. Inside this stronghold of brotherhood were a few two-legged rats gnawing at the very foundation of honor and integrity that has stood the test of time in this honorable profession. Never could you imagine this was happening. Not in *this* town!

Tap, tap, tap, tap. Billy Slayton, who never demonstrated initiative on the job and didn't even take the exam, stood guard in the hallway while peeking through the window of the closed interior door to the day room. "Keep going," whispered Slayton as he played sentinel for Pete Brewster. After all, the fire service was just a game to him. While gripping hammer and screwdriver in hands, Brewster continued removing the pins from the hinges of the locked door that secured the chief's office. Coventry was such an idyllic New England town the chief's door probably never needed to be secure. *Tap, tap, tap, tap.*

Over the past several months, the firehouse was abuzz with newly found enthusiasm. Spirits were high, and teamwork had never been better in this department of twenty-eight men, who were divided amongst four work groups and two stations, covering fifteen square miles of some of the most prime real estate on the East Coast. Chief John Wyatt had established the first promotional exam in the department's history. After serving honorably in World War II, Chief Wyatt demonstrated his progressive leadership by turning the four-man department of "cellar savers" into a respected group of professional firefighters. Time had come for the final step to be taken in bringing this small town force into the twentieth century, and Coventry would get the leadership it desired and deserved. Men's adrenaline still ran heavy with anticipation over the outcome of this written examination several of us had taken just the day before.

Having relentlessly studied for months, my confidence was high yesterday as I calmly sat while waiting for the test proctor to announce, "You may begin." All the candidates started off briskly. However, most faded before half done as they began to fidget in their seats while grappling for answers. The oldest and most senior of the wannabe officers, Pete Brewster, looked around the room as if assessing who was flowing smoothly with little difficulty. Sitting next to Brewster, and just below him in seniority, was his fellow work group member, Tom Jacobs; he just stared at everyone in a very intimidating way as if he had daggers in his eyes. As difficult as the questions appeared to most, I seemed to have breezed along.

With the stress of the exam behind me, that evening I barbequed on the grill and enjoyed the usual family dinner with my wife, Ruth, and our three beautiful children, David, Stacy and Laura. Despite a floundering relationship with Ruth, having dinner together was a rich family value we insisted upon from the start; it was such good quality time with the kids, and it gave me an opportunity to connect with them about their day, their schoolwork, their friends, and their future. Always concluding with, "I don't want any surprises. I understand life's difficulties. If you're having any, let's talk about them so we can nip it in the bud." Laura was too young for school, so just as I had done with the other two children, I sang the ABCs to her with my own second verse, "Now I know my ABCs, let me learn my 123s." Using a do-re-mi scale from low to high, I'd sing, "One . . . two . . . three . . . four . . ." Ten would be a very high pathetic tenor and then back down the scale again, singing, "Nine . . . eight . . . seven . . . six . . ." It was fun, it was delightful, and none of them ever realized what they were learning as they waited in anticipation for their father's very poor rendition but well-aimed recital to end in a very low and drawn-out baritone voice, saying, "Zero." Despite our differences, Ruth and I had a very open relationship with our children, and they responded in kind, something that would pay off tenfold in the end.

Once the kids were settled down, I relaxed and joyfully reflected on how hard I'd studied for and how well I'd done on the promotional exam several hours earlier. It was times like this I missed having a wife I could communicate with—I could celebrate with. So instead, I sat back in my favorite chair and internalized, *I may have even topped it.* I was that confident after having completed the four-hour test. Surely no one else had put in as much time or effort. With the playing field now level, each man would have equal chance for advancement based on merit. As it turned out, this one day, this one examination would alter the course of this department for decades to come and would affect many lives.

Accomplice firefighter Tom Jacobs stared out the window of the firehouse, its apparatus doors uninvitingly closed shut on this warm fall day as if indicating Closed for Business. No Kiddy Tours Today! Jacobs's eyes darting left, then right across the near-deserted streets as he watched the falling leaves rustle in the gentle breeze. Not knowing exactly what Slayton and Brewster were up to, Jacobs stood as lookout on the first floor. "Tommy, you go downstairs on desk watch and don't worry about anything else, we'll take care of the rest," slimy little Billy Slayton said prior to beginning the threesome's loathsome activity.

With the fireman's pole being a much more versatile tool than just getting firefighters to the apparatus floor quickly, a few bangs with his ring on this shinning symbol of expedience by Jacobs would resonate to the second floor well in advance of further trouble should anyone interrupt the covert break-in. On other work groups, a few raps on the pole followed by a firefighter's holler down the pole hole, "coffee's hot!" was a useful way to communicate in this technology-challenged, turn-of-the-century building. However, this was a signal Group A, as officially recognized—the A Team, as named by others who knew their deceitful ways—used often while perpetrating firehouse pranks in the past. But this was no prank!

After checking out Captain Charles, their favorite captain, who maintained his usual position in the day room's recliner, his white shirt stretching to near-button-popping expanse with each inhalation, Billy Slayton playfully suggested to Pete Brewster, "You better remember who helped you out today." Slayton laughed a phony laugh, and Brewster cackled in vain jubilation, the portly captain's snoring preventing his sleep from surrendering to their laughter in the hallway. He was always so oblivious to his boys' devious, often-criminal activities; or he simply overlooked them, then defended his Charlie's Angels for their actions. With the beloved captain being well connected with theTown Manager and Horace Humphreys—the chairman of the Board of Selectmen—he and his boys could do no wrong in the eyes of Coventry, who collectively were just as oblivious as the captain.

On this quiet Sunday afternoon, the captain's snoring notwithstanding, the only obstacle that stood between Pete Brewster and the large brown envelope on the chief's desk containing the yet-to-be-corrected promotional exams was this locked door he was now diligently removing from its hinges. The corrupt firefighters continued their caper as their leader continued to do what he did best for over thirty years.

Three hinges, three pins. *Tap, tap, tap, tap*. Soon they were in, and their mission was accomplished!

Within ten days, the results of the exam were posted.

> "In descending order, the following candidates have successfully passed the promotional examination," read the notice.
>
> Peter Brewster
> Thomas Jacobs
> Paul Dunn
> Dominic Renaldi
>
> Signed,
> John Wyatt
> Chief of Department

Filled with excitement and a very positive feeling, I went to the station on my day off to check on the results. Bounding up the stairs two at a time, passed the pole, and into the day room, my eyes focused on the top name—Peter Brewster—then the second name on the list, Thomas Jacobs. My blood began to recede as the smile faded from my face. Finally, there it was, number four, Dominic Renaldi. I leaned my arm against the bulletin board as I lowered my head into it, my body breaking out in a cold sweat and retching as if having severe stomach cramps. Having thought I'd done better, I was very disappointed with myself. *Shocked* is probably a better word.

As Chief Wyatt passed by, he said, "Hello, Dominic," his voice interrupting the silence and sending a shiver over my body as I zoned out while shamefully looking over the exam results, reading them and rereading them in disbelief.

Somewhat recomposed, but still quite dejected, I responded with a meager, "Hi, Chief," almost embarrassed to be seen by anyone, let alone the chief of department.

"Can I see you in my office, Dominic."

"Sure thing, Chief," I said while trying to appear upbeat.

"Close the door, Dom," he said, his voice sounding a little annoyed and sympathetic at the same time.

Having followed the chief's instruction, my heart pounded as I stood on the opposite side of his desk, wondering why he had called me in behind closed doors. Surely, it was too early to appoint a new lieutenant and having apparently performed miserably, no way in hell was I any longer in the running.

The rock-solid chief spoke sternly as he looked me squarely in the eye. "Dominic, I am very disappointed in your performance on the promotional exam."

Having not only disappointed myself but also the man who has meant so much to me, I briefly winced as I first hung, then slowly shook my head. In an effort to reinflate my self-respect, I picked up my head and took a deep breath, then looked the chief right in the eye. This is how real men communicate. "I'm sorry, Chief, no one is more disappointed than me. I don't know what could have gone wrong." Continuing to shake my head from side to side, I said, "I studied day and night for months. I was ready for this test, Chief. I just don't understand how I could have blown it sooooo badly."

"Perhaps I've overestimated you, Dominic. This has thrown a real monkey wrench into my long-term plans for this department. Now I'm going to have to rethink them. That is all."

When Chief Wyatt spoke, you listened, especially when the hair on his neck stood up. I listened to that painful remark from the chief and took it on the chin without flinching. "Thank you, Chief." Closing the office door behind me as I left, I leaned against the hallway wall. As my head fell back and the pain of the chief's remarks sunk in, I wondered why I had just thanked him for admonishing me. Well-earned respect for the finest chief you'll ever meet, I guess.

Meanwhile, Slayton, Brewster, and Jacobs were in Cromwell gleefully celebrating at the Double L Steak House, as their captain proudly proclaimed, "Those are my boys who topped the exam. Group A is the best on this department!"

With the seeds of destruction from this secret, covert break-in having taken root, now seven years later, they are about to show fruition. About as much fruition as the forbidden apple in the Garden of Eden!

Hello, I am Lt. Dominic Renaldi, of the Coventry fire department, and this is my story.

Chapter 1

Entering the high school through the gymnasium/auditorium entrance, I was relieved to see such a short line. That's the one thing I hated most. Waiting in lines. I always managed to arrive at these meeting pretty early. Not only did it ensure short lines, it also ensured a good parking spot for a quick exit, and my favorite seat two thirds of the way back on the far left side of the auditorium. Precincts one and two formed one line, and precincts three and four formed another. Politely, quietly, I waited my turn in precinct 3's line. Watching the experienced women checking everybody off as they passed by, I wondered. *Why was it always the elderly who were tellers at town meetings and elections? I suppose it gives them something to do, and it does demonstrate a nice volunteer spirit in the community.* One person at a time, but efficiently, we funneled between the tables. Experienced town meeting goers were well versed in the process. Street name, street number, last name, and, finally, first name. In just a short time, I was next, "Boston Post Road" followed by a polite pause as the teller flipped to the correct page. "394," I paused again. With ruler and pen in hand the teller scrolled down the page. "Renaldi. Dominic," I concluded to the familiar face seated behind the tables, which spanned the hallway just before the gym on the left and the auditorium on the right.

The teller ran a line through my name, then, looked up over her glasses and spoke to me. "I know who you are, Dominic. You don't have to give me your name," said Mrs. Clark, who has known me since kindergarten, where her daughter and I began our twelve years of school together.

"Just making it official, you know how these meeting are." I smiled at the very pleasant woman as I continued. "Hello, Mrs. Clark. It's always nice to see you."

She smiled back, "Oh, Dominic, you're always so sweet."

Gently, I put my hand on her shoulder as I entered past her. "Thank you, Mrs. Clark. It's people like you who bring out the best in me."

After picking up a copy of the budget and town meeting warrant from the information table, then placing them on my seat, I killed some time by looking in the trophy case on the other side of the hall just outside the gym. If I wanted, I could find my name in a few locations, but it was always one picture in particular I looked at. It was our championship football team, and it was a lost friend's face I focused on.

Always with a smile, I think of my childhood friend nearly every day. My pleasant thoughts always culminate in sadness wondering why cancer had to take Neil Jefferson away from us just two weeks short of his 30th birthday. How can the lord take someone with so much to offer? Life definitely isn't fair.

Neil's passing still struck a raw nerve with me, but I could always smile at something he and I had done. This evening, I chuckled as my smile broadened and my thoughts reflected back to distant memories of a bygone time in our lives.

With the light off, we carefully descended the dark and very narrow stairs that lead to the back of the alley. "Watch out for someone coming behind us," the lead architect of the plan reminded me.

"Okay, but should we really be doing this? It's wrong, and we might get caught!"

"No. I do it all the time," said my friend who was the mastermind of mischief. "Besides, its so much fun!"

Once in position, we sprang into action, and the pins began to fall. Suddenly the light came on, and a male voice called out harshly, "Who's down there?

"Oh no! Here comes someone. Quick, Dominic, out the back door."

I didn't have to be told. As if shot out of a cannon, I was already three steps ahead of Neil. As he and I ran, we laughed an adolescent's hearty laugh. At fourteen years old, it was just innocent fun disrupting the country club's women's bowling championship. On other escapades, Neil would turn up the radios and turn on the wipers in parked cars at the club; no need to lock the car there, especially if it was a convertible with its top down! Neil and I would often burst out laughing if we were nearby on the course or sitting at the pool when suddenly a car radio would come on blaring, quickly followed by a female scream. Sometimes, a distant deeper voice could be heard, "Jefferson, did you do this?" When golf carts first came on the the scene, one night Neil wanted to steal one and take it on a joyride. That's where I drew the line. Neil and I had a penchant for innocent fun, but breaking and entering at nighttime is a felony charge. I had no interest in this and wouldn't participate. I like to think it was my unwillingness that made Neil rethink the caper because he didn't do it either.

When I was a teenager, I used to visit the Coventry Country Club as a guest of my close friend. His family had moved into a new subdivision within walking distance of my dilapidated house some five years ago. With my worn-out cut-off dungaree shorts, T-shirt, and old sneakers with holes in the sole—more hole than sole—it was easy to tell I didn't belong to the club. But Neil fit right in with his Bermuda shorts and button-down, short-sleeve shirts. He was tall, handsome, and had a wise-guy sense of humor everyone loved—well, most everyone but especially the girls.

The summertime hot spot for any teenager with entitlement was at the snack bar alongside the pool of this prestigious country club. The boys would order hamburgers and Cokes while talking to all the young ladies tanning, looking so beautiful in their two-pieced bikinis. Us lowly townies spent our time at the town pool, a large spring fed pond where nature's creatures would head for shelter once the human inhabitants invaded their space at eight thirty in the morning. It had a filtering system and a fifteen-foot deep end, which had a concrete dock, diving board, and all. Still, the "snake pit" was a pretty nice place to go and was within walking distance to the club. After tennis or golf lessons, Neil would often come down to the town pool where he and I would hook up and go off gallivanting, usually ending up back at the club.

With the likes of the Van Deusen sisters turning their noses up at me, I knew I was out of place at poolside, but what was an indigent kid living in an affluent town to do as my growing circle of friends inevitably encompassed those of privilege? So I just accepted my position in life and rolled with it. As an outstanding athlete whom the girls liked, they were polite to me. Still, while on display at the club, they couldn't show too much affection toward me; or their fathers, who could easily tell my status, would be mad at them for not paying attention to one of their own. Part of this cult-like country club ego was to make sure your daughter married into the right genes pool. After all, love doesn't really matter now, does it? Conceivably, it was my solid build and Italian heritage that made these overbearing fathers judgmental while thinking lustful sexcapade, crime, and murderous death when they checked me out. They took one look at my olive skin and told their daughters to stay away from me. On the other hand, their mothers adored me, thinking I was a genuine, polite boy who would treat their daughter with respect. Possibly, it was my sad-looking big brown eyes, which disarmed them. My female friends got sick of telling their fathers, "He's not like that at all, and he's nice!" And I got sick of fighting it! Often, we met secretly. If their fathers only knew about the moonlit walks on the golf course at ten o'clock at night! Laying on the soft grass and talking as we gazed up into the stars, we found these walks to be quite romantic. Isn't adolescent love wonderful?

Even at a young age, I sensed female instincts were much better than chauvinistic egos, and I talked to my young female friends for hours when I was invited to the club, which carried into the school year. On occasion, I'd be hassled by a young male lifeguard, Chad, who looked down on me perhaps because I beat him out in athletics before he went on to private school, and he appeared jealous of my friendships as well, which he couldn't seem to attain.

With a snicker, the little spoiled brat would ask, "What are you doing here, Renaldi, a little out of your league aren't you?" Then, he'd give me that look of privilege seeming to say, "I am so much more worthy than you. You low life." He was a perfect match for the Van Deusen sisters. Heaven forbid he should have to save anyone from drowning.

Knowing I would be ready to drop the third generation Dartmouth College bound dink on the spot, Neil would intercede by saying, "Back off, Bettencourt, he's with me." The girls would giggle at the brave lifeguard's reprove and walk away, calling him an idiot. Neil was popular in all circles, and he and I were an unlikely team that just hit it off so well.

All this was possible because of Neil's father, Ernest Jefferson, president of the Northeast Steel Company. Mr. Jefferson grew up a poor child and, while on a football scholarship, became a college all-American who turned down a professional career in the fledgling National Football League. Ernie was an avid golfer who encouraged Neil to take up golf because "It's a wonderful social sport and can be quite a useful tool in business." Mr. Jefferson, once given the chance to get to know me, liked me very much and often told Neil to give me anything I wanted at the club, thus opening the door for us to have many memorable experiences over the years.

Consequently, Neil and I played sporadic golf and tennis and spent time at the pool. In the winter months, we'd bowl in the club's two-lane bowling alley and order something to eat from the kitchen. Neil's signature on Ernie's account was all we needed. Of course, I was never allowed to attend their social events.

The dimming of the auditorium lights, and the ensuing buzz about the hallway brought me back to present day reality. The town meeting was about to begin so I took my seat. In reticence, I looked about the auditorium and silently laughed. The New England town meeting form of local government was as old as Plymouth Rock, but was it really representative of all the people? We were in an auditorium and the caste was set. That's caste, not cast. The Town Manager sat in the first seat of the front left row. This gave him easy access to and from all committees. The selectmen sat next to him. Their finance committee, whose members were "appointed by, and served at the pleasure of the selectmen," sat just behind them in the second row. The school committee sat in the front row on the right side. Seated directly behind them was the school administration. All the other town boards filled in the next several rows on either side. As the aisles filled with men in business suits and tortoise rimmed glasses, all looking like boring stuffed shirts, I couldn't help but think, *do these people ever let their guard down and become plain ordinary people?* But of course, they did have an image to uphold. The town meeting form of government was an open forum where anyone could speak. Beforehand, the Town Moderator would have been given a list of names, voters who would be speaking in support of the selectmen's position on an article. Surely, he knew them socially and they were well positioned in the audience to be easily called on at just the right time. All others were welcomed to speak after the designated speakers, but the tone would be set. People who wanted to be seen filled in behind the recognized players as they took their seats. The rest of us mere interested voters sat in the remainder of the seating toward the back. With rare exception, no other members of the fire department attended town meetings. The auditorium held five hundred people. If there were a large turnout, the overflow would gather in the gymnasium where there were observers and microphones set up in preparation. It was quite rare to have an overflow crowd. With all the committees, their spouses, and their social friends present, it was easy for a few to control the vote at most all the meetings.

The lights dimmed one final time, and shortly after, the affable Moderator called out, "The appointed hour is upon us." The annual town meeting was underway. Mr. Buckingham, who has been the moderator for years, and it was easy to see why he always ran unopposed, spoke. "I would like to caution all the speakers tonight in keeping their speeches short. Not in any way do I wish to diminish your intended point, but brevity will win you more votes than a long winded oration will." There was a light applause and laughter from all corners of the auditorium. In admiration of the man who kept these meetings flowing smoothly, I smiled warmly.

Each selectman took turns presenting the warrant articles. When it came time to present the school budget, they deferred to the school committee. Over the years I marveled at, not only their intelligence, but also, their ability to publicly speak before several hundred people while effectively making a presentation. However, one aspect I could never understand was, how could the selectmen ask the town to pass a budget without knowing what the yet to be completed bargaining negotiations with each town department would encompass? Surely, I understood goals and the parameters of fiscal constraints, but how could they possibly bargain in good faith with a set budget already in place? I did, however, understand the townspeople voting with the selectmen. They were all in the same boat, CEOs with master's degrees here, doctorates there, many were board chairmen of a variety of companies; in some quirky way, a vote against the selectmen was a vote against themselves. They expected the selectmen to know what they were doing. Besides, most were country club chums. If you wanted to stay in good graces there, you had best stick together here.

Tonight's meeting would conclude uneventfully. The local newspaper reporting, "With a light turnout of only one hundred and thirty five voters present at last night's annual town meeting, it adjourned just forty-two minutes after it began. All articles were uncontested, and passed unanimously." With the budget approved, Coventry was set for another year of business as usual.

* * *

Coventry, Massachusetts, was the wealthiest community in the Commonwealth. The elite of the elite, old New England, where the wealthy city folks had moved to escape the hustle and bustle, let alone crime and disease, a century or two ago. Where farmers could farm its rich fertile soil, and wise men bought up land. Old money and very conservative. Where visionary leadership of the 1930s created bylaws prohibiting further commercial development, thus creating a wealthy bedroom community on the western edge of metropolitan Boston. Just ten miles to the west, Coventry was blessed geographically with two major highways intersecting at its outer reaches and Boston a short jaunt away whether by train or automobile. With burgeoning neighborhoods and growing resources as new money bought its way into town, its visionary leadership now focused on creating a superb school system, quickly attaining a 99 percent graduation rate and producing college bound graduates at over 95 percent, superb by any standard.

Coventry rapidly became one of the most desirable communities in the country. In today's moneyed world, it is a wonderful place to raise a family, except that entitlement was thought to be a God-given right, or so thought by the new money.

How ironic that in the post-World War II days of the '40s and '50s, men who were unacceptable by Coventry standards—the Pizzios, the Vitalis, the D'Marcos, and other men of like origin, men who had fought bravely for *this* country—settled on the worthless and rocky land adjoining Coventry and separated from it by Route 128 in North Cromwell. A very few of these heroic men mistakenly squeezed into Coventry via property the elite found to be deplorable and undesirable, my family amongst them. Coventry men laughed at such a poor investment.

"How gauche, darling!" could be heard at the exclusive Coventry Country Club so steeped in Brahmin-silent segregation, where if you were born into the right lineage, you were granted life membership. Coventry had another country club of singular belief; Italians definitely need not apply there!

Then Route 128 became a main highway during the Eisenhower administration's plan to grid the nation for military expedience in the name of national preparedness, and the northeast United States boom was fostered. Suddenly, in the modern day version of the gold rush, the valueless rock of North Cromwell became the golden nuggets of the era; and Coventry's unacceptable men, who were forced elsewhere, sold the rock from their worthless land, which formed the base of 128, the Mass Pike Extension, Logan airport expansions, I-93, and I-95. If these "dumb guineas" hadn't become millionaires yet, surely they would when the technology boom of the '70s and '80s spurred office parks all along 128. Fortune 500 companies took advantage of the brilliant young minds of the numerous colleges and universities in and around the Boston area as venture capitalists brokered high-tech companies that flocked into these office parks with start-up computer and software companies, companies where Coventry's precocious "new money" was being made by the truckload. Entrepreneurs, CEOs, investors with their ruthless leveraging partners—to say nothing of their scoundrelous, high-profiled lawyers—all becoming wealthy off the rock piles of other men who were so ignorant as to have purchased this land after the people of Coventry didn't allow them into their town.

But beneath the thin layer of thousand dollar bills, Coventry had a negative side. Scratch the surface and smell the aroma. Despite many wonderful families, it reeked of ego, pomp, and arrogance. Where men held pride above all else. Where they couldn't see beyond the tip of their company's nose, where they measured another man's worth solely by his net assets, and where they left their lonely wives behind to fend for themselves.

Many times, I commiserated with its victims, "Coventry's most underutilized resource is its women. You're educated, intellectual, articulate, and very capable with no outlet to demonstrate your worth." Coventry women weren't Gloria Steinem "burn your bra" followers, but they rode the wave of the prevailing crusade. Believing that education would make their lives meaningful and while working hard to achieve a high level of success, they found themselves looking through a glass ceiling, which they could see but not attain. They became frustrated and floundered in the unregulated, unmandated routine of home life while living under the controlling hand of ego and arrogance. Powerless, their self-esteem plummeted. They too were pawns on their husband's chessboard, and some would succumb to the game.

Ahh, the game; achieve and maintain total control, where those in control held all the power. With power came arrogance and ego, the right to destroy anyone who stood in their way—even their wives. Don't anyone dare challenge *my* decisions no matter how wrong a decision it might be; for if you do, you will be punished severely. I don't care if you're right or not. Where being accepted by Coventry was like landing on Monopoly's Boardwalk or Park Place, where if you objected to the rules of the game and didn't buy into the ego and arrogance, you got the "go directly to jail" card with no chance to "get out of jail free!"

Surely, Coventry didn't want to open the door for minorities. During a collective bargaining session, both sides were discussing mileage limitations for how far away from Coventry a firefighter was allowed to live. With the cost of housing rising exponentially, I suggested we increase the limit from eight miles to fifteen miles from the center of town.

"If we do that, we'll be opening the door for undesirables to apply," said one member of the Board of Selectmen.

"Undesirables?" We all knew she meant minorities. I was quite taken aback by Anna Feldman's remark, and her comment was a rude awakening for me.

"We've already stretched our bottom resiliency. Do you know what I mean, Mr. Renaldi? We don't need *them* in this community. However, we understand that housing needs have changed. Why don't we just leave the contract as it is and instruct the chief to simply ignore the present constraints. Unless, of course, it's to our benefit for the chief to apply them!"

Surprised by her suggestion, I innocently countered, "We can't just manipulate a contract like that. It's unfair."

With a smile on her face, Mrs. Feldman said quite matter-of-factly, "Of course, we can."

Of all the prejudice people in Coventry, I was saddened to hear a Jewish female lawyer speaking this way. I had admired Mrs. Feldman's work on a variety of town government boards and thought she was so much better. Image is everything!

Coventry's fire department was a mirror image of the town, a classic example of "the apple doesn't fall far from the tree," where "it only takes a few bad apples to ruin the barrel."

It always made me sick to hear our bigoted and narrow-minded firemen say such things as, "We don't need no black man, we already have Renaldi." Too many times, I heard *fucking niggers*, *porch monkeys*, *dumb guineas*; or when it came to women in the fire service, I heard, "They're just dumb cunts, Renaldi. We don't need one around here, they'll only get you in trouble."

I remember one conversation in particular. One of the guys, same surname as four others on the job, who took great pride in telling everyone, "My daughter and me, we was in a check out line, and she kept staring at this spic, who was as black as the ace of spades. Finally, she said to him, 'You're funny looking!'" The whole firehouse burst out laughing, and the father took great delight in his daughter's comment. It was the 1980s, people. The 1980s!

With such redneck prejudice still entrenched in the "good ole boys" network, how could we ever expect equality to grow?

"Bullshit baffles brains," Pete Brewster often said. "Just tell them what they want to hear, give them a gold badge and make them think they're important," he said of the Board of Selectmen. With newer visionless leaders now on its board slobbering this crap up like gluttonous swines to fill their egos, all the while thinking men like Brewster and Bill Slayton were superior, the selectmen put the wrong men in power. The visionary leadership of this wonderful town was gone, and Coventry was now being controlled by ego and arrogance. I can just picture a town manager sitting at his or her desk during collective bargaining, admiring how wonderful men like Pete Brewster and Bill Slayton were. And how repulsive men like me were. With clear intuition, I could feel it deep in my bones. What lies were these gullible people being fed as their egos were being polished, and to what extent would they act upon these lies? Those who tried valiantly to alter this course would pay a heavy price. Once these double-crossing men were in position, they set out to ruin anyone with talent. To them, we were mere obstacles in the path of their game plan. Men who couldn't see beyond their bugles as they stared into the blinding glare of the gold badge they were so desperately chasing.

Capt. Pete Brewster was the weakest of these treacherous firehouse leaders. Bill Slayton, the worst, most devious predator of them all. Though not in power by title, he held complete control. Billy Slayton had the ego and arrogance. Capt. Tom Jacobs was just a very sick man, talented but a very sick man who played along in their game, his form of leadership being, "Do as I say, or I'll make life miserable for you around here!"

Slayton's personal mission statement in a disgusting perversion of an idealist young president's inspiring words was, "Ask not what I can do for my community. Ask what my community can do for me."

The only accountability Bill Slayton ever answered to was how many business cards he could hand out while issuing smoke detector certificates. "Look at my dazzling personality, am I not so wonderful?" I can do so much for you, snowplowing, landscape maintenance. I found it to be quite fitting his most successful venture was in trash collection where his customer list grew with each smoke detector approval. His men? Oh, they were left to fend for themselves back at the firehouse. "My men don't need training," Slayton would say often, a weak cover-up for his lack of technical knowledge and skills to do his job. Meanwhile, at the request of his selectman friend and while on duty, he'd use the captain's car—car 2—to give twenty-five-cent tours of the town to all the professional athletes who were moving in. Ask your newly found friends about constantly training. Ask them about preparation and learning. Often, Slayton showed up late to calls well after others had made the important decisions on the scene of an emergency. So self-centered, so incompetent! His biggest attribute being his ability to garner gifts from those rich and famous newfound friends, then flash it around the firehouse as if his own personal trophy.

AND THE CHIEF ALLOWED HIM TO OPERATE THIS WAY!

For those of us with commitment to our job and all of its possible dangers, we had to fend for ourselves, finding pride in ourselves to be ready to perform our duties at the highest levels. Fire obeys no man and follows its own rules; it's rarely convenient and can come on the worst of days in the worst of weather at the worst times of day or night. It does everything possible to assert its power, its ability to tell mere mortals, "I am devious, and I am strong. I can outthink you and outwit you. I am sly, and I am vengeful. You may strive to control me, but I will always demonstrate my rage and exact my revenge in order to remind you who is superior."

"Respect fire but don't fear it"—that was my attitude in the fire service. I became an experienced firefighter, and fire had gained my utmost respect; but if I were afraid of fire, I'd be running from it like a jackrabbit, like a Bill Slayton. *Firefighter* and *afraid* are not synonymous. Not synonymous at least to a real firefighter who constantly respects the danger and potential of his mortal enemy.

"Prepare for the worst and hope for the best," was an expression I loved to use.

If you were prepared for the worst, then you wouldn't be in shock when *the worst* confronted you. If you were confronted with *the best*, then it would be a piece of cake to handle. This would bode well for me over my thirty-two-year career.

I'm a hard-luck guy who scratched out an existence in a wealthy community, the self-described "flowering bush above the tree line with no logical reason for surviving." It seemed that the higher I climbed, the harder I got knocked down. Being acutely aware of where I'd come from, I wasn't interested in climbing to the top; all I ever wanted to do was climb to the next level. My primary mission in life was to build a good foothold for my children so *they* could climb to the top without arrogance and ego.

Coventry men looked down on me. Hell, I couldn't help them anywhere. They had nothing to gain from me, so why bother. I had no real assets. I was just their kids' coach, just their peon fireman ready and willing to risk his life for them, just the rare male school volunteer who was very well respected by faculty and staff, just their lonely wives' coffee shop friend to count on, and a good friend I was.

Coventry women found me disarming and a very good listener. Though I never understood why *charming* was often said of me. I was just being who I truly was—a caring, compassionate, and helpful person. Would a lonely Coventry woman take a friendship too far? The former female superintendent of schools used to say, "It's so refreshing speaking to you, Dominic, you're so genuine and not at all like most of Coventry."

As presumptuous as all this may seem, I had developed a keen sense for knowing what was happening to me, for feeling what was happening to me, where the pressure was coming from, and by whom it was being applied. A man can only be knocked down so much before he develops a defensive posture. Clearly, I was no angel, but by no means was I a gun slinger either. Though I was a straight shooter and, with precision accuracy, quite adept at "telling it like it is" often to my demise.

When it came to fire in the heart and soul, I was far less experienced.

Would fire strike my heart and soul where it would rage out of control? Would my lack of fear lead to severe pain? Would someone exact deepest revenge for my lack of judgment?

My fate awaits me.

Chapter 2

The chain of command in the fire department of a small town is simple. The chief is the CEO, chief executive officer. In addition to all the necessary managerial requirements, he commands the entire fire scene, or scene of emergency. Chief Wyatt was a superb commander. Second in command is the captain, who is responsible for his group of men. In Coventry, there are four captains, one each on the four work groups. Lieutenants are third in command. On our force, they usually had a captain over him and quite often took on the role of a private, ending up on an attack line as the nozzle man. The privates are below a lieutenant. In small town America, this desired chain of command was sometimes helter-skelter at the scene, especially if two of the on-duty personnel were on an ambulance call. I remember a few times the chief was on the nozzle for a short time until someone else arrived on scene. A captain or lieutenant may have to be the attending EMT in the back of the ambulance, especially if Bill Slayton was working. He became an EMT only to look good but refused to perform any direct first aid. In all the years I served, Bill Slayton has never worked on a patient in the back of the ambulance or gotten blood on his hands. In fact, Bill Slayton has broken the law by refusing to ride in the back of the ambulance while an unqualified non-EMT had to in his place. Yet again, Billy Slayton was allowed to operate this way.

Coventry fire department is a small town force with barely enough to have just two men on a truck, a far cry from the desired four men per engine and five per ladder truck. With too few fires, having four or five men on a piece was difficult to justify. We were so short of manpower when it counted the most that the pump operator would set up the pump and charge the line, then enter the building to help fight the fire. Therefore, it is vitally paramount that everyone be well trained and, without enough personnel for others to cover up one's shortcomings, be unafraid to go in and attack the fire. After all, that is the basic fire service mission: "To save life and protect property." Each man had to pull his weight and more, or you could jeopardize the lives and safety of your fellow firefighters. This was well taught at the Firefighter's Academy, which all but Slayton had attended.

Boston Post Road, the same post road where two hundred years ago, Gen. George Washington traveled while on his way to help drive the British out of Boston, was a place of many fires primarily because these houses were old and of balloon frame construction. Old wooden studs ran the full height of the building, and floor and ceiling joists sat on supports attached to these studs; unwittingly, these created a perfect draft for airflow. Today's building codes mandate house construction with built-in fire blockage to prevent this deadly path for fire to follow. This made the antique homes primed for a seriously fast-moving inferno.

During the cold and early morning hours of December 24—Christmas Eve—the height of human inconvenience, while an unsuspecting family slept, the man of the house checked the old, uninsulated, and seldom-used downstairs bathroom to the rear of the house, where he knew his son went to sneak a cigarette. And he discovered a fire in the ceiling. A fire had broken out and was now traveling in the walls of this antique house on the Boston Post Road. He immediately ran to awaken the remainder of his family before calling the fire department.

With Group A on duty, Bill Slayton, who not only wasn't academy trained but also terrified of danger, arrived with Captain Charles on the first due engine and ladder truck. The homeowner led the captain and his men to the fire's point of origin—this downstairs bathroom.

Captain Charles would take inside command while his three men began pulling hose and opening the bathroom's ceiling and outside wall in an effort to get at the fire. Already short of men to properly fight a fire, Slayton slipped away unnoticed, as always, to avoid danger. Because small town fire departments are historically hampered by this lack of manpower, they must rely heavily on off-duty personnel assisting. With a small on-call force of men to augment the permanent force, Coventry was fortunate to have three or four members living within a mile radius of the station.

I happened to be living in the oldest of these balloon-framed homes just down the street from the firehouse and arrived on the next truck. "Engine 2 to engine 1's portable," I called out.

No response.

"Engine 2 to engine 1's portable," I called out again, but no one at the scene of the fire was giving us instructions, just the wife and two daughters, who stood clad in their pajamas with blankets protecting them from the morning cold.

GOOD! I thought to myself, *they are the best Christmas presents of the season so nicely wrapped*." They'll be no rescues to have to worry about today. Thank heavens, this fire didn't occur a few hours earlier, or it may have been a different story!

"C1 to engine 2, drop a line into engine 1."

Oh good, the chief's there, was my reassuring thought. I answered back, "Message received, Chief."

Engine 2 pulled up to the hydrant with three men on the truck. The back-step man would stay at the hydrant, the driver would become engine one's pump operator after connecting the feeder line from the hydrant into its pump, and I, the third man on the piece, was left to firefight. All this was pretty much SOP (standard operating procedure) for our department, and we knew it well.

The back step man flipped the canvas cover up and pulled the feeder line from its hose bed. He wrapped it around the hydrant and gave us the signal to go. Engine two took off down the road dropping the line in the street. The driveway was about three hundred feet away and about one hundred feet long. It had three-foot snow banks on either side making it difficult for use to maneuver. The snow was over the truck's running boards and two of us struggled with getting the feeder line from engine two and into engine one's pump connection. Barely able to get one foot in front of the other, I reached for an air-pack off engine one, I threw it over my head and cinched it on to my back. Not wanting to fight my way through the snow again, I grabbed a spare air bottle too. Now top heavy with the pack on, I struggled even more to get over the snow bank and onto the rear step of the engine, from where I could pull an attack line off. Thank heavens the police always responded to our calls. Some of the policemen were always very helpful and on this morning one would help me pull the two hundred foot "pre-connected" attack line off engine one. He could stand in the plowed driveway at the rear of the truck and feed me the line as I fought my way through the thigh deep snow with the line.

When I was a recruit at the fire academy, we were blessed with outstanding instructors—seasoned veterans who had "been there, done that." We were in the classroom learning about the nature of fire and of its characteristics. While discussing how fire traveled unobstructed in the outside walls of a balloon frame structure, the instructor told us, "If you have a rapidly moving fire, it will sound like a freight train."

When he said this, I thought he was crazy and wanted to question him about it; but I also knew he knew his business, so I accepted his word. Within a year of being on the job, I experienced my first of many fires in balloon frame dwellings. The first time I heard that noise, I immediately flashed back to the day at the academy.

With the air-pack strapped over my back, a spare bottle of air in my hand and the attack line over my shoulder, I was geared up and instinctively headed for the second floor. It's a good thing I hadn't donned my face piece yet. After struggling with the line in the snow, I was now breathing very heavily and would have sucked my air tank dry before I even got close to the heavy smoke and fire. Knowing I needed to conserve my air supply, I worked to get my breathing rate back down to near normal. When I reached the top of the stairs, a wide-eyed Billy Slayton ran into me. I've fought a lot of fires while on this department and immediately knew Slayton being on the second floor of a house fire was by mistake. If he wanted to perform the job of a firefighter, he'd have had an air-pak on and an attack line in his hands, at least a tool to work with. Billy Slayton didn't realize the fire, so concealed in the walls, was as severe as it was when he ran away from it on the first floor, or he wouldn't have been on the second floor in the first place. This was a large house; he was simply trying to be "out of sight, out of mind" and got caught. Fire Chief, John Wyatt, had just arrived on the second floor. He knew his position was outside, but he also understood these big old houses and wanted a firsthand report. He asked Slayton what he had found. Slayton didn't have a good answer for the chief because he didn't know what he was doing. He wasn't wearing a mask because he never did any real firefighting nor did he truly know how.

"The second floor is clear, Chief," Slayton said, hedging in his response.

Hearing noises coming from a back room off a bedroom, that deafening sound of a fire roaring up the inside of a wall, I quickly interjected, "Sir, the fire may be in the wall over there" as I pointed in the direction of the noise. I've heard this noise before and knew exactly what it was.

"Check it out, Lieutenant Renaldi, and report back to me," He then looked at Slayton and asked, "Where's your mask, Bill?"

Slayton's response was feeble, "I, I." He shrugged his shoulders and tried to laugh his way out of the situation, but this was no laughing matter.

The chief looked at him in disgust and ordered, "Stay with Lieutenant Renaldi."

The smoke was beginning to build but not yet heavy enough for me to put my face piece on, thus conserving my air supply. Slayton was clueless as I led him toward the noise; he just hid behind me. It is innate in most firefighters to watch out for each other, but I couldn't help but to think. *This ought to be good. The fire is building somewhere, and Slayton doesn't have a mask on. Today's Billy's day to eat a belly full of smoke!*" The closer to the noise we got, the more crackling sounds we could hear; slightly perplexed, I turned to Slayton and said, "That's open fire burning. Where the hell is it?" As opposed to the fire I knew was in the wall. We walked into the bedroom, suddenly there was fire rolling up and over the top of the door to the back room.

Slayton was mortified as he exclaimed out of fear, "holy shit!" Then he froze.

Moving the door, which was stopped open against the outside wall, it fell off its hinges. The fire had broken out of the wall and up the backside of the door, which was now crackling with freely burning fire. With a quick burst of water from the nozzle, the door fire was quickly knocked down; and I immediately turned back toward Slayton, who, like a jackrabbit, was already running down the stairs as I shouted, "The fire's gone above us. I'm heading for the third floor."

Chief Wyatt grabbed me at the base of the stairs. "Stay with Slayton here on the second floor," were his instructions as he exited to assume command in front of the fire building. But Slayton, with total disregard for his fellow firefighters, was already gone out of the burning building. I've seen this before and knew he wasn't running out to mask up; he was running scared. Bill Slayton is no firefighter—never has been and never will be!

As the second floor filled with smoke, I followed the chief's orders and waited for help at the base of the stairs leading to the third floor. But no one was forthcoming. Beginning to feel like a Clydesdale being held in his stall, I was chomping at the bit to get to work.

Knowing the fire had gotten an infusion of air when it burned its way out of the wall on the second floor, I was unwilling to back down and knew we had to move fast if we were going to cut it off, so I put my face piece on and headed up the stairs to the third floor. I was too late. If Slayton and I had initially gotten up there, we might have been able to control the fire. The fire had traveled up inside of the outside wall straight to the roof. In this case, a dormered third floor with walk-up stairs. This was not unusual for these larger antique colonial houses on the post road, many once owned by some of Boston's biggest and wealthiest merchants.

Without the roof opened up, the fire's force had no place to go and would simply burn off the thin wood lathes holding the plaster on the studs even faster than it had done downstairs behind the door on the second floor. With this fueling, it naturally mushroomed to the left and to the right across the ceiling. Joist by joist, it would eat its way to the far wall. Where, yet again, with no place to go, it defied logic and demonstrated its power as it followed its own rules by turning downward. Stud by stud, bay by bay, the fire grew. This too we learned at the fire academy. The more this fire grew, the more it traveled, creating a vicious cycle, taking over the third floor in the process. The fire's fury had burned all the plaster off the walls and ceiling; it was now hot and untenable. Ben Lyons, a young and intelligent firefighter, whom most of the senior firefighters, myself included, had proudly taken under their wing, quickly met up with me. As we held our ground at the top of the stairs, we could hear the truck's outside speakers crackling with Chief Wyatt's voice asking for a second alarm bringing automatic help from neighboring communities.

Cromwell's station was just a few miles to the east, and Trowbridge's just a quick jaunt from the west. Both towns were probably listening to us already, knowing we had a job to do. The fire service was like that—ears turned and scanners locked on to the frequency of the town with the fire. A good fire alarm operator would already have his hand on the vocal arm in anticipation of their automatic response, thereby having help on the way before he or she even acknowledged a requesting town over the district radio. If our own fire alarm operator's instincts were working, he'd have already called for second alarm coverage in advance.

Within minutes, several firefighters with axes, pike poles, and hooks were masked up and ready to assist in advancing the hose line. They too were stalled on the stairs. A captain from the neighboring Cromwell department was amongst them down at the bottom of the stairs.

Inside, firefighting is serious business and needs to be done correctly, lest serious consequences occur. Observing the heavier-than-air smoke building as it fell down the stairs, the captain ordered from below as he pointed to the only window in sight, "Break out that window at the top of the stairs!"

Venting a fire from underneath would "feed" the fire the necessary oxygen it needed to take off with catastrophic results as taking out this window would've done. A fire needs to be vented from above, thus pushing its super heated gasses out of the structure and allowing the firefighters to enter from below the fire. However, with the roof not yet opened, clearly taking out the window was the wrong tactic to use in this situation. As the ax man positioned himself in front of the window and raised his arms to swing, I raised my arms and reluctantly shouted, "No wait!"

"We need to vent this floor," the Cromwell captain said sternly.

"Taking out the window will draw the fire to us, and we'll be screwed. We need to open the roof." I yelled down the stairs to the Cromwell captain, who should have known this; perhaps he was a young book smart, yet inexperienced, firefighter. The fire service was leaning toward this type of promotion.

Simultaneously, Chief Wyatt was on his radio calling Captain Charles, who was now directing outside operations at the rear of the building for the chief to get the roof opened quickly, allowing the fire's fury to rocket skyward and stop the mushrooming effect. "I have men on the third floor," he said anxiously. Hearing the chief's instruction over the radio made me feel good knowing we were on the same page. Captain Charles relayed back that with three feet of snow on the ground, snow on the roof, and the house backed into a steep hill, it was very difficult to get men and ladders in place. Eventually, they would get the roof opened; but in the meantime, the fire had way too much of a head start on us.

The Cromwell captain and I squabbled over the window issue, and as we did, Lyons, who always relied on my every word, was vacillating between wanting to obey the ranking officer and not wanting to go against my word.

"Dom, listen to the captain and let's do what he says."

"We can't, Benny. If we take out this window, the fire will roar straight for it. This whole floor will light up, and we'll be fucked for sure. We have to at least wait to see if they can get the roof opened."

The captain was getting impatient and now knelt with us near the top of the stairs. "Take out that window now, Lieutenant!" he barked.

I might have been correct; he looked so young. Being fully aware that a captain outranks a lieutenant, even if he wasn't from your own department, I did not want to be disobeying an order; but I was experienced enough to know if we broke out the window, there would be no turning back. "Captain, let's first open the top of the window and see what happens."

Finally acquiescing, the captain reluctantly instructed Lyons to "open the top of the window, but don't break it." Gingerly, Lyons tugged at the top sash, but its glass was already cracked from the heat; and when the fire roared toward us, he quickly shut it again, proving the theory correct. The captain said not a word, and I chose not to show him up. He was now a little more experienced than when his day began.

As we all impatiently waited for the fire to be vented, all the while slipping down the stairs one step at a time toward the second floor to escape the increasing heat and smoke, Lyons and the now-very-quiet Cromwell captain were running out of air and needed to exit for new air tanks. I never liked having to leave a burning building, preferring instead to stay on top of what was happening, when and where. Over time, I'd become quite adept at using my air sparingly and knew to take longer, less-frequent breaths, not putting my mask on until absolutely necessary and often taking it off where I could, which is the difference between old school and new school. The younger guys, like Lyons and Paul

Frieze, probably that Cromwell captain as well, were being taught to put their masks on outside and leave them on, which I encouraged because today's progressive fire service was teaching this practice, and it was imperative their training stay consistently up to date. I was sincere enough in my teachings with these young kids that they understood me when I said, "Do as I say, not as I do." In addition, at five feet ten inches tall, and 200 pounds while being athletically conditioned, I had a slow breathing rate, something I took pride in because this too was part of the job! Besides, I often brought a spare tank with me so I wouldn't lose my position on the nozzle.

In a confined space such as this, the wisest approach was to apply an indirect attack—water sprayed toward the ceiling, the hottest spot, not toward the fire itself. A direct attack was usually done on smaller fires such as a smouldering piece of furniture or a motor vehicle fire or as I had done to the door on the second floor. That was a direct attack.

Capt. Tom Jacobs quickly made his way up the stairs past the stalled men with another attack line. My relief was tangible as the captain put his hand on my shoulder, letting me know he was there. Jacobs was an excellent, academy-trained firefighter. He and I were incredibly alike, not only physically but in our firefighting ways too—aggressive, intelligent, and unafraid. Jacobs had only recently become a captain, and I hoped soon my own promotion would follow. We seemed to work very well together, and perhaps this fire would further demonstrate that.

With the roof finally opened enough for the fire to vent—or perhaps it just finally burned its way through self-venting at least enough for the captain and me to advance our lines—shitty-looking brown smoke and superheated gasses escaped under great pressure, rolling skyward with flashes of flame bursting just above the roofline, strongly indicating that the third floor must be close to its flash point—this is where all combustible material reaches its ignition temperature at the same time. FLASH! Everything lights up simultaneously! This was a very dangerous environment we were entering, but enter we must, if we wanted to gain control. Jacobs and I each had a one-and-a-half-inch hand line with us—the customary-sized attack hose that flowed about 120 gallons of water per minute. We'd need every bit of it too. It was hotter than hell as evidenced by the plastic light switches melting from the walls.

Having been up there the longest and knowing what was happening, I briefed the captain on the fire being to the left and surmised it was probably to the right as well. This is where you need to outthink this wicked devil, or he *will* demonstrate his rage and exact his revenge on mere mortals by consuming the building. And *all* that is in it.

"Tommy, you take the right side, and I'll go left," I suggested. Though he outranked me, Jacobs dutifully nodded; this was teamwork!

Before we moved in, knowing my air supply must be low, I asked the captain to help me exchange air bottles. Quickly, I undid the air hose from my face piece so I could breathe while Jacobs shut off the tank and unlocked it from its hold. The air I was now breathing, albeit for just a few seconds, was hot and acrid—more signs of a bad environment. Coughing as I got my first taste of it, I turned to the captain and said,

"Tommy, this smoke is pretty shitty. Be careful up here." I slipped the full air bottle over my head and into place.

"Yeah, it looks pretty bad, and I can feel the heat," Jacobs said as he reconnected my air supply, and I reconnected my air hose to the face piece. Exchanging my air bottle should have taken about twenty-five seconds. We did it in about fifteen. We were ready to move in.

The dense, thick, and yellowish brown smoke, too heavy to rise, was banked down to the floor, and it was so hot we had to slide on our bellies to progress so much as an inch. By the time we made our way down the hall, we could feel the heat singeing our ears, and our neck hair was beginning to curl. With hand signals, the captain and I acknowledged our moves in opposite directions. As I turned toward the left doorway, the whole room was involved in fire. Someone joined in ten feet behind me and provided assistance in pulling the line. It was Paul Frieze. Paul was a good firefighter, always telling other young men, "If you want to learn anything, work with Lieutenant Renaldi, he'll teach you something every day."

I tried to rise up enough to open the line, but it was so hot the back of my neck began to immediately blister. Feeling the pain, I quickly dropped back down and awkwardly rolled onto my back. Air-Paks were saviors but cumbersome at times. Lying on my backside, or at least halfway over, I lifted the line enough to be able to open the nozzle to a wide V pattern and swirl it around in a circular motion allowing the water to come in contact with as much super heated air as possible. Rule of thumb was three seconds, then shut the line down to check for results, minimizing water damage.

Having the nozzle on a wide V pattern enabled more water droplets to absorb the heat, allowing more water conversion to steam, therefore more effective fire suppression. Water converts to steam thousands of times more in volume, not only cooling the fire but also smothering it at the same time. Though very effective, it means hell for the firefighters in an environment such as we encountered on the third floor. The expanding steam came down on us like hot ash cascading from the lips of a raging volcano.

The steam was scalding hot, and I could feel my exposed skin begin to blister from my wrist and ears with the pain of a bad sunburn times ten. More ventilation was needed. I yelled back toward Frieze, "Have the ax man take out *that* window, now's the time." The three-second rule was out the window too. The steam was way too hot. More water would be needed to cool the fire down. More scalding steam cascaded on the men, and we had no choice. This room needed to be cooled down fast. Backing out wasn't an option, at least not yet.

A combination of ventilation was accomplished, enabling both crews to advance. Whenever I faced a dangerous situation like this, everything seemed to slow down, and minutes passed like hours. I wasn't sure what was happening with Jacobs on the other side of the hall, but I was certain he was experiencing the same hazardous environment and would be okay because he knew what he was doing. As Frieze and I progressed forward on our hands and knees, I shouted instructions to the inexperienced junior man, our voices muffled through the masks.

"Keep an eye on our back side, you never know when big red will come back around and bite us in the ass and trap us in here."

With the cooling effect beginning to take hold, we continued to grope deeper into the room. The environment was still hot, and the smoke was still down to the floor albeit a little cooler and a little lighter. Being in the lead, I began to feel my way up and over a menagerie of burned-out rubble. Then Frieze yelled, "The fire's behind us, Lieutenant."

I tried turning about but was entangled in something made of metal and very large. I couldn't get free! My partner took the line and knocked down the fire as I tried to free myself. The junior man, having handled the fire well, then turned to help his partner to get free. By this time, Jacobs had come over from the right side to help. He had done a thorough search, and there wasn't any fire on his side of the hall. I was surprised, but if that's what Jacobs said, then that's the way it was. Trust was implied when we worked under these conditions.

Jacobs hollered through his mask, "I broke out the windows in the front dormer for ventilation." He was dependable and knew his business well. Maybe our aggressive attack *did* cut the fire off! Captain Jacobs now teamed his line on the left side.

As it turned out, I had led us on to a burned out bed and had gotten the buckle of my bunker coat caught on the old-style metal bedspring. *They'd have a good laugh back at the station house about that,* I thought. I could hear Frieze telling everyone jovially, *Yup, old Dom, we're in the middle of a serious fire, and he climbs into bed for a nap!* The firehouse would rock with laughter over that one.

With both hose lines working together, the fire was knocked down, and the smoke had cleared enough for us to be able to see. In the end, all three rooms on the left side of the hall had burned out, and half the roof was gone. We achieved control of the fire. The third floor was well vented by now with fresher men arriving to take over. As Jacobs, Frieze, and the rest of us from the original crew—minus Slayton, of course—were resting on the third floor, Chief Wyatt came over to us.

"You guys did one hell of a job." Hearing that from a man of Chief Wyatt's stature was very gratifying to all. Turning to youthful Paul Frieze and putting my arm around his shoulder, I said, "Congratulations, young man, you've made it to the big leagues!" To which Frieze beamed broadly. The chief looked quite pleased as he watched this acceptance of sorts. Another good man brought into the fold. Well done.

Jacobs, the others, and I were ordered out of the house for rehab; and we trooped out of the building, now merely smoldering. Our helmets warped and blackened from the heat of the fire, the worst of which was finally under control.

While the sun broke the horizon, passersby stopped to observe the fire scene, amongst them a member of the Board of Selectmen. The post road was a mass of fire trucks, and the ground was laden with hose that looked like spaghetti all frozen in place. Several ambulances were on the scene, and a few men, who had inhaled some smoke, were sucking on the oxygen. The moist cold gas always felt good going into the lungs. I even took a few hits of it, my body relishing its soothing refreshment as the EMTs attended to my minor burns.

Slayton was outside the building, slithering from here to there, seeking attention by anyone of importance. Never having reentered the burning building again, he was clean and neat with no signs of exertion. He was such a perfect Eddy Haskell from the *Leave It to Beaver* show. He was such a disgrace to the fire service.

"Well, look at you," I said disrespectfully.

"What do you mean?" asked Slayton with a sly look, knowing fully what I meant.

I looked Slayton up and down and simply shook my head in disgust. "You make me sick, you know that?"

"I don't know what you're talking about, asshole. I couldn't find you, so I left. You expect me to just stand around inside a burning building like I'm waiting for a friend on a street corner?"

"You couldn't find me because I wasn't running out of the building with *you*."

As I looked down at Slayton and saw his smug face—a face I wanted smack with my fist—I heard him say, "I don't have no death wish, man. You always think you're such a hero. All you want to do is leave your old lady a widow. Real smart. You don't have to be a fireman to kill yourself, if that's what you're trying to do. Take some pills, it's easier and less painful. I might even be able to get you some!"

"I do what I signed up to do!" With my glare now penetrating Slayton, I said, "You know, Slayton, I'd have a little more respect for you if after your initial bail out, you would have entered the building again. Other guys did. Young guys, guys who are suppose to look up to you. How do you expect anybody to look up to you when all you do is run from danger?"

"Fuck you, Renaldi. I get looked up to plenty."

Knowing this was getting nowhere, and because I was tired and exhausted, I just walked away from the snake. Slayton wouldn't know anything about how a firefighter felt after a difficult battle. If anyone looked up to Slayton, it was because he knew how to play the game. Fire department politics weren't much different from country club politics or small town politics or any damn politics for that matter. Smart wasn't measured in IQ points or work ethic. It was measured in knowing which asses to kiss and which ones to avoid. It was about survival—Machiavellian survival. It was so Coventry. If this country's forefathers saw how today's politics worked, they'd roll over in their graves. Slayton had everyone in town fooled. As poor a firefighter as he was, everyone in the department, especially Slayton, seemed to take it for granted that someday in the near or distant future, Coventry's favorite son, handsome little Billy Slayton would eventually be Coventry's fire chief.

Over my dead body would he be chief!

The next day, the *Coventry Town Crier* had a picture of Bill Slayton on its front page, his helmet clean and unscratched, administering oxygen to a gasping blackened firefighter—a *real* firefighter—who was lying on the ground. Slayton had a panicked look on his face and was yelling directly into the camera. I was sure he was yelling, "Help me! Help me! Somebody please help me!" The caption over the picture was, Firefighters Battle Blaze. Firefighter? Yeah right.

Chapter 3

Liz Temple paced the kitchen floor of her five-bedroom home on Apple Blossom Lane. Her remote phone was clipped to her slim and shapely waist and her hands-free headset was carefully placed on her coiffed hair. Liz's face did not portray her usual smile that lit a room, and she wasn't usually a pacer but rather an ardent doer. However, her calm exterior began to succumb to the uneasiness starting to bubble within. She was five foot three, meticulously yet casually dressed, with every silky wavy blond strand of her hair in place. But she could feel her feisty Irish personality threaten to take over her natural eloquent radiance. It was nearly 4:00 p.m., and her husband hadn't even called. Jared's nursery school play was to begin in thirty minutes.

"Dr. Temple's office." Doctor Samuel Temple's office.

"Hi, Janet, it's me. Is he there?" Liz's usual effervescent voice disguised her tumult over her husband's invariable lateness and no-shows.

"Hi, Liz, yes, he's still in the operating room. Would you like me to transfer you?

Liz knew there was no way her husband, who was still in the O R, could make it to his son's play. Not being able to resist the slap even though she hated sounding like a whining housewife, she said, "No, no thank you, Janet. Just remind him when he gets out, he missed Jared's play." Liz was feisty enough to play a game or two of her own.

Dr. Temple's very capable longtime secretary responded with a note of sympathy in her voice, "Yes, I'll be sure to do that, Liz." They'd had this conversation several times in the past.

After having kissed Ethan, the youngest son, good-bye and securely placing him in the babysitter's arms, Jared and Liz left for the school play. "Daddy will meet us there, munchkin." At least she silently hoped this would be true, but realistically, she knew, like so many times before, the chances were slim.

When Liz and Jared arrived at the school, Officer Alan Bard of the Coventry police force was there working the police detail. "Hello, Liz, I've saved you a parking space right next to me over there," he said as he flashed his nice smile to his longtime friend while pointing to a space close to the main door.

"Thank you, Alan. I can always count on you!"

As the other parents arrived, mother and father, husband and wife together, Liz sat chatting with one of her many friends, trying hard to allow her personality to shine brightly despite the pain in her inner soul. Still, Liz couldn't help but notice all the families acting like, well, families, and she longed for this for her family. Somewhere along the way, it became clear that her husband was set in his ways and had his own priorities. Sadly, family wasn't one of them. Sam was a powerful man, and you couldn't tell him anything; all Liz could do was hope he'd see the light other than the light above the operating table.

The play went on as scheduled, each child performing adorably while their fathers moved about the room with cameras in hand. As Liz sat patiently laughing and applauding the performances of all the future stars, her mind was elsewhere, and she couldn't help but to keep one eye on the entrance in hopes her husband would show. Jared was next to perform. The thought of sitting alone for yet another event with no husband was less than she had bargained for. The thought of there being no dad for *her* son to see in the audience was beyond comprehension. Weren't these supposed to be the formative years where *both* parents participated in raising the children? Isn't that what all the books said? Liz fought back tears as she put on a good front for the watchful eyes of this small busy town.

Then it was time. Tensing, Liz's pulse increased as Jared took the stage. Though this was just a four-year-old's nursery school play, Liz, as did all the parents with their children, got nervous for her son. With no reassuring hand to hold, Liz crossed her fingers while silently wishing him good luck. This wasn't just any nursery school; this was a *Coventry* nursery school.

In Coventry, where everything and everybody was a cut above the rest, their children were expected to be the same. Such high expectations, such a pressure-filled place to raise a child where the help of both parents would be of enormous value—that's Coventry, where wandering eyes took mental note. "No Dr. Temple again, wife looks upset, this isn't the first time either, hmmmmm? I hear he's much older than she. She's so adorable, what's she doing with him? Most likely the money. Did you notice how she and that police officer acted together?" More chitchat for the gossip branches of a small town's deadly grapevine of forbidden fruit.

Liz's focus now turned from no-show husband to watchful mother. As Jared proceeded, Liz could feel herself begin to relax. He was doing such a wonderful job! Performing precisely as they had rehearsed over and over again. Jared's performance could have won an Academy Award—why not, with all the time and effort he and a nurturing mother had put in. It was becoming quite clear that Liz was annoyed with her nonparticipating husband, and she was trying so hard to be a good—better than good—parent while picking up the slack. She was a nurturing, caring mother, but the strong fatherly support just wasn't there; and it could not continue, not for Jared, not for Liz, not for their family, not for any family. Liz Temple was always prepared for any task, big or small. Knowingly, she endeavored to do something about any challenge. A change was necessary. She didn't know what she needed, but she knew she needed it. Liz Temple would figure out what her needs were and where to have these needs met both for her and her boys.

The show concluded with a standing ovation for all the performers with the actors and actresses taking their bows. They couldn't help but laugh at one adorable child who stole the show with more bows after more bows as his mother looked on with an "oh well" look to the crowd. It was a delightful and fun-filled atmosphere for most of the parents while Liz sat thinking, *Stay strong, go it alone. My children need me. Put up the front that says there's nothing wrong in our household.* Liz found Jared and gave him a big hug even as he looked searchingly over her shoulder into the crowd. "I am so, so, so proud of you!" Jared looked at his mother with a question in his eyes, the one Liz prayed he would not ask. After a moment, he simply turned away while grabbing his mother's hand as he led them to the table where cookies and juice were being served.

Liz smiled radiantly.

* * *

My attitude in life was to always stand up and defend what you believed in. To fight for your team even if it meant entering the lion's den. To do what you had to do. The April meeting of the Firefighter's Association was when we elected its officers. The association president spoke, "Next, nominations to the bargaining committee are now open."

"I believe this man will do a good job for us. I nominate Dominic Renaldi," said one member. Quickly, another member seconded the nomination.

"Are there any other nominations for the bargaining committee?" asked the presiding officer. No other nominations were made. By default, I would be elected to enter the lion's den.

As a natural leader, I accepted the responsibility, and I looked forward to the challenge. Immediately after the meeting, I went to Captain Charles and asked, "When will we be meeting to discuss this year's bargaining issues?"

"I don't believe in meeting beforehand, Renaldi. You're new to the committee, you just follow my lead."

This is not what I expected, and I wasn't crazy about the game plan, but I did know Captain Charles was the key player in the association. I bit my tongue.

A few nights later, we were standing in the hallway of the town hall waiting to be called in. I was taken by the thickness of Captain Charles' bargaining book he kept over the years. He had been chairman of the Firefighter's Association's bargaining committee since we quasi organized ten years ago and he had notes on everything. His book was the association's bargaining bible: the Holy Grail. Lose it and we lose our direction, our written history of all we had gained. Sure we had all the signed contracts, but this book contained all the dialog of every selectman that had bargained against us. Clearly, "Charlie's" binder contained all the innuendos of every bargaining session over the past ten years.

Captain Charles turned to association president, charismatic Bill Slayton and said. "You just charm them." Slayton let the captain know he understood his role by laughing his phony laugh. Then Charles turned to me and said, "You follow my lead."

Just then, the selectman's door opened and Michele, the Assistant Town Manager, announced, "The selectmen are ready for you now." One by one, we filed past her and into the room. She respectfully acknowledged the captain as he walked past her, then she smiled at Slayton as he walked by. I gave her a smile, but she iced me with her dark cold stare. Turning my attention toward the conference table, and those sitting at it, I watched as Captain Charles sat closest to Snidely Ryan, the Town Manager. Slayton was right behind Charles and began charming everyone with his pretentious ways as he sat next to his longtime captain. Everyone smiled and laughed at his amicable personality. As the newest member of the bargaining team, I politely sat down the far end of our side of the table. Settling into my chair, I sized up the selectmen and the environs of this smoky, but cold room. How ironic; here was a "NO SMOKING" sign hanging between the two windows that overlooked the town green just across the street. Surely they had no qualms about breaking the fire codes in front of the fire department.

"And this is our newest member of the bargaining team, Dominic Renaldi," said Captain Charles quite superciliously.

I rose from my seat, leaned across the table and shook their hands. "Hello, It's nice to meet you," I said sincerely to the two selectmen, taking note the middle chair was empty and that Horace Humphreys, Chairman, Board of Selectman, was not present. Then I looked down the long table at Mr. Ryan. "Hello, Mr. Ryan," I respectfully acknowledged. I didn't feel a good vibe from the man who ran the town. He was an older man, Harvard, class of '36, and has been the town manager for as many years as I've been alive. He knew everything about everyone, particularly the town employees: Whom he could trust and whom he suspected might not play on their team. He could thank his assistant, Michele, for that. She had a reputation for approaching certain town employees whom she could trust. "I need you to report everything you hear to me, can I count on you?" She would ask of them. "The town will be quite grateful to you." Sitting at her desk in the corner, she never took her eyes off our bargaining team while taking copious notes. Every now and then I'd glance over at her. The years have not been kind to this woman who, with her wrinkled face, looked ten years older then she was. I had the feeling her notes were mere impressions of those speaking against the town. Perhaps she was overworked and under paid. Nonetheless, she looked like a frustrated woman sitting there in her drab, oversized dress, and a vindictive, angry look on her face. As much as I wanted to, I didn't trust her at all.

We were an hour into the meeting and Captain Charles was making the association's pitch for a cost of living increase in pay for all our bargaining units. "We have already gone a full year without a signed contract."

Suddenly, as if a theatrical production, the door flew open, and in walked Horace Humphreys. Everyone on both sides cowered to him. "Well," he said as he looked at his watch, "at least I've made it here before nine o'clock."

"Not too bad for you, Horace," said another member of the board. Humphreys boastfully laughed. Then all present laughed with him.

Humphreys walked straight to Captain Charles and shook his hand. "Hello Charlie ole boy. Nice to see you." Then he spoke to Slayton as he made his way to his seat. "Hello, Bill. Did you get your Trash Hauler & Disposal License?"

Acting quite sheepish, Slayton said in a soft tone, "Yes, thank you."

Though I had observed him during many town meetings, I sized up Humphreys. Formidable opponent, why not? He's a Harvard grad and a powerful Boston attorney. Arrogant and egotistical certainly apply, but he has my respect.

"Who's this?" he asked while looking at me, and letting me know I was on the lowest end of the totem pole.

"This is Dominic Renaldi, Horace," Captain Charles said in such a way it gave me a feeling it wasn't the first time Humphreys had heard my name.

I rose from my seat and shook his hand. "Nice to meet you, Mr. Humphreys."

His response to my handshake was cold and calculated. "So tell me, Renaldi, why do you want to get involved in cut-throat negotiations?" He asked while removing his coat.

"I don't see collective bargaining as cut-throat, sir. It's a necessary evil mandated by state legislation a dozen or so years ago. It gives both sides an opportunity to find common ground to build on."

Removing an expensive cigar from its individualized case, Humphreys asked a loaded question. "And what happens if there is no common ground?"

"Well," I paused, then, thought for a moment. "We are all intelligent people here. Surely we can find common ground."

"But, suppose we can't find that common ground, Renaldi. What then?" asked Humphreys as he rolled his cigar around in his mouth ensuring it lit evenly.

I began feeling as though I was being tested to see what I knew about the process and, perhaps, how far I'd take it. Charles and Slayton remained silent as Humphreys grilled me. "I presume that's why the politicians up on Beacon Hill put arbitration in place when they wrote the legislation."

"Are you already suggesting arbitration, Mr. Renaldi?"

"Not at all, in fact, I view arbitration as a last resort and believe there is much common ground for both sides to work from."

Humphreys turned and looked at Captain Charles and said, "Interesting." He looked back at me and blew the smoke from his cigar into my face. With an arrogant smirk, he looked at the captain again. "Times are certainly changing, now aren't they, Charlie?"

Not wanting to back down, I quickly inquired, "That's a nice aromatic cigar, Mr. Humphreys. Where's that come from?"

Humphreys removed the green cigar from his mouth and looked at it. He held it up as if in a TV commercial and said, "This is the finest Cuban cigar you can buy. Do you smoke cigars, Renaldi?"

"No, I don't, especially not in a public building. It just smells like it has a nice flavor to it."

Humphreys burst out laughing. Then Slayton laughed his phony laugh. Humphreys inhaled on his cigar before saying, "Well, Mr. Renaldi, we relax the rules around here." He exhaled the smoke in my face again. No one laughed. Without skipping a beat, Humphreys announced, "Well, I didn't mean to interrupt. Where were we in the process?"

The Town Manager, puffing on his pipe, brought Humphreys up to speed, concluding with, "Captain Charles just reminded us the firefighters are operating without a contract and they are asking for the "cost of living" pay raise."

Humphreys jumped right in. "Have you informed them we can no longer use the "cost of living index" because it is now much too high?"

"I was just about to do that when you walked in, Horace." The Town Manager instructed his assistant. "Michele, will you please distribute the charts I asked you to make up for this meeting." She walked about the room handing out the paperwork. When she handed me my copy, I smiled and pleasantly thanked her. She acted cold and callous. As we all looked over the documents, the Town Manager said, "Unfortunately, we are out of the allotted time for this session. Can we set a date to meet two weeks from this evening?" The meeting adjourned, and our bargaining team left the room.

Gathering in the hallway for a quick debriefing, I said, "Captain, if retroactive to last year, the cost of living increase will give us a 22 percent pay raise."

The captain smiled and simply said, "nice chunk of change, isn't it?"

"It sure is, but it will cause us trouble down the road."

"I'll make it work. You just follow my lead."

Two weeks later we were back sitting opposite the Board of Selectman in another bargaining session. Similar to a senate hearing, the established seating was in order and I took my seat at the end of the table. Captain Charles opened his heavy binder, and Humphreys responded. "Charlie, I'd love to get my hands on that book of yours before you retire." At which everyone laughed; everyone but me. I thought it was a direct enticement.

Captain Charles countered with a jovial one-liner straight from the movie, The Godfather. "Make me an offer I can't refuse." Everyone laughed louder. I forced a smile. Slayton was on the floor laughing. He was their best audience. Michele was taking notes.

Humphreys got right to the point. Here is our offer for a two-year contract. We'll give you 5 percent cost of living adjustments for each of the two years, retroactive back to last year. That's a 10 percent increase over two years."

Silently, our team just sat there. We needed some sort of a rebuttal if we wanted to show strength, so I calmly said, "It's also a 12 percent decrease from the cost of living index." Captain Charles looked at me as though thinking, *good, you said it, that'll take the heat off me.* Slayton remained silent. The only time he ever spoke was to crack a joke, or state the obvious while finishing someone else's sentence for them, as long as it was a neutral comment or agreed with the selectmen.

Humphreys was quick with his planned answer, "We can no longer use that index, Mr. Renaldi. It is simply—"

Slayton jumped in interrupting Humphreys, "It's too high." Quickly, I looked at him as if asking, *whose side are you on, Bill?*

Humphreys agreed, "Yes, Bill. It is simply too high a percentage now."

"Using the cost of living index has been an "accepted past practice" in determining our pay raises for over ten years," I politely countered.

Captain Charles remained silent, and Slayton had already shown his hand.

Humphreys is a cagy Boston attorney and didn't react to my comeback. But his comment spoke volumes to me. "We have another rather pressing issue on our agenda tonight." Then he turned toward Captain Charles, "Why don't you go back to the firehouse, Charlie, and think about what I said. Snidely, let's meet again in two weeks." The Town Manager nodded and a date was set.

The meeting adjourned, and, once again, we were standing in the hall. "So what do you think Captain?" I asked. It was obvious Slayton didn't want to be a part of this conversation.

Captain Charles pondered his answer, then said, "I think we should think about what Humphreys said." His response hit me like a lightning bolt. I wasn't a distrusting person, but my instincts were quite good. I thought, *think about what, the 10 percent raise, or giving your book to Humphreys?*

A few days later, Captain Charles was working, so I went down to the firehouse on my day off. Respectfully, I asked, "Captain, may I speak to you alone in the other room?" We did serve on the bargaining committee together, and I could be counted on to come back and help out during emergencies. Still, my instincts always told me I wasn't on his most favorite list. With reluctance, he agreed to speak to me.

"What's on your mind, Renaldi?"

"I've been thinking about the town's offer of a 10 percent pay raise over a two-year contract. A 10 percent raise will still keep us amongst the highest paid departments in Massachusetts. Times are getting very difficult. I think we should accept their offer. Let them know we are willing to play ball with them during tough times. It will help us in the long run."

"I'm going to be retiring in a year, Renaldi. I want all I can get now!"

"If we get a 22 percent raise in this contract, we're going to pay for it down the road, Captain."

"I don't care about down the road. I care about the here and now."

Our discussion ended and I walked away thinking, *he's only worried about himself. This contract is going to cause long-term trouble for us and he won't be around for any of it.*

It's unethical to talk with the opposing side outside of the scheduled collective bargaining sessions, but we all know about "backroom politics."

"Captain Charles," the voice over the loudspeaker stated, "phone call on line two four."

The portly captain squirmed his way forward and out of the recliner. Breathing heavily as he waddled to the phone, he answered, "Captain Charles, may I help you?"

"Captain, Horace Humphreys here. How are you ole boy?"

"I'm fine HH, but I'd be a lot better with a little something in my pocket. What can I do for you?"

"Charlie, we have to stop using this cost of living index as an established way for determining pay raises. This Renaldi has me worried with his talk about "accepted past practice," and arbitration. Then he has the nerve to imply it was a statehouse issue. For Christ sake, Charlie, I was on the Governor's Council when the governor signed that bill. Renaldi has an authoritative look that could translate into power. Can we trust him?"

"I fought those fucking guineas in WW II. I can't trust them at all. He's an ambitious leader, Horace, and he's raising a stink about this pay raise at the firehouse. He's got everyone riled up. I can't talk him out of it."

"We can't allow this man to develop a backing at the firehouse, Charlie."

"What do you want me to do about it, HH?"

"Have your boys work on him, you know, divide and conquer."

"They've been trying to do that for years. Renaldi's too ignorant to fold. He keeps rising up. What's in this for me?"

Humphreys showed his ruthlessness. "Renaldi is correct. There is an accepted past practice for using the cost of living index to determine pay raises. You agree to writing into the firefighters contract its removal, and work on Renaldi's demise. In turn, we'll give you your 22 percent pay raise over two years. That should help to set you up for retirement too."

"Now there's an offer I can't refuse." The two men laughed heartily.

"Oh, and Charlie, I get your bargaining book when you retire."

At a specially called meeting, Captain Charles spoke before the association. "It is in our best interest to remove the cost of living index from bargaining. If we do that, the town will give us our 22 percent pay raise. The members ratified the contract, and three months later, Slayton signed a two-year deal, retroactive to eighteen months ago.

Chapter 4

In anticipation of purchasing the home of Ruth's parents when they retired—which we were set to do—I had purchased the parcel of land adjoining their property several years ago. The town had arbitrarily deemed it in the Flood Plain. Therefore, it was non-buildable and almost everyone told me not to purchase it. But it was priced right, and it afforded protection from others who were better connected in town from building on it. Years went by, but Ruth's parents never budged. With my family still living at the inn, it became increasingly clear I had to switch gears.

Coventry's local government was the personification of small town bureaucracy. Of course any registered voter could run for election to public office, but the town was controlled by a few of similar background and education that preferred to cultivate those whom should run for office. Usually, this group of five men and two women met for dinner and conversation at the exclusive and private Coventry Country Club, where most were members. The local newspaper got a tip about these "dinners" and tried to attend. When they were denied entrance at the club, the newspaper sued the town for open meeting law violations. In reference to an old New England tradition where locals would sit around the pot-bellied stove in the town's general store and discuss its politics, the newspaper called the small group the "cracker barrel crowd." The moniker stuck, but the dinners disbanded. Now forced elsewhere, the cracker barrel crowd would quietly meet at night in private homes. In secret sessions, they discussed agendas and individuals who could best promote their cause. Once again, the newspapers cried foul over open meeting law violations. The town counsel argued, "They are nothing more than private citizens merely attending cocktail parties in private homes." The plaintiff's complaint was denied, and the cracker barrel crowd flourished. The chairpersons of all the town government boards were affiliated somehow, either by marriage, business associations, or educational background. In Coventry, those in power were mostly Harvard graduates, and all attended these parties. Through Snidely Ryan, the Town Manager, Horace Humphreys, Chairman Board of Selectman, pulled all the strings controlling all the boards.

At 7:30 sharp, Chairman Whitman Poindexter, known to Coventry's upper crust as Wit, called the Board of Appeals meeting to order. Sarcastically referred to as "dimwit" by Brewster and Slayton, he nervously adjusted his bow tie, then peered over his wire-rimmed glasses. "The first order of business is Mr. Dominic Renaldi. Mr. Renaldi has applied for a special permit, which will allow him to build a single family home on a non-buildable lot in wetlands," he concluded with a snicker. "Mr. Renaldi, you may proceed."

Confounded by why I had to submit an application for a special permit, I had contacted a few local attorneys and asked them for their expertise. No one wanted to represent me. "I'm too busy," said one. Another was more direct, "There's something wrong here, Mr. Renaldi. I'm sorry, I can't help you." I prepared for the meeting as best as I could, and set up a blow up of the subject plot plan on the easel. "Thank you, Mr. Chairman. This piece of proper—"

"Excuse me, Mr. Renaldi," Poindexter interrupted me. "Please give us your name and address, for the record." Poindexter turned to his fellow board members snorting and sniggering.

"Sorry. Dominic Renaldi, 394 Boston Post Road." I started again. "This piece of property is—"

With a sinister smile, Poindexter interrupted my presentation again. "What is the address of this property? For the record." He concluded with a disturbing snicker.

With a wooden pointer in hand, I began my presentation again by underlining the title of the plan with the pointer as I spoke, "The property I am seeking a permit for is Pond View Avenue, Lot B, as defined on the plot plan before you." Sliding the pointer along a blue line, which delineated the wetlands, I continued, "As you can see, this parcel of land is not in the wetlands, but rather, it abuts the wetlands."

For the third time in as many minutes, the Chairman interrupted me again, this time rather rudely. "Mr. Renaldi, why do you wish to be in the spotlight?" Then, he gave me a sneer. Suddenly, the true meaning of this meeting came to light, and it became clear it was personal.

My body tensed with anger and I could feel my temples begin to pulse. "Mr. Poindexter, I do not wish to be in the spotlight. All I wish to do is build a home for my family. Why do you insist on shining the spotlight upon me?"

"We don't give special permits for this. Why didn't you simply ask the Building Inspector for a building permit, and let him direct you, Mr. Renaldi?" He ridiculed.

"I have studied the process, sir. I did speak to the Building Inspector about a building permit. He instructed me to speak to the Town Manager about my request. The town manager told me I needed to apply for this permit."

"Mr. Renaldi, surely the Town Manager knows the correct process. What are you insinuating about Mr. Ryan?"

"I'm not insin—" I stopped in mid sentence knowing whatever I said would work against me. It was quite apparent they were having their fun, and anything I said would only add fuel to their fire. I stood silent.

Mr. Eames, another longtime board member, who spoke up, broke the silence. "Why don't we allow Mr. Renaldi to withdraw his request without prejudice?" It was a nice gesture on my behalf. If they flat out turned down my request, by law, I could not bring this project before the town again for two years.

"Well, Mr. Renaldi?" The chairman motioned toward me with a spiteful look.

I looked toward Mr. Eames. He nodded, slightly. I looked back at Poindexter. He couldn't have been more than five feet tall, nor weigh more than eighty pounds. As an investment banker, he worked closely with Humphreys in the private sector, and town politics too. We stared at each other. Poindexter looked away. My blood was boiling. *Hold your cool,* I told myself. Glaring at the chairman, I requested, "I respectfully withdraw my application for a special permit."

Poindexter, who was uncomfortable with the stare down, quickly and nervously asked, "All those in favor?" He looked to his right, then to his left. Then, he looked at me. "By a unanimous vote, the chairman doesn't vote except to break a tie, Mr. Renaldi, the request to withdraw without prejudice is granted." He said with a sneer.

Humiliated, but standing tall, I gave the chairman a wry smile and left the room. Not wanting to go home where I'd only hear from Ruth, "I told you to give up. You'll never win," I stopped at the firehouse and went to my locker in the kitchen where I kept my paperwork. Space was tight in this old building, so three of us had our assigned lockers in this unusual location. Slayton and Jacobs were having coffee with a retired member. "How'd you make out at your meeting, Dom?" There was no sincerity in Slayton's voice.

I turned toward the steel locker and said, "If this was Snidely Ryan," and with all my might, I drove my fist into the side of the locker leaving a six-inch dent in it. I turned back to Slayton and said, "You know damned well I got fucked." I locked my locker and left.

As I was leaving, the retired member called out, "Wait, Dominic. What happened?"

I simply yelled back as I walked away, "Ask Slayton, he knows."

The next day, still feeling badly burned over being hassled at the appeals meeting, I called someone I thought might be a friend. "Hello, Mr. Eames. This is Dominic Renaldi, I'm sorry for bothering you at home."

"That's quit all right. What can I do for you?"

"I'd like to thank you for getting me off the hook last night." Then I paused to see if he would pick up the conversation.

"You're welcome. I owed you that, Mr. Renaldi."

I was confused by his comment, but sensing the door was open, I asked, naively, "Why do you owe me anything?"

"You don't remember me, do you?"

"No, I'm sorry. I haven't a clue what you're getting at."

"Several years ago there was a ferocious storm, during which our house was struck by lightning and caught fire. The fire department was stretched thin because of the storm and it took a while before help arrived. Finally, one truck with two men showed up. The fire was coming out the second floor window, but that didn't stop you. Without hesitation, you went right in by yourself and put out the fire. You saved our home, Mr. Renaldi."

"No, I'm sorry, Mr. Eames. I don't remember the incident, but anyone of the men would have done what I did."

"Maybe so, but in my case, you're the one who did, and we are grateful to you."

"Thank you. Mr. Eames. My request to build a home for my family is not unreasonable. If I might ask, why am I getting the run around?"

"It has nothing to do with your request. I've heard through the grapevine you have gone head to head with Horace Humphreys over collective bargaining. This town doesn't like people standing up to them. They will find a way to get back at you. It helps to remind others not to go down that path. It's a control issue."

I shook my head in disappointment, then, said, "I'm just a blue-collar guy with a job to do. Surely they must understand collective bargaining is mandated by law, laws made by people who are their peers."

"That's just how this town operates. This is a town of mostly managerial white-collar people. Sure they use the labor force when they need you, but they don't like labor at all. I'm afraid you're behind the eight ball, Mr. Renaldi. Let things cool down and try another approach in a few months. Call me if you need more advice."

"Thank you very much for your candor, Mr. Eames. You've been very helpful."

Chapter 5

About the only times all of Coventry's professional firefighters could get together with a semblance of sober sanity were the monthly association meetings. Guys who were on duty made sure the town wasn't burning down behind their backs while the rest acted put-upon at having to do one more mandatory thing for their job, and some were secretly happy as hell for another excuse to be out of the house and away from their wives for a change. A few of us actually took these meetings seriously.

Some of us didn't have to posture and pose. Not that we were about to go out and pose as poster boys for some calendar; we were natural manly men in a town of many manicured, white-collared men who often spent more time clothes shopping than their wives. Controlling men of arrogance and ego. More than a few of the wealthy professional men of Coventry seemed to me to be closet cases, their pretty young wives hanging around simply to act as a "beard." Sometimes I had to wonder what these marriages were all about. Now I understand love is more than sex, but what on earth was the attraction to a prissy, bow-tied little man who couldn't even shovel his own walk? Could he really treat you like a woman? Could he really satisfy you the way you wanted to be satisfied? Could he reach deep inside of you and touch you where you've never been touched before while leaving you sweaty, content, and left to sleep like a baby all night long? No, I don't think so. But the women didn't seem to mind much. They got the diamonds, the mansion, and three new cars in the garage, the wallet full of platinum cards, and in some cases, a real man on the side, perhaps a fireman. Surely, these brawny men couldn't help but notice the frustrated beauty all around town.

Out of respect for the role the association played, Chief Wyatt usually kept a low profile over our business. He ran the department, but the association was a union of sorts, and it had been formed after he became chief. As chief, he was in management. It was rather unusual when, ahead of time, he had requested a spot on the meeting agenda, and men wondered what he'd speak to them about; consequently, there was a full house tonight. Wyatt was a man of few words; he let his actions speak for themselves. I looked up to him like a son looks up to a father, if that father were the president of the United States or the first man to walk on the moon. For John Wyatt was no ordinary father figure; he stood head and shoulders above everyone.

Like most of the firemen in Coventry, I grew up on the poorer side of town although some came from less affluent areas of neighboring towns and a few, like Slayton, even from minimal wealth. Coventry was so affluent that people found it hard to believe it even *had* a poorer side. For them, poor was being able to vacation only one week per year in Cancun instead of two or driving last year's Mercedes instead of the newest one. Opposing high school athletes often made the mistake of taunting me about *my* "silver spoon," only inspiring my performance through anger. I remember telling one kid after I scored my second touchdown to "shove the silver spoon up your ass!"

No, I was poor poor. Standard-definition poor. We lived in the only four-family house in Coventry, the old rooming house built one hundred years ago for the men who built the railroad one hundred yards away. Often, I wore hand-me-down clothes and, when I was in high school, delivered Sunday newspapers for my lunch money. I'd been a roughneck high school athlete, ruggedly handsome, mainly focused on my high school life with no true understanding of what life was all about after this, and I was unsmiling, the kind of kid Coventry fathers didn't want their daughters bringing home no matter how much they liked me.

This kind of negative attention on a teenager only begot more negative behavior, whether it was drinking, vandalism, or fighting anything that looked at you sideways. In my case, just plain frustration, too much fire in my belly, no quit in my bones, a desire to forge ahead against all odds. Then John Wyatt came along. Like some Father Flannigan from the past, he took this kid—this train wreck of a kid—and showed him an outlet for his frustrations. Kids like me were usually thrill junkies. Better I learned to fight fires than get in trouble somehow. The thrill was there, and it was usually far more dangerous, but I'd be on the right side of the law rather than the wrong. I would have a career, a brighter future—even if it wasn't by Coventry standards.

Chief Wyatt first advised me to go into the military, "It will give you direction and help with your maturity."

I agreed with the chief's assessment and began the enlistment process to join the navy. Choosing this branch of service would mean a four-year obligation, but I loved the ocean and wanted to sail the seas and see the world! Before this process was completed, I got my draft notice and was ordered for a physical at the Boston navy station. I showed up for my physical with a letter from my physician explaining a shoulder injury I had received playing football. No way was this going to prevent me from being drafted, but it would better explain an existing injury to the military doctors.

Those of us with doctor's letters were directed to a separate line where a not so sympathetic doctor asked pertinent questions that usually ended with, "How does it feel right now?" If a draftee hesitated, or said fine, he was told, "You're good enough to be a soldier!" and was sent on in the process. As the doctor read my letter explaining my "partial and reoccurring separation of the right shoulder," I was asked *the* question. Without hesitation, I said, "I have a constant dull pain, and it pops out whenever I make a sudden move with my arm, particularly if I lift it over my head."

The doctor looked up at me and stared for a few seconds before saying, "Go see that man over there" as he pointed to another doctor standing in an open space in front of the windows.

I flinched and recoiled my right arm as this doctor articulated it six ways to Sunday; then he wrote something down on my chart before saying, "Go to that man over there" as he pointed to a soldier at the end of the table. While the soldier read what the doctor wrote on my chart, he reached for this big square stamp unlike the one used on everyone else. He pressed it into the inkpad and then slammed it down on my chart.

REJECTED now appeared in big bold red letters at the top of my chart. That quickly, it was over. To this day, I have no idea how that happened. Some of my friends told me it happened that way because I wasn't trying to get out of the service; I was being truthful and honest. Maybe I just got lucky?

Deep down inside, I knew the military would be good for me; but at the time, it was the height of the Vietnam War, and I looked upon that conflict with enormous disdain. The politicians in Washington were playing chess with Russia in the rice paddies of Southeast Asia, and this country's young men were their pawns. Despicable at best! Because of this, I did not fight having been rejected by the military. Something I very much would grow to regret. Most of Coventry's firefighters had beaten the draft by joining the National Guard—a six-year commitment sitting around a National Guard Armory and drinking beer every other weekend. A far cry from what it is today. Billy Slayton's family connections got him out of the service completely. Captain Charles, who fought in WWII, in Africa against the Italians, called me a draft dodger and would always see me as a rebellious product of the '60s.

The fire service would be a good fit for me. In high school, I proved my worth as a class officer, student body leader, and four-year varsity letter winner while being honored with a prestigious award for outstanding athletic achievement, sportsmanship and leadership. I was caring, willing to do anything to help the team win, and it worked. I joined the fire department right out of high school. And for the first time in my young life, I was channeling my aimless wrath in a positive direction. Sure, at first I screwed up my share of times. Changes don't happen overnight, and I was rough-hewn for sure! But Chief Wyatt was stern as well as forgiving. Figuratively, he'd kick my young ass, then tell me to get back in the game on the condition that I not make the same mistake twice. I never did.

* * *

Before the meeting was called to order, Bill Slayton sat at the small table in front of the members. He was in animated laughter. That's all he ever did; laugh a phony laugh.

Why couldn't people see what this man was really like, I wondered to myself. Perhaps I had a different view of him. His older brother and I were friends, so I knew him long before we teamed up on the fire department, and I had watched him in action for years. Slayton knew how to climb the ladder because he had the enormous ability to suck up to the right people. He also had a proclivity for stepping all over the guys on the bottom rungs of the ladder. He seemed to take great pleasure in this.

One day, Group A was painting the walls of the apparatus floor. With but a few men on duty, there was plenty for everyone to do, except Billy Slayton. He didn't lift a finger all day and spent much of it up at the bank sucking up to his friend, Brian Rehrig, the bank president. Or he was at the coffee shop chumming it up.

All day, Firefighter Larry Davenport toiled. Larry was a needy guy from Cromwell. The story is he was abused and neglected, but he'd give you the shirt off his back in the middle of a snowstorm if you needed it. I had befriended Larry because, well, he needed a friend. But Slayton took full advantage of his weakness. Larry had painted for six straight hours, the last one with Slayton standing there, looking out the window, as the chief backed his cruiser into his parking spot. Finally, Slayton abruptly said, "Let me have the brush, Larry, I'll do some painting."

Angrily, Larry said, "It's about time you did something, Slayton." Then he handed the brush to Slayton and sat down to light up a cigarette.

No sooner had he taken a drag from his cigarette when the chief walked in. "What are you doing sitting there smoking a butt while Billy does all the work? Get up and do your part, Davenport."

As the chief walked away, he turned to Slayton and said, "Nice job, Slayton." Slayton acknowledged the chief with his innocent smile. Davenport fumed with anger, and Slayton laughed.

Slayton was a real snake, but I seemed to be the only one who could see it. What he did to Ruth before we were married was the final straw for me. I knew who she was because we both spent a lot of time in the same small town. She was the attractive blonde with long legs who worked in the center of town and frequented the coffee shop. After all, it was the only coffee shop in town. She had the biggest, bluest eyes you ever saw. I was a fireman who was stationed in the center of town. Ruth and I would enjoy small chitchat and exchange pleasantries when we saw each other there. Bill Slayton was the young town stud whom all the girls wanted to date, though he never seemed to date them more than once.

One day I was carrying out one of the rookie chores, I was getting coffee for the guys, and I bumped into Ruth along the way. Surely this beauty didn't want to date me, but what the hell. I asked her out. To my surprise, she said yes. I was thrilled. Smiling as I returned to the firehouse, Pete Brewster asked, "What's that smile all about?" Gleefully, I told him about my date with Ruth. "No way," he exclaimed.

"Yes, this Saturday night. We're going to that new club up on Route Nine."

Brewster told Slayton about my date with Ruth, and Slayton responded just as I would have anticipated. With his cocky, deceptive smile, he said, "I guess I'll just have to go out with her before he does."

The next night I was sitting in front of the fire station while on duty when Slayton drove by. He tooted his horn and showed off his trophy. Ruth was sitting on the passenger side. She didn't look as they drove past.

Though I had never dated Ruth, I wasn't happy as I thought, *fucking Slayton.* After I got off duty, I was having breakfast in the coffee shop when Ruth walked in. With hesitation, she joined me in my booth. Intentionally, I avoided questions about her date the night before. After all, she was free to date whomever she wished.

After a few minutes, Slayton sauntered in. I watched Ruth closely. She stared at him as he walked down the isle, and walked right past her without even looking. She looked slightly dejected. "Well, how was your date with Mr. Wonderful last night?" I asked in utter sarcasm.

"Dominic, I knew you were working, and I asked him not to drive past the station, but he insisted. The date was okay." She left it at that. I did too.

Ruth continued to stare at Slayton, and I couldn't contain myself, "Why don't you go sit with him, Ruth? That's obviously what you want."

Frustrated, she said, "He won't even look at me."

With the whole story of last night revealed by their actions, I disrespectfully said, "You must have fucked him."

Astonished by my rude comment, all Ruth could do was blurt out, "I did not!" Then she turned beet red and rolled her eyes left and right.

"Ruth, we've never dated and I am not looking to control you. You can do anything you want, but I know Bill Slayton very, very well. If you didn't have sex with him last night, he'd have spoken to you this morning, and then he would pursue you until you did."

"I don't remember much about last night. He got me pretty drunk." She said in shallow defense of her actions.

"Look, Ruth. I like you, and I don't hold what you did against you. All the women want to date Slayton. Lord only knows what they see in him, but sooner or later you're all going to figure out what he's really like."

Ruth kept looking at Slayton. Disappointment began to reign on her face. "I must say he was nice to me."

"Yeah. Nice until he got what he wanted. Now he won't even speak to you. He can't even say good morning to you. Was he worth it, Ruth? Was Mr. Perfect worth it?"

It was a rhetorical question, but she looked at me with a dissatisfied purse of her lips and held up her baby finger. "It was this big. I had to ask him if it was in."

"Now you know why he can't face women the next day." I laughed at my own joke.

* * *

Association president Bill Slayton hit the gavel. "Our next speaker needs no introduction." A few guys chuckled at Slayton's demeanor.

Wyatt was up out of his seat before Slayton could finish his little spiel. "Just get on with the next agenda item, Billy." Slayton was a charismatic little guy, a real character, but Wyatt sometimes had trouble hiding his displeasure for him. Actors belonged in Hollywood, not in real life and death situations. Though the chief hired this townie, he learned Slayton couldn't be counted on.

Slayton gave the chief the floor with a theatrical flourish, wordlessly getting in the last word. Truth be told, the feelings were mutual. Slayton knew Wyatt never liked him, but Slayton was savvy enough to know not to cross him. Wyatt had far too much power in this small town even more than did the well-connected Slayton.

The chief ran his fingers through his thick wiry salt-and-pepper hair atop his thin six-foot-four-inch frame as we patiently waited. "Next month, I'll be sixty years old." A few guys hooted and shouted out funny little comments. But Wyatt's face was a blank; he wasn't saying this because he wanted to remind us to buy him a birthday cake. "I could have retired a few years back, but I stayed not just because I could use a little larger pension but because I love this." He paused for a moment. No one said a word. "I love this job."

A few guys respectfully clapped, but it was a nervous reaction at best. Something was wrong here.

Yes, something was wrong indeed, and I feared I knew where it was going. Not only was I not ready to lose this towering figure in my life, but this department didn't have anyone ready to take over. The next few months would be critical to its long-term destiny.

"I told myself a few years ago that when I turned sixty, I was going to retire. Maybe I'll still teach a little at the fire academy or something like that. But I don't want to hang around here long enough to be a liability."

Again, silence. For another man, there might have been more catcalls and good-natured fooling. But for Wyatt, nothing was more important than firefighting. Nothing meant more than serving your community bravely and with dignity. When he talked about someday being a liability, he meant it, and it had to have eaten him up inside. Chief Wyatt was an active chief. A man who didn't just talk the talk like others on the job did when an emergency came up, leaving the actual firefighting to the expendable guys. Chief John Wyatt walked the walk, he worked a fire, and he commanded the respect of all.

"So tomorrow, I'm giving notice to the Board of Selectmen. I will be retiring in thirty days." We sat in stunned silenced as the chief continued. "I suspect they'll want to promote from within, no reason why not to. You're a bunch of fine fellows, and I'm sure there are half a dozen good chiefs among you. You guys may want to talk it over amongst yourselves; that would be a good idea. You should have a united front, be ready to support a particular man. Don't be squabbling. That's bullshit, and you all know it. An appointed committee will probably ask for my recommendation, but I'll hold my tongue until you guys have a chance to think it through." Small towns always appointed ad hoc committees to serve at the pleasure of the selectmen. More bureaucratic layers, more fence walkers, making recommendations solely based on not wanting to hurt themselves at the club or at the office. "Stay out of the spotlight and just make yourself look good." Heaven forbid, an action or comment might put them at odds with a powerful Boston attorney, or the likes, so full of pomp and ego with mental notes of *get even* and *screw them over* throbbing on their frontal lobes.

"I hope the committee doesn't have any crazy ideas of their own. They've been known to do such things. In the end, it's their decision. But I think if we settled this amongst ourselves, they'd give their blessings to the new man, whoever he may be.

"So I guess in closing, I don't want to get all weepy on you, but I'm gonna miss this job." And for the first time any of us could recall, John Wyatt was not true to his word. He *did* get weepy on us, tears filling his eyes and his voice cracking, "I love you, guys."

We weren't the kind of men who hugged and cried. Sure, sometimes someone might break down when a tragedy occurred on our watch, a citizen reached too late in a burning house, or worse, a child dying in your arms after being rescued from a mangled auto wreck, but never as a group. We've never had that kind of tragedy in our department. Brewster, as usual, was the first to the chief, weakly acknowledging a much stronger man. I was one of the first men out of his seat, wrapping my arms around Chief Wyatt as others soon joined us in a huddle. I'd never done this before; it was just spontaneous and seemed so right.

Slayton sat alone at the front of the room, clearly upstaged. No one ever knew what scheming thoughts ran behind the calm repose of Pretty Boy Slayton's face.

He twiddled the wooden gavel between his fingers, evidently bored. Bill Slayton hated playing second fiddle to anyone and stared at Brewster and me as if we were Batman and Robin. Brewster and I were a good team he was my captain and I was his go-to guy, whom he could always count on and always turned to when the shit hit the fan. Without giving it much thought, I'd say he'd be the next chief.

The meeting continued to its prescribed conclusion, but focus had been completely lost from the proceedings. As guys fought for face time with the outgoing chief, Pete Brewster approached Tom Jacobs. "Jesus Christ. I haven't seen anything like this since Ted Williams retired."

Jacobs's gave him that stony look. "Before my time," he practically hissed in response, then turned away.

Jacobs's gears were already turning. Jacobs and Brewster were the two senior captains. Technically, that made them next in line for the chief's job. Of course, it didn't always go down that way; but more often than not, it did. Jacobs had to have been acutely aware that Brewster had seniority on him. We all knew the chain of command, and Brewster was ahead of Jacobs in the structure as Jacobs was of me. Was the Williams remark his little way of reminding Jacobs? Naw, that couldn't be it. Brewster was much too literal to think of anything that clever. I watched this brief exchange from across the room and couldn't help but notice Jacobs's eyes, which were very distant. "Still waters run deep." Jacobs and I worked very well together, and I liked him a lot, but there was something brewing in this guy somewhere. What underlying current was driving this man? No one seemed to know. What we did know was that his personal life didn't fit the image of a firefighter. He was abusive to his wife, and he had driven his son to drugs; he was obviously too demanding, too harsh, and had no empathy with no understanding of a nurturing way at all.

Meanwhile, Slayton had moved from behind his wooden table at the front of the room and was suddenly slithering and snaking through everybody to find a place for himself practically inside of Chief Wyatt's shirt.

Jacobs's eyes never left Slayton. As I looked over the room, I could see him tense up, and I overheard him saying out of the side of his mouth, "Look at that fucking Slayton!" His jealousy for Slayton's charismatic personality was too overpowering to contain him.

Jacobs knew as well as anyone that Slayton was no firefighter. But "politics makes strange bed partners." Bring that into the equation, and it was anybody's ballgame. Some towns were hiring total civilians, guys with no experience at all to be public safety directors and other ill-conceived ideas. Taking care of some rich bastard's ne'er-do-well cousin or what have you. Politics. It sucked when it didn't go your way, and it could be very destructive.

Everyone was up for an impromptu party—hell, any excuse for a party—but Wyatt looked uncomfortable and seemed to be pulling back a bit. "Excuse me a minute, guys, while I drain the old fire hose." It was corny but apropos, considering the crowd and the setting, and it still got a few chuckles. A joke that evoked laughter from years ago, and it gave the chief an exit. He said what he had come to say, and now it was time to leave the association to its business.

When the chief passed by the main room, he quickly grabbed me by my sleeve before anyone else could see him. "C'mere." I wasn't the kind to question anything Chief Wyatt said, and I followed him into his office.

Chief Wyatt closed the door behind us and got close enough to me to be able to talk clearly in only a whisper. "What do you think?"

"Think? I think I'm in total disbelief at the moment, Chief. I can't get over it. I thought you'd do this job forever. You're ageless. I never would have guessed you for being a day over fifty."

"Dominic, I'm not asking for a eulogy. I'll be getting enough of those when you mugs throw me a going-away party next month. I'm asking you what you think about the future, about the department, about who's best suited to lead it."

With a confused look on my face, I stood silently.

"Let me make myself more clear. Who do you think should be the next chief?"

Now I looked *really* confused. "I don't know. I haven't had time to digest your announcement yet. I'm serious, totally blown away by all of this. No one can fill your shoes, Chief."

"So think fast. That's what I taught you. Think fast. React. Use your training and make the right decision. Don't ponder, don't dawdle, seconds mean lives. Who should be the next chief? Some one has to be!"

"Straight from my hip, I'd say, m . . . m . . ."

"Right."

"What?"

"I. You. Think about it. You as fire chief."

Unable to think of anything to say, I just looked at Chief Wyatt as if he had just grown a big green third eyeball on his forehead. With my heart pounding in my chest, I tried to speak, "No . . ." That's all that would come out as my voice trailed off.

"Why not?"

"I'm not ready."

"Why not? Who is?"

"I'm . . . I'm . . ."

Wyatt looked at me with a friendly smirk. "You can't answer me, Dominic, because you can't think of a good answer."

"I'm too young, Chief. I got on the job at eighteen. I was promoted young. I need more time, Chief. Besides, I'm embroiled with the town over building a house, and they won't even let me do that."

"Ah, bullshit. I've had this job since I was thirty-one. You're old enough. You know more about firefighting than every guy in that room out there. You take the courses, you go to the lectures, the seminars, and you read the magazines. You're as progressive as we have on this department. The only other guy I know who takes this stuff as seriously as you do is me, and I'm out of here."

"But Brewster and Jacobs are the senior captains. If I jumped over them, the firehouse would be divided. The respect of the men wouldn't be there. No, I couldn't do it."

"Dominic, don't you realize how much the men respect you now? Is there any other guy they'd rather go into a crisis with than you? You're a coach, Dom, a real teacher and a natural leader. Think about it and answer me honestly, whose hands would they sooner put their own lives in? Whose?"

Looking down at the floor, I was unable to muster the ego to answer the question. But I knew the answer. I knew, and Chief Wyatt knew. And Chief Wyatt knew that I knew. Finally, looking up with mixed emotions, I said, "Chief, I'd do it for you in a second if you order me to. But outside of that, it's not right. Someday, yes. Yes, I'd be honored to be Coventry's fire chief, but not today. The time's not right. It's in the best interest of morale. It should be someone else, maybe Brewster or Jacobs."

A knock on the chief's door broke up our little tête-à-tête. Another man with salutations for the chief; it was Brewster. Of course, it was Brewster. He had years of dried shit on his nose.

"Think about what I said, Dominic."

Shaking the chief's hand and looking him in the eye, I said, "Thank you, sir. What you said means a great deal to me." As I left the room, Brewster looked at me like I had just grown a third eye.

It didn't go unnoticed that I exited the chief's office from behind closed doors. Some chuckled and said to hold on to your helmets while others shook their heads and said, "Here we go!" Captain Charles stood and glared as I walked away. It was clear he'd developed a dislike for Italians, and I became the hot button that ignited ill feelings inside the WWII veteran. This growing notion would trickle down through his men. Because of this, Group A tagged me as not liking authority. The fact is, I respect authority; I just don't like bad authority. Charles leaned toward Jacobs and whispered, "Watch out for Renaldi, I don't trust the fucking guinea at all. He's not one of us, do you know what I mean?"

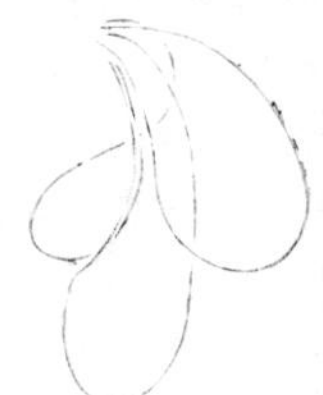

Chapter 6

The relationship between Ruth and me was so bad that when I pulled up to the house in my pickup truck, I cringed at the thought of her still being up, her pain not yet having succumbed to sleep. As I glanced at the antique windows from this angle, the full moon high in the night sky bounced off the panes, making it difficult at first glance to tell if Ruth had the TV on in our bedroom. "Damn, she's still awake."

We lived in a caretaker's apartment behind a historic Revolutionary War inn. Many of the Coventry firemen worked other jobs to supplement their incomes; this was my unique way of embracing the necessity of a second job, and it also afforded me the opportunity to commit to my primary job, the fire department. I was available to work fire alarm, short notice overtime, and most importantly, respond to emergencies. Living just a quarter mile from the firehouse, I was dependable 100 percent of the time.

The Plumes of Feathers Inn was built in 1751 and was a very successful inn on the road to Boston—the Boston Post Road. The inn flourished with servants who had their own quarters, an in-house post office, a ballroom, and vegetable gardens for fresh produce for the daily meals. There was a well-stocked pantry and an inviting dining room on the first floor with something good always cooking in the kitchen. In addition, there were fields of hay that covered the two-hundred-acre site for livestock, which were raised for the dinner table. Over time, acreage was sold off. The inn now sits on twenty acres with maintained plush green grass surrounding it.

The inn's owner was a Tory sympathizer during the revolutionary days and quietly concealed others of like mind who were passing through. In fact, British general Gates had stayed there on occasion. During the Civil War period, the inn harbored slaves in the Underground Railroad. A secret room was built behind the 1800s kitchen fireplace and was now a part of the caretaker's quarters. To access this room, one would remove the false wall to the very shallow closet on the left side of the fireplace. Ruth and I knew this well as the inn was today a museum, and we were occasionally asked to lead tour groups. Adjoining the inn to the rear was a two-story woodshed. This shed was very large, and during the 1960s, along with a portion of the original tavern, it was the apartment for a caretaker.

Coventry did indeed have some wonderful people in town, most all of whom seemed to be volunteer innkeepers for this brilliant affiliation of old money and whom Ruth and I grew to admire and respect. Shortly after our marriage, Ruth and I would become those caretakers in exchange for extraordinarily low rent. We were a young couple who had much to learn and who did more work than any previous caretaker had done. This was a perfect marriage. We were what the inn wanted, and the inn was what two struggling young adults needed on a fireman's salary.

Now, I thought, if only my marriage to Ruth was as satisfying. I don't know where we went wrong. Ruth was what I wanted. She was fun, certainly attractive enough, and unpretentious. We both came from Coventry's meager side, mine more meager than hers. We could grow together; we could help each other from steerage to second class. With Ruth's looks and my never-say-die attitude, I was certain we had the right genes to raise a family without signs of entitlement as long as the kids looked like her! We can do this; I'll lead the way. After years of trying, it became quite clear I had underestimated the anchor, which did not allow Ruth to break away from her parents.

Removing my boots and hanging up my heavy winter coat, I doubted that the television in the bedroom I shared with Ruth would be turned off by the time I reached the top of the stairs. Even if it were, it was unlikely she would be asleep. Damn! A coward's choice—stay downstairs watching the other TV until she was asleep or go upstairs and face the misery now. The latter was a way to get it over with more quickly; the former would only postpone it until the morning. The hour was late; I was tired and more than a little tipsy. I would face the music now; it would be less painful for both of us.

Tiptoeing—rather, tripping up the old stairs—even if she had been dozing, the loud creaks from my weight on old wood would have awakened her. *Well*, I thought, *here goes nothing.*

As I entered the bedroom, Ruth did not turn to look at me. I checked; her eyes were open. That was bad. The silent treatment. No man can really handle the silent treatment. It works every time. Her arms were crossed across her chest. Bad again. Stubborn body language. Her makeup had long since been washed off, and her long blond hair was matted against the headboard, a few stray locks hanging diagonally over her forehead just above her left eye. With those big blue eyes, she was still an attractive woman—beautiful, in fact. Yet marriage, certain marriages, tends to skew even the visual perceptions. The allure was gone from both sides. Fore our joint history, our collective baggage had made her a guilt factor for me—a problem to be avoided. With mirror images, the shoe fit perfectly on the other foot as well. And so I did avoided Ruth more and more. We both avoided each other more and more.

Trying to see how long I could play the silence game, I unbuttoned my shirt, pulled my undershirt over my head, dropped my pants and underwear, removed my socks, and placed them all in the laundry basket in the bathroom just off our bedroom. Back in the day, this might have even been a prelude to lovemaking. Ruth saying, "Yeah, baby" as I played along, suddenly acting like a clumsy Chippendale dancer, strip teasing for her prior to joining her in bed. But that was years ago. That was when I looked forward to coming home from work and actually told my wife I loved her!

I slid under the covers as if I was afraid too much movement would set off a sensitive bomb. *Dumb*, I thought. *She's still awake. Who cares how much I move around?* I hated these moments; they were very painful for the both of us. But certain habits had begun to be ingrained in me. In the younger days of our marriage, I'd try to make enough noise and movement to rouse her so I could seduce her no matter what the hour. That morphed into politely entering the room at night quietly, respectful of her sleep, especially when the children were babies. And now, it had become a ritual to avoid getting bitched at, derided for simply being who I was—a man, a fireman, a person who worked odd hours for very little pay despite the risky job.

Turned away from Ruth, I stared at the digital clock radio on my nightstand. Two-thirty in the morning. This was bad. It *shouldn't* have been bad. I hadn't done anything wrong, illegal, or immoral. But since I also got chewed out for coming in late after legitimately working, coming in this late when I was off duty and ostensibly at an association meeting was really bad news.

I closed my eyes, wishing I could cuddle, my large powerful hand holding my wife's firm breast as we fell asleep, but she had cast that aspiration aside long ago. Nor could I blame her for that. Ruth was making me too tense to sleep. Perhaps it was my own sadness for the situation that made me too tense. But I lay there, kept awake by the dread of how and when the tumult would start. No, I wasn't afraid of her. But our relationship had become one of perpetual annoyance. No one is afraid of the stone in their shoe; it just hurts like hell and drives you crazier with each step. Ruth had become the stone in my shoe; her defense being that I had become the stone in hers.

After twenty minutes or so, it finally occurred to me that it was pushing three o'clock, and Ruth still had that damn television blaring. "Are you watching something?" It was a dumb question. Of course, she wasn't watching anything. What the hell was on TV at that hour but infomercials and bad movies?

"Why? Does it bother you?" The shrillness of her voice could cut glass. She'd been waiting for this moment, and I had fallen right into her trap. *Damn*, I thought. *Stupid, stupid, stupid!* It was times like this when I shouldered the responsibility of our failed marriage. Ruth's pain hurt me deeply, neither one of us deserving it but too paralyzed to do anything about it.

"Do you want me to sleep downstairs?" If she really wanted to watch TV, shouldn't *she* be the one to sleep on the sofa in the family room? But TV was not at all what this was about, and I knew it.

"Do what you want; you always do."

I thought for an instant and then slowly began to get out of bed.

"You're going downstairs?"

This fight would be confusing to me even if I hadn't gone out for beers after the association meeting. I turned to Ruth in a tired, exasperated manner, saying, "What do you want?" It was a plea, a prayer. Get thee out of my shoe, damned stone. Leave me the hell alone.

"I want a husband." As much as she seemed wound up and ready to unleash a barrage of expletives and criticisms, Ruth stopped short after this one quick, sharp blow. "Let him deal with that," she seemed to say. And it worked. My heart ached as I winced.

"And what am I, the postman? Can I turn the bills over to some other guy since I'm not your husband anymore? Can I ask some other guy to stand here every day and night and listen to your shit instead of me 'cause isn't that a husband's job? And I mean, if I'm being relieved of duty—"

"You should have been home hours ago! I know those meetings, they end at a reasonable hour. Then you guys go out for what you really get together for—booze and broads. Did you all go to a strip club? Huh?"

"A few did, the rest of us went to the Double L in Cromwell where we had some beers and talked shop."

Ruth harrumphed. "Yeah sure. I know what you guys are like together."

Suddenly, I realized I was standing there naked. Not that it should have mattered. But when arguing with one's wife, having your most vulnerable regions exposed can be downright dangerous. It makes aiming for a target that much easier. I began to pull on a pair of gym shorts I had lying near the bed, which I always wore to bed, and would have tonight, if not so tipsy, another unusual event for me!

"So you're going downstairs?"

"I can't tell if that's a question or an observation. What does it look like I'm doing?"

"Goddamn bastard," Ruth murmured.

"Listen! I work hard, I bring home money, and I'm faithful. What the hell else do you want? Ruth, I am sorry I'm the cause of your misery. It breaks my heart"—my voice now quivering—"it breaks my heart to see you this way."

"Why do you have to go out with those guys after meetings?"

"It's important. After the meetings is when all the real business gets done. They put the damn gavel away, and we talk and work things out. It's important. I'm trying to move up, do right by my family." In a perfect world, I wanted to sweep into the house with a big grin on my face, telling my beautiful wife that my mentor had just tapped me to become fire chief, my idol. The man who gave me a future. She'd jump out of bed and smother me with kisses. But that woman disappeared long ago. The shrew in my bed was the enemy. Yes, I knew I was half the cause, hence the pain. I still wanted to share with her the news about chief's retirement; but if I did it now, she'd only use it as a weapon against me, taunting me for being a dreamer and getting my hopes up.

"Yeah right. Did you schmooze with some selectman who promised you a variance on that white elephant you bought?"

"Go to hell," I muttered.

Ruth knew one of my weak points. "Yeah, going out drinking with the boys, maybe some selectman will join you. Some rich guy slumming it with you bums, maybe some guy up for reelection looking for some votes from you firehouse guys."

"No, that's Bill Slayton's domain."

"Yeah, and they laugh at guys like you. You, someone who buys a piece of property that can't be built on."

Boy, this was going to be a tough night. Ruth was driving the knife deeper. This property wasn't a rock pile to be used for roadbeds; it was my rock of Gibraltar to be used as a base for my children while creating their road to success. Such a beautiful piece of property with a southern exposure overlooking a pond where wildlife abounds and where children could play and learn in the natural beauty of such an environment, all nestled in an undesirable section of town that Coventry had arbitrarily declared a Flood Plain Zone. The necessary perk test was excellent. Surely, common sense would say the rise on the edge of the flood zone was buildable, if the line was placed in a more accurate location. There was only one house on this one and a half-acre rise in the middle of half acre zoning, and it had never flooded. The road had never flooded, and none of the houses across the street had ever flooded. Besides, Coventry center would be underwater before any of this occurred, and Noah would have to build another ark. Suffice it to say, Coventry center, with its firehouse and all, had never flooded, and Noah has yet to build another ark. With a clear delineation between aquatic and terrestrial plant life, scientific evidence did in fact support the Flood Plain Line was incorrect; and a simple adjustment by the Planning Board, a more accurate placement of the line, would render this a buildable house lot. Where, for a short $15,000, payments for which were spread over five years with zero interest, we'd have a house lot to build on in Coventry. Our family would have a house to call their home. Something they so richly deserved, and our children could begin building their life's foundations through their education. It might not be Park Place, but we'd be quite pleased with Marvin Gardens.

"What kind of idiot does a thing like that?" Ruth spoke harshly. "Think any of these rich guys is that stupid? Then you give me the Mr. Big Shot act, like 'I'm a fireman. I'm important in this town. Everyone looks up to me. I'll just go to selectman so-and-so who owns his own software company and tell him my problems, and presto! Everything will work out fine. He'll get me a variance, and I'll build a real home that my family wouldn't be squished into like a can of sardines. All I need is to buy the guy a couple of beers, and he'll be my pal for life. I mean, the guy is a multimillionaire. He couldn't possibly afford his own beer.' These guys can buy their own brewery, Dominic. They laugh at guys like you."

"And their wives look down at you. You, who can't move more than three blocks away from your mommy."

"Who cares, Dom? My parents help us. What do your parents do? Huh? What do they do for us, Dom?"

"Not a god damn thing! Maybe that's why I'm busting my ass to build a better life for our kids, trying desperately to carve an easier path for them with nothing more than my bare hands. I bought that property because it adjoins your parents' property, which we were supposed to have purchased eight years ago when they moved to New Hampshire. Remember that, Ruth? But no, they're just as stuck in the mud as you. Now we're both stuck! The only option I now have is to ask for a variance from a town that's never accepted me."

The longer a couple is married, the dirtier the fights. I loathed my abusive father and had no respect for him. Ruth knew this was a soft spot as vulnerable as my private parts. *Men and women*, I thought. *Women especially*. It wasn't fair. Men grew up knowing where the invisible line was drawn. They had to, or they'd never make it out of their childhood alive. A man you could knock on his ass when he took a step too far during an argument. Other guys, some guys in the department even, were known to take a swing at their wives from time to time. Maybe they had the right idea. No, I thought again. No, they didn't, not at all. I've never hit a woman, well, except my sister, and she beat the crap out of me! But geez, if Ruth were a guy, how I'd lay into her right now. Forget words, just "bang, zoom, straight to the moon, Alice."

At least I was old enough and mature enough by now to realize that getting in the last word was not only a major coup for my wife; it was also worthless and pointless. It was easier to just give in to her. Instead of responding more, I just turned and headed toward the stairs.

"Yeah, now wake the kids, making all that noise going up and down the stairs all times of night." *WHAM*, another dagger to the heart! My eyes welled as I stopped and looked to the ceiling. The pain in my heart went even deeper, knowing my family was squeezed into small quarters because of my failure. *Screw it*, I thought. It still wasn't worth responding to. I trundled down the stairs as quietly as I could, grabbed an old afghan that lay over the top of the sofa, and pulled it over myself as I stretched out. My faithful golden retriever, Cara, came over to lie on the floor next to me. My feet hung over the arm of the old sofa. Not a perfect fit by any account. *Ruth would probably fit here perfectly*, I thought. But Ruth always got the bed, and I frequently got the couch these days. As I tried to get comfortable, I reveled in the feeling that this was the best I'd felt since I'd left the guys at the bar. I was alone. The fight had ended. Peace. I put my hand on Cara and closed my eyes.

David is sixteen, I began to think, *and he'll be out of the house in three more years. Stacy will be in five years. Then Laura will be, I counted my fingers, eight years. Just eight more years, and then I could kiss this marriage good-bye. We could kiss this marriage good-bye. We had to stick around long enough to see the kids through high school. Then hello world, I'm finally free of the misery!* I'm sure Ruth felt the same way. I just pray our children can make it that long.

Chapter 7

"Hello again, ladies." With a sincere smile, I pleasantly greeted the two familiar women in the lobby of the firehouse. How could I not be pleasant to them? They were upbeat, happy, and genuinely excited over their new business venture. They were also carrying the same set of plans as before. For the fourth time in two days, the new owners of a real estate office had come in looking for the chief. For the fourth time in two days, he wasn't in.

"We need to speak to him about this fireplace in our office before we meet with our architect."

"I'm sorry, he's not in. I did tell the chief you needed to speak to him today." The two women became frustrated. So I said, "Wait a minute while I call him. I picked up the phone and called the chief's mobile phone. A minute later, I told the woman, "He said he'll be back at around two o'clock."

"That's too late. We meet with our architect at noontime."

"I'm sorry."

Dejectedly, they said, "Thank you anyway," and began to leave.

These women were working hard at trying to do the right thing, and the fire department was letting them down. Feeling sorry for them, I wanted to do something to help. So I called out, "What is it you need to know?"

They turned around and looked back at me wordlessly.

"Perhaps I can help guide you a little better for your meeting," I said before the door closed.

Enthusiastically, they opened their plans and began to explain.

Within a short time, I gave them enough information to have a constructive conversation with their architect. Before they left, I reiterated, "But remember, this is all unofficial. You'll still have to speak to the chief. And this looks like a building inspector's issue as well."

"Thank you so much. You've been very helpful." Again, they started to walk out. Abruptly, one turned around rather exuberantly and walked back to the window while extending her hand. "Thank you again. My name is Carol, and I know a friend when I see one."

"Nice to meet you, Carol. My name is Dominic Renaldi. I'm happy to have been of assistance."

While I was helping the general public, others were elsewhere helping themselves. "So who are you supporting for chief?"

Tom Jacobs looked at Bill Slayton like he was from another planet. "Who am *I* supporting? I'm supporting myself, who the hell do you think I'm supporting?"

Slayton was not only brash; he was rude, saying, "Yeah, but do you think you've got enough support?"

"Yeah, asshole, I've got support."

"But do you have enough support?"

Jacobs pondered whether to let Slayton have it right in the side of the head or take a more intellectual approach. The little bastard could just be playing mind games, or he, maybe, he knew something. Jacobs decided it was worth taking the bait. "I'm the best choice. Me or Renaldi. And he's only a lieutenant, so it should be my turn."

"Your turn?" Slayton's voice trailed off, and he smirked that irritating, condescending smirk of his.

Jacobs spoke from the side of his mouth, "What, you don't believe in seniority? What's right is right."

"Yeah, I guess that's why Brewster will be the next chief."

If Jacobs was mildly irritated before, he was ready to throw a right cross to the jaw about now. "You know something, peanut?"

"I know that by seniority, with Captain Charles retiring too, Brewster is next in line. He'll be the senior captain, and that puts him over you, Tommy. I mean, that's if I believed in seniority." Slayton not only knew how to get under your skin; he was a good counterpuncher too.

"Yeah, that's if he gets it. Like I said, my vote is for myself. I'm a better fireman than Brewster. I'm a better leader. It should be mine."

"Yeah, well, I'd like to be chief too."

Jacobs had a hard time hiding his incredulity. "You? I don't want to hurt your feelings, Billy boy, but you're not even an officer, and you don't even know how to fight a fire."

"I'll be an officer if Brewster becomes chief."

"How do you figure that, Billy?"

"You have a short memory, Tommy. How do you think you and Brewster got promoted several years ago?"

"I had noth'n to do with that," said an angry Jacobs.

Slayton displayed that evil smile. "Accomplice, Tommy, your hands are dirty, and like it or not, you're in."

"It'll be a cold day in hell when you become chief."

"You really think so? That's what they said about me getting elected association president. Look at me now. And frankly, being association president is a nice little launching pad to the big job."

"You're a terrible association president. You sold us down the river on our last contract. Your head is so far up the ass of every selectman in town. You screwed over your fellow firefighters when it got down to the nitty-gritty."

Slayton smirked that haughty smirk of his again. "And that's dumb, why?"

Jacobs stopped dead in his line of thought, *The little bastard, the little weaselly bastard.*

"You don't have to say it, Tommy. I know. And you know. I got IOUs now. And not from you lowly firefighters either. They're from the people who make all the big decisions. I could walk right in to a half-dozen homes right now and lay my case out for the selectmen and come away with the job."

An upset look crossed Jacobs's face. *Billy Slayton as fire chief? God, that'd be like Bozo the Clown as ambassador to the UN.* Jacobs couldn't face even belonging to this department the day that Slayton became its chief.

"It'll never happen."

"Is that a bet?"

"Bill, we'd all line up against you. Me, Renaldi, Brewster, even Chief Wyatt, especially Chief Wyatt. You'd be chief of nothing. Faced with that, no, the selectmen would never vote in favor of you. They don't owe you so much that they'd be willing to go out and hire a whole new department around you because you have no support from the other officers."

Jacobs decided to take the high road. All this chief talk was starting to get a lot like politics, and as much as Jacobs hated politics, crossing Bill Slayton was a politically incorrect maneuver. Slayton wasn't even an officer, but because of those family ties, he still managed to carry a modicum of weight. The only reason Slayton got hired was that he was a townie, and his family managed to rub against the right elbows in town. Jacobs, even Brewster, were from neighboring towns. Among the officers, I was the only townie, aside from Chief Wyatt, of course.

"Brewster has a legitimate claim to the position." Jacobs left it at that.

"Yeah, I suppose he does. He could probably hold it for at least a decade or so. He's in good shape. Keeps healthy. Then it will probably go to me or Renaldi."

"Are you trying to goad me into a fight? 'Cause I've half a mind to bitch-slap you right here where people can see."

Slayton was ballsy but only after a fashion. Jacobs scared him almost as much as working a fire did. But both men knew that Jacobs getting physical with him right here at the firehouse, with other guys around, would just about kill any chance Jacobs had at being chief.

"Calm down, big guy. I'm just painting a picture for you. Wyatt's been chief for almost thirty years. It isn't like the job has a term limit. I'm just saying, if Brewster gets it, he'll have it about ten years or so, am I not right?"

Jacobs's eyes slanted at Slayton with contempt, that stony look. Slayton could be fun to hang around with sometimes. Jacobs was far less the life-of-the-party type. Of course, compared to Pistol Pete Brewster, Jacobs was Robin freakin' Williams. Brewster was dry as dust, better suited to being an undertaker than a leader. He'd hang out with the guys—Brewster wasn't a snob or anything—but he added less than an empty chair. It really didn't matter whether he was in a room or not; the effect was the same.

Slayton was a lot of things. A lot of negative things, but persistent he was. Persistent when it came to watching out for number one. Finally, the shoe was on the other foot. Slayton sat down on the running board of the big rig behind him. A few other guys attended to their business in different parts of the firehouse, far enough away to be out of earshot. The truck bay door was partially open taking advantage of this relatively warm winter's day and letting in some fresh air. Tom Jacobs stood over him, wanting to walk away, feeling his foe, such that he was, had been vanquished. But somehow he knew it wouldn't likely end there. Finally, Slayton looked up at Jacobs. "I want to be chief, and I will be some day."

Jacobs was irritated, and it showed. "And I want to be quarterback for the Patriots. The line starts behind me, asshole."

Slayton smirked, then shook his head at Jacobs for his lack of understanding. "Tommy, Tommy, Tommy. Who do you think Renaldi's going to support?"

"Me."

Slayton eyeballed Jacobs and, with a menacing chuckle, said, "No, he won't."

"Why not? He likes me. We work well together."

"You're sure he isn't supporting Brewster? Brewster's his captain."

Jacobs tried to look confident and bored, but it wasn't working too well. "I haven't asked him. But if I asked Dom for his support, I think I'd get it. He has no great love for Brewster. I mean, they get along, I think everybody gets along with Brewster for that matter. What's not to like? Check that, what's *to* like? He just keeps chugging along like an old bus. He eventually gets to where he'd heading, he just isn't breaking the speed limit, if you know what I mean."

They both chuckled over a perfect description of Pete Brewster.

"Does Brewster want the job?"

Jacobs looked less than happy again. "He's probably been measured for his new uniform already."

"And he's got that seniority too, Tommy. You think he'd step aside for you? This would be his last chance, his last shot."

Slayton was probably right. "So how do you think it will play out? Seems you've been thinking about this more than I have. You're here, and it's your day off."

Slayton's smirk became more of a grin, a little less irritating. "Well, so we have you wanting the job. We have Brewster wanting the job. *I* want the job. So I guess the way I'm thinking is, if I can't get the job this time, what's my best bet to get it while I'm still young enough to enjoy it?"

Jacobs pondered. "Support me."

"So if I supported you, Tommy, you'd help me out the next time the chief's job came around?"

Supporting Slayton would kill Jacobs—absolutely kill him. Sensing this, Slayton said, "Maybe I should support Brewster."

With an agitated glare, Jacobs snapped back, "Why, you little bastard!"

"Hey, Tommy, I gave you your chance. You have to give to get. Life's a two-way street."

Both men went suddenly silent as steam poured out of their ears. This was a chess match, one that Jacobs hadn't prepared for, while Slayton's preparations were no longer working. Neither knew what the next move should be.

Finally, Slayton stood up and said, "Let's go see Renaldi."

Jacobs didn't ask why. It seemed like a good enough idea on its own merits. The two started walking toward the alarm room, where I was on shift. The ever-buoyant Slayton, Coventry's favorite son, led the way. "Hey, Dom, how's it hanging?"

Looking up from NFPA (National Fire Protection Association), Chapter 72, which I was reading, I said, "Fine."

"Hey, Dom, listen, Tom and I were wondering who's going to be the next chief."

Stroking my chin pensively with a look of distrust, I replied, "I don't know."

"You're tight with the old man. Who's he supporting?"

Knowing Slayton as well as I did, I knew there was no-good coming out of this conversation. Sucking on my lower lip, I pondered the consequences riding on my answer. Then I couldn't resist, hoping my response would hit Slayton hard. Jacobs hung in the background behind Slayton, looking on casually, almost trying to appear bored. Slayton, though, was like an agitated Chihuahua.

Acting quite cavalier about it, I said, "He asked me if I wanted the job."

Jacobs's cool look of indifference turned to slack-jawed shock, and he stiffened right up. Slayton looked as if he would piss on himself. I almost laughed at the two of them.

"He did?" asked a wide-eyed Slayton.

Remaining collected, almost embarrassed by what I'd just stated, but enjoying it nonetheless, I said, "Yup, last night in his office after his announcement. I told him I didn't want the job."

With eyes now the size of softballs, Slayton exclaimed, "You what?" as he tried to regain his composure.

"It's not my time. It should go by seniority."

Again, there was silence in the room. Slayton and Jacobs looked as if they were at a wake and didn't know what to say to the widow. Jacobs slowly backed out of the office and seeing through Slayton was as clear and easy as looking through a pane of glass.

"Yeah. Seniority. Okay, just thought to ask. Guys are wondering what's up, that's all." Slayton sounded as flustered as a kid who just got turned down asking a pretty girl to dance, quickly slipping out of the room, and after Jacobs. A handful of steps out of the alarm room, Slayton caught up with Jacobs. He asked, "Now what do we do?"

Suddenly I became an obstacle in their path.

Jacobs looked indifferent but only because he was still in shock. "Dunno."

Slayton darted ahead of Jacobs, blocking his path as if to plead, saying, "Don't leave me now, Tommy!" And he spoke obsessively, "Well, let's see. The chief wants Renaldi, but he doesn't want it—for now. So who does that leave?"

Still acting stunned, Jacobs stammered, "Me and Brewster. I think I could get Renaldi turned around. As I said, he likes me, we work well together."

"Then I'll support Brewster," said Slayton without hesitation.

"What?"

"You heard me. I could easily talk up old Pistol Pete. He has no enemies, no friends either. But he's a safe choice, a good ole boy. It's his turn. You talk a lot about turns, don't you, Tom? It's Brewster's turn. But you wouldn't want me to do that 'cause it would stab you right between the shoulder blades. There goes your shot."

"And if Brewster has it, and I retire in a few years, then Renaldi would get it, and *you'd* be shit out of luck too," Jacobs said while figuring out Slayton's plan.

"Exactly. Which leaves one last option."

Not the conniving politician, Jacobs looked at Slayton quizzically. "What?"

"Brewster would be pleased as a pig in mud to be chief if only for a day. Something to put on his tombstone. Problem is, you know and I know he'd be a piss poor chief. He's weak.

"With him as chief, we could get away with anything. Let him have the title for a little while, so what?

"We have rules around here, Bill, we'll be screwing ourselves."

"Rules were made to be broken, Tommy, remember?"

Slayton looked at Jacobs while waiting for an answer, but Jacobs just gave him a manic, stony stare.

"You really don't get it, do you, Tommy? I've already taken care of Brewster. We could run this place. And if anything goes wrong, he's the guy who'd hang for it. Old Pete has no savvy, no skills. He just lumbers through life like a big dumb ox. It takes him two hours to watch *60 Minutes*."

"So we screw over Brewster. What then?"

"That leaves you, me, and Renaldi. Renaldi can't stand me, I know that. He and I have history going back to when I was just a kid. He and my older brother palled around together in high school. He detests me. So what if I always showed up to skate after the pond was shoveled? They're the suckers, not me. Nothing would give me more pleasure than to mess with Dom Renaldi as often as I can. Nothing. And he's just as naïve in his own way as Brewster. The two of them are Boy Scouts. They should both just put on

Smokey the Bear suits and give firehouse tours for little kids all day long. Guys like you and me, Tommy, we know how things work. We could make a helluva team."

"So what do you propose?" asked Jacobs.

"We suck up to everybody, be good little boys, and throw our support behind Brewster. Everybody will hold hands and sing, 'We Are the World.' Then we set out to ruin both Brewster and Renaldi. It shouldn't be hard. I've already started the process."

"What do you mean, you've already started? What process?"

"Last month. At the association meeting." Slayton explained, "Renaldi is now so deep into going against the selectmen at collective bargaining it's a slam dunk."

"How does that hurt him?"

Slayton was in smirk-mode again. "I took the job to make kissy face with the selectmen. And it worked. Renaldi that dumb dago has been fighting them tooth and nail for the association, and he's winning. The selectmen are already beginning to hate the guy. They'll never vote him in as chief. And he'll be too stupid to understand why. Even Wyatt knew how to play politics. Renaldi hasn't a clue."

Jacobs looked down and tapped the cement floor aimlessly with his boot as he thought for a moment. Then said, "One thing we'll need to do is get Renaldi out of headquarters. He'll be too close to Brewster and the younger guys. Too much of an influence on them."

With a sly look of confident approval, Slayton responded, "Now you're thinking, Tommy. Time is on our side. There'll be opportunities, lots of them. The association is just the first one that comes to mind. Between Brewster and Renaldi, one or both of them will step in a pile of dog shit in no time. And when they do . . ."

"I'll be chief."

"And I'm next."

The impromptu self-appointed ad hoc selection committee meeting ended with both men laughing their phony and obnoxious laughs. Slayton sounding as if he was forced to laugh with exulting force at the world's best joke, and Jacobs's laughing out of the side of his mouth as he bent over, clapping his hands together and stomping his foot.

Chapter 8

As a statement of presumed fact rather than a complaint, no matter what one's personal political persuasion, few will disagree that the basic responsibility of local government is to provide protection and education. Ironically, those of us who do the most to directly provide such services are often the most undervalued. Police, soldiers, schoolteachers, and firemen. Thus, in addition to acting as caretaker at the inn, I also did private contract work around Coventry and neighboring towns, installing fire alarm equipment and systems on a very limited basis. If a contractor called, and I could fit it in around my work for the fire department, I did the favor for him. I believed my primary responsibility was to my primary job. The extra pay was lucrative as the inhabitants of these million-dollar mansions were used to paying top dollar. Quality, not price, that's what these people were looking for; to their minds, the more expensive, the better.

A lot of firemen worked second jobs—snowplowing, landscaping, painting, or general handyman businesses—we had all the trades covered. Only the very youngest guys, like Ben Lyons, still living at home, were able to live on a fireman's salary alone. The cost of living in Coventry and its environs was astronomical. Consequently, none of the local millionaires would ever be interested in an all-volunteer fire department. As if they'd risk their lives for free.

High tech had managed to grip both coasts, and Massachusetts had been riding a long wave of growth throughout the '70s and '80s—almost too much growth. The cost of living had skyrocketed, and the cost of housing had quadrupled. If you didn't own by now, you may be outpriced, hence, still living at the inn. With small towns growing faster than their tax revenues, coupled with the increased demand for services—primarily with over expanding schools exceeding their work forces—small towns were beginning to show the strains of a stretched tax base. While the midnight oils burned in town halls across the state trying to cope with this trend, Coventry was enjoying the rewards of its visionary leaders from long ago. In an effort to create properties that generated enough tax revenue to sustain growth, subdivisions were being approved everywhere in this affluent bedroom community. With the new technology boom white hot, there was plenty of money to invest in a community such as Coventry. Men in their late twenties and early thirties became instant millionaires with so much money to burn they couldn't spend it fast enough.

Several of the developers liked my work and found me very dependable, but much to their chagrin, I wasn't often available. However, I was doing some fire alarm work in a new subdivision across the street from several established million-dollar homes. The newer subdivisions overshadowed the mere million-dollar homes with enormous palaces containing six, seven, or eight bedrooms for the average family of 4.75 members; go figure! It seemed a bathroom for every day of the week and a three—or four-room suite for the nanny. There were four-car garages, tennis courts, and pools all on acres and acres of land. I sometimes wondered if a few of these behemoths would someday become the white elephants of Fifth Avenue—the austere, unsightly mansions of the McAllisters, Vanderbilts, and Asters of the era. It was along the same notion—"I must build one bigger, better, and more expensive"—driving their spires and ceilings higher and looking gaudier, all to be torn down someday as distant memories of a bygone era. Surely, these homes did not reflect the quintessential small town I was born in. Coventry was my beat, my only true home. Even then, people like me were on the outside living in neighboring towns. What a shame, the townies felt this way. Although considered lower class by some, we were nonetheless born and raised in Coventry and a part of the town. Not nouveau riche like so many of the newcomers; native Coventry, that's what we were with our own vested interest in our community. What right did others have to look down on us? Even so, every year, the place became wealthier. Working-class people became more and more the minority. The old conservative New England town was changing. It was becoming quite affluent and cosmopolitan.

Suddenly, my helper, Ben Lyons, pointed out, "Jesus, will you look at that!"

"Huh?"

"The blonde with the stroller. I'd tap that in a second."

Glancing over, then staring with raised eyebrows, I knew that Lyons was right. There were many head turners in Coventry, where there was money galore for the best of everything—makeovers, sexy designer clothes, personal trainers, and cosmetic surgery or Botox for any female who desired their aid. If you ever wanted to see a winter migration of furry animals, just go to the Coventry Wholesome Foods Market, in Coventry center, with all the women in their mink coats silently trying to outprice each other. Let's get real, people, mink coats to the market? Now there's an exclamation point to how Coventry had changed!

But this attractive young lady was primo. She couldn't have been a day over thirty, had a knockout figure, shampoo-ad golden blond hair, a whiter-than-white smile, and all packed into the most petite little frame. She wore painted-on jeans, chic furry boots, and was pushing one of those expensive three-wheeled strollers.

"Oh, Benny, that's way out of your league."

"Hey, I went to college. I got prospects. I'm good lookin'."

Wanting to snicker but afraid the blonde would think we were laughing at her like a couple of construction workers, I quietly commented, "You may think you're a lot of things, boy, but you're not good enough for that. That's a Formula 1 car, and you just got your learner's permit."

"Hey, fuck you, old man. She'd go for me a lot faster than she'd go for you."

Cocking my head with raised eyebrows while looking at Benny, I realized I'd been affably challenged by the younger buck, so I asked rhetorically, "Oh really?" I wasn't into messing around, but certainly, I knew how to tease. It was innocent fun. Stimulating, innocent, flirtatious fun.

Opportunity knocks but once. The cute blonde may have been able to afford that expensive stroller, but she didn't seem to understand much about how to properly work it and began to struggle with it as its locked wheels inhibited movement.

It's inbred in firemen to help people. I truly wanted to help fix the brakes on her stroller. Why not? It was probably an easy fix. Besides, I thought, *This'll be fun, fireman to the rescue.* Before bolting toward the locked pram, I whispered back to young Lyons with a fun look on my face, "Watch and learn." Lyons should have been doing what I was doing, but he was still on his learner's permit and could only stare as I caught up with the damsel in distress.

"Excuse me, it looks like those stroller brakes are locking. Here, let me see if I can help you. We can't have these little guys in an unsafe vehicle now, can we?" The blonde stepped back pensively, making a quick move to keep her hands near her young children. Observing her apprehensiveness, I became more careful and deliberate in movement. "Not to worry, I'm a local fireman and live right here in town." Deliberately changing my voice, I said softly, "You're safe with me, I'm not gonna hurt ya. I'll be good, I promise!"

Still, the blonde said not a word though she didn't look afraid either. I fiddled with the brakes, but they still weren't releasing. My own kids were years beyond using one of these things, and when they did, we couldn't have afforded anything this fancy. But basic mechanical principles were basic mechanical principles. Finally, I got the brakes to release, and the problem was fixed perfectly.

"There you go. Now you'll move nice and smooth. I mean, you certainly do seem to move nice and smooth. And now the stroller will too." It was a bit forward as well as a bit clumsy, and I sort of blushed, like a comedian whose joke didn't quite hit its mark. Luckily, the blonde was forgiving.

"Thank you very much. A hundred times I've asked my husba—" She stopped in midsentence and rethought, then said, "That was quite kind of you. Where did you come from? I've never seen you around here before."

"Oh, I was working across the street. Like I said, I'm a fireman in town."

"There's a fire in town?" she said with a playful smile that immediately caught my eye.

Okay, this game suddenly became another challenge, who's going to out flirt whom? "No no, there's no fire. Sheesh, if there was, I'd be all suited up and running around, no time to chat even with a pretty lady and two adorable kids."

"My, you do flatter a girl."

Feeling my face blush, I got a little flustered. "Sorry if I offended you, I didn't mean anything by it, it's just that I have a tendency to speak the truth."

"Oh no, not at all. You get on the mommy track, you don't get as many compliments as you used to. You're sweet. And helpful too."

"Yeah, well, that's what I do. A little bit of everything. Firefighter, caretaker at the inn, fire alarm installation, and handyman work too. Stuff like that. Jack of all trades."

"Stroller repair man too! Even AAA doesn't do curbside pram repair. I'm impressed. So you do all sorts of work?"

In a tone that was half professional and half flirtatious, I said, "I can take care of most all your needs. Do you have something you need taken care of? If I can't do it, I probably know someone around who can. Knowing all the local craftsmen, I can tell you who the good guys are as well as who the crooks are. What do you need?"

"Well, there's a room in my basement that's filled with all the leftover material from when we built the house. I'd like to clean it out and turn the space into a workout area. My kids are so young, it's a hassle getting to the club, and I feel so fat."

"You're kidding me. You? Fat? You look great."

"Thank you, but you guys are all the same. You tell a woman she looks fine when she's still carrying extra baby weight. Then some girl with a tight little butt and slim hips walks by, and you fall all over yourselves."

"Lady—"

"Liz. And you are?"

"Dominic."

"Dominic. I like that. Italian?" Liz smiled and seemed to inhale deeply as she straightened herself out a bit.

"Yeah, not too many of us around here. But anyway, you look terrific. Women think guys want stick figures. We don't. We want a woman with meat on her bones."

"Oh, I've got meat on my bones. Too much of it. I need to take some off."

Looking her up and down one more time, her shapely legs, narrow waist, and a perfectly sized chest under the tight-fitting winter sweater, she couldn't have weighed more than 105 pounds. "Well, I don't see the need, but I'm not going to stand around in the cold arguing with you. Sure, yeah, I could help you out. Do you live around here?"

"That house over there." She pointed to a million-dollar home, not as ostentatious as these newer ones but still an incredibly dense building with a modest setback. *Geez, this young chick must be loaded.*

"Would it be convenient to look at the job now? I was just loading my equipment into the truck over there." Pointing toward my truck across the street, my finger was aimed directly at Lyons, who was peering around from the back of the truck. Damn! Lyons is still here.

The kid was likeable, a little quick with the answers, but he was all right. Still, the college thing was weird. A lot of the firemen had gone to college and dropped out for one reason or another. Lyons got his degree and was now working to get his masters municipal management. Some of us felt the Eagle Scout wasn't who he appeared to be. A few even wondered if Mr. Peabody liked his Cub Scout troop a little too much; I wasn't one of them. No one could figure out what he was doing lugging hoses. It wasn't like he had this deep-abiding passion for it. Most guys, they grow up wanting to become firemen; and by the time they're out of third grade, the thought has gone out of their head. Others, including some guys I worked with, never got rid of the dream and were doing what they'd always wanted to do. Sadly, others at the firehouse used the place for their own personal gains. But Lyons, he was an enigma. It was almost as if the selectmen paid this smart young guy to hang out with the great unwashed and spy for them. I'd offered him the chance to pick up some extra cash doing alarm work—a chance to learn a different aspect of our real job—and actually expected the kid to turn it down. But no, Lyons answered, "Sure. I can do that." That was Lyons's personal tagline, his answer to most everything—"Sure, I can do that." You couldn't really dislike a guy who was that positive all the time.

"Oh, you have a helper. You may need him. Some of this wood is in pretty big pieces."

Right. Bring along Lyons and ruin all my fun. No way in hell. "Uh, let me ask him. I'll be right back."

Walking briskly back toward the job site with my back to the blonde and saying to Lyons, "This poor young lady has a problem in her basement. I'm gonna check it out."

"I want to check *her* out. You need a hand?"

"No way, buddy, this is a one-man job."

Lyons looked at me and began to wonder, *I've been on the department a little over two years. In that time, I'd hung around long enough to know that several of the guys had at least two women in their lives: his wife and his girlfriend. Some police and firemen were the dirty little secrets of many of the town's wealthier married women. But Dominic Renaldi never seemed to have one of those. Now that I think about it, Dom was a great flirt, but he kept it zipped up. Either he was the rare, faithful husband, or he knew how to keep a secret. Yet. Dom's wife was a hell of a lot better looking than most of the firemen's wives. Most let themselves go, all except Ruthie. Working for Dom, I'd gotten to know Ruth; we liked each other. She was very outdoorsy, very natural looking, wholesome. More my type, the only firehouse wife I would ever look at twice.*

"Hello, Benny. Earth to Benny, yihoo!" Benny seemed to be in a deep trance.

Snapping out of his spell, he asked, "Oh, so you got a little something going there, huh?"

Not wanting to encourage Lyons to go blabbing, "Dom was closing a deal with some hot number." I murmured, "Only in my dreams, Benny." Even if the butterflies in my stomach indicated something different, this attractive young lady didn't need rumors either. Besides, unlike the other guys at the firehouse, if something did develop, I didn't believe that the pinnacle of sexual prowess was bragging to the guys about it later. It was in the act itself—the act of pleasing a woman. And lately with Ruth, the acts were practically nonexistent and less pleasurable.

Beginning a short dissertation to young Mr. Lyons, I said, "One thing I learned quite a long time ago, Benny, the way to a woman's heart is through her children. Not to diminish my work with kids, but it is true. Most men from this town are unable to, or not inclined to, participate in raising their children. They have wives and nannies for that. When kids in this town are befriended by a good, solid male role model, their mothers take notice, not in a sexual way but in an appreciative way.

"This job is on the up and up, Benny. Now go peddle your papers, we're done for the day. Thanks for the help. I'll pay you on Thursday."

"Sure you don't need a hand with the blonde? She looks like she could handle us both."

"Get your mind out of the gutter, Benny. Just doin' a job." I turned and walked away before Lyons could think of a wisecrack. My butterflies were still flying.

Thoughts began running through my mind. *This is exactly what Ruth was always accusing me of. Why am I suddenly feeling this way? The irony was that I was one of the few guys on the squad keeping it clean, not running around on the side. Slayton was tapping a saleswoman whose husband was injured in the war and lying in a military hospital in Europe. Jacobs had some brunette broad from his hometown, and Lyons was still wet behind the ears. I hadn't been with another woman since I started dating Ruth. It made a guy wonder what it was all about anymore. Would women still find me attractive? How would it feel to be with another woman? Would I feel guilty? Would I push things just so far, then get wracked with guilt and not be able to go through with it? Jesus, did guys actually have these kinds of anxieties? I'd grown so comfortable with Ruth.*

The sound of a passing car brought me back to reality. *Just goin' to look at a small job, a little fast cash, so what if she's beautiful!* my inner mind unconvincingly told itself as I walked back to her.

"Naw, he's got a class to get to. I'll take a look at what you've got. If it's too much for me to handle, I can come back another day."

"Okay," she said with a radiant smile.

As I walked along with her toward the front door, the stroller seemed to be operating well. Just to make small talk, I asked, "How's the stroller working?"

"Fine fine, thank you again." Liz seemed as anxious as me.

Looking down at her kids, I saw them meticulously dressed in winter outfits and perfectly tucked under a down blanket. Looking back up at me, they smiled.

I asked casually, "Who are these guys?"

Liz came to life quickly, responding, "Oh, this is Jared, and this is Ethan. Jared is four, and Ethan is almost sixteen-months." She was always proud and happy to talk about her boys.

I could see her watching me as I playfully said hello to the boys, my face lighting up when the sixteen-month-old smiled back. "A big smile for me, thank you, thank you, thank you," I said, not expecting a response, but Ethan giggled even more. A baby's innocent smile is so soothing to the soul, even that of a hot-headed Italian.

Liz smiled warmly as she observed the interaction of her child and this stranger.

"Young. Very young. Cute kids, though. Betcha can't tell I love kids?"

"Do you have any? Kids, that is."

"Sure. A boy and two girls, much older though. David, the oldest is sixteen."

"That old. You don't look old enough to have kids that age."

How strange, I thought. This was the kind of sweet talk the guy was supposed to be doing to the girl. This Liz had an air of self-confidence I found very refreshing. "Yeah, well, I'm quite a bit older than you, but thank you."

"I'm sure you're younger than my husband. He's fifty-nine."

"Fifty nine. Damn, that's old." I turned away. That was a rude thing to say. Geez, was I off my game. Out of practice, I guess!

But Liz only smiled demurely. "Yeah, there's quite an age difference. He has two grown kids from his first marriage. He's a doctor, a heart surgeon. He also owns a few radio stations."

"Oh, that's impressive."

"Yeah, I suppose." She sounded distant as we walked up the blues stone walk leading to the front door. "Here we are."

The front entry was double-door wide with carved solid oak doors meticulously finished. The diminutive beauty led us into the foyer. As an experienced firefighter, I instinctively did a quick size-up, looked around, checked the environment, and used my senses.

Suddenly, we had entered Never Never Land—the white marble floor, the matching décor, and the cathedral ceiling that seemed to reach to heaven. The grand staircase leading to the second floor was just in front of us all with an aroma of freshness and cleanliness with freshly cut flowers in a glass vase. Looking to the left, I could see a living room the size of my first floor. Fully carpeted with plush, opulent wall-to-wall white furniture perfectly set around the fireplace, giving it feel of a Madison Avenue showcase. Beautiful paintings graced the walls, probably Van Gogh, Monet, or Picasso. Beyond the living room was a set of French doors leading to a study. Everything was so white and so pristine with an air of sophistication.

Liz left the boys in the care of her au pair. "I'll show you the room in the basement." As we walked through the house, I couldn't help but notice everything was in place, not a speck of dust anywhere. To the right was the formal dining room with Queen Anne styled furniture, which appeared to be dark solid mahogany, an oval table that could seat ten, the highboy china cabinet filled with fine china and not a fingerprint to be found anywhere. On the other side of the room was a sideboard of the same style and elegance; its top displaying a large collection of family heirloom silver. The centerpiece, dripping from the ceiling, was a chandelier made of crystal and centered perfectly above the table as it majestically hung from the ten-foot-high ceiling. I couldn't help but marvel at its seemingly thousand pieces of glass glistening in the sunlight, beaming through the nearly floor-to-ceiling windows. As we passed through each room, there was more art, more detailed crown molding. This place was impeccable; surely the pearly white gates of heaven must be just around the corner. I'd been in too many Coventry homes over the years to be in awe, but there was something very different here. I couldn't put my finger on it, but it was very different.

Still in the lead, the mistress of the house took me through a door and down a set of stairs, which led to a finished basement with more crown molding, recessed lighting, and walls exhibiting a more eclectic Edward Hopper style artwork, perhaps insight into her innermost feeling. We passed a small open kitchen, a media room with a big-screen TV, and wall-to-wall carpeting. A state-of-the-art computer center was off to the right, and her husband's wine cellar was farther right against the outside wall near the garage entrance. All this also so nicely done with exquisite taste; I presumed hers.

"Very nice. What's there to clean up?"

"Well, this is the nice part," said Liz as she removed her heavy outer sweater and continued. "Here, let me show you the part I'm thinking about." Liz seemed slightly flustered over an apparent misuse of words. And I should have been flustered by my apparent misuse of a stare, but I couldn't help noticing her nicely shaped chest and flat tummy now more accentuated under her tight-fitting blouse.

Liz then led me around a corner and opened another door. If I had my bearings right, we were under the study. Indeed, there was an unfinished section with plywood and sheetrock lying here and there. There were some partial rolls of insulation and stray pieces of molding.

Looking here and there, I got the lay of the land. "Well, this is doable. Would you mind if I cut up any of this? It would be easier to get out." Turning around, I was suddenly staring at her breasts where the top of her head should have been.

"Up here, silly." She giggled and smiled with a smile that lit up the room. She had climbed atop two rolls of excess carpeting.

"I imagine you tell guys all the time to raise their eyes when they talk to you," I said with a flirtatious smile. For having just accidentally met, we were hitting it off quite like friends.

Liz giggled some more, then with a wee scream, grabbed my shoulders as she began to lose her balance on the unstable rolls. I, in turn, grasped her around the waist. It wasn't intentional flirtation on either's part—just a reaction to steady her balance—and we both laughed about the slight folly. But she kept her hands on my shoulders, and my hands remained on her slim waist as if we were dance partners. Electricity seemed to flow right away, and my heart began pounding. *Oh shit, here we go*. Instinctively, I pulled her tight against my body as our lips got tantalizingly closer together. The room was silent as we slowly drifted closer. I lowered my hands slightly, spreading my fingers and feeling her womanly hips as I pressed my hands more firmly against her taut body and began to slowly rub her. She didn't say a word as we gazed at each other, she smiling and occasionally giggling nervously. The more I looked, the more she smiled. The more she smiled, the more I smiled.

Don't do it. Don't do it, I kept telling myself, but this woman was irresistible. Uncharacteristically, I leaned in and pressed my lips against hers. Liz did not retreat. She wrapped her arms around me while feeling my powerful physique. Then she slid her hands all over my arms and back, feeling my muscle. Her response indicated my touch and warm kiss felt good to her. Pulling her closer and inserting my tongue into her open mouth, she vigorously responded to the desire. Then politely yet firmly pushed away from me. Suddenly, I felt faint as if all my blood just rushed from me.

"I'm sorry. I can't." Yet she still maintained her radiant smile.

I stammered and stuttered, "No no, it's my fault. I looked down in embarrassment. "I shouldn't have. I apologize. I just thought . . ." And my voice trailed off.

Liz was as flustered as me, saying, "I made you think that. It's my fault." Liz was now speaking in a higher octave as if inner pressure had built. "What am I doing? I don't even know your last name and invite you into my house. You must think I'm a nymph or something."

"No no. I'm flattered and attracted to you. I just read it wrong." Being Italian, I reached toward her and kissed her again.

Liz responded favorably again, but she suddenly extended her hand, straight-arming me to the chest, keeping me at bay with mixed signals. "I . . . I think you should go. I'm sorry. It's not your fault, it's mine. Please . . . just go."

My chest and shoulders wilted. Damn, this was bad. This was wrong on so many levels. At least, if something had happened, it might have been worth it. But here I was, left high and dry, and all I'd have to show for it was frustration and the possibility that Lyons might be back at the firehouse at that very moment, running his mouth off. Then with my luck, it would get back to Ruth, and I'd really be in the doghouse. And for what? A closemouthed kiss? To say nothing of this woman being tainted by rumors at the firehouse. Stupid, stupid, stupid.

Shuffling out the way I came in, then suddenly stopping on the stairs leading back to the main floor, I looked back. Liz was slowly following behind me at a safe, discreet distance.

"My name, it's Dominic Renaldi."

Liz ran her fingers through her hair, still looking embarrassed as if some stranger had walked in on her naked. Even so, the electricity seemed to still be flowing in her.

"Liz Temple. I'm Liz Temple."

"Pleased to meet you, Liz Temple."

"Me too," said Liz with that radiant smile back on her face.

Chapter 9

With the selectman's decision final, Peter Brewster was quickly appointed chief. As soon as he lifted his hand from the bible at his swearing in, the department's demise began. Guys like Jacobs rolled their eyes and laughed derisively from the back of the room. He'd supported the chump, as did most men, albeit with little genuine enthusiasm. Slayton, on the other hand, stood shoulder to shoulder with the new chief as if Brewster was a newly ordained conquering king of the masses, Slayton's charismatic personality shining brightly for all to see. *Which one of these men was being sworn in anyway?* I wondered as I politely stood off to the side mixing in with the other members of our association.

Within two weeks, Brewster gave all the selectmen gold badges for their wallets.

Though, the now, former Chief Wyatt had initiated promotional exams several years ago, they were not a part of our contract. The first order of business for the newly appointed chief, Brewster, was to revoke the promotional examination process. This allowed him to promote anyone he wanted. Still association president, Bill Slayton informed us, "With this department not a part of the civil service program, there was no recourse to fight Brewster's arbitrary decision."

Brewster's first personnel decision would eventually prove to be a vital mistake.

Brewster had been my captain, and I had supported him as chief. We had a very open and friendly relationship. In fact, he listened to me often and relied on my word. But we would disagree on this decision with good reason.

TO: All Personnel
RE: Promotions
FROM: Chief of Department

Firefighter William Slayton is hereby promoted to the rank of lieutenant effective immediately.

Signed
Peter Brewster
Chief of Department

cc Board of Selectmen

"Why on earth would you have promoted Bill Slayton?" I asked the new Chief Brewster.

Showing weakness right from the start, Brewster told me, "You don't have to call me chief, Dominic. We've been friends for a long time, you can call me Pete."

"You're the chief now, and with that comes respect for the position. I shall continue to speak to you openly and frankly, but I have to address you as chief."

Brewster acted as if he'd just learned something and then asked a profound question, "What was I suppose to do about Slayton?"

"Anything but this!" I exclaimed to the chief. "Now I see why you did away with the exams."

"Exams are no good, they don't always allow you to promote whom you want, Lieutenant." More insight into the troubled waters Brewster was heading toward.

"So you'll denigrate the whole department just to appease a selectman who is friendly with Slayton? Make him pass an exam just like the rest of us and then promote him."

"What the fuck was I suppose to do, Renaldi?"

"Well, chief, all I know is that Bill Slayton has never fought a fire in his career, he has refused to ride in the back of the ambulance, and he has never done his housework around here. Now he's a lieutenant, what does that do for morale, chief? What does that say to all the men who do their work around here?"

"In my eyes, Bill Slayton deserved his promotion," the chief said angrily, however, unconvincingly.

"Not in anyone's eyes does he deserve a promotion. Bill Slayton will be the biggest mistake you ever make in the fire service, and history will bear me out on that. Mark my words!"

Brewster dropped his head, and with a backhanded flick of his hand from behind his desk, silently ordered me out of his office.

A few weeks later, the new station assignments were announced. I questioned the chief as to why I was being assigned to station 2. Never before has an officer been assigned to station 2. With my fire alarm responsibilities such as they were and with all the necessary meetings about fire alarm codes and regulations, clearly I belonged in headquarters with the chief, where we could work together.

Once Brewster became chief, he changed unexpectedly. He no longer relied on the men who had helped him get the gold badge he had desperately pursued, but rather, he was accommodating those who didn't want him in power. And he was clueless. Unconvincingly, Brewster told me, "Captain Jacobs and Lieutenant Slayton suggested it, and I thought it was a good idea. We needed an officer over there to oversee the house." His reason for my reassignment was bullshit. Perhaps he was trying to put me in a corner.

When I asked Brewster if I could purchase a set of NFPA books out of my fire alarm budget, he went ballistic. NFPA, National Fire Protection Association, is composed of the industry's standard-bearer. They were the authority all building codes adopted as part of their regulations. These codes designated the fire chief to be "the authority having jurisdiction." The code further stated, "Or his designee." Brewster had jurisdiction, but I was his designee on all fire alarm matters.

"What the hell do you want to do that for? It's a waste of money!"

"Chief, it will be the best money you spend around here. How am I supposed to approve auxiliary fire alarm system plans for the schools, churches, and office buildings if I don't know the codes and can't reference them?"

"Fire alarm is just one chapter, I'll buy that one for you."

"As it is, chief, the chapter 72, fire alarm systems, version we do have is outdated and obsolete. In addition to 72, there are other chapters: chapter 10, portable fire extinguishers; chapter 13, sprinkler systems; chapter 14, standpipe systems; and chapter 101, life safety. If this isn't enough to convince you, having a complete set of reference materials for aspiring young members will be enormously beneficial to their growth and development."

"I'm still not going to purchase them."

"Chief, I've done the math, there's a conservative $1.5 billion of property protected by auxiliary fire alarm systems in Coventry, to say nothing of human life, especially in the old dorms at the college and private schools with their inadequate fire alarm protection, and we are responsible for it. You are responsible for this. You're putting this community at risk for a multimillion-dollar lawsuit, and I'm the one who'll hang for it because you designated me to oversee the codes."

With head down, Brewster said nothing. Two weeks later, there was a complete set of NFPA books in his office at headquarters. Two weeks later, I was transferred to station 2. Brewster wasn't interested in others having knowledge; he wasn't interested in the growth of others, and it became clear he had his mind set on throttling down anyone with ambition and desire. With this mentality, Brewster pulled down his own family. He took them to near bankruptcy while trying to get their son out of his horrifying situation—a drug addiction most believe Brewster drove him to.

Dealing with these men reminds me of dealing with my father. Senior year in high school, I was co-captain of the basketball team, and we were playing archrival, Trowbridge, in their new domed fieldhouse. The place was packed with two thousand strong. I loved to play against Trowbridge; it gave me an adrenaline rush. This night was no different, and I had one of those nights you dreamed about. I scored over thirty points and received a standing ovation when I left the floor with 20 seconds to play and victory in hand. I was still excited when I got home. Only to be greeted by my father, who barked brusquely, "If you didn't miss those lay-ups, you'd have scored forty points."

Ya, nice to see you too, shithead, I said to myself as I dejectedly turned. I walked away from him, and went to bed. I was willing to accept a win, and a thirty-plus point performance points against our archrival on their court. In my home, I was never able to do anything right in my father's eyes. I was always being knocked down or cast aside. Kick in the ass, that's what he liked to do both verbally and physically. I swear if you x-rayed my spine, you'd find my coccyx broken a few times. Suddenly, I knew how Brewster's and Jacobs's sons must have felt.

Putting my best foot forward, I welcomed the new assignment at station 2. Working out of this remote station about five miles away from headquarters, it was often quiet and lonely. The most activity was the flashing set of traffic lights out on the two-lane state highway in front of the building. On this foggy night, the blinking lights reminded me of a distant lighthouse being observed by a lone ship at sea.

Coventry wasn't into meeting state-mandated minority staffing levels; there were no blacks and no Hispanics. In an effort to appease the state, they did staff the schools with outstanding female teachers and support staff, and they did hire a very qualified female police officer. When Brewster became chief, the selectmen immediately pressured him to hire a female firefighter. Slayton and Jacobs were adamantly against this, but I was in favor of it. If a female were hired, Slayton and Jacobs would have no control over her—a chink in the armor of their game plan. I felt a female presence was just what this macho house needed. Jacobs would say, "They're just untouchable fucking cunts."

Barbara Pickens was hired, and the house of testosterone was shaken. Several guys fumbled with the newest addition like a first date in junior high school while others loathed her presence. Seeing it as a welcome change, I went right up to Barbara and said, "Congratulations, young lady, you've already made history. Now you have a great deal to prove if you want to make it here."

Barbara warmly shook my hand and smiled. I'd hoped Brewster told her I'd be on her side, and I'm sure the secretary did. I was equally sure that a few members told her to stay away from me. However, a new friendship was born. Barbara made a few politically incorrect mistakes right away, and some guys immediately complained to Jacobs about her. To Jacobs they complained, not the chief! When I caught wind of what she'd done, I went to her and said, "Barbara, I welcome you here, and I'm on your side. But I'm not going to allow you to fail because of some narrow-minded, visionless people around here, so I am going to give you some friendly advice that will help you survive in this snake pit."

"What did I do, Lieutenant?" Barbara seemed slightly put off.

"First off, you cannot refuse to clean the bathrooms. We all do it, and if you get away with not having to, you'll be blackballed around here in a heartbeat. If that happens, you'll never get off the list. I beg you to trust me on that one, Barbara."

"I'm not going to clear up their stinky and smelly shit."

I couldn't help but think some of Jacobs's disciples would intentionally piss all over, or worse, then make her clean this mess up, so I offered a compromise, "I'll see if I can make it so you just clean the ladies' room." Surely, the men could clean the men's room.

Barbara was a good firefighter and an excellent truck driver whom I helped nurture and guide through her probationary period. Over the next several months, we became professional friends. I very much enjoyed her company. There was one night when Coventry went on mutual aid to Cromwell. Barbara complained she didn't want to go and asked if I'd go instead. This was impossible as the procedure called for one officer to stay back—a policy established by Brewster so Lieutenant Slayton wouldn't have to cover at an out-of-town firehouse. However, I felt empathy for her having to go into the anal world of masculine behavior. I said, "I can't do that for you. If I do, you'll never live it down. Renaldi's protecting his little girl. You need to go and stand up to them. I'm sorry, Barbara. Just go do your job, and you'll be fine!" I truly did have compassion for her. She was breaking new ground, and it had to be difficult. However, she could not succumb to ego and arrogance of the chauvinistic male.

This night, engine 1 wasn't in Cromwell for thirty minutes before being dispatched to a house fire—a one-room fire as it would turn out to be. I sat at the fire alarm desk in Coventry, listening to the scanner and laughing my ass off, thinking Barbara had just hit a fire in "machoville." Cromwell didn't have any female firefighters. When our engine returned home, I sought out Paul Frieze, who was on the covering piece, and asked, "How'd Barbara do?"

Much to my delight, Frieze said, "She took the line and went in putting out the fire with ease." Frieze was happy for her, and I was happier. Paul Frieze was a good man.

Stir that estrogen into your tea of testosterone, Slayton and Jacobs! I said to myself.

When the dust settled and only the on-duty crew of five was left, I spoke to Barbara about the incident.

"Firefighter Pickens to the fire alarm office please," I requested with mock authority and a playful tone.

Entering the office happy as one can be, Barbara asked, "You looking for me?"

"As a matter-of-fact, I am." I also had a happy face on. "Now tell me something, young lady, what would have happened if I went to cover in your place?"

As she smiled, I answered my own question.

"They'd have called me an asshole for covering for you, and they would have been pissed that I hit another fire. They'd say you're nothing but a protected little c—, um, just a protected species. And you would not be able to live it down." Barbara just sat listening to the dissertation with a broad smile on her face as I continued, "Instead, you did your job and won their respect. Way to go! Now wipe that shitty grin off your face and give me a hug."

Obligingly, she did both and simply said, "Thank you, Dom."

"Just keep doing your job, and you'll blow them out of the water, Barbara."

* * *

Much to the dismay of Jacobs, young Ben Lyons had become my regular partner at station 2. Lyons seemed to develop an interest in the municipal fire alarm system and worked with me frequently on it. Now working together at station 2, we created a good work schedule outside of our regular shift. Consequently, he was also spending a lot of time at my house where he'd developed a friendly relationship with my family. Benny helped all of us with computer questions, and Ruth found him to be adorable. "I'd like to teach him a few things," she would playfully say after he left.

To appease a few, Brewster had changed the departments work schedule too. We now worked twenty-four-hour shifts—twenty-four hours on, twenty-four hours off, twenty-four hours on, and then five days off. It was an eight-day cycle. This new schedule was the primary reason that a lot of Coventry's firefighters' interests strayed outside their primary job and centered on their personal side businesses and other interests—something I deplored. I didn't have a problem with the men working outside the department or owning their own businesses. Some guys had successful small businesses, but their primary focus remained on the fire department, their primary job. However, the same could not be said of others. With Slayton leading the way, their focus was not on the fire department but on their personal side business. Slayton was boasting about what a young Coventry kid said. "I want to get on the fire department and use it to start my own business just like Bill Slayton did." Proud as a peacock, Slayton would strut around the firehouse every time he told the story. And he told it often! Could Brewster not see this, or was he blind? Maybe he was just too weak and appeasing. Interesting how our new schedule fit so well with Slayton's new lake house. Stay in Coventry for three days, and then go to the lake for five.

As I sat in the day room watching the end of the ten o'clock nightly news, Lyons already in bed, the alarm went off, and the house lights came on. We were going somewhere. As I got out of my chair, the voice over the loudspeaker said, "One hundred Balliet Drive, a woman giving birth." The paramedics from Edwin Morris Hospital were also responding; they'd be the last to arrive because of the distance they had to travel.

For decades, the emergency medical services (EMS) customarily was handled by the police department. They had station wagons for cruisers and had a stretcher in each car. Once on the scene, they'd scoop and shoot to the hospital often with the victim getting little or no care at all. In defense of the police, this is how the system had operated. It was also the weak link in the chain of patient care, and in the early '70s, "the system" got smart by mandating certified ambulances with certified technicians on board. Now a town faced two choices—contract the service out or give it to the fire department. Coventry chose the latter, and why not, the affluent and demanding taxpayers weren't accustomed to waiting long for anything, certainly not an ambulance.

At the time, departments across the state were slashing budgets and cutting men; we needed this emergency service for our own survival. The union tried bargaining for eight additional men to provide this service—two men per group to cover the ambulance. I wasn't in favor of the proposal. "Take the ambulance, and we'll make it work," was my suggestion, but I was only one of two men who felt this way. Paul Dunn was the other man with the same view. The association lost their battle, and in eighteen months, the fire department would take over the town's EMS. Chief Wyatt tapped me to become an EMT and assist with bringing this new venture into our department. "You have the commitment and the spirit to make this work, Dominic, and you'll make an excellent EMT. I need you to talk this up and make it happen," the chief said at the time.

Within months, four of us became the original EMTs—and some of the state's first—who got this service off the ground and turned it into a first-class operation, providing Coventry professional first responder care. Neither Brewster, Slayton, or Jacobs were one of the four original EMTs. Now fifteen years later, with all the younger guys on the job, they haven't a clue about any of this. Surely, the three stooges weren't going to give credit where credit was due. In fact, Slayton and Jacobs were telling the new EMTs how bad an EMT I was and not to listen to me.

With the onset of the ambulance service, a new category of firefighter was established—firefighter/EMT. The reclassification gave the EMTs an edge and made us more qualified for advancement. Strange how, under Brewster, the other three original EMTs had been banished one way or another, opening the door for Slayton's further advancement.

"You awake, Benny?"

"Yeah, I was in bed studying. Baby patrol, huh?"

"Yep. I actually look forward to these kinds of calls. They usually have happy endings. You know where you're going?"

"Sure do, old man."

Always wanted to deliver a baby. *Yes!* I thought. *This might be my chance*. After all, delivering a baby wasn't that difficult; the mother did all the work, right? Over the years, the rescue squad had several calls for childbirth, usually on the highway. The mother was brought to the nearest hospital before giving birth. On a few occasions, however, the EMTs did deliver a baby in town. All pretty routine. But it made the adrenaline pump a little harder even though life and limb would not likely be at risk—at least not for the responders.

As Benny and I left the station, the fog was thick as a pea soup. The two and a half mile run to Balliet Drive would be a slow one tonight. Surely, a police cruiser would be there before us—they usually were—and the mother would have received immediate help; however, I was disappointed because I very much wanted to deliver a baby. Just once. Just to get it out of my system.

The ride took us into thicker fog as we descended the steep hill toward Balliet. Lyons was being very slow and cautious in operating engine 3; you couldn't see a foot in front of the engine. We turned right on Maiseville Road, barely seeing it until we got right on top of it, under the Mass Pike and back up another hill we went. Surely, the fog would be lighter the higher we climbed. But this wasn't happening, and Benny kept saying, "I can't see anything, Dom. I can't see a damn thing."

"Neither can I, you're doing just fine, Benny. Just go slowly, and we'll find our way." My thoughts now turned from childbirth to the weather. We could worry about the incident once we got there, *if* we get there.

Balliet Drive was at the very top of a long hill. As we crested the hill, neither of us could see the road on the right. Suddenly, out of the fog, the road appeared, and we made a quick turn onto Balliet. This was not the time for bad weather conditions; it now became impossible to see the addresses in the fog. As we tried to pierce the fog with our eyes, I said to Benny, "With any luck, the police are there, and we'll see their cruiser." All the trucks were equipped with scanners, and we could hear the police crosstalk, but I hadn't heard the cruiser sign off yet. This was unusual. They should've been there by now. In the thick of the fog was a glimmer of blue light. Prophetically, a police cruiser seemed to just be pulling up to what must have been the house. Officer Alan Bard signed off just ahead of us.

"Look up ahead, Benny."

With a sigh of relief in his voice, Lyons said, "Yes, I see it!"

Signing off on the radio and jumping out of the truck, I grabbed the medical kit from the compartment directly behind the passenger door. The house, an old English Tudor, was well lit. The front door was wide open; seeing the engine coming up behind him, the cop had left it that way.

Racing through the open door, I yelled, "Hello," thinking a response would come from the second floor. To my startled surprise, a weak female voice emanated, saying, "In here" from my immediate left, just inside the door. Turning, I found a woman lying on the floor. In a terrified voice and a grimacing look on her face, she said, "I can't deliver this baby here, I need to get to the hospital. This is a breeched birth, and the baby has a prolapsed cord. We know this already, and I'm scheduled for a C-section tomorrow."

As I began getting to work, I asked, "Where's the cop?"

"He went upstairs to check on my sleeping son."

I though to myself, *Great, here's a woman giving birth, and he's upstairs checking on a sleeping child. Now there's immediate first aid.* I thought some more, *Perhaps he was upstairs rifling the woman's jewelry for the after-hours illicit activities the honorable police officer was known for. More dirty secrets of an idyllic puritan town.*

As reassuringly as possible, I gently removed the distraught mother's designer maturity pants and was confronted with a presentation. Immediately turning to Lyons, I said something not often spoken, "Get the OB kit ready."

The OB kit, such as it is, is just a small sealed package in each first aid kit containing sterile gloves, blanket, scissors, and clamps—a far cry from a hospital setting.

Lyons was also an EMT though inexperienced but very capable. The mother, hearing talk of the OB kit, panicked even more and fearfully crying, "No no. Not here." She was on the verge of losing it.

Can you imagine how she must have felt? I mean, here she was lying on the floor at near midnight, half exposed to three male strangers, her husband still two hundred miles away, and she was about to give birth. No woman should have to go through the sanctity of childbirth this way.

"Are you sure you know what you're doing?" A voice sounded from behind me. It was officer Bard, who joined the police force soon after high school and who managed to keep fairly discreet his long-term affair with a night nurse at the local extended care facility and a few other affairs he was having with Coventry women. And there was a strong rumor he dealt in "second-hand" jewelry. I didn't know why, but of late, he had turned a cold shoulder to me.

Just staring at him with a look of displeasure on my face and thinking, *What the hell did you say that for? Especially in front of the mother.* Then I spoke calmly, "The ambulance hasn't gotten here yet, and the baby is crowning. We really shouldn't move her. We have to get started right here right now, we don't have a choice. Yes, we can do this." I wondered if I was saying the words for the benefit of Bard and the mother or for myself. I was confident in my abilities, but a breeched birth with a prolapsed cord? *Why wasn't anything ever easy for me?*

The woman began to sob even more. I'm sure the cop's words didn't set well with her. "My husband is on the way home from New York." Begging, she pleaded, "Please just take me to the hospital."

Compassionate and reassuring, I spoke very briefly and softly to the mother, "We can't leave. The ambulance isn't even here yet, and the baby has a mind of its own. We'll be okay." I'm not sure if the words helped, but it was as gentle as I could express the cold, hard facts to her while my own mind was gearing itself for this very extraordinary event.

Everything was happening so fast, yet it seemed like slow motion. I was in my element. I was kneeling directly in the doorway to a small den, making it very tight quarters.

As I hastily unbuckled my fire coat, I asked, "Alan, could you remove my fire coat?" Reaching my arms behind myself one at a time, the coat came off like it was greased. "Benny, put the sterile gloves from the OB kit on my hands." The gloves slipped right on. I wasn't even sure if they were on the right hands or not and didn't have enough time to worry about it. Settling into God's plan, I looked at the presentation, then asked, "Are you sure of the breeched birth? Because I'm looking at what appears to be a head of hair."

Very tearfully, mother responded, "Yes, I'm sure, please just take me to the hospital!" Poor mom was not understanding me there was no ambulance to take her to the hospital. Not yet anyway. The tension was mounting; the atmosphere somewhere in the twilight zone—very *slow* motion.

As she was writhing with more anxiety—her own body telling her something was happening—her water broke. Suddenly, out popped a small foot and leg. Startled, my first reaction was a quick squirm, then I exclaimed, "Yup, it's a breeched birth all right!"

The ambulance had now arrived, and I began instructing the crew. "Jack, come over here and assist me. Barbara, you take the mother's head and comfort her." Neither EMT asked questions; they just dug in and began lending a hand.

The doorway became a mass of humanity stepping and climbing over one another with apparent orchestrated, synchronized efficiency. Ben Lyons squeezed in silently behind us all, his face reflecting a look of awe. If ever there was a far-fetched analogy to "how many kids can you fit into a phone booth," this doorway was it.

Slipping my fingers around the baby's exposed leg and gently into the side of the mother's vagina, the baby's very slippery second foot and leg also popped out. Never before had "slipping my fingers into a woman's vagina" have a less sexual connotation. This was strictly a medical procedure and a fight to save two lives. What I intentionally neglected to tell the mother was that the umbilical cord was not only wrapped around the baby but was also between the baby's legs. This was not going to be easy at all, but we forged ahead valiantly. "Ya gotta do what ya gotta do when ya gotta do it," was a favorite expression of mine, and I repeated it in silence. What choice did we have? Even if we panicked and ran, we'd still be doing this in the ambulance; and the fog was so thick we'd never make it to the hospital. Hold your ground and do the job you were trained for, was the best course of action. We'd have the paramedics for support shortly.

"Dom, we really should try to get her to the hospital now." Barbara may have been new to the job, but she wasn't inexperienced, having worked for an ambulance company for five years prior to joining our force. She was a Joan of Arc, and she looked concerned.

"We're too far along. We can't leave. This has to be done here and now."

All this talk about not knowing what we were doing and questioning whether we should just panic and leave was getting to the mother. She began to cry desperately, "My baby's going to die, my baby's going to die, please, just get me to the hospital!" It was a sickening sound, and the scene was beginning to panic everyone. Strangely, the worse the anxiety got around me the more I got into the zone, leaving my own concerns behind.

"Cut the cord, Dom," someone said urgently.

"We can't. It's the baby's lifeline, and if this process stalls with the baby halfway out of the womb, she'll suffocate. We can't—not yet!"

Trying to slip the cord out from between the baby's legs, I noticed how tight it was and tough too. The umbilical cord would be stretched beyond the tearing point before we were done. Pushing down hard on the baby, I slipped my fingers under the cord and started to get them around its leg as I timed my one-word instruction to mother.

"Push," I said with command.

The panicked mother did so, and miraculously, the cord slipped from between the baby's legs as I gently maneuvered it about. I exhaled a great sigh of relief; however, the cord was now wrapped around the baby's stomach. Keeping the process moving, mother and I were in perfect unison.

"Push again," I instructed with stronger command.

She did, and with my assistance, the cord slipped up higher. Unfortunately, it lodged around the baby's neck and was tighter than hell. The process seemed to stall. Suddenly, this wasn't going so well; the mother began to get hysterical. Trying to sit up, she screamed uncontrollably, "My baby's going to die, my baby's going to die, isn't it? Please just get me to the hospital." The look of despair was etched on the rescuer's faces. The poor mother's anguish was real, very real.

As I looked at this hapless child, so swollen and so very blue, I was thinking, *This baby is already dead. It sure looks like it.* Self-pity took my emotions over for a second as time seemed to completely stop. *My entire career, I wanted to deliver a baby, and when I finally get my chance, the baby's going to die.* This lasted but a split second. The sight of this child—this lifeless, helpless child hanging by its head from its mother's womb, all swollen and blue, and now stuck by its umbilical cord wrapped tightly around its neck in a strangulation hold—kicked me into a place I'd never been before.

One final time, the mother sprang to a near sitting position looking down at her lifeless child, and in a distressed state that only a mother could understand, let out a blood-curdling screamed, "My baby is dead, isn't it? Oh my god, look! My baby is dead!"

In silence, I couldn't help but agree with her assessment; nonetheless, generated from a mother's desperate cry, an insurmountable power built inside of her and me, which motivated me to lean forward and say to her in a voice of both compassion and command, "This baby is not going to die on my watch." I became very stern and much in control. "When I tell you to push, you push as hard as you possibly can."

Thinking for sure the panic-stricken mother's vagina muscles would begin to constrict from her tension, I figured we had one more shot to make this happen. Positioning my fingers under the cord the best I could, and with my other hand under the baby, I implored the mother, "PUSH!"

To which the mother responded with a grunt and a sustained push with all she could muster. At the same time, I forced the cord up. The next few seconds is a sequence I'll never forget. It will be etched in my mind forever. First, the baby's chin sprang up as the cord began to rise, then suddenly down as the cord temporarily lodged in the infant's mouth as I continued to assist with an upward pressure on it. Up over the baby's tiny upper gums, the cord slid pulling her upper lip up and then squishing her nose first up, then flat as it passed over. The eyebrow region of her forehead was the final obstacle for her lifeline to clear. "Keep pushing, Mom," I encouraged, and she did. Somehow, the cord slipped up over the baby's head, and she popped right out and into my waiting hand. *This poor tiny infant. If she ever survives, she'll be tough as nails,* I thought to myself. For a second, I just stared at the little girl in amazement as I continued to think, *Holy crap, we pulled this off.* She still looked dead though, so swollen and very, very blue. Did mother just give birth, or did the human body just self-abort? Still, we were only halfway home, and that answer was yet to be determined.

"Benny, get on over here." Lyons elbowed his way closer. "Suction the baby's mouth using the suction bulb in the OB kit."

Fast and furiously, Lyons began. But the baby wouldn't start to breathe. Lyons looked timid and unsure of himself. "It's not working, Dom."

"Do it again!" But still no breathing.

"Tilt the head back," Barbara added. It was a good idea.

Her partner, Jack Maley, stuck the oxygen line in front of Lyons with the infant mask on the end of it. "Try the oxygen."

"No, it might force an obstruction deeper and lodge it," I interjected as I continued, "Jack, just flow the oxygen close to her. Maybe she can get some into herself somehow."

The mother was beyond reproach and was crying her eyes out. Barbara, holding her head in her arms with care, tried consoling her.

Shaking my head as we continued, the baby's limp arms and legs hanging off my hand, I thought to myself in remorse, *Shit, this baby is dead!*

"Ben, cut the umbilical cord just in case we had to bolt with the baby." Hearing this, the poor mother became even more hysterical. Lyons calmly and effectively clamped off the cord on both sides of where he would make the cut just as we were taught in school. EMTs were always instructed not to cut the cord except in extreme emergencies. This was an extreme emergency.

As Ben cut the cord, I brought Barbara into the action. "Don't worry about any damage you may do to the baby's throat. I want you to push that syringe as far down her throat as you can and see if we can clear the airway."

Barbara repositioned herself and carried out her instructions like a true professional. As she did, the baby gagged and suddenly came to life.

Never before had the sound of gagging and choking sounded so sweet to the ear. I couldn't contain myself. I said, "OH MY GOD, SHE'S ALIVE!" The atmosphere in the house became euphoric with mother crying and laughing with an exultant smile of very mixed emotions.

No way in hell could a man understand what this poor mother had just gone through. I mean, first, conception is miraculous to begin with; then a woman grows a human being inside of her—this, only a woman can truly understand. For nine months, a child is carried inside of her womb, her responsibility, her very own being; the feeling associated with this must be heavenly. The true love only a mother could understand. Suddenly, the child's life seems to be snatched away from her in apparent full-term stillborn delivery on a cold living room floor with nothing but strangers around, driving the mother into desperate despair over horrific failure, then returning to euphoric heights in a matter of seconds with this successful resuscitation.

Though the rescuers could feel their pent-up emotions released, I stared in disbelief over what had just been accomplished. Barbara said, "Give the baby to the mother, Dom." Spoken like a true woman. Jack held out the sterile blanket to wrap the infant in, and I laid her on her mother's chest. Mother clutched the baby as she wrapped and kissed her child with her unrestrained love. The paramedics arrived and wanted to take the baby aside for an Apgar test—the traditional ten-point assessment test done to make sure the child is functionally well. I interceded one last time and asked for mother and child to be allowed a minute together, "They've just been through hell!" After asking a few good pertinent questions about their health, the compassionate medics agreed to wait a minute. After they took the baby, I spontaneously leaned over and hugged the mother on the floor as she hugged me back and cried in my ear, "Thank you, fireman. Thank you."

The baby had a perfect Apgar score. She *is* tough as nails! As Barbara and Jack finally prepared to transport the mother and child to Children's Hospital Boston, with the paramedics on board, I held the baby for a moment, saying, "Bless your heart, you beautiful little thing," and I kissed her on the forehead. It was very emotional. Before the ambulance left the scene, I walked around to everyone, shaking their hands and telling them what a terrific job they did.

"Geez, helluva job, old man."

"Thanks, Benny. Thanks."

The official incident report would show a mere ten minutes passed from the time engine 3 signed off until delivery.

Within a few days, the *Coventry Town Crier* ran a picture of baby, mother, father, and me splashed across its front page. A few of our men congratulated me for my role, and one told me something else. "I hope you don't think you did anything any one of us couldn't have done," Paul Dunn angrily and emphatically stated.

"No, not for one second do I think that, Dunn!" was my response to this bitter man.

Word began to spread through the Coventry grapevine about the childbirth, and many townspeople were congratulating me.

As I sat in the coffee shop having a light breakfast with Henry—a local businessman—Molly, owner of the Coffee Shop, refilled our coffee as she put her arm around my shoulder and said, "Congratulations, hon."

"Thank you, Molly."

Yet again I was congratulated by another patron, which prompted Henry to ask, "Why is everyone congratulating you, Dominic?"

Henry looked on with admiration and astonishment as I quietly explained the incident to him. "How the hell can you put people's lives in your hands like that? You are a hero, Renaldi!" he said with excitement as he flashed his hands about, making sure all the gold rings and Rolex watch could be seen.

"That's not how I look at it, Henry."

How can you not look at it that way?"

"It's my job. I did what I'm trained to do. What you do is far more heroic than what I do," I said to the president of Coventry Wholesome Foods."

"How do you figure that?" Henry actually seemed sincere in asking.

"You have fifty employees, all of whom have mortgages or rent to pay, most with families to support, and many with student loans to pay. Right?"

"Yeah, so?"

One wrong move by you, and there goes their home, their family health insurance, and their kids college education. And you face this burden on a day-to-day basis. I'd say you're the hero!"

Henry fluffed his feathers in acceptance of my adulation, then looked at me with a look of "Where the hell did that come from? I never would have imagined you had that in you." He said, "Dominic, that is one helluva way to look at the world, and I appreciate what you just said. But you're still the hero, and I still can't believe you did what you did!" Henry, always needing to be the center of attention, was now smiling and demonstratively pounding the table in excitement.

I just sat there shaking my head as we looked at each other and laughed.

Shortly after our conversation ended, Henry got up to leave. While standing at the cash register, he said to Molly, "Give that man anything he wants. It's on me!"

Knowing Molly since I was eight years old—and Molly was seventeen then—when she first started working in the coffee shop, I ate for free every day for two weeks. Molly would laugh each day as she put my bill on Henry's tab, saying, "He can afford it!" Knowing Henry since Wholesome Foods sponsored my Red Sox little league team, cookout, and all, he wouldn't mind!

One of the younger guys tacked up the *Town Crier* picture on the firehouse bulletin board. Captain Jacobs and Lieutenant Slayton looked it over with disdain.

"Bastard managed to be in the right place at the right time. Fucking asshole!"

Slayton was not as easily placated. He turned and shouted to whomever was within earshot. "Who put Renaldi's picture up here?"

Lyons, who was off duty but hanging around, his breast feathers still puffed with pride over his participation in the event, jogged on over and said, "I did, Bill. What's the problem?"

"Who gave you permission to put it up?"

Lyons furrowed his brow. "I didn't know you needed permission to put something on the bulletin board."

"Of course, you do. We have rules around here," said Slayton.

"But . . . it's about the squad. It's not some ad to sell my car or something."

"It's not about the squad," said Slayton, "it's about one guy on the squad. He didn't do anything anyone else wouldn't have done. And it's not your job to put it up on the bulletin board. You have to run it by an officer first."

"Dom's an officer," Lyons replied sheepishly.

"Did he tell you to put it up? He probably did. Renaldi is always thinking of himself first. Have you noticed that working with him, Lyons? The guy's got an ego the size of an ice cream truck."

"No, I hadn't noticed that, and Dom didn't tell me to put it up," said Lyons, still feeling scolded. "What's your problem, Bill? He saved two lives the other night!"

"Lyons, if you want some advice, here it is, Dominic Renaldi is just out for Dominic Renaldi. He'll get you in trouble, or he'll get you killed. You want to be like him, you'll never have a career in this department. Is that what you want?"

"No, I like it here."

"Then don't go waving Renaldi's flag for him. He does enough of that himself. You think Renaldi was a hero the other night? He should have gotten that woman to the hospital immediately. He fucked up. He always fucks up. He thinks he's a cartoon character in a movie. Nothing will ever happen to him. He thinks he's unbreakable. Well, he's not. You've got a future here, Lyons. Guys like me and Jacobs, we can take care of you. Listen to us, not Renaldi, or you'll be on our shit list."

Lyons thought for a moment. "I can do that, yeah, I can do that," he said and left the room.

Slayton turned to Jacobs and said, "We've got to do something to change the focus here."

To which Jacobs replied, "I'll take care of that!"

Chapter 10

With my responsibility for the municipal fire alarm system, I was in and out of headquarters quite a bit. This responsibility was much greater than just the outside physical plant. There were nearly three hundred fireboxes in Coventry, a third of which had interior fire alarm systems attached to them, automatically notifying the fire department if the alarm went off. We had auxiliary fire alarm systems that protected schools, dormitories, churches, the few office parks, and the housing-for-the-elderly complexes in town. The town leadership did deserve credit for going against its own bylaws and creating millions of dollars in revenue with good use of some highway-locked land. Approval of these systems and overseeing the owner's commitments for their maintenance and testing, as required by code, was very time consuming. Building code knowledge—NFPA code knowledge—reading complicated and comprehensive plans, this responsibility was far greater than just running a shift, responsibility for human life excluded. None of the other officers had responsibilities that stretched outside their neat two twenty-four-hour shifts every eight days, then off for five days. I had agreed to take on 24/7 responsibilities. The mechanic and I were the only two so tied to their jobs.

Though the chief had final say, he acquiesced with my recommendations most of the time. Brewster was an intelligent man who, having worked fire alarm earlier in his career, knew it well. In fact, he had taught me quite a bit when he was my captain. Not having as good a grip on fire alarm as he once did, and in an effort to contact me, the chief gave me a department pager to wear. Communications between just him and me. There were meetings with architects, engineers, building owners, and contractors—meetings held at the convenience of others. Who was I to hold up a multi-million dollar projects because I wasn't *on duty*? The system worked well, but others fumed over my closeness to Brewster and the power of these responsibilities. Power used so correctly. Why did all these other professionals, whom I'd met through these meetings, find me to be so cooperative, understanding, and easy to work with? Brewster began pulling in my reins.

Purely by fate and coincidence, I was tromping through the melting snow, salt, and sand in the backyard to the firehouse when Liz Temple spied me from the Wholesome Food Market next door. *Oh shit,* I thought as I vacillated between fantasizing about that day in her basement and trying to push it completely out of my mind. Sexual harassment. That's all I'd need on my permanent record. That would get my ass kicked off the squad as well as out of my home and marriage.

As I glanced over, I saw that shining head of radiant blond hair and quickly turned away, ducking my chin into my chest. *Damn, she saw me!* Funny, Ruth's hair was the same color, only straighter and longer. Weren't men in long-term relationships supposed to be more attracted to opposites? Women totally unlike their own? I should have been chasing redheads or brunettes. Or perhaps, it was safer not to chase anyone at all. But I was a sucker for blue-eyed blonds. They just make me melt.

Entering through the rear door of the station house, I fastidiously wiped off my boots. It had been an unusually long hard winter, and we were all sick of the mess. Back when I was just a private, I recalled all those menial tasks of mopping the floors over and over again in those New England winter months. As mind numbing as it was, I took pride in it, and I liked a clean place. Once they got promoted, many guys like Jacobs or Slayton would drag in as much dirt as possible, not even stopping for an instant to use the doormat, then point to the mess they'd made and say, "Looks like the rookies have been laying down on the job again." It was as cretinous as any other macho initiation to humiliate and dominate the new young guys, instilling in them nothing more than the desire to grow old with the program simply in order to dish out the same sort of punishment to others. The circle of mindless abuse. I always felt this was wrong and knew it was destructive, having my father to thank for my far better understanding of what *not* to do. Never would I treat the younger guys like that. "Build them up, don't tear them down," was my modus operandi.

"Lieutenant Renaldi, there's a lady here to see you." The sounds rang over the speakers from the front of the house, and I wished I could vaporize. *Ah shit. Here it comes.* I marched stoically toward the front door.

The blond was with her stroller again, Jared—the elder of her two boys far more rambunctious this time—climbing out of the stroller, yelping, and waving happy as hell. "Hi."

Not wanting to look at Liz yet, I took the opportunity to focus on her exuberant son. A feeble hope that perhaps the men at the station would ignore me and especially her. But ignoring an attractive woman at the firehouse was very unlikely. "Hi, how are you, Jared?" My head still hanging down, eyes still somewhat averted, the feeling of being called on the carpet for doing something wrong still controlled my manner.

"Hi, Dominic, remember me?"

No, I'm always trying to kiss beautiful married young women I've just met in the basement of their homes. It happens so often I've lost count. Were you Tuesday's or

Wednesday's? I thought. I know it was important to look someone in the eye, so I looked up and said, "Of course, I do. Hello, Mrs. Temple."

"I saw your picture in the paper. Congratulations."

Unless this golden beauty was the insanely sneaky type who set up her prey in order to lower the boom all the more acutely, this was going quite well. She didn't seem pissed at me at all.

Still, I remained cautious, nodding my head in appreciation. "Thank you. That's nice of you to say. It was quite an experience for all of us." I smiled in recall of the incident.

Looking around in hopes the chief hadn't been called in or, worse, the police, I noticed the young fireman who answered the front door, standing behind her, mouthing words like *hot!* and *oh, man!* while acting like a juvenile humping the air. He was such a classy guy. I tried hard not to laugh.

Liz's eldest must have been on a sugar high; he was doing everything but eating the tires on his stroller and piercing our eardrums with his happy screeches.

For once, the word retreat came to my mind. Do or die, see what this "visit" was about. "Hey, would the little guy like to see a real firehouse?"

"Would you like that, Jared? Huh? Want to play on a real fire truck?" The little all-boy excitedly agreed. Yes! This is a good sign. Perhaps I was worried over nothing.

As we walked toward the apparatus floor, Liz asked the question, "How did you ever pull off that childbirth?"

"Shit luck," I said instantly.

"It had to have been more than that."

"That's what retired Chief Wyatt said too, saying, 'It wasn't luck, it was a very good man doing what he was trained to do and doing it very well.' Man, could he lead!"

"I do know a little something about the medical field, and I've had two kids of my own. I agree with the retired chief. The new chief must be pleased. What is his name again?"

"Chief Brewster, Peter Brewster. And no, he has never said a word about it to me."

"Here we are, Jared," I said. There were few firemen who enjoyed giving kids tours of the apparatus. Hell, I loved kids. My own children liked fooling around at the firehouse. Short of vacations at the beach, it was some of our happy times together, especially when their school classes used to visit and their dad put on a show for their friends to admire. Most other guys only went through the motions as if it was a big chore. In fact, when Brewster was my captain, he once told me, "You spend way too much time with the kids. Show them a few things and get them the hell out!"

What the hell was his problem? Our job was something kids were fascinated by. If you were an accountant, what would you do, show kids tax forms? Jared was really getting into it, having himself a ball, almost as much fun as I had giving the tour. The sound of Liz's giggle was striking a cord inside of me. "Here," I said as I opened the engine door; "would you like to sit in the truck, Jared?" Jared eagerly stretched from his mother's arms toward the seat. As I slipped my hands around the child's chest to hoist him higher than his mother could reach, I accidentally rubbed across Liz's breasts. It was meaningless and not the first time it has happened as I lifted many active children from their mothers' arms. on a firehouse tour; except this time, that damned electricity seemed to flow again! Liz's reaction was silent, but her facial expression indicated she felt it too.

The tour continued. "Here, let's turn on some lights for you." All the red and white warning lights are always a big hit with the kids as the light's brilliance reflected off the windows and walls of the apparatus bays. Extending my arms toward Jared, I said, "Wanna see the lights out here?" Jared came to me immediately and held me around the neck as we walked about the truck with me proclaiming, "Pretty cool, huh?"

When I glanced at Liz, I sensed how pleased she was for Jared as she stood warmly smiling at Jared and me.

Putting Jared back in the driver's seat with all the lights flashing, I told him, "If you're going to drive the truck, you need to put your helmet on," my voice inflecting humor and lightheartedness. I placed my helmet on his head; my warped and beat-up helmet. With a big smile on his face, Jared was picture perfect sitting up there with the helmet on.

His mother exclaimed, "I wish I had a camera!"

With thoughts of sexual harassment fading, I couldn't resist looking at her with a smile and saying, "I guess you'll just have to come back again."

Liz smiled warmly and said, "I guess so!" then paused briefly before turning to say, "Wow, that helmet's pretty old and worn."

"Ya, we've been through a lot together."

"I guess you have. I didn't realize this town had bad fires."

"All fires are bad, Liz, no matter what town they happen in, but some of us aren't afraid to go in and get it."

Liz seemed to flinch when I said that and smiled demurely at me as if hiding something.

I began dropping my guard a bit more as we continued to walk around the apparatus floor. Jared was having so much fun. The three of us were having so much fun. Liz was pleasant and sweet, acting as if the other day had never happened at all. This was good. I'd put out a couple of innuendoes, and she never demonstrated a negative reaction. This was very good. Knowing this fun tour was coming to an end, I started to pay more attention to Liz's expressions in hope I could pick up a vibe or two. Much to my satisfaction, she seemed quite delighted with her son's pleasurable experience, and I so hoped this would reflect on me.

"Oh look, Jared, here's the fireman's pole we read about from your book."

"Would you like me to slide down the pole for you, Jared?" Asking this question to a thousand other kids over the years, I already knew the answer. So I began making my way up the open stairs to the upper level of the living quarter's mezzanine. With Liz holding Jared at the base of the pole, I slid down once to great delight and a second time for an encore. Lightheartedly, Liz screamed and laughed in the excitement of the moment as I hit the floor and swept the little boy out of his mother's arms.

"Oh my," was all Liz could muster as she playfully fanned her red face.

I asked him, "Would you like to slide the pole, Jared?" Holding the boy up as high as I could reach, I slid Jared gently down the pole. He loved it as he laughed and giggled; he was definitely his mother's child.

I turned back to Liz and playfully said, "Okay, now it's Mom's turn to slide the pole, Jared." I stared at Liz with a warm friendly smile as I teased her.

"Oh no. I don't think so. Thank you just the same," said a blushing Liz while laughing and covering her face a bit.

"Chicken!" I said. She laughed some more.

I never expected Liz to slide the pole, but it was a fun moment.

We were professional firefighters who had to live at the station when we were on duty and needed to have some diversions. Besides, we needed to be in shape and ready to go. Our lives depended on it; other lives did too. Liz, Jared, and I eventually wound our way into the weight room just off the apparatus floor.

"Yes, now this is what I'm talking about."

"Huh?"

"This is what I want in that big cluttered room in my basement."

Reality snuck back into the picture; the lioness had roared. But she was smiling, still acting like nothing had happened. *Had* nothing happened? Maybe I dreamed the whole thing up, some Walter Mitty like unrequited sexual fantasy.

Liz turned to me. Quietly, she asked, "Would you still be interested in coming over to help me?"

I stared at her, contemplating my answer. I found her irresistible. "Yeah. Sure, I'm available. Here." And I pulled out two business cards, handing one to her in the usual manner, then pulled out a pen and handed her the other. "Why don't you write down your phone number on the back of this one."

"Okay. I'll put my pager number on here too. I don't keep my cell phone on. You'll have to page me, and I'll return the call." A smile never left her face the entire time.

This is good. Oh so good, I thought as I stood waiting, slightly trembling. I'd never done anything like this before.

"And by the way, Dom, my name is Liz, not Mrs. Temple."

"Sorry. We just met the other day, and we were in the firehouse. I was just trying to be professional."

"From now on, my name is Liz!" she said with that sparkling and inviting smile.

Playtime was over for the three of us. I walked Jared and Liz out of the firehouse and to her parked car. "This yours?"

"Yeah, this is me." It was a Gold Lexus GX470. Nice and new, probably the premier mom mobile.

"What's LEGNO?"

"Oh, my vanity plate?"

"Yeah." We talked as I helped her with the pram.

"It's Italian for 'woodwind instrument.' I play the flute. My husband is a classical music nut. He owns two classical radio stations just so he has something to listen to."

"Wow. So *legno* means 'flute.'"

We lifted the pram into the back of Liz's car. It gave us a close proximity, and we stopped, briefly gazing at each other. Her scent drove me crazy, and the electricity was so heavy I could feel the arc between us. We both fought back the urge as Liz ran her hand over mine. Quickly, she picked up the conversation where we had left off.

"Actually, no, *flauto* means 'flute.' But my husband thought that *flauto* sounded too much like something you'd order in a Mexican restaurant. So we went more generic."

"And here I thought it had something to do with your nice legs." I smiled.

Liz laughed. "My husband's plate says FAGOTO."

"You've got to be kidding me." And I rolled my eyes and smiled again.

"It means 'bassoon.' His first choice was *corno* for 'horn,' but it was already taken."

"I'm sure I don't have to tell you what those words sound like."

Liz smiled at me as she buckled up her seatbelt as I stood at her door. "I guess it takes a special kind of man to want to drive around with *fagoto* or *corno* on his car. Do you play any musical instrument?"

"I tried organ lessons at church when I was really young. Gave up after only a short time."

I sensed the dynamo of a cutie was flirting with me when she came out with, "That would be *organo*. Did you ever think you'd be getting a lesson in Italian today?"

"My name's Renaldi. Shouldn't I be the one teaching you?"

Liz winked at me before putting on her sunglasses. "Well, come on over to my place. Maybe there's something else you can teach me."

"Ciao!"

Liz drove off with that brilliant smile. As she did, I laughed my ass off. After watching her disappear up the road, I walked into the firehouse and thought, *I'd like to teach you how it feels to have my "organo" between your "legnos" instead of being with some "fagoto."*

Chapter 11

After delivering the baby about a week ago, I was still on a personal high when I reported for duty at the firehouse to begin of our next eight-day cycle. The morning ritual was to get your gear out and place it beside the engine, then wait respectfully for the other departing crew members to put their gear away.

Paul Dunn and Bob St. James were on duty. Dunn was the guy passed over for promotion, and I seemed to be the thorn in his side over it. St. James was just an angry man who complained about everything. Quite selfish for him since he's the one who came from Coventry wealth. Old Yankee money. His family owned hundreds of acres of land, and he lived mortgage free in a family owned house. Nonetheless, he still complained about how much money I made at the fire department. As his older brother had worked his way into town politics, St. James became increasingly vociferous about how the fire department spent its money, in particular, the fire alarm budget. "Renaldi's an asshole, we should take his money away from him," he would say to anyone who would listen.

Ben Lyons was already a friend of St. James, and Captain Jacobs saw an opportunity here to chum with St. James. In short time, St. James would become one of Jacobs's disciples. Donald St. James, the soon-to-be candidate for selectman, was listening intently to Jacobs's warped view of both Brewster and me and how the department was being run. This became a very untenable situation for Brewster. He began to feel handcuffed.

When the younger St. James first got on the job—after having worked part-time for both the police and the highway departments, neither department wanting him—I welcomed him as I did all new firefighters. Why not? This was a team, and a warm welcome made for good team cohesiveness. However, it would be a school function that made me see this man differently.

St. James's daughter and my daughter were assigned to the same elementary school class one year, and it was back-to-school night. As I had done for all my children's elementary school classes, I volunteered to speak to the class about fire safety. I would bring in my gear for the kids to try on, a STOP, DROP, AND ROLL poster for the teacher to hang in their classroom and another EDITH poster—Exit Drill in the Home. The teacher would introduce me to the class as they gathered around with excitement.

Even in a classroom setting, I was always assessing while looking over the students as I spoke. With such an intriguing subject, I had their attention; but there was always a troubled student, whom I could easily pick out. When it came time for a volunteer to dress up, I would ask this student to help me. First, I picked up the child and slid him into my boots, which came up to his crotch. Then I put my fire coat on him. The coat would hang to the floor and well over his hands. His classmates laughed in fun as I made this troubled child the center of attention. When I put the coat's heavy collar up, it covered half his head and face. With everyone laughing and this child feeling good, I'd put the crowning jewel on his head. My helmet would come down over his forehead and cover the remainder of the student's face. As this child stood before his peers, who were hysterically laughing with him, I could feel the joy in his heart as he felt acceptance for one fleeting moment. Always, the teacher warmly looked on, knowing exactly what I was doing. I'd speak for an hour but could have spent five hours there. I always had more fun than the kids did and wished I could do this every week.

This particular evening, Mrs. Allyard—Laura's second grade teacher—and I were talking when St. James came over. Mrs. Allyard, being the eloquent person she is, extended a handshake and spoke, "Mr. Renaldi just volunteered to come in and speak to the children about fire safety, Mr. St. James. Would you like to do the same?" Her warm smile should have made anyone say yes.

St. James, who with his tall thin build and curly red hair, looked just like the bushy redhead on the cover of *MAD* Magazine, said defiantly, "I'm not coming in to speak to anyone unless I get paid overtime to do so. And he shouldn't be doing that either," angrily pointing his finger at me.

I looked tersely at St. James. He had embarrassed both the teacher and the fire department. Giving back to the community would never register with this guy.

I walked around looking throughout the fire station, and kept asking myself, "What the hell did I do with my boots? I know I put them away on my last tour." I looked everywhere; still couldn't find them. Walking into the dayroom, I saw Dunn and St. James. I said, "Good morning." Dunn barely elicited a gruff grunt. But it was St. James whom I made eye contact with. Wordlessly, he spoke volumes with his body language. He could not look at me—always a telltale sign of guilt. I was sure I found the culprit who'd taken my boots and was tampering with equipment.

Not having full turnout gear on when responding on a call was a violation of department regulations, and I didn't want to be called on it, so I called HQ and spoke to by my captain.

"Are you sure they're missing?" he asked.

"I'm certain, I've looked everywhere."

"Look again."

"I've already checked twice, they're no where to be found!"

"Well, I'm working on my '57 Chevy, and I have to make some calls for my landscape company, so I don't want to be bothered by having to come over with a new pair for you. Maybe later."

"Okay, but don't blame me for showing up not wearing any boots."

Lyons and I carried out our daily housework and sat down for a cup of coffee when the bell hit and houselights came on. "E-3 and C-2, Coventry High School for an alarm sounding."

Off we went just down the street less than a mile away. The alarm turned out to be a false, and we returned to the station. When Lyons backed engine 3 in, my boots were sitting right outside my door on the apparatus floor, right where I would have put them. Now how in hell's name did that happen? I called my captain back to let him know.

"They must have been there the entire time, Dom."

You've got to be kidding me. "Do you really think I'd have missed seeing them, Captain?"

"You must have, how else did they get there?"

"Someone is fucking with me."

"First, *someone* would have to come in here and take your boots, then listen to their scanner or, somehow knowing you weren't here, return to put them back. I don't think so, Dominic."

"Captain, I am a sane man and an astute firefighter. I did not miss seeing my boots."

"Look, Renaldi, Jacobs already hates me, and he'll probably be the next chief, so I might as well not fight him."

With someone messing with my gear, my captain oblivious to what was happening, or simply burying his head in the sand, I began to look around. As I diligently looked over engine 3 and S-1—the fire alarm truck—I found air hoses disconnected from their bottles on the engine's air-paks and tools missing from S-1, or the cherry picker as the general public called it. Part of my responsibility of the municipal fire alarm system was being responsible for S-1's equipment.

I liked my captain personally, and we were friends, so I didn't want a riff between us. With evidence mounting, I called him back to brief him on what I'd found, concluding, "Do you still think I just didn't see my boots, Captain?"

Now very perturbed, the captain said, "I'll speak to the chief about it, Dom." He wasn't happy to have been put in the middle of whatever was happening. Heaven forbid, he had to protect one of his men.

The next workday, my boots were missing again. This time, I called the chief. I will never forget his reaction or what he said though it should not have surprised me.

"What the fuck am I supposed to do about it?" he yelled over the phone and was actually mad at me for this.

"Let's put it this way, Chief, somebody is dangerously messing with me and with the equipment over here. If it happens again, I'll consider it a threat to my life and will be calling the state attorney general's office."

"Go ahead!" said the angry chief as he slammed the phone down.

At 6:00 a.m., we went to 115 Country Drive for reported smoke inside the house. Engine 3 was the first due engine, and I signed off, "Nothing showing." By the time that my captain got there, we had the origin of the smoke isolated to an overheated garage door opener, and I had just climbed up a stepladder to investigate. By now, the captain and the woman of the house stood there with me. Reaching into my bunker coat pocket for my gloves, they were gone. Turning to the captain with total disregard for anyone else present, in fact, wanting a resident to hear me, I said, "They stole my fucking glove, Captain."

The homeowner hastily asked, "Who did?"

"I presume someone at the firehouse," I said while raising my eyebrows.

"How childish," she quipped. "Does that really go on?"

"More than you'll ever know," I said in exasperation.

With a disgruntled look on his face, my captain handed me his gloves and said, "Use these." After that incident and when all apparatus had been returned to their respective quarters, the captain called me aside, scolding, "Dom, in the future, don't swear in front of a resident like you did, you make me look bad. Ya know what I mean?"

"Yes, sir, I know what you mean." What he meant was he was only worried about how he looked in front of other people and not worried about the well-being of his men.

I had purposefully created a light schedule for today, leaving enough wiggle room for possible unexpected activities with a new customer. Suddenly, this missing-gear business was now on my front burner. I'd given up speaking to my wife about the firehouse. All she ever said was, "No, they wouldn't do that!" So I decided to call the state attorney general's office in Boston. I knew there would be serious ramifications to my actions, but I had no other recourse if I wanted this crap to stop. Most of the department liked me, but they also knew the department's controlling influences did not like me. For their own good, most members had to stay away from me. A state trooper, who passed me along to an assistant DA, first screened my call.

"Hello, Lieutenant Renaldi, this is ADA Jonathan Piermont. Trooper Murray has briefed me. Who do you feel is stealing your gear and disconnecting the air hoses?

"It could be one of three men."

"I presume you've spoken to your chief about this, Lieutenant?

"Yes, I have, sir, but he seemed to have buried his head in the sand over it."

"Well, sooner or later, the chief has got to step to the plate here."

"Therein lies the problem, sir. The chief doesn't even know where the plate is, let alone step up to it."

"That's not good for your department, Lieutenant, but give it a few more days. Speak to your chief again, and if no action comes from him, call me back. I've documented your call today, and I'll take action at that time."

"Thank you, sir, I'll be sure to do that."

After this conversation, I called the chief.

"What the fuck did you do that for, you asshole."

"I was forced to take this action because of your INACTIONS, Chief. Do you honestly think I wanted to do this?"

"What did the DA say?" he asked quite angrily.

As pissed as I was, I was suddenly worried about ramifications from the chief.

"He said, 'Sooner or later, the chief will have to step to the plate. If he doesn't within a few days, call me back, and I'll take action.'

"Batter up, Chief," I quipped.

Smirking, he smartly retorted, "Okay, Dominic." The conversation ended abruptly, and I went off to work.

Brewster got on the phone and made a call. "Do you know what the fucking asshole just did?" And the heat intensified exponentially at the firehouse.

Someone had loosened the fuel pump on the fire alarm truck, and it leaked gas all over the hot engine. The truck should have burst into flames. Then there was the time the front brake lines were loosened, so the truck wouldn't stop well. Someone was always putting water in the gas tank. Ha, ha, ha. Ha, ha, ha.

I rang the doorbell, and the heavy oak door swung open. An older woman or nanny of some sort greeted me. "Is Liz—I mean, is Mrs. Temple here?"

"No." The woman shook her head, her face a sour scowl. She appeared in all likelihood the type of domestic help who never broke a smile, too bad too. So many people in this world who didn't enjoy what they did for a living, whether rich or poor, didn't smile.

The stern, but polite, servant instructed me to go back around and enter through the garage where she would meet me. As I entered the garage, the "spare car," a three-year-old Mercedes, was in the third bay over; and she was standing in a doorway, leading back to the basement where I had been a few days earlier. Without Liz, the room seemed cold and depressing, lacking the life she brought to it. The work was fairly easy. The excess sheetrock broke up easily so that I could manage getting it out by myself. There was a lot of natural wood, most likely excess exposed beams, which would make great fuel for my wood-burning stove at home.

I started at a hearty pace at first, hoping Liz would come downstairs at some point and see a hardworking, blue-collared guy, but I slowed to almost a crawl as time went by—the pretty lady was nowhere in sight. *Oh well*, I thought. Perhaps the other day at the firehouse was just to let me know that she still wanted me—as a laborer.

Filling the back of my blue pickup with the remains, I headed home. On the way, I received a call from a friendly face at the firehouse.

"Hi, Lieutenant, this is Barkeefe." It was the Mad Russian, a wild and crazy guy who raced cars at a few regional tracks and whom we also called AJ, short for A. J. Foyt of racing car fame. He was a good guy. "Have you seen the latest notice put out by the chief?" he asked.

I had no idea. Fearing the worst, I got a lump in my throat. Knowing Brewster, he had probably demoted me without a hearing. "No, I haven't seen it, what's it say?"

"It's titled Personal Harassment and goes on to say anyone caught messing with anyone else's gear or personal belongings would be severely punished. It then goes on. Want me to read it?"

"No, thank you, AJ. I'll look at it tomorrow."

"Nice going, Dom, maybe this will help to stop all this crap that's been going on."

"Thanks, AJ."

WOW, he actually took action. All it took was three incidents and a phone call to the DA's office!

The missing gear business would end with this notice. One of Jacobs's disciples even came to me and said, "I'm not the one fuck'n with you. I don't need a DA breathing down my back!"

I'd started the job at Liz Temple's around 10:00 a.m., and now it was about midday as I pulled into my driveway at the apartment behind the inn. As I was getting out of the truck, I saw a familiar Lexus SUV with that vanity plate parked at the hardware store across the street.

For some reason, not wanting to shout her name, I walked over to a location where Liz was the only one who could see me. I quietly called out, "Over here!"

She smiled. What a contrast to Ruth. Ruth who never seemed to smile anymore. Ruth who always seemed pensive and nervous, uncomfortable and insecure, unable to allow life to bring her out of her sheltered existence. Liz ran over to where I was. She had no kids.

"I was going to drop by the firehouse to pay you. Now you've saved me a trip. You did a great job today, thank you."

As she walked with me around the backside of the inn, we chatted, "No problem. If you don't mind, I took some firewood. We burn it here in the house."

"Oh wow. This is really quaint."

It truly was too. The innkeepers had done a splendid job restoring the inn back to original form, and the apartment was tied in beautifully.

Liz may have actually meant what she said, which would have been quite kind. It actually was a pretty nifty place to live, if you were into the whole rustic thing. "Thanks. Want a tour?"

"Geez, every time I see you, you're giving me a tour." With that, she entered into the front door.

"Hello?" No answer. Safe.

"Wow, this is cool."

"Are you just saying that, or is that for real?"

"What do you mean?"

I looked at her with a wink in my eye. "Oh, come on now, Little Miss Princess, it's not the Taj Mahal. It's a caretaker's apartment. I'm the caretaker of the museum, remember?"

"Busy guy. Any job you don't do?"

"Yeah, any job that makes money."

Liz chuckled. "There are enough people around town with those jobs."

"I'd be happy to trade with them."

"Dominic, believe me when I tell you, it's not what it's cracked up to be!"

She sounded convincing. Liz continued to peruse the place as I pointed out this and that. She was not being condescending in her interest, or at least, it didn't appear so. Nice.

As we found ourselves back in the foyer, we stood like two teenagers on a first date, each looking at the floor and then making eye contact, then shuffling our feet. *What the hell am I doing?* I thought. *What am I, crazy?*

I didn't have to think much longer. Liz suddenly got on her tiptoes and lunged forward and up to meet my lips. I had no other option than to respond in kind. The kissing immediately became passionate, pressing, insistent, and ravenous. My mind exploded, and soon, we were going down, down, down, each sinking deeper and deeper toward the floor, pawing each other, tearing at each other breathlessly. I wanted to appreciate every second of it, and yet I couldn't; time would not stand still that long. It didn't matter how hard the floor was or that the cold winter air seeped underneath the front door, blowing on us. What we were doing was thoughtless, thoughtless on every level.

I was thrown by how aggressive this petite woman was. Ruth hadn't moved like this in ages, if ever. Liz was like a small wild animal, thrusting and heaving and clawing at me with savage intent but yet in such a feminine way. We continued far beyond the point of turning back, and turn back we did not, would not, or could not. Liz smiled in anticipation when she wrapped her hand around my plentiful endowment.

Knowing time was limited, I immediately went down to taste the nectar of the woman I was about to make love to. Mmmmmmm, so sweet and delicious! I wanted more, but no way was there enough time for me to please Liz the way I was accustomed to pleasing a woman. So I quickly got on my knees between Liz's legs. Wrapping my arms under her legs with my hands holding her thighs tightly, I picked up her legs and pulled her closer as I began penetrating her. Liz's eyes opened wide in delight, and she smiled in satisfaction as I began thrusting deep inside of her. Liz was moist as I pumped harder and harder, and she winced in pleasure every time I pushed my final inch of reserve deeper. Soon, her lean stomach arched taut, and her thin neck turned red with veins popping. "Touch me. Touch me," she implored of me in a guttural voice as she took my hand and placed in just the right spot. The moment lasted briefly, but intensely, more intense than I had ever felt in my life. Spent, I laid down on top of Liz and kissed her passionately before we both laid back, searching for breath, drenched in sweat, chilled even more now by the leaky wooden door.

Neither of us said a word. I didn't know whether to mentally savor the moment or begin immediately worrying that Ruth could walk in at any moment, and there would be nothing we could have done about it, compromised as we were.

Finally, Liz, flushed with color and a warm smile, began to gather herself, still rather wordlessly unless *wow* was much of a word. Most of our clothes had never gotten removed but were twisted and turned this way and that. I rose to my feet and immediately looked out the front door window, acting as sentry. No action. No Ruth. No divorce. Not today. Not yet anyway.

The quiet was now awkward as she put herself back together, occasionally catching me staring at her, smiling when she did. "Well, that was something."

I didn't respond. Too confused. Still too out of body and mind to make conversation. Finally, I said, "I enjoyed that."

"Well, I gathered that." And she smiled at me again. The woman was definitely in control.

"You know how to get out of here?"

Now she looked at me strangely. "It's a small town, cowboy. I know where I'm at, thank you."

With that, she got up on her tiptoes again and kissed me, this time more puckishly as if we had a mutual secret. She then quickly pushed open the door and left, just like that, quickly and assertively. Mission accomplished. No good-byes, no long talks, no postgame analysis. She hobbled to her car, got in, started it up, and drove off as I stared at the taillights through the window.

I can't remember a more eclectic day I've ever experienced in my life. The good, the bad, and the ugly topped off with the beautiful and the sweet!

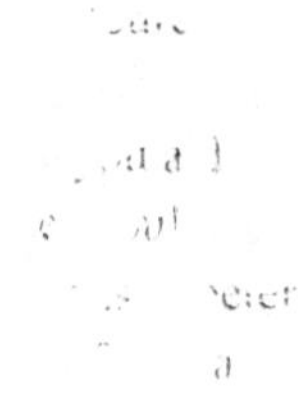

Chapter 12

"Mmmm, don't these cookies taste delicious, sweetie? Here, let's put another batch in the oven." Ethan and his mother were having fun. He was Liz's quiet child. She loved her boys. Still, something was missing in her life. She thought a little more. "Ethan, why don't we deliver some cookies to the firehouse? Mommy has some errands to run and maybe that nice Lieutenant Renaldi will be there."

They finished baking the cookies and quickly cleaned up. First, Ethan and Liz stopped at the bank, then the cleaners. Ethan had worked sooooo hard he was now beginning to doze in the stroller. "Don't fall asleep yet, munchkin, just one more stop!" As they walked toward the firehouse, Liz noticed my truck, which brought a smile to her face. *Regain your composure, don't let on*, she internalized. Meanwhile, Ethan was internalizing ZZZZZZs; he'd fallen asleep.

While covering headquarters for an ambulance call, I stood staring out the window and thought back over the past few months. Had they occurred at any other time of my life, I would have I would have regarded them as exciting, more memorable. Chief Wyatt had officially stepped down, Pete Brewster became the new chief, and I had been elected the new association president.

Pete Brewster's inauguration as fire chief was fairly pathetic in its own way. Brewster was choked up as if he'd just won an Oscar or something. John Wyatt put a professional face on the procedure, but he too had to have been a bit disappointed. His own tenure had been so meritorious, and the department had developed into such a proud and gallant force, providing innumerable services to the community. Now here he was turning over the reins to, at best, a dullard, at worst, an incompetent.

Just as Slayton and Jacobs had planned, I was elected association president. Just as they had also predicted, I enthusiastically gave a speech outlining my goals and objectives for the coming year. "And going into our contract negotiations, I can assure you all, we are not going to roll over and play dead like we have in the past. We are all overworked and underpaid. We risk our lives yet struggle to make ends meet. I vow to you all, our efforts will be respected, and our salaries and benefits will reflect that. This community can afford it. Times are changing in the fire service, and they're getting the best squad in the state. We should be paid accordingly."

As cheers and whistles filled the room, Slayton and Jacobs tucked their heads in their shirts while eyeballing one another, giggling like schoolgirls. Oh, what a sucker. Such a sucker!

I turned my thoughts back to Liz Temple.

Waking up each day and looking at Ruth, her unsmiling face, her drab appearance, she seemed lifeless. For years, I felt responsible. I couldn't help but feel I should have been a better husband to her. Now I felt guilty about my marital indiscretion; nonetheless, I couldn't help thinking about Liz's smile or my exhilarating experience with her. I was torn. Every time the phone rang, I knew it had to be Liz, perhaps calling to make a tearful confession and apology to Ruth or acting as the woman scorned, determined to fix me good by ratting me out to my wife. And so with each ring of the phone, my nerves jumped, and then I pounced on the phone. Each time, it was someone else for someone else about something else.

Now I wanted more—the energy, the desire, a woman who actually wanted to be in my arms. This was exciting and seemed to give me an infusion of life while offering hope for a better existence. I wanted to call Liz, to make contact, to find out where I stood. Did she want a repeat performance? Or was she just looking for a quickie to get something out of her system. As to my own feelings, I was excited. This woman was sexy, self-assured, young, and beautiful. She dressed impeccably, even in her casual attire, and kept everything about herself in perfect form as if on her way to a modeling assignment. *Of all the men she could have, surely she couldn't possibly want me!* I fought to keep myself from diving in headfirst. Deep inside, I knew that the inevitable comparison to Ruth was unfair. Marriage was about becoming so comfortable with another person that he or she no longer needed to close the bathroom door and could go to bed sans makeup—not that Ruth wore much anyway nor did she need to. You got to see their worst foibles and human faults.

You also fought. Fighting between a couple in a failing marriage is as inevitable as a rainstorm. It may not happen every day, but it happens often enough, sometimes for long consecutive streaks that can seem unending and unbearable. It leaves you hopeless and feeling depressed. After a while, these fights also become as commonplace and predictable as that same rain from the sky. You've seen it once; you've seen it a hundred times. Only when it presents itself uniquely or dramatically does it truly catch the eye. Otherwise, it's the same old same old. After umpteen years together, fights with Ruth had become verbatim repeats of the same two or three fights over and over and over again ad nauseam. And I, for one, had just about had it. The fighting had taken away my desire for her and hers for me. Yes, we still had sex, but now it was the obligatory kind. "You're here, I'm here. We both need this, let's get it over with."

As I continued to look out the window, I spotted Liz as she was heading right for the firehouse. I didn't know how to react when she came sauntering in much as she had a few weeks prior. Again, the stroller was attached to her hands. Ethan perfectly tucked in and fast asleep. She approached me.

"So it's been a while. Any particular reason for that?" Liz started the conversation.

For the first time I could recall, Liz Temple's face was less than sunny, her personality turned to feisty. Even in this frame of mind, she was still adorable.

"Uh . . . I didn't know what to do."

"It's simple. You pick up the phone, you drop by. It's that simple. That's if you ever wanted to see me again. If not, then you were acting perfectly. Message received."

"No no, it's not like that. Not like that at all. I just . . . just didn't know how to go about it. This is the first time I've ever . . ." My voice trailed off again.

"As I said, you go about it by showing interest and treating me like a lady. None of this slam bam thank you ma'am."

I gently laughed at her.

"Stop laughing at me," she said curtly. "This isn't a laughing matter!"

"I'm sorry, Liz. But even while showing your feisty Irish temper, you're still adorable, and it cracks me. Please forgive me." I became all the more flustered. "I never meant to make you feel badly. I definitely would like to see you again. But you know how it is. It's complicated. You're . . . and I'm . . ." Any idiot knew that *married* was the word I was reticent to say. "Herpes simplex 2" or "genital warts" would have been just as hard to spit out.

"Well, it's all in how you look at it. Life's for the living, don't you agree?"

"Well, yeah, I guess so. Look"—and I lowered my voice even more—"I *really* enjoyed the other day. It was a wonderful experience."

Liz lightened up only slightly. "So if it was, why have you left me hanging? I've never done anything like this before either, Dominic, and I'm not just someone to have a quickie with. I want more from a relationship . . . Hell, I can get *that* from my husband!"

"Well, it's not like we talked at all about it afterward. You just kind of left."

"I left happy. With a kiss and a smile on my face. Look, if you're not interested, it's okay. I'm not here to stalk you. I don't beg."

My eyes looked heavenward, even grabbed humorously at my chest. "Oh dear Lord, you must be kidding! Of course, I'm interested. I'd do that again anytime you wanted. I loved it."

As the noose slipped around the necks of the helpless preys, Liz flirted, "Loved it as in you'd love it with anybody who'd do *it* with you?"

"No no, I don't do that sort of thing. I don't . . ." and I almost said, "Cheat on my wife," but again I held my tongue.

"Well, I loved it too. And I'd be open to doing it again . . . with you . . . if you felt the same way. But first you'd have to promise that I wouldn't have to come chasing you after waiting another two weeks."

"I understand, Liz." Then I smiled affectionately at her and said, "Message received."

Liz laughed at my use of her words and said, "Good, in that case, I have a little present for you. You did a favor for me, now I'm doing a favor for you." Liz reached into the stroller, her son still sound asleep, and pulled out a pretty gift bag. "Ethan and I were baking cookies, and I thought of you. Here, something from me, something yummy for you. Consider it a thank-you."

"But you already paid me for the work in the basement."

In her adorable, flirtatious way, she said in a high pitched voice, "That's not the only thing I have to thank you for." She smiled a devilish smile. "Mornings are best for me. Weekdays after eight but before noon." With that, Liz Temple sassily turned and strutted out of the firehouse, pushing her stroller. As I held the door open for her, I couldn't take my eyes off her undulating posterior. As if fully aware of my attentions, she presumptuously swayed and sashayed from side to side with each step. *Damn*, I thought. *I'm hooked!*

As she finally faded from view, I brought the bag closer to my face and began to smell what were obviously some delectable baked goods inside. Naturally, Bill Slayton and Tom Jacobs were lurking around the corner in the firehouse and descended upon me with, "Geez, Dom, that woman was *fine*. What the hell was that all about?"

"Nothing. I did some work at her house the other day."

"Man, I'd work her over any day she'd like. Did you get some?"

"You guys never grow up, do you? It was all on the up and up. She even brought me something to eat." Opening up the bag, I stared down at homemade oatmeal cookies. "See. Cookies. Women don't bake you cookies for fooling around with them."

Quick on the uptake, Slayton said, "Mine do," followed by an obnoxious laugh.

I shot back just as quickly, "If they do, it's only because they hope it'll make you grow."

Slayton turned beet red. Even Jacobs laughed at that one. "Hey, Dom, share the wealth. Those cookies look good."

Food at the firehouse was like food sent to summer camp or to a military base. It was customarily shared and immediately devoured.

Just then, a voice came over the house speakers, "Lieutenant Renaldi, phone call on 28."

Walking away to answer the phone call, I said, "Mange, Mange."

Jacobs said, "I'll make the coffee."

Slayton said, "I'll bring the cookies into the kitchen." As Jacobs turned left into the kitchen, Slayton went right and disappeared for a few minutes.

"Where'd you go?" Jacobs asked Slayton upon his entering the kitchen.

"Nowhere," said Slayton with a self-satisfied smirk on his face.

Rejoining them in the kitchen, the three of us poured our coffee and sat at the table, I reached for the bag, and Jacobs grabbed for it too, tearing it in our eagerness like starving children. As the cookies tumbled out, something else fell from the bag. Slayton quickly grabbed for it and suddenly held up a short roll of condoms. "Uh, excuse me, Dom?"

All action stopped. Slayton smiled wildly, Jacobs nearly choked on his cookie, and my jaw dropped open; instantaneously, all the blood seemed to drain to my toes.

"What the fuck is that?" Jacobs finally sputtered.

Now it was my face that turned fire engine red. Impulsively, I reached to grab the condoms from Slayton, then pulled my own arm down, afraid of claiming the prize for myself. Standing and then briskly walking away in embarrassment, I mumbled almost inaudibly, "I don't know."

Jacobs and Slayton were left to stare incredulously at one another, shooting quick glances back to figure out where I went. "Ho-ly shit," Jacobs finally said, each syllable punctuated with shock and awe.

As for Slayton, there was no wiping the smile off his face. "Tom, this guy's making our job easy as shooting fish in a barrel."

"What do you mean?"

"You heard their conversation. Mr. Boy Scout has a married honey on the side!"

"Yeah, sooooo?"

Slayton held up the condoms and shook them like a noisemaker. "Uh, hello? How do you think that's going to play out in a town this small? Dog shit, Tommy, dog shit!" Triumphantly, they both laughed.

Chapter 13

One of the benefits of a greater net worth was being able to donate to worthy causes. Many did so through sincere beliefs; others did it purely for tax reasons or personal gain. Dr. Samuel Temple stood looking at himself in the mirror, proud of himself for the fact that he could still fit into his very first tuxedo. Indeed, the doctor was slim, ate well but meagerly, and exercised frequently. He had Liz to thank for this; after all, she's the one who set the diet, bought the food, researched the best health club to join, and encouraged her husband toward fitness. But Sam Temple never would see it that way. He was the master of his universe. Unfortunately, Dr. Temple was fifty-nine years old, and he had bought the tuxedo when he was twenty-one. Thus, in order to give himself this particularly egotistical conversation starter at black-tie events, Sam Temple wore a thirty-eight year-old garment. And even though tuxedo styles do not change drastically over the years, to the eye trained in subtlety, they do evolve incrementally. Liz Temple hated that ratty old tuxedo and dreaded every time it had to come out of the closet. That piece of pretentious clothing symbolized everything she had grown to abhor about her relationship with Sam. The tuxedo and the man were old, worn, unfashionable, unattractive, trite, and full of self-indulgent, self-serving, egotistical pomp. They also only spent time with her on a more and more infrequent basis.

"Let me see what you're wearing," Sam said to Liz, who was buried deep inside the entrails of her walk-in closet, a room big enough to house a small family. Sam Temple was controlling, the master chess player and champion of his game. Liz huffed. One of the many downsides to marrying an older man was his unspoken insistence on treating her like a child rather than his equal. Check that. Dr. Samuel Temple knew no one was his equal. Liz dutifully, yet reluctantly, padded out of the closet, wearing a modest, beige dress—classy and elegant as befitted the charity function they were to attend that evening. Sam looked her up and down meticulously. This was a man used to sizing up a situation with great haste. "No. Won't do. Too frumpy."

"Frumpy? This is incredibly chic. It's Chaiken."

"Never heard of him. Put something else on."

"He's a she. Shows how much you know." Despite her protests, she turned and went back for something else. This was their routine, part of the game. Dr. Samuel Temple was a graduate of both Harvard College as well as Harvard Medical School. For an American Jew, his money was relatively old. By Coventry standards, he represented new money. His ego was ingrained in him and fortified through his life and education.

"Something younger. More attractive."

Liz knew what this meant in Sam-speak. It meant something more revealing and sexier. What was the point in having a young trophy wife if she dressed ten years older than her age?

A few moments later, Liz came back out from inside the closet, this time dressed in something a successful call girl would wear—low cut, backless, with a long slit up the side barely leaving anything to the imagination. It was from long ago, but she too could still fit into it. She'd never think of wearing it anymore, but it would make her point tonight. "Is this what you meant?"

"I don't see the humor, Liz." Samuel Temple's cold eyes peered down at his wife, unable to see the beauty or her own intellect, let alone her pain. "Don't play me for a fool," he said harshly. Sam Temple may be a successful surgeon at the hospital, but he's a coldhearted man.

Indeed, Sam was completely humorless even when hobnobbing with other wealthy professionals from the same MetroWest clique at these dull parties. It gave him an air of superiority to listen to a fellow tell a joke and, no matter how funny or well told, to grimace into his drink as if to tell the man, "You're not that funny, you're not that bright, and although I have demonstrated none of these qualities myself, you are still beneath me."

Some women took joy in finding excuses to dress to the nines and having a closet full of choices at their fingertips; it gave them security. Liz Temple was not one of them. Oh, perhaps in the beginning, it was fun. It was different. Different from being with the young men she dated—all the Dutch treats, the mediocre restaurants, the movies, and a burger. Sam Temple in his Mercedes, taking her to gala balls in the city, now *that* was a move up. He was the first older man—the first divorced man—she'd dated. Dr. Temple's success had given him the one tool he needed to win a woman over—money. When he began dating Liz, the wealthy doctor bought her a new car and paid off her college debt. Liz was swept off her feet. When he asked her to marry him, the size of the enormous diamond blinded her.

Suddenly, all of this could be hers forever. And for an older man, a man old enough to be her father, he wasn't smelly, fat, or gross. Balding, yes, but he swam, played tennis, or golfed. Their sex life was satisfactory. But as time went by, his prowess as a lover waned, not due to biological issues (Viagra took care of that) but due to simple disinterest. Liz thought she would be the one to lose interest in him, suspecting he might become more decrepit and unattractive in short time. But no, it seemed that she was nothing more than a conquest he had won. He pulled her out of the closet as he did the thirty-eight year-old tuxedo. She served a similar purpose.

Liz was a powerful woman in her own right and didn't like being controlled, but she knew how to play the game. "What about this?" She now wore the classic "little black dress and sexy open heels." In that closet, there were at least a dozen little black dresses, so she always had choices.

"Fine," he said, and nothing more. Liz looked at herself in the mirror. She looked more than fine. She looked *fine*. Liz longed to hear how beautiful she looked, but that simple compliment would not be made. Not tonight. These days, now that he had a steady, attractive young wife on his arm with two new children, the game was won. "Oh, you little rascal, you old bird, congratulations!" The other players would say in admiration. Sam Temple would preen and smile.

Sam bragged about the kids based solely upon what Liz had told him about them, for he spent no time with them at all. Recently, Ethan had some sort of cold. Liz handed the baby to Sam. "You're a doctor. What's wrong with your son? Does he need something?" She was feisty, sometimes not being able to contain her unhappiness.

Sam backed away from the child in fright, the way another person would a severed head. "I'm a heart surgeon. I don't do pediatrics. Call Dr. Earle!" Heaven forbid, he actually parented. Sam had two grown children from marriage number one. They grew up as emotionally distant as their father. Or perhaps, giving them the benefit of the doubt, they acted that way only toward him. Payback.

"Which one of these events are we going to again?"

"The hospital's fund-raiser gala ball. It's at the Ritz-Carlton."

"All the way into Boston?" Liz said with a whine. If it had been something at the country club or out in the nearby suburbs, perhaps she could muster up the facade to tolerate an hour or two. Liz loved the city. In fact, had received her master's degree from Boston College and was quite accustomed to the theatre district, fine restaurants, museums, and of course, Newbury Street. But if they were driving into Boston, she knew this would be a long night, another in a long line of nights under Sam's control.

As if reading her mind, Sam adjusted his tie and said, "Don't drink too much."

"It's the only way I can stand it."

"You used to like these things."

"Yes, once. I'll try almost anything once. Now we go to these kinds of things about once every week or two. I hate them. They're boring."

"Only boring people are bored," he replied.

"When do we ever do what I want to do?"

"I buy you everything you want. You wanted a big house, I bought you a big house. You want clothes, I give you money for clothes. You wanted a vacation home on the Vineyard, I bought you that too. You've got nothing to complain about."

"Yes, you give me money. You buy me off. But we never spend time together doing anything I want to do."

"We're spending time together tonight."

"You're not listening. You don't get it. I don't want to go to another stuffy, pretentious, black-tie cocktail event. Why can't we ever spend time together? We bought the place in the Vineyard; I go there alone. If you ever manage to come down at all, you spend the whole time reading a book or on your cell phone while ignoring the kids and me. You don't even know your own children."

"Liz"—he sighed—"I don't have time for this. My time is valuable. I make time for things like tonight because it's good for business."

"Good for business? No one comes to you because they met you at a cocktail party. They come to you because you're a good surgeon. Your reputation is established. You should even consider retiring, it's not like we need the money. Face it, you do this because this is who you are. This is your crowd, and they talk about the things you care about. It fills your needs. Well, it's not my crowd, and it's not what I want to talk about, and it doesn't fill my needs at all."

"Quite a few of our friends from Coventry will be there. Whenever we go," Sam countered, "you always find someone to talk to. By the way, please don't embarrass me by talking to the wife of the chief of staff so much. People think you're sucking up to her, and that's a bad reflection on my image."

Liz was shocked by Sam's remark. "You make me sick. Jennifer and I serve on committees together, doesn't that count for anything? Oh yes, you're right. Dr and Mrs. Samuel Temple, we're part of a clique—wealthy west suburban Boston clique—but it's your clique." Liz didn't back down as she continued to parlay her displeasures. "At all these events, of course, I can find someone to talk to. I can find someone because I'm young, because I'm vivacious, and because I'm more attractive than a dull *fine*. Oh, I'll find someone, don't worry about that Sam, I'll find someone!" Liz was now on the verge of tears as she poured another glass of wine.

Sam Temple was too caught up in himself to even understand what his wife had just said to him. Straightening his bowtie for the final time while looking at himself in the mirror, he asked, "Did you have the car cleaned for tonight?"

Dutifully, but sarcastically, Liz called out, "Yes, dear. I brought it to the carwash when you got home. I had them clean it inside and out just as I have always done for your special occasions."

The Ritz-Carton, Boston's most posh address, was the perfect setting for the elite to assemble. Politicians mingled with men in black ties, their right hand extended for a handshake while their left hand worked the coffers of MetroWest wealth. When Dr. and Mrs. Samuel Temple made their entrance, Sam held Liz by the arm, and she captivated everyone with her beautiful smile. Together, they walked as if on a runway at a Paris fashion show. Liz deplored the spotlight but obediently performed. As the night went along, men regaled with insincere laughter, and woman found their niche. The other thirty-something's chatted about their rich husband's success: about his money and about how unfulfilled their lives are. For the first time, Liz patiently listened.

"My husband is so aloof, I've taken up with my contractor," said one golden beauty. "You should try it. It's very stimulating."

Suddenly, Liz became more interested in the conversation. "Why don't you just get divorced?" she asked while trying to sound the most naive of the group. Everyone laughed.

"Because I'm not going to give up this kind of lifestyle," she replied as she cast her arm about the room, encompassing all the wealth it represented. Again, all the women laughed in agreement.

With enough to absorb at the moment, Liz walked away with Jennifer. She and Liz have children in the same class at school, and they both serve on the Coventry Enrichment Committee.

"Do you really think there are quite a few woman who do this kind of thing, Jennifer?" Liz wasn't sure if she was inquiring as a possibility or if she was trying to justify her experience on the floor a few weeks ago.

"Of course, they do, Liz. Look, our husbands are never around. When they are, they're not really there. I haven't had sex with my husband in months."

Liz was surprised by the comment. She turned and asked, "Does that mean that you're . . ." She stopped speaking and looked at her friend.

"I've already said too much, Liz. Just think about it for a while. Think about your needs and if they are truly being met. As you walk around the room tonight, look to see if you can tell who is and who isn't."

Their conversation was interrupted by someone wanting to speak to Jennifer. Liz excused herself and walked away, looking for her husband. He was with a group of men who were preoccupied. She looked for their wives. They were all sitting around as if old maids. She looked back toward the group of women talking about their extracurricular activities. They were alive. They were happy, and they were excited. As Liz rejoined the younger crowd with their champagne, the conversation had loosen up to gossip, which inevitably led to the whispered confessions of sexual frustration and young lovers on the side.

"The secret is to not fall in love with your lover," laughingly said one.

"That would ruin a good thing, now wouldn't it?" blurted another to everyone's laughter.

Unexpectedly, one of the loosened-up members of the club asked, "Have you tried it yet, Liz?"

Caught off guard, Liz was shocked, dumbfounded, at a loss for words. "I don't know what you're talking about," she said breathlessly.

"Of course, you do. I can see it in your expression. Don't worry, we're on your side. We're all in this together, sister."

Not knowing how to react, quickly Liz walked away and sought out Jennifer. "Do you have a lover?" Liz asked inquisitively but rather abruptly.

With both guilt and compassion, Jennifer spoke in a whisper, "Liz"—then a brief pause—"out at the club, we all have lovers. The money is great, and the lifestyle is wonderful, but there are voids to fill. Here's my friendly word of advice. I've watched too many woman fall to their husband's demands. Don't let it happen to you. Your husband is older and not about to change. You're still young and beautiful. Find someone who can lift you up. Find someone who can make you happy." Jennifer's eyes were moist, and her voice trembled slightly. "Find someone who will love you for who you are."

Jennifer had struck a cord. Liz was visibly upset and needed to regain her composure. "Thank you for your advice." Liz tried walking away looking composed with a face that said, "I am fine. I wasn't just told to go have an affair. On with the show!"

She had no idea where she was walking, but she kept walking as if with purpose. All the while, she thought to herself, *A woman's primal instinct in this situation is to turn toward safety, comfort, a place of protection*. But she found herself thinking about what they just said. *Though I've only felt his warmth for one fleeting moment, why am I wishing Dom were here right now ravenously taking me in his arms, being a hero fireman and sweeping me away in the safety of his grasp?*

Jennifer's advice seemed to unlock a door in Liz's inner soul, and suddenly, everything was turning, churning, swirling around in a vortex of emotion. As titillating as it was, the thought of taking on a lover filled her fantasies, but made no practical sense—until Dom, that is. She still couldn't believe she did it. It was four or five years of pent-up frustration all pouring out into one hot, sweaty pile. Did she feel guilty about it? Unbelievably so; she came back home that day and cried. Then Sam came home late as usual, and instead of using some form of mental telepathy to understand that the woman he was suppose to be in love with was a woman with desperate needs, he ignored her as always. Did he not even know his wife? Did he not even know the mother of his children? Sam went straight to his study from where he would treat his wife as if his secretary. Day after day, this continued. Sam was not about to change. This only made her wonder why she'd ever felt guilty about it in the first place. Now this evening! Liz just sat bewildered, lost in thought, shaking her head in wonderment.

As they drove home, not a word was spoken. Still caught in the vortex of her emotions, Liz gazed out the window.

"Liz, how could you get caught up in that loud crowd of young women who drink too much, then talk about their fantasies?"

"Oh, shut up, Sam!" The final nail in his coffin had just been set.

Having made up her mind, Liz set about creating with Dom, this near stranger, a semiregular affair in hopes it would grow into the love she yearned for. He may not have known that was her plan, but nevertheless, it was what she had decided. Liz would take Jennifer's advice and not ask Sam for a divorce, not just yet. The boys were still young, and Liz didn't wish to burn that bridge. After all, she had invested her best years in this relationship and wasn't about to run from it empty-handed, at least not without first looking at all her options.

Dominic seemed to spark something in Liz right from the beginning. He seemed so caring and genuine a person. As wonderful as the sex was with him, she could only dream something more might come of it. Would he perhaps spend some time with her? Surely, he seemed to want to. Would he talk to her about something other than ways to spend money? Would he be someone who could appreciate her for who *she* was? Would he tell her how beautiful he thinks she was? He's already told her that more than Sam has! And great sex on top of *that*!

It's been years since Liz Temple had passion in her life. Equally disconcerting was how long she'd gone without simple companionship. Dom was fun, reliable, and oh, those hands! Perhaps this was her chance to regain the simple pleasures of life.

Chapter 14

Nervous as hell, I aimlessly drove my truck around without a plan but with the hope that a plan would develop from this phone call. Who would answer the phone? What if it's her husband? What was his schedule? She did say between eight and noon was best. Should I hang up if it's not her? So many things to think about. The phone was answered on the third ring, "Hello," said that wonderful, captivating voice. Phew, it was her.

My demeanor changed as we exchanged pleasantries; in a voice that gravitated from low to medium high, I acknowledged, "Hello."

Liz, such a smart ass in a very fun way, said, "See, calling's not that difficult."

I could feel her bright smile being emitted over the phone as she said that, and we laughed together, her giggle sending waves of yearning through me. Finally, I said, "I just thought I'd call to say hello."

"I'm glad you did. I was thinking about you all last night," Liz said rather sultry like.

"Mmmm. That's nice to hear," I said as seductively as I knew how.

Liz was far more nervous than the first coupling on the floor of my house. That was fairly spontaneous. This was planned. *This man would be over in a matter of minutes, and I knew exactly what he was coming for* ran through her mind. A thousand things ran through her mind.

Liz scurried around in that enormous closet of hers, looking for just the right thing to wear. *Somehow, total seduction wear would be too, too over the top. It was daytime, and our time together was limited. He's a jeans kind of guy. Maybe jeans and a sexy top; besides, the most important part of the outfit would be my underwear. That's where a woman wants to look really good for a man.* With excitement building, she scurried and thought some more, *Jared was in daycare, and the nanny had taken Ethan out for a while, then she would pick up Jared at school. Okay, we have a few hours.*

She looked around her bedroom. *Here? Should I make love with him here, right where I slept with my husband? Possibly. That gives me a perverse feeling—a good, perverse feeling. That'll hit the bastard hard. Maybe the guest room, unemotional there?* But she was still undecided. *If things were like they were the last time, we might never make it up the stairs.*

"Oh my god, what was that?" she said out loud. The doorbell had rung, and it startled her. It sounded amplified, louder than ever before, her imagination obviously. Tension. Nerves. The show was about to begin.

Liz bounced down the stairs like an excited teenager. *Look at my chest, it glistened with sweat, I'm not that out of shape.* Nerves. Nerves again. *Talk about getting a girl hot.* Liz fanned her face briefly.

Just before she was about to open the door, she got into character. Composed. Sexy. Alluring. That was how she wanted to portray herself. Not anxious and apprehensive, not to mention guilty as sin. Geez, this was more difficult than she thought!

"Hi," Liz finally said coquettishly, opening the door and trying to act demure at the same time.

I tried to act nonchalant, but it wasn't working very well. "Hey" I said, melting a little more while looking at that smile I was not yet used to seeing with every greeting.

Good! thought Liz. *He looks as nervous as I feel.* "Come in."

I had been inside Liz's house before, but still, I ambled in, looking at everything as if for the first time. Frankly, this was nothing more than the defense mechanism ingrained in me. Whether I knew it or not, I was looking for danger, no different from when I went into a house fire. As straightforward as a situation appeared, there was always the little voice in my head saying, "Her husband is going to walk in. He's hiding in the closet. And he could have a gun."

"What have you got there?" Liz smiled and asked, 'Something for *me*?" as she pointed at the plastic grocery bag I carried.

"Oh yeah. A little gift for you."

Liz reached into the bag and pulled out two little red plastic fire helmets and two gold plastic badges.

"They're for your boys. I wasn't really ready for you the last time you brought them to the firehouse."

Liz looked at the trinkets and became visibly upset.

"What's the matter? Did I do something wrong?"

She just stared at the souvenirs and shook her head slightly. "Do you want some coffee? I could use some coffee," and she turned and walked away, so I couldn't see her face. But I instinctively knew.

I briskly followed. "Is something wrong, Liz? You look upset."

She walked past the dining room on the right, past the basement door on the left, and we entered a huge kitchen. I demurely sat down. I looked around at the custom-built cherry cabinets, top-of-the-line Sub-Zero appliances, with matching wood panel fronts, of course, and a sliding door opposite where I was sitting which looked out to a huge deck.

Still, she said not a word, not answering me at all. Liz began pulling out coffee cups, acting like a woman entertaining the local undertaker who had just come with bad news.

"C'mon, what did I do wrong? I thought they'd like them."

Visibly nervous, she continued her ministrations, soon producing two steaming cups of java. "Sorry, no cream. The one percent milk is here, sugar's on the counter."

Liz sat opposite me, not at all like someone who had invited me over to jump my bones. I knew something was suddenly wrong and wanted to keep asking the same questions over and over, but Liz appeared to want to compose herself, take the lead.

"Look, Dom, the gifts were sweet of you. They just threw me."

"Why?"

She fidgeted in her chair and then stared me in the eyes. "You've never done this before, have you?"

"What do you mean?"

"You're married, right?"

"Yeah."

"And you've been faithful. I mean, up until a little while ago. Am I right?"

I looked down into my coffee. "Basically."

"So why me? Why now?"

I pondered her question as I fell into her blue eyes. "Why *me*?" I asked with raised eyebrows and a slight tilt of the head.

Liz gave me no answer, but I could tell she was conflicted. It was as if she just wanted Joe the Town Stud to come over and ravish her and be done with it—a professional, so to speak. Then I come over, bearing presents for her kids, and then demonstrate genuine concern for her. It was too much for her.

I broke into Liz's thoughts. "Look, I think you're very attractive. And no, I don't do this sort of thing all the time. I'm married and have three kids whom I love."

"And what about your wife?"

I went back to staring into my coffee. "It's been better."

"Do you think it'll get better again?"

With one arm draped over the back of the chair, I sat back pondering in thought as I stared out the slider. "No."

"Same here."

We both sipped our coffee in silence. For no rational reason, we both looked calmer than any time since I arrived.

"Look, I didn't invite you over to be my therapist. That's too much of a burden to place on a near stranger, and I don't want you to think I'm a ditsy blond."

"No, it's okay. We can talk. I'm a great listener. And no way in hell are you a ditsy blond. You're at the opposite end of that spectrum, Liz, that's written all over you."

Liz stared deeply at me. Yes, I was a near stranger. And yet this moment was sweeter than any Liz had spent with Sam in years. Simple. Uncomplicated. Mellow. Gradually, she smiled, and I smiled back. We gazed at each other.

Conversation was light. Liz was doing most of the talking as I listened patiently. Once again, I felt in the zone where the world seemed to stop. Unfortunately, this time it did not.

There were several cross town routes to travel in Coventry, and most used the main drag right up the middle. Little did I know that Bill Slayton had altered his usual ride today. As he glanced up the Temples' driveway, he saw my blue pickup truck parked there and quickly got on his cell phone checking in with Tom Jacobs. "Guess whose truck is parked in the Temples' driveway?"

"Renaldi's?" Jacobs replied.

To which Slayton said, "I smell dog shit, Tommy!" and then that fucking laugh of his.

In the meantime, Liz beautifully articulated to me about several committees she served on, the daycare association, and Coventry's Educational Enrichment Fund. I am a good listener, and it was clear that Liz enjoyed someone who wanted to listen to her talk about her life. We must have talked for an hour straight.

Quietly, I sat there with a refreshing smile on my face while this adorable 'Energizer Bunny' demonstratively babbled as time passed by quickly. With an empty coffee cup in hand, I made my way to the sink where I placed my cup. Liz, still talking, still articulating, followed my actions. From the start, I was never sure where this day would lead. Liz's talk was incessant, and I just let her continue while we stood at the kitchen counter. Besides, I was thoroughly enjoying this dynamo of a petite woman, her actions, her smile, and her vivaciousness all so appealing to me.

Suddenly, the urge was too strong for me. In midsentence, I put my hands on her cheeks and tilted her head back for her lips to meet mine. I gave her a long wet kiss. Her welcoming reaction assured me I did the right thing.

Her response to my kiss seemed just as spontaneous. Wrapping one leg around my leg, she invitingly opened her mouth and pulled me closer. My arms wrapped around her.

As we darted our tongues in and out of each other's mouths, Liz abruptly said, "Come with me." She pulled my hand and led me up the stairs.

"Okay." I followed without resistance.

When we reached the top of the stairs, the master bedroom to the right, I took Liz into my arms and kissed her passionately.

"Hmmmm, what's that hardness I feel pressing against me?" she asked with an inviting smile as she slid her hand down and began rubbing. Then said, "Not here, c'mon."

Liz led me into the master bedroom and said, "I want you in my bed with me." Then she pulled the covers down. We lay on the bed and began kissing and embracing. Soon, we were removing each other's shirts. With tongues rolling and salivating, we continued to remove our clothing. I undid the front of Liz's bra. Her supple breasts felt so good in my hands. And her erect brown nipples were tantalizing me.

Liz closed her eyes and sighed, then moaned in pleasure as I gently squeezed her nipples between my fingers. "Your hands, Dom, they feel warm and strong."

I looked down at her. We exchanged smiles while I massaged her breasts. "I'm going to make love to you the way I like to please a woman, Liz."

"Please do, Dominic. Please do."

I laid back down with Liz, our warm bodies pressing against each other. We could feel each other's heart pounding. Our kisses were more voracious than before. I caressed my way down, and kissed her nipples as I run my tongue around it, finally sucking on the erectness of her nipple. Tenderly, I nibbled on its firmness. Liz moaned, "Yes" as she yearned for more pleasure. I found her to be so sweet and delicious.

Frantically, we remove our pants. As I knelt naked in front of Liz, she looked at me. "Oh, Dom, it's beautiful. Look at how big it is. I want you inside of me," she said with a trembling voice. Then she sat up and began sucking on my manhood.

I grabbed her by the back of her head and guided her. She definitely knew what she was doing. "Oh my good geezus, Liz. You're going to make me come."

"Not yet, you're not. I want this to last."

"Then stop. Give me your tongue in my mouth." Now both completely naked, we were laying there pressing, feeling, and rubbing. It was hot, and it was passionate.

Liz tried to put me inside of her, but I wouldn't let her. "Yes, please, Dom."

I wiggled her close to the edge of the bed where I slid onto the floor. With her legs hanging over the edge, she knew what I wanted. She wanted the same thing. Liz picked up her legs and spread them for me. "Liz, your pussy is sooooo inviting." And I rubbed it for just a minute. Just enough to feel how wet it was.

Liz took my hand and placed it for her pleasure. "There, touch me right there." As I did, she gasped and moaned loudly.

Sensing Liz was climaxing, I went down on her and began touching her special spot with my tongue, flicking it back and forth, then sucking gently. Liz arched and stiffened while bellowing a constant moan as she immediately climaxed again. I began eating and sucking her. My tongue went deep, her smell so clean and her taste so delectable.

I slipped my finger in as I continued to flick with my tongue. Liz arched and screamed again. "Put it in. You have to put it in now!"

"Come again for me, Liz." I ran two fingers faster and gently sucked on her.

Liz exploded for the third time as she screamed in pleasure.

The bed was high enough for me to stand at the perfect height. I took the throbbing head of my penis and began to rub it around Liz's clit. Her wetness was making this easy to do, and it felt sooooo good too. I wanted to be inside of her as badly as she wanted me in her, but I wanted to make it last a little while longer.

I looked at her firm breasts, her rippled tummy, and her tight, shapely hips as I continued to play. Liz, you are so beautiful."

"You feel so good, Dominic. It's so warm, but you're teasing me. Please just put it in all the way before I come again. Please!"

I smiled as I slid it in just enough to bury the head, and I rubbed it around. This drove Liz insane. She arched and craved for more. I was craving too and on the verge of climaxing. So I slid it into her wetness. She was so wet my whole nine inches went right in.

Liz shrieked, "Oh my, you're huge" as she opened wider in reception.

I was surprised at this petite woman being able to take all of me, and she felt just as wonderful to me. I pick up her legs and began thrusting harder. Faster.

Liz screamed, "OH MY GOD. OH MY GOD, touch me, touch me."

My whole body stiffened as I pumped hard while rubbing her clit on her desired spot. In an explosion I've never felt before, we came together. I continued fucking her hard for who knows how long. Liz wanted as much as I had to offer. Finally, my legs weakened, and I collapsed into Liz's arms as she locked her legs around me. Intertwined, I remained in her as we held each other tightly. I caressed Liz's body where I could reach without withdrawing from inside her.

Totally wrapped around me, Liz said, "Dominic, no man has ever made me feel that way before."

It was such a wonderful feeling. We stayed there growing together until time grew short for us to be alone. It seemed like hours. It was a very special moment.

Chapter 15

As a lieutenant in the fire service, I understood no fire was good, and we never want to see any harm to anybody. As it was, this had already been an unusually busy winter for the town's fire department. Nonetheless, I always wanted to see action when I was on duty even on an overtime shift like tonight. However, on this very cold dark February night, all we wanted was a nice quiet evening. The normal complement of personnel—five in headquarters and two at Station 2—was entered in the log. The balance of the log was filled out, day of week, weather, and temperature. "Thursday, clear, -4 degrees," was entered.

The night was crystal clear. The inefficient heating system to our brick building was rumbling and hissing as it huffed to keep us warm. Even so, I wore my long johns and turtleneck that night. Boyles always wore his even in May.

The shift started out just as it had a million times before, behind the eight ball. With seven men on duty, we were already down eight men to man two engines, a ladder truck, and a fire alarm office as prescribed by the National Fire Protection Association (NFPA), the industry's standard. Sure, we managed to dodge the bullet on many occasions; but when the shit hit the fan, we sucked wind fast!

It was very quiet throughout the area. No radios were squawking; it appeared that all of metropolitan Boston was hunkering down for a cold winter's night. The phones weren't even ringing.

The three-story home had big rooms with high ceilings and a two-story addition off the back. Over time, this former woodshed had been turned into a storage room with an incinerator on the first level and a now unused bedroom on the second floor. The Crescents' house was "preexisting and nonconforming," which meant, in part, it was legal to maintain the inside incinerator, however unwise. Before leaving for the weekly Rotary Club meeting, Kenneth Crescent, a founding member, had started the incinerator, burning all their trash. before he and his wife, Marion, leave the following day to go on their annual extended trip to Florida. Inside trash burning was very dangerous, but old habits are tough to break.

In the quiet of the evening, I was talking on the phone to Liz. Nights at the firehouse were a good time for us to talk, and talk we did—for hours. Liz was so involved in all she did; she used me as a sounding board. This was fine with me. I found her lively conversation refreshing, articulate, and informed. All of which just drew me closer to this beautiful woman. "Hold on, Liz, the other line is ringing."

It was 2323, the emergency line. It was pre-911, and this was our hotline. "Coventry Fire Department, Lieutenant Renaldi," I answered on the second ring. A steady and firm female voice spoke with urgent clarity. "This is Marion Crescent at 218 Boston Post Road. I have a crackling noise on the third floor of my house. I think it's a fire."

After a minute or so of waiting, Liz would hang up on her own knowing I suddenly got busy. She'd grown to understand that it was en emergency if I didn't even quickly return to say good-bye.

While writing the address on a pad of paper for Boyles, the deskman, I repeated the address, "That's 218 Boston Post Road, house fire. Is everyone out of the house, Mrs. Crescent?"

"Yes, I am the only one here."

We'll be right there."

In a flash, I sprung into action. I sounded the vocal alarm, which notifies both stations simultaneously. "Striking a box for a house fire at 218 Boston Post Road," I said just as urgently as Mrs. Crescent had articulated. When the captain hit the apparatus floor, he asked if I was sure it was a fire. I confirmed, "She said it was a crackling noise over her head." The captain went with my instincts and trusted my word. With lights flashing and sirens blaring, engine 1 and ladder 1, Frieze at the wheel, roared out of the station and we headed east on the post road. I remember telling Frieze on the way, "This is the real deal, Paul."

"How do you know that?"

"I can feel it, trust me, we have a job to do!"

E-1 signed off at the house. We heard the commanding officer radioing in, "Heavy smoke showing. This is a working fire." The ladder was right behind. A working fire would automatically mean an additional engine to the fire. Engine 3 from Station 2, but it would be seven to eight minutes before they got to the fire. With just two men on a piece, I masked up as the captain told me to get a 1 1/2-inch attack line. He and I entered the front door and turned left through the dining room filled with fine antique furniture and smoke too. Pointing to a closed door, the captain said, "There's the fire, see it around the opening?" Sure enough, you could see the glow all around the door. I positioned myself low and opened the door as we expected some sort of reaction when the oxygen-rich fresh air come in contact with this glowing red room, but nothing happened.

Standing up to see what the hell was happening, I saw this wasn't a room but a small shallow closet, which we learned was located directly behind the old incinerator. I could see the fire had already burned a hole big enough for me to look up and see that the fire had drafted up the wall and to the second floor. In addition to traveling vertically, fire would also travel horizontally across open ceiling joists. Damn, another old house with a fire that had a huge head start. "You better get a lot of help here in a hurry, Captain." He quickly radioed in for a second alarm on the box, my observation verifying what he was already feeling. It seemed every place we turned, there was fire. Every wall had fire in it. Unfortunately, the chief was down in the south shore area having dinner. He wouldn't arrive for at least a half hour. With second-alarm apparatus arriving shortly, the captain exited to take command. This put us down another man to fight fire. I was now alone on the line. The National Fire Protection Association shuddered at this practice as did the Firefighter's Union, but it was not unusual to have a lone firefighter on a line in a small department. Sure, we knew it was wrong; but with just two men on a truck, it was almost impossible to have it any other way. Too many jobs to accomplish with too few men. We were accustomed to operating this way. Under Chief Wyatt's leadership, the Coventry Fire Department had gained enormous respect from all of metro Boston for being an "inside" firefighting department. Something we took great pride in.

Quickly ascending the stairs, I got to the second-floor landing. It was halfway up the stairs where the landing turned 90 degrees. I then began chasing the fire and could hear open-fire crackling. Again, staying low and out of the path of the doorway, I opened the door to the spare bedroom over the storage shed. The room was heavily involved in fire and not yet vented. This time the fire rolled out from the top of the doorway, and I began hitting it with a fog pattern of water, which produced blinding steam and smoke. With line in hand and fearing a burned-out hole in front of me, I carefully felt my way as I crawled into the room and along the wall to my left until *bang*, my helmet hit the corner. *Okay, if I turn right, this should be the outside wall*, I thought to myself. I crawled with my hands. Somebody must have been feeding me the line from below, because it kept coming with me as I moved in deeper. Still feeling along in front, I groped until I found a window. I grabbed something off the floor—in this case, an old portable TV—and threw it through the window. Cleaning out the remainder of the glass with the nozzle, I began power venting out the window. Power venting is a useful method for removing heat and smoke by opening up the nozzle in a fog pattern out the window and drawing out the air from behind it. Fortunately, the room was small and cleared quickly.

Then I turned back in the room to chase "big red" farther up the stairs. Chuck Allen, my lifelong friend and a hell of a firefighter, met up with me on the landing where we tried to make the third floor. It was heavily engulfed in fire by now. Lord only knows why, but I stared at him; Chuck hadn't donned a mask. When he first arrived on scene, he probably was given an order outside, which probably led him to another order pulling hose just inside the door, where yet another order sent him a little deeper into the fray—the drawbacks of a small department. Before making his way out for an air-pak, he assured me, "I'll be back, Dom."

Lt. Bill Slayton had arrived on the same truck with Chuck. He was outside the building, ducking behind trucks just trying to look busy while going unnoticed so he wouldn't be ordered to mask up and go inside. He had this maneuver down pat.

Chief Brewster arrived on scene and, after observing the heavy, dense smoke pulsing from the eaves, ordered an additional engine and ladder from Cromwell to the scene. This was very rare for our department to request an additional engine and ladder above a second-alarm response. His experience was telling him that fires in these three-story colonials were fast-moving and unpredictable. For all his shortcomings, Brewster was a very good fire officer.

We were so close to the fire on the third floor, I could taste it. The fire was crackling and the usual shitty-looking yellowish brown smoke from incomplete combustion was rolling from the room just inches away from me. The color of the smoke indicated the fire was beginning to starve for oxygen. When this happens, the fire produces more smoke than fire, and the flames begin to subside as it is smothered by its own smoke. But it doesn't lose much heat in the process because of the confined space inside a building. I was an experienced firefighter and had been through this before. I should have read the signs better.

As I waited for help, the fire progressed unchecked. Time was short. If this fire found even a cubic inch of additional air, it would take off in either a rapid flashover or an explosive backdraft. Both scenarios are very dangerous.

I had to make a move. I was confident moving in because I knew Chuck would be right along. The fire wasn't as hot as others I've been in, so I slowly crawled into the room, advancing into the thick brown smoke. It was unusually dark, and things were about to turn ugly. Just as I got set to hit the fire, the whole room exploded in a backdraft. With a whooshing sound, a hot air blast of red and yellow flames sent me flying across the room, and the ceiling caved in. I lost my line, I lost my hand light, and I had no idea which way was out. Having been knocked on my ass, I began to regain my senses and heard a bell ringing. *Shit, it's my alarm bell on my Air-Pak! Stay cool and find your line,* I told myself. With my air supply running low, I groped for the line in the dark, in the pitch dark. Yes! I found it and began following the line out, but it led me into a pile of heavy timber-type rubble, so I turned around and went the other way. SHIT! The nozzle—the end of the line. I also found myself sucking harder to get air. *This may well be the end of the line—for me!* I thought for sure I was about to lose my life! In all my years as a firefighter, I had never had that feeling before. Still while trying to find my way, I ran out of air. Disconnecting the face piece hose from its regulator and shoving my face tight to the floor in hopes there was that small space of fresh air found very close to the floor, I began following the line back to where it had tangled in fallen debris. I was coughing and choking and thought for sure I was fucked. This was not good. Thinking, hoping, the way out was on the other side of the debris, I started to bull my way through. My instincts were correct. I heard Chuck's voice. "Dom, Lieutenant Renaldi." Chuck had returned to where he had last left me. He followed the line to where it led him—right to the doorway. Chuck reached for me just as I got to the stair rails, and as he pulled, we fell onto the stairs, tumbling down to the landing where the small bedroom was. Gasping for air, I tore my mask from my face. "Never in my life have I been so fucking glad to see you, Chuck!"

Chuck looked on in disbelief and said, "What the hell happened?"

This was no time for long explanations. All I could say was, "Some kind of a backdraft or collapse." I'd swallowed a lot of smoke and heat, and my lungs were burning.

Several men were rushing up the stairs led by Paul Frieze. Paul looked pretty funny; he looked like he was leading the cavalry into battle after having been given the order to CHARGE! Frieze helped me from the building while the others teamed with Chuck to continue the attack on the fire.

Slayton was still outside, still trying to be inconspicuously busy. How many times can you open and close compartment doors? No way in hell did he want to go into a burning building!

Sitting on the side of the ladder truck just outside the front door, Frieze grabbed the oxygen mask from the EMTs. "Give me that." He was a little excited as he shoved the mask in my face. Slightly dazed and confused, I was then led to an ambulance where my vital signs were taken. The EMTs on board were insisting I go to the hospital. I refused.

Rollie was the attending EMT. He was an instructor when we went through EMT training years ago, and he liked me. We all had respect for him. His Massachusetts certification number was 01. He was the first EMT certified in the state.

"Your BP is elevated."

"No shit!" I exclaimed in jest. "I'm OK, Rollie, I feel fine, just took in some smoke that's all." After a brief rest, I insisted on going back in. Rollie may have silently worried he'd be doing huff and puff on me shortly, but he let me go.

The captain asked if I was all right and wanted me to get checked out at the hospital, but I told him I was okay. Chief Brewster asked me to go get checked out, but I told him, "I've been here from the beginning, chief, I'm staying to the end." He knew my style from when he used to be my captain. Chuck and I would go through three cylinders of air at this fire, as would several other men. Realistically, I thought we were going to lose the whole damned place, and I didn't want to miss the bonfire. Another hour or so later, and only after an aggressive attack, did we get the fire out. Though many of us took a terrible beating while fighting this fire, Slayton never donned a mask and still can't tell you the color of the wallpaper on the first floor.

Chapter 16

With the association's contract due to expire in six months, we began the bargaining process with the town again. Captain Charles had retired and through lack of other's interest, or fear to face Horace Humphreys, I was now association president and the chairman of our bargaining committee at the same time. My first order of business was to get Captain Charles's bargaining book in my hands. I went to the file cabinet to retrieve it, but it wasn't there. I called him at home.

"Hi, Captain. This is Dominic Renaldi."

"I thought I was done with you. What do you want, Renaldi?"

"I'm not that easy to get rid of, am I Captain?" I said smartly to him; our true feelings finally surfacing. "I am looking for your bargaining book, but can't seem to find it. Do you know where it might be?" I asked innocently enough, but repulsed knowing it was a loaded question for the Captain to squirm away from.

"No. I don't know where it is. I left it in the file cabinet. Did you look there?"

"That's the first place I looked. Seems it isn't there."

"Well, someone must have it then."

I fumed inside as I thought to myself, *Yeah, someone must have it all right, but who?* "I'll keep looking for it. Thank you, Captain." But I already knew where it was.

Several nights later, I led the bargaining team into the selectmen's office, where a smiling Horace Humphreys greeted us. "Well, Mr. Renaldi, I see you've taken over for Charlie. Did you get his book too?" Humphreys laughed an egotistical laugh, then, lit up a victory cigar.

"No, as a matter of fact, I looked for it, but couldn't find it." looking into Humphreys' eyes, I asked, "Perhaps you know where it is?"

Humphreys' face quickly tightened as we stared each other down. Neither one of us blinked. Finally, he snickered. "Now how would I know where Captain Charles's bargaining book might be, Mr. Renaldi?" Then, he laughed loud and obnoxiously, and said, "I wish I did."

Humphreys was powerful, arrogant, and he had an ego the size of Harvard Square, but I wasn't afraid of him when I said, "Just a wild guess on my part."

From his chair at the end of the table, Snidely Ryan broke the tension, "We have to bargain with all our departments this year, so we would like to have these sessions be very direct and to the point. What are the firefighters looking for this year, Mr. Renaldi?"

Short of our 22 percent raise a few years back, the town seemed to be set on giving a 3.5 percent raise each year. No matter how direct they expected us to be, I was still going to leave a little wiggle room for negotiations. The firefighters are asking for a 5 percent pay raise, EMT incentive pay, a guarantee for minimum staffing levels, and a paid holiday for Martin Luther King Day. The selectmen nodded affirmatively for their understanding of our request. It was no reflection on how they would respond. The Town Manager spoke for the board, "We are in receipt of your request, but we want to hear from all our employee groups before we respond. Let's meet again in two weeks." The meeting adjourned.

One of the common courtesies of collective bargaining was to stop at the firehouse after a session and brief the men on what progress, if any, had been accomplished. This night, there was no progress to report, and it was never a good idea to give out too much information. However, I did say to the on-duty crew, "This is going to be a very difficult contract to negotiate. The selectmen are adamant about not giving an inch." Just prior to leaving, I wished I could see Liz. Not for sex as nice as that always was. But to decompress, just to talk, just to receive that special support we gave each other. With text messaging still years away, like a light switch turning on in my imagination, I got this fun idea and wondered if her pager was still on. Hastily, I went to a phone with a pad of paper and pen in hand and began looking at the keypad—46636444896. Carefully, I double-checked the corresponding letters of the alphabet to the numbers, then dialed her pager number and sent out the page as I laughed at the thought, *She'll never understand what this is*. I left the building with a smile on my face.

* * *

Instead of going out after the executive session of the town selectmen's meeting, I dutifully came home to Ruth. Still smiling, I kicked the slushy grime off my boots before going in, then removed them and placed them neatly on the boot tray inside the front door. I'd been doing a lot of this lately, despite which, nothing much had changed for us in the Renaldi household. It was a guilt move. I had become so afraid that Ruth might find out about Liz and me that I spent every moment at home when I wasn't working. Thoughts of mysterious phone calls tipping Ruth off flooded my head. I no longer feared they'd originate from Liz herself. But we lived in a small town with a fertile grapevine.

Indeed, I knew I had enemies but never quite understood why. Surely, it wasn't wealth, and I wasn't a threat to these guys in town. I'd never purposefully hurt anyone. I helped out everywhere I could and was as civic minded as anyone I knew, especially for a town servant. I did notice from an early age that I always got along better with women than with men. Not that I was a Casanova—far from *that*. I'd always thought it was because I was a good listener. So was it jealousy? I had no idea what anyone would be jealous of me for. At least, 90 percent of the town probably looked down their noses at me. Perhaps it was my tendency to speak my mind. I did get a heck of a vibe about this earlier this evening at that selectman's meeting.

"I'm home!"

Ruth ignored me, which wasn't unusual for either of us to do. What was she mad about now? Of course, our relationship had declined to a point where we no longer needed a specific reason to be angry or unhappy. These were simply our states of being.

My behavior was changing since I'd taken up with Liz, and I could feel it. In typical male fashion, I didn't trust the inner workings of the silent female. If Ruth knew something, I figured, there might be a heck of a chance I'd have to drag it out of her, or else she'd spring it on me when I least expected it and was least prepared to deal with it. And so, I talked. I chattered more to Ruth over the past month than I had in the past three years of our marriage. Was I happier of late because of Liz? Had her chattiness rubbed off on me? Or was it a subconscious ploy to draw something out of Ruth, make her reveal what she knew? Either way, nothing worked—she was either the world's best secret keeper, or she knew nothing.

"Geez, that meeting was difficult. Do you know those bastards are hanging us up over a quarter of a percent? That's how far apart we are, a quarter of a percent. We want a 3.5 percent raise, they're sticking to 3.25 percent. They're willing to send this to arbitration over a lousy quarter of a percent!"

Ruth remained silent. The more she did, the more I sweated. And the more I sweated, the more I talked.

"They say they can't afford it. Can you believe that? They could give us a 10 percent raise every year for the next ten years and still be able to afford it. Not that we'd ever ask for 10 percent in these times; as president, I wouldn't let that happen. I mean, we have to be reasonable, but a lousy quarter of one percent? Lemme tell you, the reason they're so rich is because they're so tight. If they can't wear it, live in it, or park it in their driveway, it's of no value to them. *We're* of no value to them, Ruth, just a number. The EMTs, no incentive pay. Then they have the gall to ask me directly why we can't recruit more EMTs. They're not stupid. They know why. I give them the answer, and then they ask me again, like, 'Give us an answer that costs no money, otherwise, we can't hear you.' Goddamn bastards."

I was now in the bedroom stripping down. Ruth was sitting in bed in her bathrobe, reading a book, a lemon-sucking look on her mouth as she barely observed me. I stared at her as if to try to figure out if she'd heard a word I said.

"They even threatened to close Station 2 because they think we get too much overtime. You think I'm making this up? They do that. I told them, see how quickly we jump up to go back and cover the ambulance service. Let it be *their* family that puts in a call some night. Then they'll know who they're messing with."

Ruth finally arose from the dead. "Oh, so you threatened the selectmen. That's bright."

"I didn't threaten them. I merely informed the selectmen that if they did close Station 2, in an effort to make ends meet, the men might have to put their time and energy elsewhere."

"It sounds like you threatened them."

"I didn't even realize you were listening to me."

"You mean you've been talking to yourself this whole time? Figures."

"If I am, it's only because you never talk, you never start a conversation yourself. If it weren't for me, the only thing we'd hear in this house would be the animals and the kids."

Ruth continued staring into her book, the only thing that seemed to interest her. Her unhappy face never seemed to change. How long had she been this way? I wondered. Was it really this bad before Liz? Or had it gotten worse recently? God, I was so wracked with guilt, so torn not knowing which way to turn. Maybe I should just begin a civil discussion about divorce. Surely, Ruth would go for that. We seemed to have lost all our love for each other years ago. Why were we still together? It was as if out of obligation; both of us felt stuck in the rut of life, powerless to make things any better or to move on.

Divorce would be far less cruel than her finding out about Liz and me. What an embarrassment. It was a close-knit town. Things like that happened frequently, and when they did, the participants were like the walking dead. You become the Scarlet Letter—the husband or the wife would come into the local grocery store, and everyone would stare and whisper. *There goes Rob Robbins. You know, his wife just left him for John Interdonato, the CPA. They'd been fooling around behind his back for years.* As much as I loved my time with Liz, I didn't wish such a fate on Ruth. She didn't deserve that. We've just grown so far apart.

Ruth broke into my internal dialogue. "So you started a fight with the selectmen?"

"I wouldn't call it a fight. I just told them what was right and stood my ground. I'm not going to cave in like Billy Slayton."

"Oh, you mean the Billy Slayton who has a big landscaping business and snowplowing business? That Billy Slayton?"

"He got that by selling us out and kissing up to Brian Rehrig, the selectman, the banker."

"And this makes him dumber than you? How?"

I fumed with anger in silence, then I said, "Don't ever compare me to that snake."

"So how's that variance coming on your unbuildable lot, Mr. Trump? Did you bring that up at tonight's meeting?"

"This was a private executive session to discuss a contract negation, nothing more. Personal business has nothing to do with collective bargaining nor should it!"

"Yeah, I'm sure that's how Billy Slayton would have handled it."

"No, that's not how Slayton would have handled it. He would have sold the firemen down the river, which is exactly what he did two years ago, and then he would have kissed Rehrig's ass again and gotten his variance."

"Like I said, and this makes you better than him, how?"

"I represent the association, and I stand with its members. Bill Slayton stands for himself."

Whatever goodwill and cool I'd walked into the house with was now gone. "You could have had Billy Slayton years ago before me. You fucked him one time and told me he had a dick the size of your baby finger. Well, that's how big of a man he is too. I wouldn't have to be fighting a tough fight if he had the balls to do what he should have done as association president. But no, little Slayton is out for himself, and he'll fuck over anyone to gain an edge. People are just pawns to him. Why didn't you have a second date with him, Ruth? I'll tell you why, because all he wanted to do was to fuck you before I did. You were just a notch to him, nothing more. Welcome to Slayton's world, Ruth. Ya still think he's so wonderful?"

Now Ruth was making eye contact with me, and it wasn't of a sensual nature. I don't think I've seen her as mad as she was. I had no intention of hurting her as I did, but she had to know what I was dealing with, what I was going through both at the firehouse and with the town. Still, that never registered with her and never would.

"Don't talk to the mother of your children that way. Who the hell do you think you are? Grow up! This is my house. My children are downstairs and still awake. I don't want them to hear that kind of language in here."

"*Your* house? *Your* children? What am I, some guy just passing through?"

If ever there was a time when Ruth would be liable to blurt out that she knew of my indiscretions with Liz, it was now. But for all the vitriol she spewed out, nothing of that sort was uttered.

Ruth went back to her book, probably as a ploy to get away from this argument. I don't know how she could've possibly started reading again. I backed down. Part of this whole "be at home more, talk to Ruth more" thing was a crazy last-ditch effort to repair my relationship with her. Strange how an extramarital affair could set your mind in such a direction, but I saw how I was with Liz Temple. I was a better man with her. Liz lifted me up, made me feel wanted again. I was the man I once hoped to be with Ruth. Granted, Liz and I were in a honeymoon period, so to speak, but it reminded me of the old days with Ruth and how I wanted life to take us in a different direction. As much as I was becoming enamored with Liz, I strongly doubted anything would come of it. It was like one of those cheesy romance novels, the one where the princess falls or appears to fall for the poor stable boy. In real life, things never went that way, not unless the stable boy grew up to become a wealthy surgeon.

Two week later, we were at the bargaining table again. Mr. Ryan started the meeting off by addressing the selectmen. "Horace has a meeting in Boston and will be about an hour late."

Brian Rehrig tried to show strength in Humphreys' absence, but was ineffective. "What do we have on the table?" He perused a list in front of him, then spoke, "A pay raise, EMT incentive, and an additional holiday. Let's skip over the pay raise for now, will that be okay?"

With out hesitation, I nodded my head and said, "Sure, we can come back to that later."

Rehrig continued, "Having the ambulance is the fire department's savior, Mr. Renaldi. Without it, there would be lost jobs at the firehouse."

This wasn't the first time we had this theme, but I hoped it would be the last. "Mr. Rehrig, if you are going to cut jobs, then cut them. If you're not going to, then stop threatening us with it." It was bold, and perhaps insightful. I could feel the other members of the bargaining team wince, but it needed to be said once and for all.

Rehrig didn't like being stood up to and was quick with his response, albeit weak. "Then what do you suggest, Mr. Renaldi?"

"I agree the ambulance will become the savior of many small town fire departments, but holding jobs over our head won't accomplish anything. Offer an added stipend; give the men an incentive to become an EMT. Let the men know that the EMTs are the cream of the crop. We all need to embrace the coming of emergency medical services, and we need to recognize those who are willing to provide it. No matter what the stipend, it will still be far less costly to the town than a private ambulance service. And it will probably be a more timely service as well."

As I spoke, Mrs. Feldman wrote something down and slid it in front of Rehrig. Then, Rehrig asked, "Could you give us a few minutes to discuss this?" Gladly, we excused ourselves from the room.

"What do you think they're talking about, Dominic?" asked one of my colleagues.

"They're going to give us an EMT stipend," I said with a confident smile.

"Are you sure they're not going to cut jobs?"

"No way. This town does not want an outside private company to handle the ambulance."

Several minutes later Michele came out to get us, and we were listening to Rehrig speak, "We are willing to give you an EMT stipend on the condition you maintain no fewer EMTs than required to provide the ambulance service."

I was ready to jump out of my skin, but out of courtesy I looked at my fellow negotiators. They all nodded in the affirmative. "Thank you very much, Mr. Rehrig. We accept the offer. Now, what is next? Oh yes, Martin Luther King Day as a paid holiday?"

Snidely Ryan, the Town Manager, spoke, "It is the intent of the town to give all bargaining units this day as a paid holiday; which is consistent with all the federal holidays."

I looked at the selectmen and asked, "So, we agree on this item?" Both selectmen nodded yes.

The Town Manager informed the selectmen that they had to move on in their agenda. Our bargaining session ended with handshakes and without Humphreys ever showing up.

At out final bargaining sessions the following week, Mrs. Feldman recapped all the points both sides had come to an agreement on, with the exception of one—our pay raise percentage. Humphreys quickly interrupted her, "Wait. What? Have I missed something here?"

Immediately, I knew he wasn't happy and that he had never given his blessing to his colleagues' actions. Lightheartedly, Mrs. Feldman replied, "Oh, yes, Horace, perhaps we failed to mention this to you. We came to agreement on several issues at our last meeting. The one you weren't present at."

Humphreys glared at me for a moment, then said, "Oh okay, if it's already been agreed upon." He was very unconvincing, looking like a five-year-old who just had his favorite toy taken away. For several hours, we hammered away over a pay raise, but it became clear Humphreys' nose was out of joint and he was not going to budge an inch. It also became clear he was going to push this into arbitration where he was likely to win. "Mr. Renaldi, we just cannot afford a 3.5 percent pay raise on both years of a two-year contract. A 3.25 percent on the second year is the best we can do. I would say we are at a stalemate."

Our final "good faith" bargaining meeting was at an impasse and the meeting adjourned. We were headed for arbitration.

Chapter 17

One Saturday morning several weeks later, the stalemate between the association and the town came to a head. The arbitrator sat at the head of the conference room table and explained the process to both sides. She was perhaps in her mid-forties and appeared to know her job quite well. Humphreys looked perturbed. Surely he was above this mere arbitrator.

"Who will be speaking for the town?" she asked while carefully listening to the response.

"I will," Humphreys said, harshly. The arbitrator wrote it down.

"And who will speak for the firefighters?" Once again, she listened intently.

Respectfully, I said, "I'll speak on behalf of the association." She wrote that down too.

While professionally carrying out her game plan, she instructed our bargaining team to go into another room while she spoke to the selectmen. We exited to a small kitchen just off the conference room. After a few minutes, she came in and spoke to us. "I find it easier to separate each side so I can get an honest answer to my questions."

Fair enough, I thought as I continued to listen to her.

"Mr. Humphreys and I will direct our response to you, Mr. Renaldi. Mr. Humphreys insists the town can't afford a 3.5 percent pay raise in each of the two years of a two-year contract. He is offering you a 3.25 percent raise on the second year of your contract."

I started off calmly in my response to her. "The firefighters' association has every intention of cooperating with you by bargaining in good faith, but that's just bullshit." I got more intense, "This is Coventry, Massachusetts. They can afford to meet our reasonable request."

The arbitrator kind of nodded affirmatively and I got the impression my response was okay. She asked, "Do you have a counter offer you'd like to make?"

Never having been through this process before, I paused and thought for a moment. I knew making us go to arbitration was never about the money, but rather, it was about power and control, all of which Humphreys was accustomed to having. Clearly, any arbitrator would understand Coventry had the means to meet our demands without suffering any financial strain. I broke my silence. "I'd like to be able to tell you," I curtly began, "to go back in there and tell Mr. Humphreys 3.5 percent on both years of the contract. And for a lousy quarter of one percent, let's get the hell out of here for two years!"

The arbitrator lit up with a bright face and opened eyes, then said, "I'm going in there and telling Mr. Humphreys exactly what you said, and I'm going to use the same tone of voice you did."

I was fired up and could only reply, "Please do!" She left the room and the other members of the bargaining team looked at me. One said, "We're in trouble now."

I said, "No, the association is not in trouble. I am."

Within five minutes the arbitrator returned. She looked directly at me and smiled. "Your response was very effective. Mr. Humphreys accepts your offer. He wanted me to tell you that he particularly liked the part about not having to bargain for two years."

Several weeks later, a contract was signed which included a 3.5 percent pay raise for each of the two years, EMT incentive pay, and an addendum stating the town would not close Station 2.

With a better picture of how the town was going to be treating us in the future, the association finally joined "The firefighters' union. Up until now, we were happy with our small town " The firefighters' association, but it was time to support the brother/sisterhood of professional firefighters. Brewster wasn't happy about this and worried he'd have trouble fending off such a powerful affiliation as the International Association of Firefighters. Now feeling pressure from too many sides, Brewster was beginning to fold like a bed of hose. In a desperate attempt to show he was in control, he arbitrarily changed our shift's starting time from 0800 hours to 0700 hours—that is 7:00 a.m. Jacobs and Slayton were off duty but managed to stop by every day. It was their way of keeping their finger on the pulse of what was happening in the firehouse. "He's a fucking asshole!" Jacobs said of the chief. Starting our shifts an hour earlier became just a perceived excuse for others not to do their job, especially Slayton, who never made it to work on time at 0800 hours. He was really pissed at the move. "What the hell are we going to do at seven o'clock in the morning? I can't make an appointment for smoke detector approvals that early in the morning. People will be furious with me," he said while shaking his head in disapproval.

Quickly, I said, "We can fight fires or go on ambulance calls. It's just a start time. Our job hasn't changed." Not able to resist, I concluded, "If it's too early to be in other's homes, Slayton, perhaps you can do some in-house work at the firehouse. You can train your men for an hour a day, Lieutenant," I said as though it was a new revelation.

Slayton got really angry at my remark and gave me a look of contempt.

We were sitting at the kitchen table in the firehouse having coffee when my pager went off. It was Liz. I'd given her my pager number as a quiet link between us. Of course, Ruth had my pager number too but found high tech too intimidating and never paged me.

I returned Liz's call to her house, and after pleasant good mornings, she asked if I'd tried to page her last night. *Yes, it worked!* I said to myself with a gratifying smile.

"I did indeed page you last night."

"It came through incorrectly. It wasn't a phone number."

"It wasn't meant to be a phone number."

"What was it then?"

"Wanting to be with you last night, but not able to, I was just having some fun and sent a message to you. Figure it out."

"How do I do that?"

"Look at the keypad of a phone and associate a letter with the number."

"Oh brother, I don't have that kind of time on my hands."

"Busy girl, huh, Liz"—the doer, the Energizer Bunny—"Come on. This'll be fun. I'll give you a hint. It's something often said before bedtime."

Okay, I'll do it just for you. I'll call you back in a bit. Bye."

Feeling her smile coming over the phone, I hung up and returned to the kitchen.

The heating system in the firehouse was so ancient that when Paul Frieze came into the kitchen, he opened the window halfway in order to balance out the stifling hot temperature.

"Where'd Slayton and Jacobs go?" I asked in a distrusting tone.

"Jacobs went off to work, and I don't know where Slayton went. He said he needed to get something from his locker, then he left too."

"Good. I'm sorry, Paul, but I always feel uncomfortable when they're around."

While ignoring my comment, Frieze, who always felt undernourished, asked, "watcha eating?"

With a mouth full of food and coffee in front of me, I looked up. "Strudel."

"Is it good? It looks good!"

I looked over my cup at Frieze while I took a sip of coffee. I came from a poor family and have three brothers and a sister. All of them were good eaters, but having enough food in the house for everyone was rare. Thus, it took me years to get over the starvation mentality when it came to food. When you're poor, you always wonder if the meal in front of you is the last one you'll see for a while, especially when it's good; and this strudel was definitely good. "Of course, it's good, I made it!"

Suddenly, my whole abdomen was vibrating. My pager went off again, and it was Liz again. *Boy, that was quick*, I thought. This time, I used the phone in the kitchen for the return call so I could keep an eye on my strudel.

Without so much as a hello, "You wished me a good night over the pager," said this cutie with giggles and laughter. "How sweet!"

Giggles and laughter I so loved to hear, she just exuded so much life, so much fun, much of what I needed. With a broad smile on my face, I responded, "I did indeed!"

Liz seemed ecstatic at my simple gesture. "This could be our way of communicating with each other—by coded messages."

"Yes, it could, and not that difficult either. Frieze, don't touch that, Frieze!" My attention was temporarily sidetracked.

"What are you doing? To whom are you speaking?" a confused Liz asked.

"I'm talking to young Mr. Frieze who's trying to eat my apple strudel." *Shit,* I caught myself. *Too late!*

"What are you doing eating strudel, especially before ten o'clock in the morning, Dominic," said the stern overseer of good health.

Man, you can't slip anything past this astute woman. "Sorry, but if I don't eat it, someone else will."

"Good, let them. Okay, I'll leave it to your imaginative mind to come up with something for our pagers. You're good at figuring out things like that. For now, I've got to go, bye."

Laughingly, I said, "Yes, I will enjoy my strudel too. Bye, sweetheart." And I hung up the phone.

Frieze was looking at my plate like someone who hadn't had a meal in a week, which was crazy because Frieze ate like a horse. He was a young guy; one of the "cement heads" as some of the older guys called them. Frieze and the other cement heads burned off all their calories by lifting weights for hours a day, so they were constantly hungry yet rarely had much fat on them. Of course, guys like me also envied their youthful metabolism. I worked hard at keeping the spare tire from developing around my middle—a curse of middle age. Furthermore, I was spending a lot of time in bed with a certified hard-bodied beauty named Liz Temple, and she was forever encouraging me to lose weight. Not that I looked bad—in fact, pretty good for my age—but I wanted to look better for her. She was so health conscious; she didn't want an ounce of fat on me. That wasn't going to happen, but I too was hitting the weights a bit more than usual although nothing like these young guys. *Now if only they'd be as studious about learning their firefighting and emergency skills*, I thought. Then they'd be something. In their defense, with Brewster removing promotional exams from the process, there was no incentive to study, no incentive to work hard, and time would show the negative affects of his ill-conceived plan.

Frieze was angling for a bite or two of my strudel, but it was the last piece, and damn, it was so good. I'd have some playful fun with him.

"Can I have a bite?"

"No."

"C'mon, don't be a dick."

"I'm not being a dick, I'm merely sacrificing myself for the good of *your* waistline."

"Yeah right."

"Hey, Paul, if I had more I'd share, but I don't, so I can't."

"You mean you won't. That's different than can't."

"Look, it isn't like you're starving. You eat everything that doesn't move in this place and some things that do. If you ever stop lifting weights, you're going to look like a blimp."

"C'mon, lemme just have a bite." Frieze started moving his fork in for the kill until it hovered over my plate.

"I'm warning you, don't take one bite of this strudel," I said playfully.

"Look, you're old, you're getting fat. What do you need strudel for?" Frieze's fork remained poised to attack.

Our playful camaraderie continued. This was how you hung around with the young guys. "I'm not getting fat, that's my winter weight," I said with a smile.

"I want that strudel," Frieze continued.

"I'll spit on it."

"You wouldn't dare."

"It's *my* strudel. I'll spit on it if I want to. It's only going to go in my mouth anyway, so why would I care if my spit was on it?"

"Oh please, don't spit on it please! You can't do something that nasty to a pretty little piece of strudel like that. That would be wrong, just plain wrong." Frieze's fork got closer and closer.

"I'll do it, I swear I will." I dipped my head and started to produce a wad of spittle, his total obsession making it nearly impossible for me not to burst out laughing. Silently, I hoped I wouldn't have to actually spit on my own food just to fend off a hungry cement head, but I was having way too much fun with the good young kid not to carry through.

BAH BOOM!

Suddenly, an explosion rocked the kitchen in the firehouse. The blast occurred directly under my chair. The table deflexed the shock wave away from Frieze, but I took the brunt of it. I jumped and flailed. The table was knocked over, and I was thrown off my chair. Landing on my side, my hip cracking off the hard linoleum floor; Frieze jumped back from his chair almost like he was shot from a cannon and flew back against the wall. "What the fuck was that?"

My head jerked in reaction to the acrid smell of gunpowder wafting up my nostrils. A pain shot down my neck as I looked up to see what was happening. There was a faint haze of smoke, but it was already dissipating. I looked in the direction of the window while climbing to my hands and knees. Watching Frieze, I wanted to get up and look, but my ears were killing me. I couldn't hear right. There was a loud tone, sounding like a note from a pipe organ that wouldn't stop. Bringing both my hands up to my ears and cupping them, nothing changed. The sound just kept reverberating in my head.

"Fucking bastards, I'll kill them."

"Kill who?" I asked as I continued climbing to my feet.

Frieze didn't answer but bolted out of the room to give chase. Groggily, I got to my feet but didn't follow him. My hip hurt, and my ears felt as if someone had stuck a knitting needle in one ear and out the other. Rehashing what just happened, I remembered hearing running footsteps and laughter—male laughter—outside just prior to the explosion. A familiar, obnoxious laugh now that I think about it. Frieze must have heard it too, for he ran to the window to check immediately after the explosion.

Doing some quick recon in the room, what the hell *was* it? What had just happened? I sniffed around like a dog. Finally, I observed a burn pattern on the floor near where my foot had been underneath the table. Some kind of explosive. It hadn't ripped the floor up or anything. It wasn't dynamite or anything that serious. But the closeness of the blast was enough to scare the hell of both of us, and that ringing in my ears was annoying as hell. Worst of all, my strudel was now all over the floor.

I went to the window and saw Frieze standing, looking down the street, agitated as hell, his head turning from side to side, trying to decide which way the culprits went. He looked like a raging bull with smoke coming out of his mouth as he screamed, "Get back here, you little pussies! I'll fucking kill you!"

He then started dashing off down the street but stopped when he reached the nearest intersection, looking both ways, not certain which way to go. He was mad as hell.

Frustrated, Frieze turned jogging back to the firehouse. Another young firefighter had joined him outside, and I finally made my way down to the door.

"Get in your cars. Get in the trucks. Some little pricks just tried to blow us up. Let's kick some ass!" Frieze pushed past me and the other firemen, heading for the fire truck.

"I think it was an M-80 (an explosive device larger than a cherry bomb) or something like that."

"What?"

I repeated, "An M-80. It wasn't a grenade or anything, but it was loud as hell. I can't hear right. My ears are all messed up."

"Let's go teach those little bastards a lesson first. I'll bet they're still running. If we all circle around, we'll find them. I'll beat the piss out of them."

Both of my ears were hurting, the pain now extending down my neck like a whiplash affect. Loss of hearing didn't make my decision-making any easier, but I said, "Paul, Paul, slow down. You're not taking the truck out to chase destructive kids, if they were in fact kids. Call the cops and have them do it. Meanwhile, I've got to sit down, I think my eardrums were punctured." While sitting down, I put my head in my lap and closed my eyes. The ringing felt like a laser beam searing a hole through my head.

"I wanna kick some ass! This is broad daylight! Who throws an M-80 into a fire station in the middle of the day? That's disrespect! Why aren't they in school?"

Why indeed? It was a Tuesday, around 9:00 a.m. It wasn't a holiday. Town kids would be in school. Besides, with my reputation in the schools, kids wouldn't have done this.

"Did you see them?" I asked of Frieze.

"There was more than one. I only saw them from the back for a second. The one lagging behind was kind of short, and he had on a Celtics jacket and a knit hat."

I mulled this information over, *Celtics jacket short, hmmm.* "What color was the hat?" I asked quizzically.

Frieze gave me an irritated look.

"What do you mean 'what color was the hat?' What am I, *Queer Eye for the Straight Guy?* It was a knit hat."

"Was it green? Did it match the Celtics jacket?"

Frieze finally seemed to calm a little as he pondered. "Yeah, I think it was. I'm not totally sure, but it sounds right."

"Are you sure he looked like a kid? I mean, was he in good shape, running fast?"

Frieze thought again. "No no, not really. He was a little thick legged, now that you mention it. He looked like he was pushing another guy, a taller guy, who was ahead of him. There might have been three, it was hard to tell. But yeah, the Celtics guy was shorter, slower . . . yeah, probably not in the best of shape. Why?"

I thought for a moment, *Explosion, Celtics jacket given to him by his insider friend, the box of M-80s he kept in his locker, and that laugh I heard.* "Fucking Slayton!"

* * *

While settling into the evening portion of our shift at the firehouse, I tried forgetting about what had happened this morning by concentrating on Liz. My ears were ringing loudly, and it was tough to concentrate. Whenever I got feeling low, I always managed to think about her. It lifted me up and always made me feel better.

"How can I do this?" My gears began to turn. That's it! Liz and I can use the firebox numbers, which are all over town, to set up locations to meet. Okay, 552 is the retirement home where we meet in the large remote parking lot; we'd made love in her car there many times. Reckless, yes, but both of us were sexually frustrated by our mates. Frustrated by the lack of feeling associated with lovemaking. Finding a partner with which to stretch our carnal limits was rapturous. Sex wasn't the only thing on our minds. We met almost every day just for coffee. Liz enjoyed spending oodles of money on me and never wanted anything material in return, so I always bought the coffee. It wasn't that I owed her. It was just easiest to keep it consistent. We figured this out innocently one day when we both showed up with coffee and bagels. We laughed and marveled at how "on the same page" we were with each other—black with two sugars and a sesame seed bagel toasted with raspberry jelly and cream cheese, if it was before noon. By now, I knew this by heart.

Then there was number 17, an office building right by the entrance to the Mass Pike, a good place to meet and take off for one- to two-hour day trips we shared together. Number 21 was an athletic field in an adjacent community where we had coffee and walked. No sex there, just a secluded place to meet for walks and talks as we sipped on a cup of coffee together. Number 46, Holy Trinity College, a small Catholic girl's school in Coventry that had numerous secluded spots; 461 was a quiet unassuming café in one of their buildings where we would meet for coffee or lunch. Then, of course, 911 would be reserved for absolute emergency messages. Never had either one of us sent this page, but we talked about it. If these three dreaded digits appeared, drop everything and call.

Okay, now we've established *where*, what about the *when*? *Let's see*, I thought, *if we wanted to meet in the parking lot at the college at 3:00 p.m., the page would be 46 300.* It was ingenious. I burst out laughing thinking how much fun this was.

I sat back and ran it all through my mind. Yes, all this will work, but it was the bagels and raspberry jelly that made me smile, and think deeper. Liz and I had made arrangements to meet for coffee in the parking lot of the retirement home. Liz was already there when I arrived. I got into her SUV, and we greeted each other with a warm smile and a kiss just as we had a thousand times before. She looked beautiful in her silk blouse, slightly open, and her short—not too short—skirt. "Liz." I paused and looked her up and down again, "You look terrific."

She smiled and said, "Why, thank you. I have a meeting to go to."

We sipped on our coffee as Liz talked about her presentation she would be making at this meeting. As she ate her bagel, a small drop of jelly fell off. Fortunately, it missed her blouse and landed on her chest. Liz went to wipe it off. "No wait. Let me do that," I said with a broad smile.

I leaned toward her chest and licked the jelly off with my tongue. Then I went up and inserted it into Liz's mouth. She sucked the jelly off my tongue, and a passionate kiss ensued.

As quickly as gas ignites a fire, Liz said, "We don't have much time." She slipped between the bucket seats with ease and into the rear seat of her SUV.

Quickly, I followed with a smile on my face. Without a wasted moment, she was straddling me with her skirt hiked up over her waist.

"Don't wrinkle my blouse, Dom. Take it off of me."

In doing so, I revealed a red bra with matching bikini undies. "Liz, you are so sexy. You drive me crazy with passion."

"Drive me crazy with your lovemaking, Dom. You always do."

I undid her bra and buried my face in her breasts. Liz wrapped her arms around my head and squeezed me tighter. Lowering my hand, I moved her panties aside. Then I inserted my finger. She was wet. Liz began to frantically unbuckle my belt and unzipped my fly. I wiggled my pants down just far enough as our tongues darted inside of each other's mouth. Liz shuddered as she slid down on me. With beautifully shaped muscular legs, she began pushing up and down as she rode every inch of me. I cupped her breasts. She pumped harder and harder. She pumped, and I pushed hard. We rode each other until we climaxed.

"Touch me, Dom. Touch me," she said while holding on to me and riding hard.

I put my finger on that spot and rubbed fast. With her veins popping and a satisfying groan, Liz exploded. When she did, I thrust and pumped as hard as I could. "Don't stop, Dom, don't stop. Harder and faster, I went until I exploded inside of her. She climaxed again with me.

Liz sighed as she sank onto me. My penetration buried deep inside of her. "Oh my lord. You feel sooo wonderful!" We stayed in that position, holding, kissing, and caressing for fifteen minutes. Finally, Liz said, "I have to go to my meeting."

Chapter 18

"Renaldi thinks you did it."

"So?" Slayton smirked as he sipped from his frosted mug of Heineken. Glancing sideways at Jacobs, the two of them sat at the bar in the Double L Steak House, a watering hole and restaurant located in the west end of Cromwell. Coventry was too puritanical to allow sale of alcoholic beverages. Leo kept upscaling the food at the Double L to suit the ritzy Coventry clientele; but the bar, with its understated lighting, was still a classic wooden place on which to rest your elbows after a hard day.

"Well, did you?"

Slayton laughed. "If I told you, I'd have to kill you."

"So did you?"

"Look, Jacobs, if I said to you I did, you'd be an accessory after the fact. Why would you want me to do that? For now, let's just say I think it's funny, and it couldn't have happened to a nicer guy."

Jacobs took another mouthful of beer. "Did you do it by yourself?"

"You're trying to backdoor me, compadre. I ain't answering."

"Frieze said he saw at least two guys running."

"If we tried to figure out who does *not* belong to the Dominic Renaldi fan club, I'm sure there would be a lot more than one suspect in this case."

"Frieze may kill you if Renaldi doesn't."

"Frieze is okay. He'll get over it. Take Lyons. He used to like Renaldi too. Look how quickly *that* changed." Slayton's face was lighting up with a look of accomplishment. "Wait till you see what Lyons is going to do for the cause. He's really going to enjoy this task." Slayton bellowed his phony laughter.

"What are you talking about? What's Lyons have to do with it?"

"As I said, Lyons is a good soldier."

"What is Lyons going to do?"

"We'll take down Renaldi one way or another." Deviously, Slayton looked at Jacobs.

Jacobs shook his head, confused and disagreeable. "This M-80 thing was pretty immature. I don't know *who* would have thought it would accomplish anything in the long run. It was a dumb prank."

"Well, let's see now. We have Renaldi all banged up and injured. Who knows, maybe he won't come back. That would wrap things up rather nicely for him. I mean, he could even draw disability. Those 'kids' would have done him a big favor."

"And if this rumor keeps spreading that another firefighter had something to do with it, that would really suck for morale in the department. People would start choosing sides. If you were Chief Brewster, you wouldn't want that, would you?"

"No."

"Renaldi might make a big stink of it. That'll just draw negative attention to the department. That's not good for the chief."

Jacobs kept looking at Slayton with greater and greater admiration. Damn, this guy was clever. Best not to ever cross him.

"Of course, I doubt old Brewster would know what to do about it. He'd probably just bumble around, pissing off both sides."

"Also good for the next guy in line to be chief."

"Uh-huh."

"Geez, Slayton, those kids who threw that M-80 through the firehouse window were pretty damn smart."

"Goddamn geniuses, I'd say." Slayton laughed.

* * *

Before going into the chief's office, I paged Liz 4812. A while back, she told me about a children's poem. The gist of it was this: four hugs a day for love, eight hugs a day to sustain life, and twelve hugs a day for growth. For us, 4812 grew to represent hugs and kisses whenever we felt like giving them; and with total understanding, they were coming right back at you with support.

I held my breath, then marched into the chief's office. "I want an investigation."

The chief rocked back and forth on his heels like a child's punching bag with his head down and his hands in his pockets unable to look me in the eye. "Dom, Dom, Dom," he said in a singsong voice.

"Tinnitus. That's what the doctor called it. I had him write it down 'cause I couldn't even hear him right because MY EARS DON'T WORK RIGHT!"

"So what do you want me to do about it?"

"Chief, are you kidding me? I just told you, conduct an investigation."

"Investigation?"

"Yes, Chief, an investigation."

"Dom, it was just a firehouse prank. Harold, Town Counsel, told me that's all it was."

"Slayton did it. Call it a precognition, but I know he did it. You know he did it."

"I do not. I know nothing," said an ineffectual chief.

"Chief, with all due respect, what are you, that dumb incompetent on *Hogan's Heroes*? Frieze did everything but get his damn fingerprints."

"Dom, listen to me. Frieze saw a couple of guys running away from the scene. He thinks one of them looked like Slayton. You didn't even see them yourself. You're just taking Frieze's word for it. And Frieze never said it until you put the words in his mouth. I think you don't like Slayton."

Smacking my forehead and rolling my eyes with indignation, I spoke, "Don't like Slayton. Christ almighty, Chief, why should I like him? He's obnoxious, he's a drain on this department, he brings nothing to the table that isn't for himself, and he's gutless—to say nothing of a disgrace to the fire service."

"What am I hearing? Some kids throw firecrackers through the window, and you use it as an excuse to try to get Slayton fired."

"Mother of god, Chief, at least you can *hear*!" I exclaimed to the chief with a combination of rage and incredulity. "Some kids, Chief, how do you know that? That's what you want to hear. I never said anything about getting Slayton fired. That would be premature to an investigation. Investigate to prove me wrong, *Chief*."

"Dominic, you have to stop being so emotional. That's your flaw, you know? Someday, it's going to cause your demise."

"Chief, if there isn't any snow on the ground when you go to bed, but when you wake up there is snow on the ground, it is safe to assume it snowed that night even though you didn't see it snowing. Right?"

"What do you mean by that?"

"I mean the facts are clear. Aside from who did it, fireworks are illegal in Massachusetts, and by all codes, the FIRE CHIEF is the AHJ (Authority Having Jurisdiction), Chief. Be the authority. Be the judicator, Chief. Do your job, Chief."

"I mean it, Dominic. You handle emergency scenes the same way. You ride on emotions, too many ups and downs, to quick a temper. Someday, you're going to make a wrong decision because you reacted instead of thinking."

With my innards boiling, I thought I'd explode. "Who made you my therapist? You're covering for Slayton. You're afraid of him because you think he's connected in this town for some reason. Well, let me set you straight, Chief, that's just a put-on. He uses it to stave off guys like you, and it works. Slayton is nothing. Or maybe he's got something on you. Yeah, maybe that's it, Slayton has something on the chief."

Brewster immediately turned his head back toward the floor.

"Oh my god, Slayton does have something on you!"

The typically blank look on Chief Brewster's face changed to one of hard malice. "You're talking to your chief, Lieutenant. I'd watch it."

Staring him down, I finally stood silent, angry, but silent.

Brewster continued, "The police were called. Who did that? You? I told them this was an internal matter, and we'd handle it." Now, furthermore, if your ears are that bad, I don't know how you're going to fight fires and go out on calls. What did the doctor say?"

"Internal matter, Chief, you trying to run me out of here? Is that the game plan, Chief?"

"Now, Dom, there you go again. I never said anything of the sort. I just asked, are you physically capable of doing this job? If not, you're entitled to compensation."

Glaring at Brewster like a linebacker on a quarterback, I said, "Even with no hearing and no arms, I'd still be more capable than Slayton." We stared briefly, but Brewster could never look anyone in the eye, so he looked away. Then I continued to speak, "The doctor gave me a few things to try. He never said anything about not being able to work. He just said it might make me uncomfortable. The hearing loss is probably permanent. It may get worse, but it's too soon to tell. He said I should keep it protected so it's not exposed to another incident."

"How do you do that?"

Sarcastically, I said, "Stay the hell away from Billy Slayton."

"C'mon, Renaldi. This is bullshit. I can't have this. Things were never this way when Wyatt was chief."

"Ya think? You just noticed that? What's the only thing that's changed around here, Chief?"

"You don't like it? You want to quit, Dom? Then quit. I can't have this kind of attitude and insubordination around here. Either you'll show me respect, or you'll have to go. I don't want to lose you, but you can't talk to me that way."

"Respect is earned, Chief. Defend one of your men injured in a violent attack at the firehouse and earn your respect."

"You're pushing the limit, Renaldi!"

For the first time, my head drooped slightly. It was obvious I couldn't quit or be fired with cause. From my childhood, I set my sights on putting all of my children through college, and nothing was going to derail that. Besides, I loved my career. Maybe, I could hook up with another department in another town. All the local chiefs knew me well and respected me. We worked big fires together, and on occasion, I'd helped them with fire alarm problems in their communities. I also helped out at the fire academy. But Coventry is my home. It meant something to me to be good at my job, to provide a service in my hometown—a town that had looked down on me all my life.

As I stood there, Brewster stammered nervously, "I'd like to put this—this thing—behind us all." Suddenly, the chief called out, "Lieutenant, Lieutenant Slayton, come into my office."

"You've got to be kidding me, Chief."

"No, this is for the good of the department, Dom."

Slayton jauntily walked in to Brewster's office. I wanted to belt the smirk right off his face. What kind of nerve did he have, standing here, smiling, when he should be cowering in shame? Just like he should have when he ran from fires.

"Now, guys, I know there's some history here, but the bad stuff has got to stop. I need you both to work together. Now, Slayton, I know you've been asked this before, but I'm going to ask you again. Did you throw that M-80 at Dominic?"

My instincts told me something wasn't right. The scene almost looked staged.

Slayton never took that sadistic smile off his face. "No."

I shook my head. "You goddamn liar. Both of you are conniving liars."

"All right, Dom. This is exactly what I'm talking about. Slayton wants to put this all behind, but you keep on stirring it up."

"Dom, I'm sorry you think I did something to you. I should be offended, but I'm trying to be the bigger man here. I'm willing to forgive your accusation if you'd apologize to me and move on," Slayton said with total lack of sincerity.

"What? Me apologize to you? It'll be a cold day in hell before I do that!"

Right on queue, Slayton turned calmly to the chief. "Well, I tried. I'm extending the hand of brotherhood, but Dom has to meet a guy halfway." To demonstrate, Slayton slowly stuck his hand out toward me.

The gesture was not reciprocated.

"Oh well. Guess old habits die hard." With that, Slayton turned his back and happily walked away, quickly laughing.

Brewster's face looked a little longer and sadder than usual. "I'm disappointed in you, Dom. Chief Wyatt always spoke so highly of you."

"You should never use that man's name. This would never had happened if *he* were still chief." With that, I too turned and walked away—far more in trouble than Slayton.

Meanwhile, Slayton was on the phone. "Hello, Lyons. I just wanted to remind you, Renaldi's going away this weekend. It might be a good opportunity for you."

"Yeah thanks. I'm having a cook-out this weekend, but it seems only one person is coming." They laughed together.

I was so livid at Brewster I could have screamed. Surely, I wanted to be in Liz's arms right now, so soothing, so supportive. Knowing that wasn't possible, I paged her, and we talked. How sad my wife wasn't the one to whom I wished to speak in troubled times, but Liz was the woman with whom I connected. She always defused me better than a bomb squad. I told her what had just transpired. She too was in disbelief over Brewster's weak response. Liz knew about the original incident when it happened. She called it childish and agreed a criminal act occurred.

I contemplated my options; if I sued the town, I might win. If I lost, and it was labeled "just a firehouse prank," I'd be out of a job. My children would be eating out of soup kitchens somewhere. No matter what I did, Slayton had just fucked me.

Finally, I concluded the best option would be to keep this matter in-house and let the chief deal harsh punishment to Slayton. Surely, every book ever written on management would support harsh punishment, perhaps even discharge, for causing bodily harm to another employee.

Liz didn't think Brewster had the guts to do anything about it. "He's fucked up his family, and now he's fucking up the fire department. You need to take this matter into your own hands."

For the protection of my children's future, I couldn't take that gamble, so I left it up to Brewster to take appropriate actions with Slayton.

An hour later, my pager went off—4812.

Chapter 19

"Bobcat hunting?"

"Yep."

"Bobcat hunting."

The first time Ruth said it, it was a question. The second time was a statement of flat incredulity.

"Yep, me, Steve, Dennis, and Jim this weekend. C'mon, you know we love to get away at least one weekend a year to hunt."

"But bobcats? You never hunted for bobcats before. What do you know about bobcats? What do you even hunt them with? Where do you hunt them? *Why* would you want to hunt them?"

I knew I'd get these questions, so I studied up on the answers. No, I had never hunted for bobcats before in my life, but I read that bobcat was the only game in season at that time of the year. "We didn't get to go bow hunting for deer last fall, so we had to think of something. It'll be fun. I enjoy it. I like getting together with the guys. We haven't gotten together in a long time."

"And where is this stag party going to take place?"

"Becket, Western Massachusetts, in the Berkshires near the New York line. That's where you'll find bobcats. There are a lot of them out there. They're a very cagey prey. You get up early in the morning and use a shotgun and calls."

Ruth pursed her lips and said, "Go ahead and have some fun. I'll find something to do." She turned her back and walked away.

I thought to myself, *Good.* I left the house to work in the yard.

Ruth was cleaning the house when the phone rang.

"Hi, Ruth. It's me, Ben Lyons."

Ruth's face lit up. "Hi, Ben."

"I'm looking for Dom. I'm having a cookout this weekend and I was hoping the two of you could come."

"Sorry, he's going away for the weekend."

"Oh, that's too bad." He paused, then asked, "Why don't you come over anyway."

Ruth thought for a moment. Then smiled and said, "Sure, I'll come over. It'll be fun."

Lyons immediately smiled as he thought, *This may be the chance I've been waiting for.* "Sure. I'd love to have you stop by."

"What can I bring?"

"Everything is all set. Just bring yourself. It will be fun."

Ruth smiled.

* * *

The guys really were going away hunting for bobcat. This wouldn't have been my first hunting trip away with them, so Ruth was used to it. I had also contacted my best friend Dennis, whom I was closest to and whom Ruth would be most likely to call if she were to check up on the trip. It was a tough call. For the first time since I'd hooked up with Liz, I was allowing someone else in on the secret. Dennis has been a lifelong friend of mine. I had never told him about Liz. If anyone could keep this secret quiet, it was Dennis of the Coventry Police.

"Do I know her?"

"Remember that cute blonde I introduced you to in front of the firehouse one day?"

"Yeah, short with a beautiful smile."

"That's Liz!" I said as my demeanor lit up.

"You're fucking *that?* Good for you, you old bastard. Is she worth it?"

It was an odd question. "Was she worth it?" I wasn't just getting my jollies off now and then with a woman without a last name. This was a full-blown affair. Liz had managed to arrange to be away that weekend at her vacation home in Martha's Vineyard. For all the time we had been spending together, all the beds we had mussed and sweated upon, we had never yet had the chance to spend a night in each other's arms. This would be heaven. Now all I had to do was figure out a way to get out of the house for an entire weekend alone. The hours we spent talking on the phone notwithstanding, I managed to get over to Liz's place at least two mornings a week. Tuesday mornings were always reserved for Liz and me to see each other at her house—no kids, no house cleaner, and no husband. We had made love in every room of her house and on almost every piece of furniture. In between, we often did it in cars parked discreetly at the far end of a parking lot or at the end of a private road. We fit other occasions in where we could. We took risks—no doubt about that—but so far, we'd been lucky. Oh, once or twice, there was the unexpected phone call. One experience will always stand out.

During one of our first rendezvous at Liz's house, suddenly, a male voice spoke, "Lieutenant Renaldi, call fire alarm." My heart skipped a beat as Liz screamed and pushed me off of her. It was my mini receiver from the fire department. We all carried one on our belt. After that, I always made sure it was off.

Once or twice during one of our "outings," we narrowly escaped the prying eyes of strangers, which brought more laughter and excitement to our already exhilarating relationship, but so far, so good. I had no desire to brag about my good fortune to the guys at the firehouse. I'm sure enough of that was going on there already. Half the women in Coventry had their reputations tarnished by firehouse gossip, most of it embarrassing but true; sometimes, not so true. Slayton was in everyone's business, needing the smut on everyone and then sharing it with his inner circle. More info for "the book" he and Jacobs kept on everyone—more perceived power.

"Yeah, Dennis, she's something special. You should see her. She's got the tightest body, the greatest face. She looks like Elizabeth Shue and has a body like Halle Berry."

"And I'm sure blond hair and blue eyes too, Dom." Dennis knew me well. Again, he asked, "But is she worth it?" I was brought back to reality. Dennis didn't want naughty stories. He was asking his friend if he knew what he was doing and whether he was willing to risk everything with his family to have this affair. It was a damn good question.

"Yeah, Dennis, yes, she is. There's definitely something there. I've never felt this way with a woman before."

"This woman, Dominic. She seems familiar to me. I've seen her around somewhere." Dennis began to think. "Yes, I've seen her talking to Alan Bard here at the police station."

"Yes, she is friendly with Bard, Dennis. They swim together at the college."

"Well, then I'd be very careful with her, Dom, you know Bard. He'll fuck anything that moves. Just last year, he was fucking that broad up on the post road. He backed the cruiser out of her driveway late one night and totaled it into an oncoming car. Then he lied, 'I was just turning around in the driveway.' I'm sorry, Dom. If Bard is that friendly with her, he's fucking her."

The shot hurt me. "I just don't know, Dennis. This is our only difficulty. I'm trying hard to trust her when she tells me they're just friends."

"I ask you again, Dominic. Is she worth it? Is she worth risking everything?"

I thought for a minute. *Dennis may be right, but she seemed to take all my troubles away, and she made me feel so good.* "Yes, Dennis. Yes, she is worth it. I feel as if I am failing in life. Liz is stopping me from doing that. There's definitely something there. I've never felt this way with a woman before. I don't know where it's headed, but I'm there. You know what I mean? It's real."

* * *

That Friday, I parked my car at a firehouse in a nearby town just off the highway and waited for Liz to pick me up. Checking in, I left my keys with the firefighter at the watch desk. It was a common courtesy when we traveled out of town; firemen from other towns often parked their vehicles at the Coventry firehouse overnight.

When Liz arrived, there were smiles but no overt public displays of affection. This was our burden alone. It wasn't until we were well on our way that both of us were able to let down our guard and relax our anxieties.

"I am *so* happy," she mused.

When we were together, I drove her SUV, and she contently purred. She melted into her car seat, curling up and reaching around to hold on to my arm. "*So* happy."

"Me too," I said running my powerful hand on Liz's thigh.

Liz brought her leg a little closer to my outstretched arm as she said with a sigh, "Oh, that hand feels good." She closed her eyes and leaned her head back with a smile.

Miles went by, the sun was shining brightly, and all was fine with the world. What Dennis had said stuck in my mind, but I didn't quite know what to do with it. From time to time, I'd look over at Liz. We were both rather quiet. Liz's left hand was now intertwined with my right hand in a symbiotic way. It felt perfect. If there was a picture of relaxation, this was it. But I kept being bucked by internal conflict, wondering when would be the right time to talk about our situation beyond the here and now. The answer always came back the same—not here, not now, some other time.

We arrived at Woods Hole for the 11:30 a.m. ferry. We were as far away from the Berkshires as logistically possible due east rather than due west. Not that Ruth was going to go trekking out looking for me, but still, it gave me a shiver. I had never done anything like this before. There was never a moment of true, utter peace. Even when I had one of my most ecstatic moments with Liz, I would return to my truck, and then the worrying would set in. I could set my watch by it. I wondered if Liz had the same anxieties. She never showed any, but then again, I never showed her mine. Even we had secrets from one another.

The ferry crew began boarding the vehicles in their usual systematic way. Trucks to the center, cars to the outside—this would keep the ferry balanced. Once our car was positioned near the front of the left outside row, Liz began making good use of her time by doing some work on her laptop. Not nearly as accustomed to the forty-five-minute jaunt across the Vineyard Sound, I headed for the deck. As a frustrated seaman of sorts, I wanted to capture the full experience of the captain and his vessel. Being the only person on the bow, but it was a beautiful spring day albeit cold, I nodded to the captain on the bridge. With lines cast off, the captain engaged the propellers, and we were under way. With deft precision, he backed his vessel out from the dock, then slipped into neutral as the vessel glided backward until just the right time, then forward—smooth as silk. Marveling at the captain's handling of his responsibilities, I watched as we exited the harbor. Soon we were steaming across the sound. There was nothing but water in sight. With the sun shining and the wind in my face, I felt at ease.

Suddenly, I was interrupted by a familiar voice. "There you are. I should have known you'd be up at the bow." Liz wrapped her arms around me, the two of us standing on the port side and feeling the cool wind and spray of a chilly New England spring. I opened my parka and wrapped Liz inside with me as I said, "I could be on water all the time."

"I love this. I could do this all the time."

"What, be on the water?"

"No, silly. Be out in public with you, like a real couple. No hiding, just being free, being in love."

Smiling, I kissed the top of her head. New couples always have that "love" thing hanging over them like cupid. Somehow, Liz had managed to slip it in unobtrusively without saying the classic line "I love you." Cute. Very cute.

"So picture we could do that. Would you? Would you face the music, stand up to receive some pain in order to create a happy ending like this?"

Liz hugged me tighter. "I don't know. Must we talk about it?"

I thought for a few moments, then I said, "Yeah, I think maybe we should. Or if we're not going to talk about it, maybe we should talk about that."

"You're confusing me."

I undid the warm wrap and put my hands on Liz's shoulders. "Sweetheart, we're both playing with fire. You know that. Sooner or later, something's going to happen, something bad. I just want to know what's going to happen when it does. Is it every man for himself or what?"

I couldn't make out Liz's eyes through her large dark sunglasses. For the first time, there was a barrier, a wall between us. We hadn't broached this subject before, and she was being cagy and avoided answering my question.

"I . . . I don't know. Look, Dom, let's just enjoy ourselves. This weekend is going to be incredible. I just know it. Wait till you see what I've got planned."

My mind immediately thought, *So it was every man for himself.*

*   *   *

The captain maneuvered his vessel into magical Edgartown Harbor with deftness his years of experience had brought, her bow coming to rest against the padded piers of the slip as gently as a mother lays a baby's head on a pillow. Liz and I climbed back into her SUV. As I began exiting the ferry hold, Liz was already at work with her list of things to do. I started turning to the left when Liz blurted, "No, to the right!"

Quickly, but safely, I swerved right, which made Liz scream slightly as I said, "Hey, give me a break, I don't know where I'm going." Then she laughed. The fun had already begun as we headed cross island toward her place in Chilmark. It was Liz's favorite place to be. Chilmark was remote and exclusive—the summer playground of Kennedys, Cronkites, Simons, and others. I could not be more out of place. Still, I enjoyed the views, the areas left natural in their rugged beauty. Once on the island, Liz was different; she was in her zone.

While driving up the winding, crushed-seashell driveway, I just shook my head as I pictured the wildlife bounding from the adjoining preservation's land. The home was set back off the road and partially hidden from view—secluded. What a place; like Liz Temple, it was elegant but not ostentatious. Though it was still early spring, there were crocuses and daffodils in the sunnier flowerbeds, and I could just imagine the lush beauty the dormant gardens would bring to life on a sun-soaked summer's day. We sat in the car for a bit as I took in the life a place like this may have brought.

No, not today's world of the rich and famous, but of yester world—of three-mast schooners and captains who guided their ships, not by GPS and radar but by the stars, the weather, and the seat of their pants. Just imagine yourself sailing out of Martha's Vineyard halfway around the world to the West Indies, across the treacherous high seas of mutiny and piracy, perhaps a run-in with Cape Cod's very own pirate Black Sam Bellamy, and back again to a harbor filled with docks and the busy life of an island seaport where proud sea captains sailed their beloveds into the harbor, riding low in the water full of bounty, and maybe, a little booty too. "Home at last, home at last, thank God Almighty, home at last," might have been quite appropriate. Home to a heroes welcome as they returned with the necessary goods for the island's survival. Home to their women waiting dockside.

As I daydreamed, I thought, *Even today, I'd go back into that world in a second.*

Everything about Liz exuded style and grace. This house was no different; its style was a combination of an eighteenth-century sea captain's home, complete with widow's walk, and a beautiful old English mansion. Visitors were welcomed at the front door after passing by four columns, which supported the second floor forming a full-length front porch. The gambrel design had large dormers on the front and a full dormer across the south facing back full of hinged windows with flower boxes under each one. I could just imagine young children, jubilant in laughter, playing inside and out, plenty of wonderful sunshine splashing on them and the ocean breeze on their faces. The rear of the house also had four columns and a full veranda-style porch. *Someday*, I thought, *Liz and I would sit there sipping cocktails as we watched what would be a magnificent sunset off to the west.* All this flowed from green grass to a narrow band of sandy sea grass with plenty of wild rose bushes. Beyond the roses was a sandy beach with rolling ocean waves. There was a kitchen addition to the left with a long vista of the ocean. To the right side of the house was a grape arbor bordering the perfect island patio for a glass of afternoon iced tea while sitting in the shade. The rear sunroom off the kitchen was new, windows on all sides and skylights, a nautical compass inlaid in its floor, and natural wicker furniture. Liz had this room added on; it helped to make her mark on this home. The weathered shingles gave it a look of old New England charm.

"Paradise!" I said as we walked in through the front door.

"Excuse me?"

"Which room is Peter Pan's and which is Tinker Bell's?" With a look of childish bewilderment, I exclaimed, "Oh, there she goes!" as my glance drifted across the room as if following her in flight.

"What on earth are you talking about, Dom?" Liz inquired laughingly.

"Oh, that's right, you're Tinker Bell! Hey! Does that make me Peter Pan?"

Now we were both laughing. "You've totally lost me, Dom!"

"This is paradise, Liz, and I never want to leave it, I already know that."

"We'll worry about that tomorrow, for now, just kiss me."

Our embrace, just as it had been a million times before, was sincere, sweet, and pure, culminating in a locked hug.

"Seriously, Liz, this is magnificent."

Little Miss Busybody, now breaking away from our hold, said, "Thank you. I picked it out myself. I had the kitchen done when we first bought the place. The sunroom I had done just last year. It's my favorite room."

"You spend your husband's money well."

Liz responded with silence while I chuckled a little at my own comment to indicate I was joking. Again, I repeated, smiling, "Besides, Liz, you *do* know how to spend money well."

"It's my Irish heritage, I guess," Liz said as she moved from room to room. Though she called in advance to have the house automatically turn the heat up, Liz was running around checking to make sure it was functioning. I followed like a perfect dance partner. "If I didn't spend his money, we'd be living in the 1960s. I mean, all he's focused on is the operating room. Sometimes, he doesn't even know the children and I exist." Her husband's lack of interest was a hot button issue for Liz, but I was always willing to listen as she vented. She was such a feisty little thing. It made me smile as I watched her vent.

I shook my head. "How the hell could he ever forget he was married to you?"

"He's in his own world, Dom. Come on, check out the upstairs."

Following Liz was like being on high speed. I managed to keep up. We walked into an incredibly airy bedroom, where two skylights allowed in all of heaven's brightness. Two bay windows overlooked the ocean.

"I could definitely handle this," I exclaimed as I looked out over the ocean.

Liz looked at me with that beautiful inviting smile as she put her arms around me and said, "So handle me, Dom, handle me."

No sooner were we in the room before we began passionately embracing each other.

Through lips muted by kisses, Liz said, "It's still freezing in here. Sorry. We have to get under the covers."

Liz jumped under the covers with her clothes on, and I followed. Like teenagers, we kissed and hugged and played for a while until finally we removed each other's clothing.

Maybe it's my Italian heritage, but when I make love, my primary objective isn't to please myself—it's to please my partner first. Lovemaking with Liz always started off with me kissing her tender lips as I gazed into her blue eyes. There was something about her look that ignited something deep inside me. Holding her tightly, I insisted on slowly removing each piece of Liz's close-fitting outfit. With the unbuttoning of each button, I enjoyed her perfect body, succulently kissing and caressing her bare skin as it was revealed. I ran my lips across her shoulder, then down her arm, stopping to suck each fingertip before returning to her yearning lips. Our tongues darted around and intertwined as we locked our love together. Casting the covers aside, I slipped farther and farther down, sumptuously caressing her body from top to bottom. Welcoming my desires, Liz undid the front snap of her bra and instructed me. "Put your hands on my breasts, Dom" as she guided them with a seductive smile.

I cupped her milky white breasts in my hands. Soothingly, I massaged them. She closed her eyes and writhed in pleasure. "Oh, those hands," she moaned as she undid her pants for me. A peck on the roundness of her breast, which stood tall in the fullness of my hands as I pushed up and, gently, squeezed my fingers around them. A brush across an aroused nipple elicited a quiver from Liz, an acknowledgment of her consent. Then I paused to kiss and flick my tongue on her belly button, knowing this would send shivers through Liz's body. It always did. Liz giggled and shook. I grabbed her black-laced undies by the top. I pulled on them just enough for me to run my tongue inside, stopping just as I got to the good part, her aroma sumptuously inviting. She was beginning to arch. I tugged on her pants enough for them to slide down to her thigh. Just to let her know what was to come, I briefly sucked on her through her underwear. She moaned and parted her legs. Gently, I nibbled at her loins.

"Liz, even with your underpants still on, I can taste how sweet you are." She smiled at me in acceptance.

Sliding my hand down her leg, I slowly and methodically removed her pants one leg at a time. Silently granting me access, she raised her leg. First, a kiss to her thigh, then her knee, her calf, and finally sliding her pant leg off, where I could softly kiss each toe as she stretched her leg out to accompany the rough but tender touch of this silent man. She moaned in delight.

With each one of my movements, Liz countered, deftly removing my clothes. Soon the covers were on the floor, and we were nearly naked.

I started up the backside of this heavenly woman's well-developed leg. She raised it invitingly as I stopped long enough to suck and nibble on her round calf, so tender and sweet. I could spend all day doing this, but Liz's excitement was growing.

"Come up here, Dom," she implored as she pulled on me. "Come up here. I'm going to come."

But I didn't budge, just muttered, "Uh-uhhh." I turned toward her inner thigh. My lips lightly caressing every inch of her as I made my way closer to where I could feel her wetness. I inhaled deeply. Her wonderful scent made her more delectable. I caressed and licked on the very edge of her undies, occasionally running my tongue inside of them. When I did, Liz shuddered in delight and moaned. Upon the touch of my tongue, she gasped and spread her legs invitingly in anticipation. She thrust herself toward me as she came. Her taste made it nearly impossible for me not to bury my face in her sweetness.

"I want you inside of me now, Dom." But I just brushed across her tender spot and onto the other inner thigh. She was begging for me to "Put it in. Put it in now." She continued pulling on me.

"Not yet, sweetheart." My hot pointed tongue encircled her already-engorged clit.

"Yes . . . there . . . more . . . yes yes . . . more . . . now, please," she panted. I pushed my tongue into her warm wetness. With her sweetness on my tongue, I withdrew and went right up to her waiting mouth where I inserted my tongue. Our kisses were passionate, and Liz was so volatile. "Fuck me, Dom, please fuck me now."

I took my throbbing member and ran it around her swollen clit. Still with her silk undies on, I pushed myself into Liz's wet opening. She begged and clutched as she pulled her underwear to the side so I could enter her. "Now, Dom. Please now!" She began to touch herself on that special spot.

"Not yet. You taste too good. I'm going to eat you first." I rubbed the head of my erection on her dripping opening, making sure it touched her clit.

Liz was in wild, splendid delirium. Barely able to fit her hands around my swollen dick, she tried guiding it in. "Please," she whispered while throwing her head from side to side, arching her back, waiting for the final barrier of her panties to be removed. "Please, Dom, she pleaded again. "Please."

I brought my erection up to her full lips. "Lick the wetness from me please, sweetheart." Liz opened her mouth and sucked. I withdrew, then went down and embraced her lips.

Finally, I started to remove her panties just as slowly and methodically as I removed her pants. With one leg to go, I slid both my hands over her calf, my fingers undulating every curve of her shapely leg. My tongue ran behind all the way down.

Liz moaned, "Oh, Dom. Those hands, they're so powerful and just rough enough. They feel so good when you rub them on me like you do."

Her silky wet undies and my lips arrived together at her foot. Her scent filled the air. I buried my face in them. Spontaneously, I took the scented silk in my mouth and slid them off. My hands pressed against her body all the way down to her toes where I gently, quickly, gave them a soothing massage as my fingers passed by. Liz moaned and writhed as she spread her legs wide, aching for me elsewhere.

With her sopping wet panties still in my mouth, I brushed them, teasingly, up her leg and dropped them just as I got to her lions. I licked her lush tenderness. She was dripping wet, and I opened my mouth wide. Completely encompassing her pussy in my mouth, I sucked gently, my tongue entering her. Liz screamed in pleasure and instantly climaxed. Sucking harder as she did, I consumed her juices. Then I slid my tongue up her wonderful body and inserted it in her mouth. We slobbered and sucked on our tongues in decadent behavior. All the while, Liz's supple breasts fit perfectly into my powerful hands. Soothingly, I caressed them. Her erect nipples seemed to be an inch long. I ran my finger inside of her wetness, then a second finger. It was so hot. When I did, Liz climaxed again. I took my wet fingers and ran them all around one of her breasts. It became slippery and succulent. The firmness of her nipple, the milky contrast of her skin, I sucked and licked the wetness off both her breast and my fingers at the same time. Her nipples were incredible. I nibbled on them and licked some more. Back and forth I went, orchestrated by Liz's moaning signals. I bit onto a nipple and raised her breast. She screamed in torturous pleasure. I released it from my grasp; then I plunged my lips into her breast with sucking desire, soothing her with my tongue. This was as passionate as I could ever remember being. But I was not yet done. Liz was insanely turned on. I was too. I was oozing and ready to come. Still, I went down on her again. Liz shuddered and shook, her neck so red and her veins popping out as she arched and screamed out loud in utter, sexual pleasure.

After several minutes of this luscious enjoyment, I knelt before Liz and rubbed the firm head of my stiffness all around her wetness as she spread her legs even wider while lurching for me to be deeper inside of her. But I wasn't letting it happen.

Liz wreathed in pleasurable anguish. "You're teasing me."

I just smiled warmly at her and said, "You're so wet and feel so good. I want to enjoy it for as long as possible. You are so beautiful, Liz."

We smiled at each other for a few more seconds. I watched in enjoyment as the head of my throbbing hard-on separated Liz's moist pussy lip. Slowly, I ran it in just a few inches, and slowly, I pulled it out. Each time, I savored the feeling and such a gorgeous sight. Finally, I couldn't take it any longer. I thrust inside of her. Liz gasped as I pierced her deeply. I pumped as hard as I could. She was so wet. The full length of my thick pulsing dick slid in and out of her with no resistance at all. It felt so wonderful. I lied down on top of her. Liz moaned in complete acceptance as she wrapped her arms and legs around me while I buried myself in carnal pleasure.

Her scent was making me dizzy with ecstasy. I was lost in an aphrodisiac of love. My body was tense. I could feel the pressure starting deep inside of me as I thrust into her. Our intensity rose together as the shackles of fear and anxiety were stripped away much as our clothes had been. I pumped harder. My legs tightened, my toes tingled, and I began to erupt. I was numb with pleasure as I fucked as hard as I could. Our bodies were dripping in sweat. Then moans turned to shouts, which turned to screams. "Touch me, Dom. Touch me. Don't stop, don't stop. Come with me, Dom. Please come with me."

"I'm going to, Liz. I'm coming right now." My entire body tensed like never before. I let out a harsh groan of satisfaction. "Geezus. You feel so good. I'm coming, I'm . . . OH SSSSSHIT. It feels so good!" Harder. Faster I thrust. My juices burst inside of her. I gave her everything I had, and she took it all.

Liz and I were in perfect symbiotic unison. As the spasms of her orgasm contracted, she screamed with me, "OH MY GOD, OHHHHH! Harder. Faster. OHHHH MY GOD." Liz was trembling. "Don't stop, don't stop. Keep going. You're so big. You fill me up. Your warmth inside of me, it feels sooooo good." Liz was tonguing me profusely as she locked her legs around me. "OHHHHH, I can feel you coming. OH, DOM. Don't stop, please don't ever stop." I pumped and fucked her until my muscles were so tight they wouldn't move anymore. We collapsed into each other's embrace. This was freedom. This was heaven. This is what Liz inspired me to do.

With our arms and legs completely entwined as one, I laid on top of Liz, still inside of her. Sweaty and completely spent, I pecked her forehead, her nose, her eyes, and her cheeks. I was still showing the affection Liz had drawn from deep inside of me.

"Where did you ever learn to make love like this?"

"You bring it out of me, Liz." Our afterglow continued until we had to move. I rolled off her and collapsed on to my back. "Liz, that was so wonderful. I don't think I've made love like that before."

Liz smiled and giggled. "I know I never have." She then laid her head on my chest, and we snuggled up against each other. Pulling the covers up almost over her head, Liz said, "This is my favorite part of all."

"What is?" I asked.

Liz squeezed her arm around my chest and repositioned her head on it while I held her in my arm. Then she said, "Crawling all up inside of you. You're a gentle big teddy bear. My silent big man. I never get to do this with you. Your arms feel so good wrapped around me, and I feel so safe when I'm with you. You make me feel good both on the outside and on the inside, Dom."

I smiled. "All this could someday be yours."

The words were melancholy. All the material things around us were already hers. What was missing in her life was everything else—the love, the passion, and the companionship.

"Dom, I don't know where this is going. I'm torn. You know I love you."

"You never said that until today."

She was quick with the retort, "And you haven't said it yet."

"I love you," I said playfully.

She elbowed me gently with a giggle. "Cheater. That doesn't count. I practically cued you to say it. That's not true inspiration."

"I am truly inspired to tell you that I love you. I am *in* love with you. What's *not* to love? That's why I'm being such a headache this weekend."

Liz pondered. "I know. I'm sorry. I wish this was how it could always be."

"Are we talking about the lifestyle? The big house, the vacation home on the Vineyard?"

"I wish I knew. You can hate me if you want, but you don't know what it's like to have something like this and toss it all away. It's easier if you never had it."

"But if you divorced your husband, you wouldn't be left high and dry, for Christ's sake."

"I signed a prenup. Sam's lawyers drew it up. It's obviously written in his favor."

"Yeah, but there's poverty, and then there's *poverty*. You're the mother, you'll definitely get the kids. And with the kids, you'll have to get child support. C'mon, you're not going to be living out of a cardboard box. He'll have to allow you to maintain your lifestyle."

Liz squeezed me tighter and said nothing more. It was not a gesture of disagreement. Perhaps I was winning her over. I certainly hoped that was the case.

The rest of the weekend was a hedonist's paradise. Despite the spring cold, we cruised the beach holding hands and embracing as we walked and talked. "We could make love here and here and here." I pointed to every romantic spot I saw, and Liz laughed heartily.

"Yes, and if it were summer, I would—in a minute," said Liz as she wrapped her arms around me and drew herself tightly against me.

Liz is such a capable woman, who did everything so meticulously well. I often thought, *What a shame it was that so many talented, educated women were buried under the success of their controlling husbands*. Conversely, Liz would look at me and see a caring, compassionate man who understood her needs and allowed her to take the lead. *Her husband may give Liz everything she needs, but I give her everything she longed for.*

That evening, we went to a wonderful restaurant in Oak Bluffs and dined by candlelight on duck and venison. "I brought you here because, I mean, you *are* on a hunting trip." Then the giggle, so irresistible!

"Funny. The only wild game I'm having this weekend is you." The banter was playful. We both laughed.

Suddenly, Liz stopped and stared at me, her eyes glistened in the flicker of the candlelight. "No, seriously, Dom." She reached across the table and held both my hands, saying, "I chose this restaurant because I knew you'd love it here. It's perfect for us."

The wine was smooth, the atmosphere dark and romantic, the company delightful, and the meal extravagant. We luxuriated for hours until we were the last to leave.

While walking back to the car, Liz and I held hands. When we got to her door, I took her in my arms and kissed her. "Dinner was wonderful. Thank you very much, sweetheart."

Liz had a warm glow about her. She smiled up at me and said, "You've very welcome. It was my pleasure."

As we drove home, I playfully asked, "So ya wanna go parking?"

Liz smiled seductively. "I want you to take me home. I have a special dessert for you," she said with a sly look and a wink.

With a smile, I floored the accelerator. We laughed at my gesture, and I reached to pull her closer as I drove. In no time at all, we were back at her place. We relaxed in the sunroom for a bit. The ambiance was wonderful. With lights turned low, Liz lit a few candles. We snuggled on a cozy love seat and listened to the soothing sound of waves crashing onshore at high tide. The moon was bright, and the stars shined in the clear sky. I had my arm around Liz as she rested her head on my shoulder. Silently, we gazed into another world. It was very romantic. We began kissing. Liz and I did this often, and we loved doing so, but this was special. I had never felt like this before.

Abruptly, Liz took my by the hand. "Let's go upstairs, Dom. Tonight, I want to please you the way you did me this afternoon." I smiled warmly and blew out the candles.

While Liz finished up in the bathroom, I got undressed to my underwear and was laying on the bed with a hard-on that was throbbing in anticipation. Liz came out of the bathroom wearing a short see-through powder blue nightie with matching bikini undies. With her beautiful smile, that gorgeous face, and a magnificent body, I almost came right there. "Liz, seeing you standing there is the most beautiful sight I have ever seen." My heart was pounding, and I wanted to devour her all over again.

Liz smiled warmly and said, "Thank you." She then pranced over and jumped onto the bed. Kneeling at my side, she said, "I love it when you give me compliments." She gave me a broad smile.

"You look so inviting. I want to make love to you right now, Liz."

She smiled at me again. "Uh-uhhh. Not until I'm done satisfying you." She had a smile that said, "I am the seductress."

"Kiss me right now, sweetheart." Liz leaned in, and we began kissing . . . . It didn't take long for us to get hot. My hands were caressing her back as she began her decent. Liz enjoyed kissing my nipples. She sucked and nibbled one, then the other. She drove me crazy.

"Come back up here," I asked. We looked into each other's eyes and smiled. Placing my hands on her face, I pulled her closer while still gazing into her eyes. Softly, I said, "I love you."

Her heart was full, and her eyes welled up with tears. She had a warm smile. Then she said softly, "I love you too." Quickly, ravenously, she began to suck every inch of me. She tore off my underpants and wrapped both hands around my huge member as she looked down. "Dominic, he is so beautiful." And she began stroking me.

"Don't, Liz. Don't do that. You're going to make me come."

I want you to, Dom,"

"Oh no. Not yet, Liz," I begged her.

She went down anyway. She began sucking on the tip of my dick. "I love how you taste and how firm and meaty it is. That ridge right there." And she ran her tongue slowly over it. My whole lower body shivered. "I can't begin to tell you how good that feels when you're pushing in and out of me." I was already totally erect and dripping when Liz brought herself up to my mouth and began kissing me. "Don't you taste good, Dom? Don't we taste even better together?" she asked as she ran her tongue back into my mouth.

It was decadently enjoyable. "Not nearly as good as you taste, sweetheart." I then lifted her nightie over her head, reveling her beautiful skin. I pulled her in close, and we kissed passionately. Her warmth felt so good against me.

Abruptly, she slid down and took my dick deeply into her mouth. With her lips wrapped tightly, she began stroking up and down. The sensation was out of this world. "Slower, sweetheart. God, slow down! Make it last longer."

Liz obligingly followed my request. Sucking on me and stroking me with her fingers, I grabbed hold of her hand and blurted. "STOP!" My body stiffened as I tried desperately to stop the eruption.

Liz looked up and smiled. Lustfully, I requested, "Turn around and get on top of me."

In no time, we were in a sixty-nine position, and I was removing her powder blue undies as she was sucking me off. I was shaking with desire. Liz was slurping long and hard as I buried my face into her hot wet love nest. I licked her pussy until it soaked. Muffled by a mouthful, she shuddered and screamed. Realizing she was coming, I sucked harder. Occasionally, Liz took me out of her mouth and, with her fingers, gently dragged her nails along my member up and down. The sensation was making me shudder. When she started sucking on my balls, I thought I'd erupt. "Oh god, Liz, put it inside of you somewhere. Put it in anywhere, I'm going to come." I arched high as it lifted her off the bed with just my dick holding her. We were both loving this.

Liz went back up and began sucking on my head again. I inserted two fingers inside her and began running them in and out as hard as I could. When she flicked her tongue on the underside of my head, I erupted. She went down deeper into her throat and sucked me dry. I buried my tongue and ran my fingers. Liz came again and again. I could feel her muscles tremble each time.

She turned around quickly and climbed on top of me. She looked at me with sheer lust as she buried her tongue in my welcoming mouth. I received it readily. My lips were wrapped around her tongue as she slid it in and out of my mouth. It was unadulterated pleasure.

I was still hard as a rock, and neither of us was ready to stop. Liz climbed on top and began to ride me. "What would you like me to do to you now? she asked in a deep, lustful voice. "I want to please you."

"You do please me, Liz."

She smiled and rolled us over with me still inside of her. We began to fuck with me on top. In no time, Liz was screeching in delight. "TOUCH ME. TOUCH ME."

My hand was in the right place, and I was buried deep inside of her as we came together. My heart was pounding harder than ever. I was short of breath. While still lying on top of her, playfully I muttered, "Dear lord, if you're ever going to take me, take me right now!"

Liz kinda laughed and asked, "What?"

I was still on top of her and still inside her too. "Today has been the most wonderful day of my life. Never have I experienced anything like this."

Liz smiled. "I love you."

I answered with a huge grin, "I love you too."

That night, we both fell asleep in each other's arms. Liz snuggled tightly against me so safe and so warm. I gazed out the skylights and into the faraway stars. I thought I had found heaven.

The next morning, I awoke to find Liz looking at me with a smile on her face. I smiled back. "What are you looking at?"

"I'm just happy to see you sleeping so peacefully. It makes me smile."

Good Jesus, I thought. *How could I not love this woman?* I took her into my arms, and we began kissing.

* * *

During our last morning together on the Vineyard, neither of us wanted to return. Over breakfast, the usual coffee and bagels we often shared, this time with juice. There was a lingering reticence. Neither face could hide a smile. All movements were serene and placid.

"Lost at sea, aren't we?" I asked as I walked up behind her, wrapping my arms around her and kissing the back of her neck.

Liz continued to stare out the window. There was a magnificent view; however, I sensed she wasn't looking at it. She brought her right hand up to the side of my face. "Last night was all the love I could ever hope for." Then she paused. "You'd leave, Ruth?"

I now stood erect with my hands on Liz's shoulders and looked out over her. "I already have. It's been over for years now. We're both just going through the motions. Why do you ask?"

Liz looked back at me intensely. "So you'd really do it?"

"That's what I said."

She snickered. "You're lying. You'll never leave your wife."

"No, I mean it. I know it's a big decision, but if you want me, I'm yours."

"You have no idea what a bastard my husband can be. It could get ugly."

"I'd kick his ass."

"Dominic, it's not like that. Sam is ruthless. Nothing matters more to egotistical men like him than their pride. He'd do whatever he could to ruin you."

"And what would he do to you?"

Liz paced. "That's the thing that worries me the most. That's why I've put you off for so long. He scares me, Dom. He really does scare me."

"If he hurt you, I swear—"

"Dom, the Sam Temples of the world don't operate that way. You just don't understand his world. There are much worse things you can do to a person than punch them in the nose. You can make their life a living hell. You can make it so they have nowhere to turn. Money talks, Dom."

"Liz, as long as I'm alive, you'll always have someone to turn to."

Liz's eyes began to well up with tears. "I know. I know that so well."

Chapter 20

One of the better traditions of the fire service is mutual aid—one town, or many towns helping the one in need. Perhaps this dates back to the colonial times with neighbor helping neighbor in an effort for all to survive. Nonetheless, this was professional teamwork at its finest. Men and women risking their lives for neighbors, people they didn't even know. It wasn't uncommon for Coventry to respond to adjacent communities such as Cromwell; in fact, I had fought many fires on mutual aid. It was far less common for Coventry to assist the larger urban cities, but on occasion, we did, and we were glad to be of assistance.

After having put in a hard day's work making repairs to the municipal fire alarm system, I quietly cleaned myself up at home, kissed Stacy and Laura good-bye, telling each, "I love you," and headed in to work, not even exchanging a good-bye with Ruth. David was still at his part-time job at the hardware store just across the street.

"Swap time" is a common courtesy in the fire service, and I was paying back someone who had previously worked for me. Amongst others, I would be working with Frieze and Lyons, who was working an overtime shift. Captain Jacobs was on-duty too. As I sipped on a cold drink, I watched the news. Jack Williams, news anchor for Channel 4, said, "It was ten years ago today that the city of Lynn was nearly consumed by fire. We'll be right back with the story."

I called out to the young firefighters, "Frieze, Lyons, come watch this." Both firefighters hustled into the day room. Jacobs's ears must have perked; he could hear a pin drop from one hundred yards away, let alone hearing my yell from the bunkroom with its door open.

"What's happening, Lieutenant?" Frieze asked.

"Watch this, it was *unbelievable*!" I said excitedly.

"Watch what?"

With a friendly smirk on my face, I said to the two capable men I'd taught so much, "The news, you'll see what real firefighting is about." Both Frieze and Lyons couldn't help but notice my excitement. This wasn't typical Renaldi. Surely, if something newsworthy had occurred, they'd have heard about it.

"You okay, old man?" Frieze asked in a good-natured way, "Just watch." I said with a smile and an upward nod of my head.

As the TV switched to archive tapes of the raging inferno, this powerful force sweeping across street after street, consuming factory after factory, unimpeded and increasing its self-propelled winds into a firestorm of havoc and swirling flames, the young firefighters' jaws fell open.

"Holy shit!" exclaimed Frieze as they sat to watch.

When the segment was over, Frieze said, "Geezus, that must have been something to see."

"It sure was."

"Did you see it, Dom?"

"See it? We were there fighting it!"

Frieze's eyes popped out of his head. "NO SHIT. Tell us about it, Dom."

I thought back to that day when Lynn's cry for help brought us to this old New England mill city north of Boston. Sliding forward in my chair, I began to speak.

"The scene was like a war zone, five-story brick buildings were gutted by fire and falling like dominoes. I'm talking massive mills, like maybe two hundred, three hundred feet wide by several hundred feet long. I'll never forget how tight the whirlpooling funnels of fire were, I mean, they looked like the eyes of a tornado. Every mill building had a dozen of them swirling straight out horizontally from the windows. Never in our lives had we seen walls of brick five and six stories high, falling like an earthquake had struck. The scene was as ferocious as the London Blitz must have been. I'm not even sure if I can describe it with justice. Every time a wall came down, huge columns of smoke rolled into the sky with very angry-looking fire leaping out from within. Each one looked like the A-bomb mushroom without the stem." I was animated as I continued, "*It was fucking unreal*! The fire had jumped into residential neighborhoods adjacent to the mills and began eating up wooden three-story tenements as if they were a pile of kindling."

Being the next truck on the list of available pumpers, Coventry was positioned in Edison Square, thrust into the vortex of this unremitting rage in an attempt to stop the old wooden seven-story Edison Hotel from going up in flames. If the fire leaped here, there was nothing stopping the wind-driven conflagration from sweeping across the whole city of Lynn.

Do or die, take a stand, and hold your ground. Make it happen here.

Our crew was deployed to the rooftop of the building next to the Edison. I was on the nozzle of the typical handline. Danger was all around as acetylene and oxygen bottles exploded from the body shop just below us. Would the next explosion rock the building we were on? It was unnerving. There were 120-foot chimneys wavering like treetops in the wind, no telling when one would come crashing down. Several had already fallen.

As we watched one chimney in particular, which teetered back and forth, aiming right for us, the two other guys on the line with me left out of fear, but I held my ground. "The chimney won't fall like a tree, it will tip and crumble unable to reach us," I said to them as they ran. "When you signed up for this job, you took an oath to stand in harm's way," I yelled louder as the distance between us grew.

But man, that chimney was damned close to us!

The raging inferno must not reach the Edison, no matter what the cost, so I stood alone on a small flat roof and played my line on the fire through the dormer window of the burning building. Several ladder pipes, heavy appliances attached to the end of the aerial ladder just like you've seen on the news, had set up an effective water curtain, and my line was slowing the fire's interior progress in hopes that inside help would soon be arriving. A Lynn deputy chief followed our line up through the hotel and out a third floor window where the crew had jumped the three- or four-foot gap between buildings and onto the flat part of the fire building's roof. The chief was shocked to find a lone firefighter.

"How did you get over there?"

"We jumped the alley, sir"

"Where are the other men?"

"They were worried about that chimney over there," I said as I pointed behind myself, "so they bailed."

The chief, unable to view the chimney because he was standing in the window of the hotel, wasn't happy I was left alone.

"Stay right where you are and don't go in the fire building. I'll get some help for you."

With a nod of the head, I acknowledged the chief and held my ground. Just then, a ladder pipe dumped one thousand five hundred gallons per minute of water on me not knowing I was squeezed into no-man's-land. I didn't give an inch as the Lynn chief used his portable radio to call command.

"Have the ladder company in Edison Square reposition their ladder pipe, I have a firefighter back there!" The chief was reluctant to leave me alone, especially after what he just witnessed, but he knew he needed to get to the street if he was going to get more help. The radios were clogged with traffic. "Firefighter," the chief called out to me.

Looking like a drowned rat by now, I silently looked at him.

Again, the chief yelled emphatically, "Do not go in! I will be back."

I held my ground. I worried things may be deteriorating around me rapidly. Eventually, to my surprise, I saw a straight stream of water directed at the fire from inside the fire building. The chief had come through, help had arrived, and the fire could now be contained. Over the course of the next few hours, the Edison Hotel was saved, as was the city of Lynn. It would still take several more hours to put the fires out, some burning for days. As for the chimney, it never fell.

The Lynn deputy made his rounds well into the night. When he got back to the square, he told my captain what an outstanding job we had done. Pointing to me, he said, "That man is one hell of a firefighter." Though I wasn't looking for the compliment, I still remain quite proud to have heard it. In my head, I was thinking, *There are some country bumpkins who can play with the big boys when we have to.*

On the cover of the next month's most-read fire magazine was a picture of our engine in the middle of Edison Square completely stripped of all its equipment with the raging fire in the background.

The title on the cover was CONFLAGRATION IN LYNN, MASS.

Of all the trucks at the fire, I don't know why we made the cover. What I do know is, I've fought four major conflagrations in my career. Each and every time, I am proud to serve beside the brave men and woman in the fire service.

"It was a helluva battle to win," I concluded as I sat back and relaxed as though I'd just fought the fire all over again.

Meanwhile, unbeknownst to the enthralled audience, or the storyteller, Captain Jacobs had entered the room and was quietly listening from the doorway. Stiffening up, he'd heard enough. "Frieze, Lyons, come with me. We have work to do," he said angrily.

I just shook my head knowing the kids were in trouble.

"I told you two to stay away from Renaldi, not to be pumping up his ego. He's a fucking asshole."

"But, but, Captain," said Frieze.

Jacobs, who couldn't handle anyone who didn't immediately agree with him, quickly tensed as he rebuked the innocent young firefighter, "Don't you 'but, but, Captain,' me, Frieze. You just sit there with your mouth shut. You haven't been around here long enough to have an opinion. Don't be listening to Renaldi, or you'll be on my shit list."

I just shook my head in disgust and retreated to a phone in another room. I paged Liz 4663 64448 4812—good night with hugs and kisses—and then I retired to my cell.

This is something we had grown accustomed to. In anticipation, and an early riser, Liz would turn her pager on as soon as she got up. Faithfully, every morning, I rolled out of bed and paged her 4663 6676464. "I love receiving your early morning pages, Dom. They start each day off with something for me to look forward to, and they are so meaningful to me."

In a short time, we each became familiar with certain numeric orders. The number 4663 was *good* and 667464, *morning*. We became quite good at this. In the evening, it was 46639 64448—*good night*. Sometimes, we'd have to get out a pen and paper to figure out a message. But we'd developed our own unique way of communicating, and we loved it. Always, we looked forward to receiving an inexplicable page at any hour of the day. We were connected to each other.

Twenty minutes later, my pager went off—456838 4812—I love you with hugs and kisses.

I now had a smile on my face while locked in hell.

Chapter 21

Departing this magnificent ocean front retreat was difficult at best. As I took one final look at Liz's beach house, I promised myself I would return. The trip home was bittersweet, neither Liz nor I wanting to leave our forbidden paradise. In an effort to savor every last minute together, I sat with her in her car as the ferry pounded the choppy waters of Vineyard Sound back to Woods Hole late in the afternoon. Talk was quiet and mostly about the island and how short our time together there was. Conversation was a cornerstone of our friendship. I'd learned to get my words of encouragement in where I could, but I so enjoyed hearing her cohesive thoughts. I loved to just sit back and listen to her elaborate, but today, there wasn't much elaboration. We each took a few minutes to organize and separate our belongings for an easy parting back at my truck. By the time we disembarked at the terminal, we were both pretty exhausted; it had definitely been an action-packed overnight trip. As was our customary practice, I drove. The sun had now set on our enchanted time, and the atmosphere, though loving, was somber. Lost in thought as I drove, the highway was illuminated by the headlights. Each dash of the lane markings passed by just as quickly as the minutes of this glorious weekend. I'd wondered if, in fact, I would ever see that magic kingdom again.

Symbiotic was a word Liz used to describe our relationship more than a few times. Last night, we grew together in a gloriously loving way, and it continued on our ride home. We held hands with intertwined fingers as if our hands had grown as one, and we'd smile as Liz made calls on her cell phone. When she put her finger to her mouth to say, "Shhhh," I knew she was calling home. Every now and then, I'd make a funny comment about turning around and going back; at which, we both laughed just a little, knowing it wasn't possible. Traffic was light and trouble free. Before we knew it, I was pulling into the parking lot behind the fire station where I'd left my truck. It was dark back there, so before I got out of the car, we made out like teenagers as the car idled. One last quick display of affection culminating in "I love you."

It was early Sunday evening, and there were a lot of cars there, guys probably watching a Celtics or a Bruins game together; it was play-off time, which drew enhanced excitement. A few years back, the same would be true in our station; now, it might be the same, if the right group was working. Firefighting wasn't just a job; it was a lifestyle. A brotherhood. Guys would be paid to work about forty-two hours a week at the fire station, but in-between, they would hang around at least another forty. The camaraderie was unlike most other jobs. I loved it, I nurtured it, and I built on it. It reminded me of the necessary teamwork in athletics, the importance of working together and creating team unity.

I could also feel the team deriding in our own fire department. As I've said before, small towns relied on off-duty members coming back to assist during emergencies. In Coventry, each work group was becoming isolated with the department's new leadership, those in power anyway, failing to understand that all four work groups made up the entire team and not just a chosen few men. The chosen few remind me of a city gang of thugs. It was imperative other members from other groups came back to fill out a full assignment of firefighters—a full team to handle the emergency. This type of teamwork is uniquely different in that you couldn't just call a time-out because you didn't have enough players on the field.

Jacobs was the mastermind behind this "divide and conquer" attitude; Slayton taught him well. I remember one day while working on Jacobs's shift and being assigned to the desk because he didn't want me going out on calls. Putting an officer on the desk for that reason alone was in of itself a sign of divisiveness. We hit a fire that night. As the off-duty men came back, I hollered to two as they ran by the fire alarm office, "Wait for the third man, he's coming in right behind you." To which one of Jacobs's disciples, St. James, also the brother of the town selectman, said to the other, "Fuck Renaldi, he's an asshole!" Under Chief Wyatt, this would have been insubordination; and the man would be punished, at least, reprimanded for his actions. Today, this kind of attitude, so sickening, was so pervasive. In retrospect, I should have walked away. I should have concentrated on my outside interests and not worried so much about our department. I should have just sucked out a good paycheck and been done with it. I should have been a Bill Slayton. But it wasn't in my blood to abandon my town, and I certainly didn't have it in me to back down from Brewster, Slayton, and Jacobs.

"Come back down to earth, spaceman." Liz chuckled with that special giggle I loved so much. "I've got to go home."

"Jesus, where the hell did I just go?" I asked Liz. My pulse was rapid, and I was sweating, almost disoriented.

"Maybe back to Martha's Vineyard?" Liz questioned delightfully as though completely satisfied with her suggestion.

With a long face and a toned down voice, I replied, "No. No, I was a long, long way away from there, sweetheart!"

Refocusing with a broad wise-guy smile on my face, I gave Liz a second answer to her query. "Besides, if we went back into that world, I'd have to find a place for reentry." I got out of the car and retrieved my belongings from the backseat. I leaned back into the driver's window for one last kiss as Liz slid over from the passenger seat.

"C'mon, Dom, time to revert back to who we really are. Time to leave behind those happy people we were in Martha's Vineyard and become the gloomy people we are back in Coventry."

Feeling melancholy and a little blue, I said, "It doesn't have to be that way, Liz. I'm happy when we get together no matter where we are. Aren't you?"

"Of course, I am. But this weekend spoiled me. I finally found what I need, and I want more, but I know I can't have it."

"Oh yes, you can. You can if you want to, Liz."

Liz looked at me unhappily. "Dom, please don't go there. I gotta go," and she abruptly drove off.

Walking toward my truck, I stopped dead in my tracks. My blue pickup was covered with something—eggs, it looked like. As I got closer, it was indeed eggs. The entire windshield was covered with at least a dozen of them, coating the entire hood and windshield. It didn't just happen. It appeared to have baked in the sun, then overnight in cool weather of an early New England spring. I touched it; it was hard.

Shit, I said to myself as visions of Slayton and Jacobs flashed in my mind. *Goddamn sons of bitches.*

Trying to be cool and not show my anger, I went into the firehouse where I walked up to a group of men. With frustration in my voice, I asked anyone who would listen. "Does anybody here know what happened to that blue pickup out back?" A voice from the small crowd around the large screen TV turned and said, "Oh, the one with the eggs? Is that yours?"

I looked toward him. "Yeah, you know anything about how it got that way?"

With shrugging shoulders and shaking heads, the other firefighters all looked at one another, then back at me. Another guy said, "We all seen it, but none of us did it. Not that I know of. Everyone commented on it when they got here. Is it yours?"

I thought to myself, *Dumb question. Of course, it was mine. If it weren't, why would I be asking?* But I bit my tongue. If I were a police detective, I'd have told my partner as we walked away, "They know more than they're telling us. That guy who said, 'We all seen it,' do you think he did it?"

Slayton. He had to be behind this somehow. How he knew I had parked my truck here, God only knows. But firemen are a fraternity, and this was less than five miles away from Coventry. Now that I think about it, there was a loudmouth from this department who works for Slayton collecting trash. Slayton got around; he prided himself on that. As much as I despised him, I also knew that he had the gift of gab. He could talk the talk. But that's all he could do. As I've said before, he's a real Eddie Haskell type, all goody, goody two-shoes when it served his purposes but a cowardly backstabber. Slayton ran his own agenda. Always had, always would.

Asking for buckets of hot water, I cleaned up the mess. It was dark and a pain in the ass, but I got it cleaned. I'd work on it some more tomorrow.

Starting back home to my mundane life with Ruth, I thought about the egging as I drove the short distance up the highway. This incident wasn't over two married people sneaking away for the weekend; it was deeper than that, and some SOB was behind it. "What a perfect Dominic Renaldi ending to a wonderful experience." Despairingly, I shook my head. Inside, I seethed at Slayton, Brewster, and Jacobs. Somehow, somewhere, one of them, or all three of them were behind this; but for Liz's protection, I had to keep my mouth shut. If it was her husband behind the egging, I could understand, but I wasn't doing anything these three stooges hadn't done before me. Ah, that Coventry mentality—"It's okay for me to do it but not for you!" Sometimes, I wished I could line up the three of them and just drive my fist right though their faces. Oh to have lived in the Wild West.

Just before reaching home, I paged Liz 45683968—I love you. Though we would not communicate that night, I'm sure Liz loved receiving the page. In time, this message became the hallmark of our unusual system of communication. A few of our most frequently used messages got abbreviated, most always ending with 4812—a hugs and kisses.

When I got home, I noticed both David's and Ruth's cars were gone. Though I'd like to see David, he's the cream of the crop in our household, it was good that Ruth wasn't home. I could ease back in. Walking in the door, I was greeted by Stacy.

"Hi ya, Daddy-o," she said as she jumped up out of the chair, giving me a hug and a kiss.

Accepting her greeting warmly, I was happy with her innocent happiness. "Hi, sweetheart, where is everyone?"

"David's off playing his guitar at Rob's, Mom and Laura went to the chateau with Gram and Grampy. I had too much homework, so they're bringing something home for me."

"That a girl, sweetheart. Were you able to finish your work?"

"Yup. All done."

"Perfect! I'm going to jump in the shower before they get home."

"Okay, Daddy-o."

She was so innocent and pure, so unknowing of her father's demise. *How long could I survive this charade? Could I get my children to where they need to be before I fall?* It was becoming a desperate struggle for me.

Though not in any way did I want to involve my children in my indiscretion, it was perfect. I put my clothes away and started the laundry. I was able to shower and get myself back into this reality.

When Ruth and Laura got home, Laura also greeted me with a kiss and hug.

"Hi, Pops!" She was my full-of-life daughter—so much like a younger Liz—and she always made me laugh, to say nothing of being the best athlete in the family.

Ruth seemed happy too and actually gave me a kiss. It made me want to ask in sarcasm, "What, are you horny or something?" Later on, when she and I were alone, she seemed talkative, more outgoing and had great color to which I asked in fun, "Did you just get laid or something?" Ruth rolled those big blue eyes left and right with an intentional look of innocence, which is her trademark comeback if she wanted to playfully deny without speaking a word. I was a little taken by her reaction. Having lived with her for so long, it was telling. My bobcat hunting never even came up in conversation. Apparently, the both of us had other things on our minds. That night, Ruth and I had the hottest most passionate sex we've had in years brought on by her. Go figure. Having been where I'd been the night before, I did feel guilty, but what was I to do? It would have been quite unlike me to reject such an enticing offer from my still-attractive wife.

The following day, I went to the firehouse early, before the daily activities began, straight to the mechanic's shop/office where Slayton, Jacobs, and a few of their cronies had coffee with the mechanic before they all went off to work. It was a morning, almost cult-like, ritual you could set your watch by. The closer I got to the door, the more my anger built. Doing something to this little weasel would only get me in trouble. At this point, I didn't care.

I walked straight in the door. My eyes focused on Slayton. Guys separated like the Red Sea, allowing me to make a beeline straight for him. I blurted, "Well well well, if it isn't the little chicken with all the eggs!"

Jacobs smirked from the side of his mouth with a look of sickness in his eyes as if thinking, *Kill the little weasel. He'll be dead, you'll be in jail, and I'll be in control of this place.*

Slayton's face betrayed guilt; then there was fear, yes, but also a blank look only a consummate liar can portray. Slayton would make a helluva professional poker player.

Rather than run, Slayton stood for the show. He'd be safe amongst all his men. He'd have witnesses—the only time he ever showed anything that resembled bravery or valor staged in the perfect setting where a director could yell, "Cut," and it would all end. I grabbed him by his thin, little throat and hauled him up against the nearest wall. "What the hell did you do to my truck?"

Slayton's eyes bulged out of his head. I really wasn't grabbing him that tightly, but Slayton acted like he was in a hangman's noose. "What are you talking about?" he managed to squeeze out of his narrowed throat.

"My truck. You were behind my truck getting egged."

"You're crazy. I didn't do anything to you. Let me go."

A pair of hands grabbed me from behind, pulling me away from the smaller Slayton. "C'mon, Dominic, let him go." It was Ted, the mechanic, well liked by everybody—a real top-shelf kind of guy and a helluva firefighter.

"Slayton, don't ask me how, but I know you're behind my gear being stolen, I know you were behind the M-80, and I know it was you with the eggs. You better start thinking twice before you do something again."

"Dominic, you go cool off somewhere," the friendly mechanic admonished.

As I walked past Jacobs, I curtly said, "Wipe that smirk off your face. If he's Butch Cassidy, you're the Sundance Kid!" Jacobs wouldn't look at me. His distant eyes stared away. With that side-mouthed smirk of his, his face was showing his mindful, out-of-focus distortion. He knew I knew.

Slayton rubbed his neck like a bad actor involved in an accident, still feigning that he was nearly the victim of strangulation. "That guy needs serious mental help, and Brewster better do something about it. Did you guys see what he just did to me?"

Ted was pissed, and the only guy with enough courage to speak up. Looking at Slayton, he yelled, "You're ruining this place, and something very bad is going to happen if you don't wake the fuck up."

The other men looked on confused. Honest Abe, one of the veterans, this was the same firefighter who retreated from the rooftop in Lynn. He murmured to no one in particular, "Which side is winning, that's the team I'm on." Quietly, he turned to the younger guys and continued, "Something bad is brewing, this place has become a ticking time bomb."

Ted retorted, "It's our friends who are causing it."

Sadly, neither man would ever approach anybody about the deteriorating situation in the firehouse.

Jacobs sidled up to Slayton. "Now you're egging his truck? What are you, twelve years old?"

Slayton was regaining his composure. "I didn't do it."

For a moment, Jacobs thought he saw Slayton actually wink. "The hell you didn't."

"I didn't, Chief."

Jacobs interrupted, "Stop calling me chief, asshole."

Slayton's contrite smirk turned into an egotistical grin as he continued, "Maybe someone told our brothers down the road Renaldi wasn't a union man. Ya know, that twenty-four-hour tape machine in the fire alarm office holds a lot of secrets, Jacobs."

"Oh, so now you're breaking Federal Communications Commission [FCC] laws. That's a federal offense! What next, Slayton?"

"Tommy, Tommy, Tommy, we were just looking for an incident on the tapes. It was an emergency," Slayton said slyly, "and we accidentally came across some information. No laws were broken."

"What incident were you looking for?"

"Turned out to be nothing, Tommy. Don't worry about it."

Jacobs looked around to see if anyone else was listening to them, then spoke, "Okay, so explain this plan to me. You're going to harass Renaldi as if you were both in seventh grade, and then what?"

Gleefully, Slayton explained to Jacobs how bad the fire department was getting. "I don't know what you're talking about. But it sure looks like someone doesn't like our pal Renaldi. And lemme tell you, Brewster isn't doing a very good job of managing this place either. Guys are accusing each other of malicious mischief, I'm telling you, it's out of control, and he has no handle on it. Brewster's losing control of his department, Chief."

Angrily, Jacobs snorted, "Smart ass, I told you to stop calling me chief." Then he paused before asking, "How do you figure the selectmen give a shit about stuff like this? They could care less if we brawled here every night of the week just as long as we show up when the time comes. I've heard the chairman in the coffee shop talking like a big shot to that new member of the board who just came over from the school committee. 'All we care about is that the chief delivers the budget to us. How he runs his department is his business'—I've heard it straight from the horse's mouth, Bill. They're more clueless than Brewster is."

"Is that a fact? Well, maybe, but a fire starts with just a little flame, you know what I mean? And the flame gets higher and hotter and bigger. Pretty soon, it's an inferno, and you can't ignore it."

"I still don't get it."

Just then, the recently ordained newest member of the cult, young Lyons, came into the shop and made his way right over to where Slayton and Jacobs were standing.

Slayton looked eager to see him. "Hey, how was your weekend, stud?"

Lyons grinned from ear to ear. "Sweet. A very good weekend. Very hot, very nice. Everything I hoped it would be."

Slayton smiled back. "I told you it would be. Very good, my man, very good. Ah, to be young, virile, and handsome again like you. Yes yes yes. You've got the world on a string."

Lyons was still smiling broadly.

"What was that all about?" asked a confused Jacobs.

"It seems the young stud was with Renaldi's wife this weekend. Lyons is a good soldier in our army!" The satisfied Slayton smirked.

Jacobs smiled and shook his head up and down as if to say, "Yes, he is." Then they both laughed out loud.

* * *

When Brewster got to work that morning, he was greeted by one of Slayton's cronies, firefighter Dunn, who reported what had happened between Slayton and me, asking, "What are you going to do about Renaldi?"

In his usual, ineffectual manner, Brewster called Slayton to his office and talked to him about it.

Slayton pulled his best TV act out of the bag. "Chief, you heard what happened, I was just sitting there minding my own business, and this nut case comes busting into the room accusing me of egging his truck. Then he grabs me by the throat and threatens me. I tell ya, you've got to do something about Renaldi. He's lost it, and he's gonna hurt someone."

"Did you egg his truck?"

Unable to look Brewster in the eye, he stammered, "N . . . no, I didn't. Chief, you ask too many questions. It's best that you don't know any more than you have to. Gives you deniability." Then he laughed.

Brewster just cowered in helpless fashion as they exited his office, Brewster out of the building and Slayton to his men.

Jacobs tried to get a message from Slayton's eyes. "You're a scary guy."

Slayton smiled at the admiration. "I'll just tell you this, the selectmen will come down on this place if what goes on here starts to affect other members of the community, and they find out about it."

"What are you planning to do? Have us not answer fire calls?"

"Nothing like that. That would make you and me look bad now, wouldn't it? We can't have that, Jacobs!"

"What then?"

"As I said, just lay back and watch the fireworks."

* * *

When Brewster left his office, he came looking for me. He wasn't happy when he finally caught up with me at a job site. When I saw his cruiser pull up, it was quite obvious why he was there, so I went over to him before he was in earshot of anyone else.

"Lieutenant, what happened at the firehouse this morning?"

"Is this on the record or off the record, Chief?"

"Off the record, Dominic."

"Well, if you're going to continue to cover Slayton's ass, I'm going to have to take matters in my own hands, Chief. I'm not putting up with this shit anymore."

"I'm not covering Slayton's ass!"

"Chief, do you even know what 'cause and effect' means?"

"Of course, I do—what, you think I'm stupid or something?"

"Then why are you always punishing the effects instead of going after the causes?"

Brewster, in typical fashion, just lowered his head.

With contempt and growing disrespect for the chief—the man who used to be my captain, used to be my friend, and used to show so much promise—I took full advantage of talking off the record. "Of course, you're covering for Slayton. It's quite obvious you are, and everyone knows it! I don't know what he has on you. But it must be good!" Brewster's head dropped to his chin. "Look at you, Chief. You expect anyone to believe you when you hang your head like that? Look me in the eye and tell me you're not covering that little shithead's ass. Look at me, Chief, look at me and tell me."

Still unable to look me in the eye, Brewster whimpered, "I want to help you, Dom."

"There you go lying again!"

Brewster held up five fingers as he said, "I can count the number of friends I have at the firehouse on one hand, and you're one of them."

"Well, you can put your thumb down then."

"This is bullshit, Renaldi!"

"Yes, it is bullshit, and it's all coming from you and Slayton. Now if this meeting is still off the record, I'm through talking to you, and I have work to finish. Go back and play your firehouse games, Chief."

"No one is playing games, Lieutenant." The chief turned and walked to his cruiser. As he stood by his open door, he yelled his parting words to me, "Dominic, nobody is after you. I want you to get help. I'm available anytime to arrange it."

I walked closer toward him and said, "I'm not the one who needs the help. Look in a mirror, and when you do, see if you don't see a weak coward." I walked away in total disrespect of my chief.

A few days later, Slayton sat in his car just outside of Massachusetts General Hospital. His insignia allowed him to park in a restricted space. Not the fire identity, but the police insignia he displayed more prominently on his car. Yes, he was tight there too. It was this connection that gave him more power. *Ah, the entitlements of office,* he thought. It was a long, long wait, and he made the best of it by trying to figure out what FAGOTO meant. He made calls on his cell phone; he listened to the scanner, more interested in what the police were doing than what the fire department was doing. All the while, he stared at this one car, this one car with FAGOTO on its plate, parked in front of an impressive-looking reserved sign. But no sign could match the impressiveness of the car itself—a brand-new black Mercedes Benz CL600 coupe.

Slayton continued to stare. "Geez, this car cost more than I make in a year. I want to be seen in one of these cars." Slayton was becoming self-obsessed again. "I need a car like this if I'm going to become Coventry's fire chief. Oh yes, me becoming chief. Mental note to self, *Start figuring a way to get rid of Jacobs too*. "God, I want that car, I need that car."

Slayton became absorbed within himself. *Hello. I'm Chief Bill Slayton, and this is my brand-new Mercedes CL600. Maybe with all this, they'll vote me in as a member of the country club too. Oh, life would be grand.*

The guy who owned this car may have been book smart, but Slayton was street-smart. People misjudged him, and most lived to regret it. He'd screwed over more than a few people as the years went by, and they still haven't figured it out, suckers soothingly being drained of their money by charisma and charm. Just tell them what they want to hear, act the way they want you to act, then rob 'em blind. Slayton was a master craftsman at this.

I found him despicable and despised him from the time he first moved into town and started pushing around my younger troubled cousin, who also lived in the four-family home owned by my family. Slayton lived just down the street from us. It wasn't easy being smaller than most kids, and Slayton was the perfect little wise guy picking on the easy targets. As a big-ass athlete in high school, and being a few years older, I wanted to give Slayton a taste of his own medicine. So I pushed him around for how he treated my cousin.

Billy Slayton never forgot that, and he kept a list. When he grew up, he never got out of his parents' house. When he got married, the house was given to him. If you ever visited Slayton's house and used the upstairs bathroom, you'd find his list posted—Bill Slayton's shit list.

There were a number of names on it. Some he might never get a chance to get even with—guys who had moved away. Teachers who had died. Girls who had spurned him, laughed at his ineptness, got married, then changed their names. Slayton had his own mental problems—the little guy syndrome, the Irish curse. But my name stared back at him every day while he sat on his porcelain throne. Slayton had become obsessed with the thought of getting me as payback.

Finally, after hours of sitting in his car, Slayton observed a balding, white-haired tall thin man briskly walked out of the hospital toward the Mercedes.

"Dr. Temple?"

The man looked up.

"Dr. Samuel Temple?" Slayton asked again.

"What?" said Sam Temple, irritated as usual.

"I'm with the Coventry Fire Department."

It made Sam Temple stop for just a moment, wondering what the fire department wanted with him.

"We have a mutual interest. I think you should know something."

Chapter 22

Parking my pickup at the rear of the building next to all the other vehicles of the working-class, I eyeballed one of Slayton's dumpsters as I walked past it. It was blocking fire department access to the rear of the building. *Typical,* I thought as I shook my head in disbelief and displeasure. *Slayton is more interested in his trash business than he is in the fire department.* I had studied the comprehensive plans for this renovation for two weeks I was well prepared for the initial preconstruction meeting. The chief, as the authority having jurisdiction, was also invited to attend, but I doubted he'd show up. The only time he ever attended meetings of this type was if the Town Manager was present. Most all the heavy hitters in town government belonged to this club, and the chief knew there would be conflict here.

"Good morning, I'm Lieutenant Renaldi of the Coventry Fire Department," I said to the conservatively dressed but attractive receptionist.

"Good morning, sir," she said with a professional greeting. "Today's meeting will be in the upstairs conference room. You may go right up."

Ascending the flowing long stairs with an overlooking balcony, I walked into the conference room where the project manager for the Walsh Construction Company greeted me.

"Good morning, Lieutenant," he said while extending a handshake to me. The usual key players were in attendance—the general contractor and his subcontractors, the architect, the electrical engineer, all except Brewster. James Ackers represented the building owner and was also the chairman of the club's renovations committee. Mr. Ackers owned a software company and was new to town.

As I politely listened to the project manager concisely running the meeting, I couldn't help but wonder where Brewster was. "Why did he always leave me hanging at these meetings? These are his decisions to make, especially for renovations to this potentially dangerous building. Now is the time for the fire chief to show his strength. Now is the time for the fire department to apply the necessary leverage to ensure a safe and successful project while making sure all codes were adhered to and, perhaps, convince the building owner to make some upgrades not required by the code as well. I found it rather unusual the building inspector never attended these meetings either. He is, after all, designated the code enforcer. Why hadn't Brewster, the building inspector, and I sat down for our own preconstruction meeting to discuss a plan? Why didn't Brewster conduct monthly staff meetings to discuss game plans and vision for the department? Christ, even I did that with my little league coaches!

Finally, they got to me. "Do you have any concerns, Lieutenant?"

"Just a few basic concerns, thank you, sir."

Rising from my seat, I addressed the attendees in a quiet professional manner. "The chief has asked me to apologize for him not being present, too many meetings to attend in a given day." I tried to cover for the chief's ineptness. Continuing to address the meeting, I said, "This building is old and, over the years, has been renovated and added on to several times, surely you already know this. Because of the nature of this building, it is of enormous concern to the fire department going into this demolition phase."

I definitely had their attention, especially Acker's. "To the fullest extent possible, both the fire alarm system and the sprinkler system shall remain intact and be operational at the end of each workday." With heads nodding and slight mumbles, all present were acknowledging in the affirmative.

"In addition, all demolition debris shall be removed from the building on a daily basis." With stern emphasis, I concluded, "And ALL dumpsters shall be at least fifty feet from the building and shall not impede fire department access to any part of this building at any time."

The project manager interjected, "I assure you, Lieutenant, all of the aforementioned concerns are of equal concern to my company, and we shall strictly adhere to your very reasonable requests."

"Thank you, I am quite confident that you will."

Here comes the pitch where the fire department is asking for something beneficial but not required by the code. "Now I've noted that there are no plans to upgrade the existing fire alarm system with smoke detectors."

Defensively, the electrical engineer interrupted me, "The building code does not require us to upgrade the fire alarm system. In fact, we intentionally did not exceed the percentage threshold of renovation, which would have required us to do so."

"And how does one measure this threshold of a renovation, sir?" I asked rather sardonically, already knowing the answer.

The electrical engineer stumbled, "Well, the code is vague here, really, it is up to the building inspector to determine if the work falls under major renovations or simply renovations, Lieutenant,"

With no building inspector present, I couldn't hammer the point home.

Nonetheless, looking straight at the renovations committee chairman, I tried. "The fire department thinks it would be in the best interest of the building owner and the town if this building had smoke detection." As Mr. Ackers looked away, I concluded, "I believe, Mr. Ackers"—drawing his attention back to me—"if you checked with your insurance company, they would agree with me." This was quite sardonic as well. I knew it would box him in.

Sheepishly, Ackers responded, "I will bring it before the committee, Lieutenant Renaldi."

The meeting ended with handshakes and a "let's get started" attitude. As we all walked down the stairs and out the front door, I turned left and cut through the pool area while on my way to my truck. I paused for just a moment and couldn't help but to smile as I observed teenaged boys chatting with the girls at poolside. Whimsically, I wondered if they were planning a moonlit rendezvous. I smiled warmly as I walked through the back gate and into the rear parking lot.

Several days later, I received a call from Jim Ackers. "Hello, Lieutenant, nice to speak to you again."

I smelled a rat. Coventry men weren't nice to me unless it was to their advantage.

"I've checked with our insurance company, and they say smoke detectors will not save the club any money on our premiums, just the sprinkler system will, and we already have that in place." Mr. Ackers was quite victorious in voice.

I already knew this. But it was such a superficial answer that they continued digging a deeper hole for themselves. *Smoke detectors save lives, and sprinkler systems save buildings,* was on my mind. This expression was an insurance industry excuse to keep premiums high. But it made no sense to me at all.

I shot right back at Ackers with my weakest defense first, "Yes, that is what insurance companies say. However, I promise you that if there's a fire before, during, or after construction in your club, the sprinkler system may contain the fire to a $100,000 loss, but a smoke detection system would detect the same fire in its incipiency, and you may suffer only a $10,000 loss."

"I'm sorry, Mr. Renaldi. I took this committee over because they were already over budget, and I am not going to commit to more unnecessary spending."

Unnecessary spending? I thought to myself. Translated, it means, "I'm not going to look bad in front of the other club members. I have a reputation to uphold."

Unable to comprehend this way of thinking, I became abrupt when I defiantly asked, "Does your insurance company know about the illegal occupants living above the locker room? And if so, what do they say about that, Mr. Ackers?"

Suddenly, Ackers was not happy with me. He hemmed and hawed as if I wasn't supposed to know about the kitchen help living in their six-by-eight rooms with an old light fixture dangling from the ceiling by frayed cloth cords. Not in this town. "They don't actually live up there, they have rooms to go to on their breaks."

"Mr. Ackers, you don't know me from Adam, but I assure you, I have the best interest of the Coventry Country Club in mind when I say they do live up there. It is an illegal operation, and you people aren't even interested in providing them with a smoke detector for their safety. All you're concerned with is the insurance premium and cost overruns. What happens if there's a fatal fire over there, Mr. Ackers? A smoky, acrid fire not hot enough to set off the sprinkler system." I continued, "Your insurance company probably won't pay you a dime, and you'll have a million-dollar lawsuit on your hands, to say nothing of the very negative publicity the club will receive. In addition, you are putting the fire department at risk. And I am not going to let this happen, Mr. Ackers."

A very disconsolate chairman of renovations somberly closed with, "I'll look into it a little more thoroughly, Lieutenant Renaldi."

I hung up. Immediately, I walked into the chief's office and told him about the meeting at the club and the conversation I just had with its renovations chairman. In weak approval with lips moving and no words emitting, the chief acknowledged the professional correctness of my actions, the political incorrectness notwithstanding.

"This is why you need to be present at these meetings, Chief. These are your decisions to be made. With not so much as a sit down between you and me, I'm flying by the seat of my pants."

Brewster just looked down at the floor.

Within two days, the electrical engineer set up a meeting with me—to discuss the possibilities of upgrading the fire alarm system to include smoke detection.

Once word got around about the meeting, some of the men praised me for my ballsy action while Slayton steamed into Brewster's office. "Your friend has overstepped his bounds, Chief. Who runs this place anyway? What are you going to do about it?"

"What on earth are you talking about, Bill?" Brewster knew what he was talking about, but Slayton had caught him off guard.

"The country club called me about my dumpsters blocking rear access to the building, and they're not very happy with Renaldi for being so authoritative. If he screws up my reputation, or my contract with the club, Chief, there'll be hell to pay."

Brewster was caught between Slayton and me once again. He knew the codes supported my actions, and he knew Slayton was in tight at the club. Neutralized by Slayton's conflict of interest, Brewster simply told Slayton, "He's an asshole for doing what he did."

* * *

It's a cliché to say, "The heart wants what the heart wants," but many times, the heart wants more than is reasonable and feasible. The heart can also be greedy and selfish; like all things greedy and selfish, the heart does not rationally and realistically care or consider the ramifications of such actions.

Liz and I continued our affair. It was akin to an addiction to true love with one acting as the necessary "fix" for the other. It was hot. It was passionate. Faithfully, I continued to page Liz every morning 466366—good morning. Seeing each other every day had become a necessity, and we altered our schedules accordingly. The only breather we had were the two days I was at work. Even then, it wasn't completely isolated. We shared lunch together when I worked at station 2. Often, Liz would stop by for a chat in her car, and we talked on the phone two or three times a day while I was at work. We went to Boston for lunch, followed by a walk on Castle Island. Liz always stood aside as I paid my solemn respects to Firefighter Richard Green. His statue memorialized a fallen hero. For some unknown reason I felt a strong bond with him. Knowing I somehow was in touch with this man's spirit, Liz would wrap her arms around me from behind and place her head against my back if I stared too long at it. I ran errands with her three or four times a week, we shared coffee in every community east of the Housatonic River, or so it seemed. One of the more fun things we did was to make love everywhere imaginable—back roads on private country club property, parking lots, and fields. It was exhilarating to say the least.

Cold Springs Park was our favorite place to go. Often, we'd go for lunch, then go on a two- or three-mile walk. There was a grassy knoll overlooking a field, and it had a soft patch of green grass where the sun would shine warmly on us. Secluded from the path, it was a wonderful place to make love. With my toes dug into the hillside as I thrust uphill, sometimes I'd slip from the driving force, which made us laugh. The first time we made love there, I said to Liz, "This gives me a whole new meaning of 'the grassy knoll.'"

The pager worked well as our beacon day and night as we silently set time and location to meet. I found ways to have dinner at her house on a few occasions too; one time, there was the overdone risotto.

While Liz was cooking, I started a fire in the fireplace, which we sat in front of and shared a glass of wine. The ambiance was too much for both of us, so Liz climbed from her chair and on to my lap without touching the floor and was smiling the entire time. We kissed and slid to the floor where we made love in front of the fire as the risotto simmered on the burner. Afterward, Liz hurriedly stood naked in front of the stove while rescuing the risotto. Seeing her naked beauty cooking in the kitchen, all I could think was, *Geezus, I have to be on Fantasy Island.* She was something to behold.

A while later, as we ate dry risotto, we laughed about "no more having dessert before dinner!" We were in love, and we were addicted to it. Neither one, though, made a serious move toward ending the relationship we had with our own spouses. Not since the dream weekend on the Vineyard had we hinted at it only obliquely, occasionally saying something on the order of, "I wish it could always be like this," or "I wish we didn't have to sneak around." But that would be the end of it. I never understood Liz's reasons, but I clearly knew my only reasons for staying married—David, Stacy, and Laura.

Yes, I agree, it isn't always wisest to stay together for the children's sake; but in this case, it seemed to be. There wasn't enough money to sustain everyone and who knew what type of a school system our children would end up in. If I divorced Ruth now, it would uproot these wonderful kids from a system that, though not socially kind to them, would propel them into higher education and a far better path for them in the long run. Coventry would help build mental toughness in them through the obnoxious behavior of its entitled children. Communication, nurturing, commitment, and love from their parents would help sooth their wounds and get them through the pain of being looked down on by entitled children of privilege. A father's seemingly pointless dissertations about life, hard work, about the haves and have-nots, about staying strong, and how "in the long run you will be far better for it" may show fruition someday. "You might not understand what I'm saying until you're eighteen, twenty-five, or maybe not until you have children of your own, but I beg of you to listen to me and trust me on this."

Though borderline dysfunctional, the family had to stay together right where we were. Many times, I felt as if a father speaking to his children from his deathbed. Surely, something was bound to bring this game of Russian roulette to a head.

Liz always expressed her concern for my position in life, telling me I needed to get out of both my marriage and my job. As correct as she may have been, backing out was not an option, and I frustrated her with my answer. "As difficult as my situation may be, my children need a foundation from which to build a future, and this is the only way I can set the footing under that foundation." To make my point perfectly clear to Liz, I concluded, "I will turn into the dirt beneath their feet to accomplish this if need be. My children will not fall!"

Caught in a vicious cycle of life, the firehouse was my living, and Liz Temple was my savior. One was grinding me up from the outside while the other was eating me away from the inside. I knew I was falling and that I had no choice but to suck it up and hold my ground until I could safely set my children down.

Very sadly, Ruth never understood what was happening to me. Had she, we may have made it together, and I definitely would not have strayed. She lived in a Cinderella world that I could not breach. A world of make believe where a magic wand made everything right. When we were first married, I did try talking to her, but all she'd say was, "You'll find a way."

I remember one day in particular. I was asking Ruth for her help in financially supporting the household. I was trying to make my point in quite an "out of the box" way since nothing else had worked. Getting down on my knees and crossing my fingers in prayer, I implored to Ruth, "I cannot do this alone, and I need your help."

To which she said her standard line, "Oh, you'll find a way."

I seemed to have more of a conscience about publicly embarrassing Ruth than Liz felt toward her husband. Rarely did I talk at all about Ruth to Liz, but Liz frequently complained to me about Sam.

"He's a control freak. Crazy as it sounds, I used to admire it. He was the most powerful man I'd ever met. All the other boys in my life tiptoed around me, so afraid they'd lose me. Sam let me know who was boss right from the start. He wanted me, no question about that. But I always knew it would be on his terms."

"I have a hard time picturing you agreeing to that."

"Me too. I was a different person when I met him. Or maybe it was just how different he was. I don't know if this makes much sense, but being dominated by a man who dominated everyone else around him made me feel more powerful around others. After marrying Sam, I would go into department stores or car dealerships and treat everyone the way Sam treated me. I learned that from him. There was a pecking order—Sam was God, and I was number two. Everyone else was below us."

I never said it, but in my mind, I found talk like that to be the least attractive thing about her. I'd spent my life around women like that, rich women who felt superior to everyone else. The people who worked in the sales or service businesses of Coventry were far poorer than the people they served. Both parties knew that going in. For the customer to lord it over the help even more was simply cruel. I'm glad I never saw that side of Liz.

Some people get sloppy and careless with a secret over time. Liz and I were quite the opposite. The longer our affair went on, the more ways we imagined we could get caught. We plugged up holes as we discovered them, getting downright paranoid that someday what we had could all come crumbling down.

And so, it did not strike me as totally odd when I received a page—17 200, the office building by the Mass Pike at 2:00 p.m. Usually, when we met there, we had already discussed our schedules and knew we had enough time for a trip to an out-of-town destination. Yet there were other times when we simply wanted a chance to see each other and talk. By this time, there was no coyness or confusion about things. We were in love, and people in love do things like that.

I sent a return page—65, OK.

The agreed upon hour had arrived, and as I pulled up in my blue pickup, I saw Liz's familiar gold Lexus SUV. My mood elevated like that of a schoolboy, and my adrenaline flowed like when I got a fire call. I pulled up behind her and got out. Her car door opened. Out stepped Sam Temple.

I stopped dead in my tracks. I stared at the man and knew immediately who he was. Although we had never officially met, I'd seen pictures of him around his house.

Sam Temple glared at me through fighter's eyes. As I tried digesting the scene, frozen like a statue but lucid enough to move quickly if need be, the other door of the Lexus opened. Liz got out. My full attention was drawn to sizing her up. Her blond hair was a shock of sunshine here in my darkest moment, but the despair on her face worried me, and she had been crying. She didn't look beaten; I was more concerned for her life and her not making it through the night. Temple, who had been staring at me, quickly switched his attentions to Liz and then back to me. Back and forth, back and forth, until he finally disrespectfully said, "Get back in the car, you whore."

Silently, she meekly obeyed.

"So you're the stud."

My throat was dry and my mind a mess. I didn't want to give the doctor a harder time than he was already going through, but I couldn't give an inch. I had to push back. "No, I'm not the stud, I'm Liz's friend."

"I brought her along because I wanted to be sure. I'm sure now. It's written all over your face, you uneducated loser, and the little whore's face too. So you're the guy who's been screwing my wife." Then there was silence as he looked me up and down.

Physically, Sam Temple was too weak to fistfight, but I remained poised for a sudden move. *Watch his hands, don't let him reach for anything.* I glanced around to make sure others weren't going to jump me from behind. Was this going to be a fight? If I'd had been in his shoes, that's certainly how I would have gone down; then again, it would have been over by now.

"What's the matter? Cat got your tongue, you loser?"

"Ball appears to be in your court, Doctor. Cat got your tongue?"

"Dominic Renaldi. Your wife's name is Ruth. Your children's names are David, Stacy, and Laura."

"This is an adult matter. you leave my children out of this." Not even the Mafia involved the wife and certainly not the children.

"Oh, like you stayed away from mine."

Now I was getting angry. "If you dare do anything to my kids"—pointing my finger at the doctor—"I will . . ." Then I paused before threatening him. "You hear me?"

"You don't scare me."

"I'm not trying to scare you, just telling you to stay away from my children, or you'll regret it."

"Are you threatening me? Well, then, hit me, why don't you? Go ahead. Make my day. It's broad daylight. People are in that building behind you there. I'm sure someone up there is looking out of his or her window. Let's give them a show. I'll have you arrested for that."

"Wouldn't you love to have me arrested, Doctor? Well, I'm not going to fall into the trap. I don't believe I threatened you at all, Doctor. Wouldn't I be the brave hero kicking the shit out of a weak sixty-year-old doctor. How macho of me."

"How much money do you have, Mr. Renaldi? Can you afford a good attorney? 'Cause I can. I can get anyone I want. And I will. I will take you down for ruining my marriage."

"I didn't ruin your marriage, you did. I just came along at the right time to pick up the broken pieces of a pained woman and helped her back together again. And she did the same for me."

Sam Temple was less than understanding and rather pissed I'd just hit a nerve.

"I will ruin you, Renaldi, and it will be slow and painful."

Ah, the arrogant sound of money talking. "I'm already ruined, Dr. Temple. Go ahead," I countered.

"I'll ruin you even more. Let me explain to you, Renaldi. Here's what's going to happen. You've just seen the last of my wife. I hope you enjoyed it. Next, I will be going to see *your* wife to let her know what I know. Then I'm going to see your boss, you're a fireman, aren't you? As a citizen of this town, I don't appreciate my civil servants fucking my wife while I'm at work. That's not what I pay you for."

"Stop right there. Hold it. I'll be the one to talk to my wife. She should hear it from me."

Temple chuckled irreverently. "Yeah right. Like I can trust you."

Feisty Liz had gotten out of the car and was now standing next to her husband, unsure of what he might do.

"I'm a man of my word, Temple. She will hear it from me first," I said angrily.

"What makes you think you have any bargaining position on anything?"

Liz interceded, "Sam, if that's what Dom said, then that's what he's going to do. At least give him that much."

"I'll give you until ten o'clock tonight, then I'm calling your wife. Now get out of here, you no-good loser!"

Looking directly at Liz with concern for her safety, I said, "I'm not leaving until I'm sure you'll be okay, Liz."

Temple got infuriated and moved toward me in anger. I so hoped he would start a fight.

Suddenly, Liz jumped right in between us, so feisty and quick. "Stop it. The both of you."

"You're through with my wife, Renaldi."

"That may be so, but you are too, and I don't trust you anymore than you trust me. I'm not leaving until I know she'll be safe."

"I'll be fine, Dom, please, just go."

"I'm worried about what he may do to you."

"I'll be fine. He won't hurt me, not here. He's goading you."

"Page me later, so I know you're okay, please?" Liz acknowledged with her eyes.

As Liz got back into the car, I shouted to him, "That's right, you bastard, I am much more than just a stud. I am your wife's soul mate and her confidant!" He never heard my words, but then again, he wouldn't have heard them if I were six inches away. Men of ego and arrogance only hear themselves.

As he pulled away, I stared, trying to see if I could make out Liz through the tinted windows; but it was useless. I was concerned for her well-being, but I now had my own fires to put out. For an indeterminable length of time, I simply stood there, pacing around aimlessly, trying to gather my thoughts. *My life is over. No longer would I be living under the same roof with my children. Would they be living under the same roof they've grown to call home? God, that scared me. Could they continue in the same school system that had taken them this far?* If I reacted this way in a fire, the flag would be at half-mast and the firefighters would be wearing black bands over their badges.

Hurting the ego of a man like Temple was akin to poking a wounded lion with a sharp stick as you stood between it and a raw piece of meat. The unwritten rules of Coventry's power game did not require Sam Temple to look into the mirror in self-assessment but, rather, to destroy the person who hurt his ego. His wife's pain would never be considered in the equation. Temple will get to my chief, and he will get to the selectmen. This cannot be good! But for my children's safety, the worst had happened; my magical odyssey with Liz was over, and that unraveled me. I was suddenly alone, lost and desperately seeking an anchor to ground me.

Finally, I cloaked myself in determination to keep to my word and tell Ruth the entire, sordid truth. We weren't happy together. Maybe this was fate pushing us in the long over due direction of positive change. Like a heavyweight boxer who just took one in the chin, I staggered about only able to focus on one issue at a time. Ruth was number one at the moment. It was time to tell my wife I'd been having an affair. Suddenly, the thought of her pain made me feel sick. I worried about Ruth; this scenario just did not fit into her closed little world. How will she handle Temple? I worried for her. I know, I know, I know. I should have thought about that way back when this whole thing started.

It was time to come clean, and I had but a few hours to do it.

Chapter 23

With shaken resiliency and feeling like a player on the way to defeat, I pulled up in front of the house. This is it. Here comes the divorce. David, Stacy, and Laura, how would they react? More importantly, how will they survive? What about Ruth? She had suffered enough already; I didn't wish for her to suffer more because of my indiscretion. All these questions surfaced, coming at me like machinegun fire. There's only one day in my life that comes close to how I'm feeling right now.

For those of us in emergency services who have faced the death of others many times over, we were accustomed to knowing either "we did the best we could," or it was simply "their time to go." Death is a part of life, a part that I coldly accepted. But sometimes, death is unjust and torturous. I'm sure I speak for all when I say, especially when it comes to the death of a child.

Unlike schoolteachers, who epitomize true, humane characteristics through their tireless dedication, firefighters, cops, and soldiers seem to lose their human identity as they don their anonymous uniforms for battle. They seem to become immortal and invincible in their quest for victory on the battlefield. The human aspect so internalized, they ultimately remain faceless as they perform their heroic duties. As stoic warriors, we are never allowed to show emotion. Tears are out of character for these heroes. "Don't let anyone see your tears." Surely, this wouldn't be cool.

Bullshit! Of course, we were human beings, human beings who had emotions, human beings who did have the right to show grief, compassion, and understanding toward fellow man. Brewster must have had his head up his ass when he told me, "That's your problem, Dom, you're too emotional." In my eyes, having emotion was quite manly as well as healthy.

Several years prior, we responded to a frantic call of an automobile accident with serious injury. The cops were hollering to "step on it," never a good sign. Gutless Slayton would later say, "I was just down the street from the accident, but after hearing the police on my scanner, I avoided the accident and shot right home to make sure my family was okay." He could never be the first to arrive on the scene of an emergency. He was a no-good piece of gutless shit who never stood up to do the job.

First to arrive on scene, we found devastating wreckage. Passersby were screaming. Women covered their faces. A mother was wailing in agonized grief, "My daughter. My daughter." Traffic had stopped on the busy road as the mangled car straddled the yellow line, and the dump truck had careened over the embankment and came to rest overturned; its rear dual axle detached and looked very ominous in the middle of the road. Nobody went near the car. Another bad sign. I grabbed the first-aid kit and sized up the scene as I ran toward the car. There was smoke coming from under the hood and no time to worry about it. Fire was not the most pressing issue at the moment.

The entire left side of the car was twisted and torn apart with a child's car seat, dislodged in the backseat. No child in it. All mental notes. Snapshots began to click in my brain later to be conveyed to the hospital staff. When I reached the left rear window, I was horrified. On the seat lay an unconscious little girl of about five years old. Her head propped against the back of the seat with her chin forced to her chest, her white T-shirt saturated and dripping bright red blood. She had arterial bleeding from somewhere, and her brain matter was on the back of the seat. She was gasping for air. The bottoms of her feet were pushed together as her legs limply fell open, her face angelic, yet the scene was grotesque. The automatic blinders went on as I fearlessly climbed into a world of death and destruction. This was called the golden hour, the time from which a person was first injured until the end of time a hospital team has to save the life—now reduced to nanoseconds. Some guy, redhead with a beard, I'll never forget his face, flashed a badge through the window and told me he was an off-duty firefighter/EMT from another town. He must have been a callman somewhere, no beards allowed. Taking his word for it, I asked him to check under the hood for my partner and me. As I checked for a pulse, I instructed my partner to get the oxygen and portable suction from the ambulance. "DOUBLE TIME IT!"

A couple of our guys showed up off duty and pitched in. Never having enough hands, this was always a welcoming sight. One helped the bearded volunteer with the hood while another readied the ambulance for rapid departure as my partner and I diligently labored in the backseat of despair.

The little girl's pulse was rapid and weak, erratically all over the map; her pupils were fixed and dilated. This poor little angel wasn't going to make it. I knew it. We saturated her face with oxygen in hopes that she might be able to take in a little by any means possible as I suctioned the blood and other matter from her throat in hopes of maintaining an airway. The volunteer firefighter reported all was okay under the hood and that they'd disconnected the battery as a precaution. Thanking him without looking, I continued my focus on the little girl. I could, however, subconsciously put to rest my concerns of a flash fire sneaking in on us. Further protocol would suggest full immobilization, but surely, we didn't have time for that, so I instructed my partner to hold her head in traction as we transitioned her onto the short backboard and into the waiting ambulance. This is BTLS—basic trauma life support—a glorified expression that really means, "You're screwed, and you know it, get to the hospital as quickly as you can."

All the while, I frantically worked on this girl as I begged her, "Don't die on me, sweetheart, please don't die on me." Her very shallow breathing would come and go, and I just knew that one of these times it was going to go and not come back. The nearest hospital was about three miles away.

As I mentioned before, when it came to children, emergency services responded with a special kind of care drawn from their deepest, rarely seen, and very protected passions. Someone, probably the Coventry police, had gotten to the Cromwell Police Department, and they had all intersections stopped by police allowing us immediate passage to the emergency entrance driveway at the Cromwell Hospital. The situation in the back of the ambulance was grave. We were losing this little girl, and she was taking a part of me with her. As we climbed the hilly emergency entrance, she breathed her last breath, that sudden gasp defining life's final moment, which we'd heard so many unemotional times in the past. In my heart, I knew she'd just died, and there wasn't a fucking thing I could do to change it. In retrospect, I wish I had just held her in hopes she would feel wrapped in the arms of someone who cared. With the absence of a loved one, perhaps the tender touch might have helped her slip away more peacefully.

As the ambulance's rear door flew open, a massive medical team greeted us, prepared to take whatever action was necessary to save this little innocent life. My partner continued to hold traction, and I continued to work on her as we transferred care to the hospital team. Being the last to exit, but still the one tied closest to her, I clearly and distinctly said, "She just died." No one wanted to hear it. With a "we can do this" attitude, they rushed her into the emergency room where doctors hastily called out instructions, and their support teams magnificently responded with dedicated professionalism and compassion. It was commonplace for the attending EMT to interact with the medical team telling of the mechanism of injury, damage to the car, and obviously what care we'd rendered at the scene. As the lead doctor called for IVs, blood transfusions, x-rays, and CAT scans, they found "no pulse, begin CPR," so prepared and willing to do whatever it took to save this precious life.

Curtly, I said, "Doctor, look at the back of her head before you go too far." My partner's hands had obscured the doctor's view of her small injured head as she lay supine on the short board.

With a slight look of reluctance, the doctor looked straight into my welled eyes before taking an immediate look, then simply said, "Stop. Everybody stop what you are doing." The room fell deafeningly silent; the only sound being heard was that of straight-line warning from the heart monitor. The official end had arrived, the fight was over, and this brave little girl was pronounced dead. Nurses wept as the doctors wrestled with their very difficult decision. I looked at my partner. We stared in silence. After a moment, slowly, quietly, we began gathering our equipment and left without uttering a word.

To Brewster's credit, he consoled me back at the firehouse. "I know how much you love children, Dominic. This must be very difficult for you."

Up until today, that had been the most difficult thing I had had to deal with in my life. Suddenly, all those emotions came roaring back. Now I had to face the music, and I had trouble imagining Ruth's pain caused by my action. If only it was a few years from now as I had hoped with the kids all grown up and able to make a better adjustment; then perhaps Liz might still be in my life. What perfect timing that would have been.

I was sitting in my truck as the passenger side door suddenly opened. Ruth got in. Jesus, I was startled. My heart pounded, and suddenly, I was short of breath. Ruth looked upset, which was not particularly unusual. She seemed blue, and I noticed her eyes were red, perhaps from crying.

"What's wrong?"

Ruth just looked at me hurt but said nothing. I fidgeted, waiting for an answer. Something was up; something wasn't right, and I got very nervous. "Are the kids okay?" I asked in desperation.

Finally, she said, "Yes, they're fine."

Something was very wrong with Ruth, and it really worried me. I still had to confess.

Neither of us seemed willing to be the first to talk. Ruth kept looking down at her lap, saying nothing. I was staring above the steering wheel, looking off into the distance, trying to gather up the courage to make my speech—a speech that would change the rest of our natural lives.

"I have something to talk to you about," I said slowly.

"I know," Ruth said it so calmly, almost as a whisper.

"What?"

"Go on. Tell me."

"I've been with someone else."

"Yes, I know, Dominic," again, Ruth literally whispered.

"I'm sorry. I didn't mean to hurt you. But things between you and me haven't been good for a while, not for a very long while. It just happened."

"Was it just sex?"

I thought for a moment. This was not the reaction I expected. It was if she already . . . "Did you know?"

Ruth tried to avoid answering, looking out of her side window, showing me the back of her head in silence. Finally, she turned back toward me. "Yes."

"How? When?"

Ruth looked back down at her lap, tears welling in her eyes. "Earlier today."

I got agitated. "Did you have a visitor? Did someone come by?"

"No, he called."

"Who called?"

"The doctor did."

"What did he say, what did he say exactly?"

"He said he'd been contacted by one of the better, more honorable firemen, who felt he should know about you and his wife."

Fucking sons of the bitches! I thought. "When did he call?"

"This morning."

"The doctor called you this morning?" I said angrily. Much as I wanted the details, this was all somewhat off topic. Ruth knew I'd been having an affair. That was the headline.

"Yes."

The bastard. The fucking bastard. He'd made me beg, and I'd been begging for something the doctor couldn't even deliver, yet he made me beg anyhow. God, he was exactly the controlling nightmare that Liz had told me he was.

"Who was the firefighter?"

"It doesn't matter, Dom. When he told me that, it hit me, like a lightbulb had just gone off in my mind. Everything suddenly became crystal clear to me. Your constant anger about work, your sudden disinterest in the department, a job you loved so much, and the telltale sign that something was wrong, your distancing yourself from the kids. I should have seen it."

"I'm sorry, Ruth. I'm sorry for you, and I'm sorry for the kids. I never wanted you to hear this from anyone else. I . . . I wanted to tell you myself. I never wanted to embarrass you, and I never wanted to hurt you." I paused for a moment. "Do the kids know?"

"Yes, I told them when they got home from school and asked for them not to disturb us when you got home."

With that, Ruth sobbed.

"I'm sorry, Ruth. I'm so, so sorry."

"There's more to it."

"What do you mean?"

"I'm sorry too."

I straightened up a little. "You have nothing to be sorry for, Ruth. This is all my fault, and I'll do whatever you want me to do. I'll move out, I'll leave tonight. You want to divorce me, I understand. Whatever you want, I'll do!"

Ruth continued seemingly out of context, "You leave me alone a lot."

"Yeah, what's that got to do with anything here?" I politely asked in confusion.

"I don't like to be alone all the time. I get lonely. I missed being with someone. I miss the way we used to be."

"I do too, Ruth. I always thought we were a perfect match."

"No, I'm sorry!" Ruth yelled. Ruth's face was an ugly, curled up, red mess with tears running down her cheeks as if I'd been pounding her with my fists for a few rounds. I didn't know what to say, what to do, or where this was going.

"Ben Lyons." Then silence.

"What about Lyons? Was he the one who told the doctor?"

"I always told you he was cute." Ruth's eyes rolled left and right with that look of innocence, and then she reached into the glove box for tissue to wipe her eyes as she tried to collect herself. "Ben Lyons. Me and Ben Lyons, Dom." Ruth was cutting her sentences short.

"You've been thinking about Lyons?"

"Thinking about? Don't you understand what I'm telling you, Dom? You and Dr. Temple's wife. Me and Ben. We were all doing the same thing."

This was the last thing I expected. I sat stunned while shaking my head. First, getting caught by Temple, then finding out Temple had told Ruth even before confronting me. Now this—Ruth having an affair with young Lyons. I focused on Lyons. Handsome kid. Always liked Ruth, and Ruth always liked him. She said way too many times, "I'd like to show Ben a thing or two." I actually liked him pretty much although we'd sort of drifted apart in recent months. I always thought that was Slayton and Jacobs pressuring him.

"So you're having an affair with Lyons." Suddenly, the lightbulb went off in my head too.

Ruth harrumphed, "It never really developed into a full-blown affair like you had. I wanted it to continue, but Ben wanted to stop, said he needed to think about his job. About his career. About his future.

"What about you and the doctor's wife?"

My shoulders contracted, and now I too looked down in my lap. "We've gone this far, Ruth, I'm going to tell you the truth, and it may be painful."

"Continue please!" Ruth said in a way that made me think she really did want to now hear it all.

"It wasn't just sex, and it's been going on for a while. I love Liz very much." God, I got it out. I actually told my wife I was in love with another woman! Ruth took several short shallow, stuttering breaths but seemed to take it much better than I anticipated. "I'm sorry, Ruth. I'm not asking for your forgiveness. That would be too much to ask for. I've been so miserable for so long, and you just never understood. When I tried talking to you about it, you just wouldn't believe me. You never comprehended what was happening to me, so I gave up. You never wanted to leave that Cinderella world. You still don't. I never even told you Chief Wyatt had asked me to be the next chief. Then suddenly shit began happening to me." My voice trailed off.

Ruth interrupted me, "Like what?"

"Slayton blew my eardrums out with an M-80 in the firehouse, no investigation. I deliver that baby, and my gear begins to disappear, no investigation, but I know Slayton's behind it. Lyons showing Slayton and Jacobs how to replay my personal calls on the twenty-four-hour tapes. My truck gets egged, and I know Slayton was behind that too. Remember Little Billy Slayton, Ruth? You were with him once. I'm sorry for venting here, but you've been sleeping with the enemy for a long, long time. And you never understood it. You never understood their ulterior motives. I can just picture the conversation now—Slayton, Jacobs, and Lyons with Slayton saying to Lyons, 'Go ahead, you can fuck her.' Lyons saying, 'I can do that, I can do that,' the good little Eagle Scout that he is. Then Slayton and Jacobs praising him. And Lyons smiling broadly in triumph. There's so much you didn't know. Nor did you ever want to hear. You were always saying, 'No, Ben wouldn't do that. Not Benny.' Well, Ben would do that, and Ben did do that. For the same reason Slayton did it to you years ago. Short of our children, you've never been on my side, and I was falling. I understand how unhappy you are, and I understand why you strayed. I strayed for the same reasons. The only difference is my extramarital affair caught fire, and you got burned in yours. You were their most valuable player, Ruth. I'm sorry for causing you pain here, but these are the cold, hard facts of life. I was in desperate need of support, and I wasn't getting any from you. You were a pawn on their chessboard, Ruth, and I had no place to turn."

I relaxed a little and gathered my thoughts. The truth was hard for her, but she seemed to accept it.

"Then Liz came along at just the right time to lift me up and take me away from all my troubles. She made me feel good again, and she was fun. She immediately understood my dilemma and soothed the wounds. She was so keen and intuitive. Isn't it ironic? Liz always said, 'Watch out for Lyons, I don't trust him at all.' And I naively said, 'He's okay.' I'm not saying this to blame it all on you or to hurt you or to turn the tables here, Ruth. All of this is my fault. And I'm sorry for the apparent rancor toward you, but you need to know how all that happened and why. You can't tell me you haven't been miserable too. I carried that burden on my shoulders knowing I was the cause. It too was crushing me, Ruth. When I came home to you, I immediately felt drained, guilty for that long, sad look on your face, and it hurt very badly. I'd escaped to Liz and found calmness. I want you to know that I didn't just go out looking for a woman to have sex with behind your back. And I certainly didn't do this to cause you pain, and I'm sorry that I have. Inexplicably, Liz and I came together. It's as simple as that. We met by fate, and we connected instantly. We could answer each other's question before it was even asked. She had her own difficulties in her marriage, and we became two ships huddled and tightly tethered together in the eye of the storm where we worked as one. I can't be anymore honest than that."

The weight of the world had been lifted from my shoulders, and I felt at ease. "Go ahead, Ruth, it's your turn to chastise me, and well you should."

"I thought, though, we'd make it," said Ruth philosophically.

I knew I'd just spoken, and now was the time to sit and listen. But this was the basis of the problem—Ruth didn't talk; she just didn't understand life outside of her world.

"How could we make it, Ruth? We were stuck in the mud, too anchored down. Did you really think anything was going to change? I'm not trying to start a fight. And your parents are wonderful people, but it's always been you and your parents, you and the kids and your parents, you and the pets and the kids and your parents. I was on the outside looking in to your little make-believe world, Ruth. You didn't ever talk about doing things differently, trying out new things, getting a job or a career. Whatever our life has been like, this is how it would probably continue to be until all the kids were out of the house. And then what? It's not like they're the reason we're unhappy."

"No, they're not. If I had to say one thing about you, Dom, it's that you're a good father."

"And you're a good mother. Many times, I've thought the good Lord put us together just to produce wonderful children. Certainly, we have them to be proud of, Ruth."

"So now what?"

"What about you and Lyons, is he the one for you?"

Ruth just shook her head in silence.

"What do you mean by that?"

"It was sex, Dom, nothing more. I was frustrated. He made me feel attractive, and he convinced me it was all right."

"You are attractive."

"Yeah, that's why you took up with the doctor's wife."

"Liz."

"I don't want to know her name. I don't want to know anything more about her. Maybe you're into that, but I'm not. Let me live in blissful ignorance. I prefer it that way. You tell me I live in my own little world, well, look what happens when I leave it."

"I fully understand your leaving your world for an extramarital affair, Ruth, and it doesn't surprise me it was with Lyons. How long has it been going on with you and him?"

"Not long. Not long at all. Just a few times."

"So why are you telling me?"

"As I said, when the doctor called me today, everything just seemed to fall into place. And the lightbulb went off in my head, Slayton, Lyons, your distancing from everything. It all suddenly made sense to me, and you've been saying it for years."

"He's single. Are you two going to try to make a go of it?"

Ruth harrumphed again. "Dom, it was not a love affair. And furthermore, it's over. To say it was purely physical is an overstatement, and I don't want to talk about it ever again." Ruth began to cry.

"Maybe I'm a glutton for punishment, but was he good in bed?"

Ruth pursed her lips while concluding, "There was no passion to it at all. This is what I mean. It all makes sense now. Lyons wasn't making love to me. He was fucking you, Dominic."

Chapter 24

A few days had now passed since that unforgettable day in the parking lot. I hadn't heard from Liz. *Surely I'd seen the last of her,* was what I thought; however, I was still worried about what that control freak of a husband would do next. While working at station 2, I received a page about 9:00 p.m. Thinking it was Liz, hoping it was Liz—after all no one else paged me—I excitedly looked to the pager. It was 911 and my home phone number.

Shit, this can't be good! Ruth had never paged me, now a 911? I quickly called home, and Ruth answered on the first ring.

"Dr. Temple just called my parents and told them about you and his wife."

Oh fuck!" I sat back in the swivel chair at the watch desk. As my head fell back, I closed my eyes and asked, "What did he say?"

"My mother was too stunned. He didn't say much, just enough to worry my parents and show how sick of a man he is. Great, now my parents are involved."

"I'm sorry, Ruth. I'll find a way to put a stop to this."

"Please do so before they find out about me too. GREAT, now my parents will find out about me too!" Rightfully upset, Ruth hung up the phone.

Now I'm irate. This man has got to be stopped. I paged Liz 911 with the phone number to station 2. Knowing what had happened, she called me right back.

"Your husband just called my in-laws."

"I know he did. We can't talk, Dom, I don't know if he has the line tapped or what he might do. I tried talking him out of it, but he's obsessed with letting the whole damned world know what happened. He's going to call Brewster next. I'll try to stop that from happening. He's going to ruin you, Dominic."

"Yeah, no shit! You okay?"

"I'm . . . things are difficult, but I'm okay. I love you, Dom, bye."

"I love you too, Liz. Call me if you need me. Bye"

The next morning, I called the police station to speak to Dennis again.

"Dennis, we need to talk."

"About what?"

"Not over the phone, Dennis, this is serious."

"Are you okay, Dom?"

"Yeah, let's just talk right away."

"Meet me in the cemetery behind the station in five minutes."

"Thanks, buddy."

It would take but five minutes for me to get to the cemetery, so I left right away. Dennis was already there and sitting in his cruiser. I jumped in.

With concern for a friend, he greeted me not with not a hello, but "what the hell is going on?"

"The doctor caught Liz and me."

"Oh shit."

"Yup, and he's calling everybody close to me."

"Like who?"

"My wife, my in-laws, and he's going to call Brewster. And I'm worried he's going to call my children."

"Jesus, this guy's out of control."

"Yes, he is. Is there anything I can do to stop him?"

"First, file a complaint to get it on record just in case."

Just then my pager went off. "Oh great, what marvelous piece of information will this page reveal?" Removing the pager from my belt, I looked at it. "It's Brewster. He wants me to call him. FUCK! I'm just gonna go down to the station and speak to him. I'll call you afterward."

"Okay, be careful, Dom," my policeman friend cautioned me.

"Thanks, buddy."

I walked into headquarters a few minutes later and went straight to the chief's office where I knocked on the open door.

"Come in, Dom, and close the door." It is never good when your boss says, "Close the door."

"I have a feeling I know what this is all about, Chief."

Brewster came close to me before speaking quietly. *Had he finally figured out that others listen to his conversations through the communication's open sleeve in the floor under his desk?* I wondered to myself.

"I just met with Liz Temple at an out-of-town park."

"Excuse me, Chief?"

"She called me first thing this morning and asked if we could meet."

With my head in hands, I shook my head and said, "Good Jesus Christ."

"She's very easy to talk to and pretty cute too."

"Ya think, Chief?"

"She cares for you very much, Dominic, and doesn't want anything to happen to you."

I just smiled and said, "I care for her very much, too, Chief."

"She warned me her husband was coming to talk to me about you."

"And?"

"I've already spoken to Town Counsel, and there's nothing I can do for either of you. It's a personal matter. But Liz is very concerned for you."

"And I'm even more concerned for my family. This man is out of control!"

"My friendly word of advice is to stay away from his wife."

"I agree, Chief, and that's the way it is right now. But it may be hard for either of us to stay away from each other for very long."

With that, the meeting ended, and I headed for seclusion. I had never hidden or backed away from another man before in my life. But this was no longer about men against men. This was about families. I'll do whatever I have to do to keep my children safe and out of this fray, away from a madman. So I headed straight for home where I held up. I didn't want trouble, but I did make sure my rifle was handy with ammo at hand. I was this worried about the doctor.

That same afternoon, Dr. Samuel Temple marched right into the firehouse. It was like a stripper walking into the St. Patrick's Cathedral. He did not fit.

"Who's in charge here? I want to speak to whomever is in charge here," he bellowed.

"Excuse me, sir? May I help you?" the agitated front deskman asked.

Temple had his hands on his hips like a man about to make a complaint to a manager in a department store, only louder and more officious. Mumbles and mutterings abounded until he insisted, "Where's the chief? I want to speak to the chief."

Thanks to Liz, Brewster was prepared for this confrontation. "I'm Chief Brewster, you must be Dr. Temple. I've been expecting you. What can I do for you?"

"Is there somewhere we can speak privately?" But Temple didn't seem too concerned if this request were to be denied. He was prepared to air his business wherever he had to. The requisition was simply a formality. Temple was full of formalities.

Brewster led him into his office but left the door half open. Brewster didn't talk too loudly and must not have expected shouting, certainly not from him.

Word had spread throughout the firehouse that I'd been caught in a love affair. Thanks to Slayton for sure. Needless to say, the other men in the station at that time conveniently shuffled near to the chief's office door. The sleazy ones went to the room under the chief's office to listen. "You have a man here by the name of Renaldi."

"Yes, Dominic Renaldi. He's one of my lieutenants."

"He's been sleeping with my wife. I'm a taxpayer in this town, so I want to know what you're going to do about it." Temple's voice was indeed loud as if he was completely devoid of shame regarding the matter. Neither Slayton nor Jacobs were in the building. Their work on this matter was already complete and now handed off to their brainwashed disciples for an intelligence-gathering recon mission. From another room right next door and from below, Jacobs's agents could hear Temple's end of the conversation as clear as a bell while straining only slightly to hear the laconic chief.

"Well, are you sure about this?" Brewster raked his hand through what was left of his graying hair he vainly combed over the balding top of his head, looking and feeling uncomfortable.

"Of course, I'm sure. You think I don't know what goes on in my own house?"

Eavesdropping firefighters snickered. "Well, apparently not."

"You think I'd come in here if I didn't have a grave concern that I want taken care of immediately?"

"Well, is there any legal record of this? Is there any proof?" asked Brewster. "This is a personal matter, and I have no jurisdiction over it."

Temple stared menacingly into Brewster's eyes. Temple's anger, his entire dominating countenance, seemed to frighten the fire chief. "Are you stupid?" He stopped there, letting it sink in that this was exactly what he thought of Brewster.

Brewster did not respond. A few men found it hard to pretend to be minding their own business and began giggling in the adjoining room as one said out loud, "More than you'll ever know."

"I want to know what you're going to do about this matter, Chief."

Brewster paused as he had no answer. In fire school, they don't teach you what to do when one of your men sleeps with the wife of a citizen.

"I'm sorry, Dr. Temple, there is nothing I can do to help you. This is a personal matter. Now if you can prove something happened at the firehouse, put it in writing, and I might be able to be of assistance."

Temple's jaw dropped. "You're talking to a very powerful and wealthy man, Chief. This isn't about writing up reports and putting notes in files. This is not kindergarten. This is not some child who called another child a name. I am a taxpayer in this community, and one of its hack employees has been carrying on with my wife behind my back. I am an aggrieved party to an act of public embarrassment and deception caused by someone whose salary I pay."

"What do you want me to do about it?"

"If you don't do something about it, I'll put a bullet in his head."

Brewster did one of his infamous pauses again but now for a different reason. "You just went from victim to villain with that statement."

"We'll see about that." With that, Temple turned and stormed out.

Men began to cackle, then guffaw loud and long, some rolling on the floor holding their sides. One was already on the phone to Slayton. All except Pete Brewster. After regaining his composure, he called the former chairman of the Board of Selectmen for advice. Horace Humphreys was the man who hired Brewster as chief and taught him the ropes of town government. They often dined at Humphreys' expense.

"Horace Humphreys. Hello, Chief, what can I do for you?" as he lit up one of his $10 cigars. The same ones he lit up at collective bargaining before blowing the smoke in our faces, the personification of ego and arrogance.

"Do you know a Dr. Samuel Temple who lives in town?"

Boastfully, Humphreys answered, "Sure, I know Sam, he and I serve on a few boards together. Is everything okay with him?"

"Apparently, one of my men has been bopping his wife."

"We can't have that, Pete. We have to take care of men like Sam Temple. You'll need to do something with this firefighter. You know what I mean, Chief? Who is it?"

"Renaldi."

"Renaldi? The one who bargained against me last year?" Humphreys seemed eager.

"Yes."

"He beat me three times in mediation for collective bargaining. Take care of him, Chief. Teach him a lesson about the Coventry way."

"There's more HH. The doctor just said, and I'll quote here, 'If you don't do something about it, I'll put a bullet in his head.'"

"So what? Take care of Renaldi, and we'll all be happy," he said revengefully. "Let's have dinner tonight and talk."

"What do I do about the threat to Renaldi's life?"

"Is it in writing?"

"No."

"Then just ignore it like it never happened. Christ's sake, Pete, I'll make a lawyer of you yet." With that, Humphreys laughed like a boastful king.

"The usual place tonight?" a cowering chief asked.

"Sure, I've got to go. We're about to ruin a small company who's a threat to one of my clients. Seven o'clock tonight, Chief." As he hung up the phone, like a proud peacock, HH inhaled deeply on his Havana cigar and thrust out his chest, then exhaled into the universe he controlled through power and dominance.

My pager went off again. Suddenly, all my pager fun I'd been enjoying wasn't so much fun anymore. It was the chief. Not wanting to leave my home unprotected, I called him back.

"I just spoke to Dr. Temple, Dominic."

"And what did the good doctor have to say?"

"He threatened to put a bullet in your head, Dominic."

"Good Jesus Christ." I shook my head in disbelief. "What are you going to do about that? You called the police right?" I asked knowingly.

"It's a personal matter, Dom."

"Chief, I'm sorry for putting the department and you in the middle of this, however, that's neither here nor there. That man has harassed my family. He has now harassed me at my place of employment, and now he's threatened my life directly to my boss. And you, my boss, don't think the police should be notified. You do know there were witnesses."

"There were no witnesses, Dominic."

"Of course, there were witnesses, they were listening to you from below your office just as they always have. Investigate that, Chief."

"They . . . they don't do that. Besides, that doesn't matter."

"I think it does." Brewster had one managerial style—avoidance. Some guys thought he should keep a jar of lollipops on his desk to hand out to any and all complainants, hoping a taste of sugar would make all difficult decisions and problems go away. I continued talking to Brewster, "So you're not going to file a police report on that threat, which several guys probably heard?"

"I'm going to have to do something with you, Lieutenant."

"Excuse me, Chief? Someone just threatened to put a bullet in my head, and you have to do something with me?"

"I'm the chief of the entire department, and I have to do what's best for all."

"Let me see if I've got this straight, Chief. Slayton blows my ears out with an M-80 in the firehouse, but I get reprimanded for my anger. Now some rich and powerful sicko, who just happens to be friends with your obnoxious buddy, Humphreys, threatens to put a bullet in my head, and instead of calling the police on this guy, you're going to punish me. Do I have this correct, Chief?

"Why do you always have to bring up the M-80 incident, Renaldi?"

"Because you never did anything about it, Chief!"

"I have to think of the town as a whole, Lieutenant."

"How much is he paying you, Chief?"

"Watch your step, Renaldi. You're not in a very good position."

"And you're not a very good chief! Go ahead. Fire me. You're too much of a gutless, yellow-bellied pussy to do that. Do you know that? No one here respects you because, except for Slayton and Jacobs, you don't stand up for the guys. You don't stand up for anything."

"Now now, Dom, don't go being that way. I don't need to hear that from you. You seem to have enough troubles as it is."

I muttered, "Fuck you" under my breath, almost inaudibly. "Go ahead, Chief. Fire me. I don't think you've got the balls to!" And I slammed the phone down.

Now I definitely had to do something to stop this madman. I called Dennis back. "He just threatened my life right in front of half a dozen witnesses."

"Do you really think he'll do it? Is he the violent type?" Dennis asked.

I mulled over Dennis's question as we sat together in a local coffee shop, both of us keeping our voices low. "I don't know. Maybe. He's a control freak. You know how some of these rich guys are. Masters of the universe, they call themselves. It wouldn't take much for a guy like that to become completely unglued, like a dictator of some sort."

Indeed, from what I had heard Liz say about her husband and the way Temple acted when I'd seen him, he made for a very believable strong-armed potentate—a Mussolini, a Khadafi, a Hussein.Those guys may have worn fancy suits and uniforms and lived in castles with hot and cold running gold and silver, but underneath it all, they were cold-blooded killers. Maybe in a country like America where they did not rule the land as a law onto themselves, it would be more likely that a Sam Temple might be more inclined to hire a good professional hit man. Great, another thing to weigh on my mind.

"My concerns for causing this man further pain are long gone, Dennis. I have to do something to stop him now. He just threatened my life. Who knows what he'll do next?"

"Well, you could file a complaint. That way, it would give greater credibility to any other accusation you ever brought against him. It's kind of like saying, 'If I die mysteriously, here's the first person to check out.'"

"He's also been calling and seeing other people. He called Ruth's parents. He called my parents. He called my brother. He even went to station 2 and offered to pay the guys to rat on me, for christ-sakes! He's telling everybody that his children have been traumatized and all kinds of shit. His children are fine, and he has Liz to thank for that. If there's anything wrong with his kids, it's from him, not me. And everything he's doing now is only making it worse on them."

"Dom, before I forget, how are your little bambinos? Are they okay?"

"Not so little anymore. I don't know if that's a blessing or a curse right now. They're okay, I guess. Seems Ruth has been straying a bit too."

"No shit!"

"Yeah. I don't want to get into it. If you haven't heard about it, then maybe that's a good thing. I wouldn't put it past the guy she did it with to go around bragging like a big ass stud."

"Wow. No, I hadn't heard about that."

"Well, at least it made things a little more even. Ruth and I haven't been getting along that well anyway, so I moved into a little one-room apartment a couple days ago. The kids are upset, but it's not like I moved to another state or something. I'll be able to see them just as much as I ever did. Ruth isn't going to do anything nasty regarding custody or anything like that. It's going to make it simple, quick divorce. Hell, the divorce may be more pleasant than the marriage." As I looked into my cup of coffee, I continued, "Dennis, I'm sorry. This man has threatened my life, and I want him arrested."

"Okay, Dom. Let's get started."

"Can it be done on the QT? Nice and quiet like."

"Yes, we'll call him down to the station and formally charge him, and he'll appear in court tomorrow morning."

"Perfect. I still hate doing this to the guy, but he's left me no choice."

"Well, my advice is this, combine the threat with the harassment, and I really think you'll have a solid official complaint. It's not like you're trying to send him to prison or anything. It'll just put him, as well as us, on notice. That usually puts an end to such shenanigans."

"Yeah, but this is going to really make things uncomfortable. His wife is going to be so embarrassed."

"You mean she's not already embarrassed by all the phone calls he's been making? Look, it's never easy. You should see when I have to convince a woman to file battery charges against her guy or a girl who's been date-raped. People are afraid of the system. They're usually just afraid—period. But this is a simple, dignified way of putting your foot down and being a man. I'm not saying you're a pussy or anything like that. If anything, I'm glad you came to talk to me. The old Dom I grew up with would have been the one putting a bullet in another guy's head. You've come a long way."

"Thanks, I think."

"I'll help you. Just come on down to the station, and we'll file a report. The rest will be up to us. We'll call you when we need you."

"Thank you, Dennis. I'm sorry for having to do this."

"You have no choice but to do this if you want it to stop. Keep your head up and your eyes open, Dominic."

That evening, Sam Temple received a call from the Coventry police requesting him to come to the station. It was suggested he have an attorney present. Sam Temple arrived at the Coventry police station with his attorney, Horace Humphreys, where, Dr. Samuel Temple, of Coventry, Massachusetts, was quietly arrested and charged with threatening to kill one, Dominic Renaldi, also of Coventry, Massachusetts. Sam Temple was booked, fingerprinted, and had his mug shot taken. With the court magistrate present, Dr. Temple was released on his own personal recognizance without spending a minute in jail.

Woe be to Dominic Renaldi.

Chapter 25

Slayton sat in the chair on what is referred to as the platform in the Coventry Savings and Loan, the area beside the tellers where more complex banking transactions take place. He leaned back as if he were a millionaire being wooed by every bank in the area, anxious to get their hands on his money. Yep, Slayton was feeling and acting like one heck of a big wheel as he imagined how others saw him, *Can you all see me up here, people? That's right, I'm Bill Slayton, and I'm up here with the big boys*. Life was good. With his trademark laugh, theatrically, little Billy Slayton performed much to the delight of all the bank tellers. He knew how to play the game.

At the approach of a well-dressed, bespectacled man in a navy blue suit, white shirt, rep tie, and of course, wing-tipped shoes, Slayton suddenly snapped to reality. "Bill, how are you?"

Slayton rose on cue and said, "Fine, Brian, and you? How are your beautiful wife and wonderful children doing?"

Brian Rehrig, bank president and town selectman, had a brief look of discomfort on his face, most likely caused by Slayton's attitude of familiarity. It was one thing for Rehrig to call Slayton "Bill"; it was another thing entirely for Slayton to call him by his first name in the bank setting. Coventry had a caste system, and few could be farther apart than blue-collar Slayton and country club member Rehrig.

"Fine fine. What brings you here today?"

"Is there someplace we can talk in private?"

Again, Rehrig looked less than comfortable. He knew Slayton wasn't a millionaire, and thus, Rehrig figured that whatever this was about, it would be more for Slayton's benefit than for him or his bank. Still, he led Slayton back to his private office.

Slayton's theatrics now took him from comedy to a dramatic role. "This is town business. I hate to bother you at work, but I thought you'd be less happy if I dropped by your house."

"Yes."

Slayton took a huff and began. "I don't know if you've noticed, since Chief Wyatt stepped down, things have really been falling apart with the fire department."

Rehrig looked nonplussed. "All we care about is that the chief delivers the budget. How he runs the department is his business. I haven't heard of any incidents."

"Well, consider us all lucky. Morale has never been so bad. Pete Brewster isn't a terrible guy, but he's not up to the job. There have been some major situations."

"Such as?"

"Well, for one thing, our new union president has been having an affair with the wife of a prominent citizen."

A stern look crossed the selectman's face. "That Renaldi character?"

"Yeah. He's a piece of work, isn't he? How's it been for you working with him on the new contract."

"He's not very reasonable. He just doesn't see it our way. He thinks we're Santa Claus with an unlimited supply of money. I know we're an affluent community, but we won't be if we have to keep raising taxes to feed the fire department."

"Right. Well, I knew that. That's why you and I got along so well."

Again, Rehrig seemed to wince a little.

"Yeah, so anyway, he's been sleeping with a doctor's wife—a taxpayer here in Coventry—and he's been out of control in the firehouse. He's Italian. You know the type. Big hothead. He started a fight with me over some crazy false accusation. Then he recently had a to-do with another fireman. Seems *that* guy's been sleeping with *Renaldi's* wife."

"What? Geez. What the hell is going on down there?"

"Precisely, Brian. Yeah, young guy Ben Lyons. I generally like the guy, but he's one of these cement heads, you know, weightlifter type, always swinging his dick around."

"Lyons, the young firefighter who lives here in town? asked a surprised Rehrig.

"Yeah, that's him." Slayton looked for a "locker room guy" nod of approval, but Rehrig again looked more uncomfortable.

Rehrig acted even more surprised and shook his head with slight disappointment. "We know him. We've had our eye on him for a while. He's helped us out a little."

"Yeah. Well, you never know who you can trust, Brian. Anyway, they almost got into it. Meanwhile, the chief is twiddling his thumbs. Doesn't know what to do. I'm telling you, the next time there's a fire, I wonder if these guys will even be willing to help one another out. They also work fire alarm together. I just don't know what one might do to the other. I want to step up and help out. I want to be a real leader, Brian."

Rehrig paused to take it all in for a moment. "Let me get this straight. First, we have this Renaldi fellow sleeping around with a married woman, and this family lives in town."

"Yeah. Dr. Samuel Temple. His wife."

Suddenly, Rehrig became quite wide-eyed, "Temple?"—pause—"I was just with him at the hospital benefit a while back. I know the man well." Pause again and still wide-eyed, then he said, "Renaldi's tagging THAT?" Rehrig then had to straighten his tie.

"Well, her old man's not too pleased. He found out about it and came down to the fire station to file a complaint and see what Brewster would do about it. Brewster basically threw the guy out. Worse than that, Renaldi reported *Temple* to the cops. Claims Temple's been harassing *him*. Can you believe it?"

"Oh my god. And Brewster did nothing about this Renaldi character?"

"Nope. Protected him. They're both good ol' boys."

"God."

"And then again, you have Renaldi starting fistfights and threatening guys on the job. This Lyons kid can handle himself if need be, but it shouldn't have to come down to that. Can you believe this is happening?"

"No, but what was he doing sleeping with Renaldi's wife?"

"Exactly. That kind of stuff never went on before. I just can't imagine doing this type of thing to one of the brothers! I like this Lyons kid, but if he has to go too, then so be it. This kind of stuff is going to rear its ugly head some time when we need all hands on deck, when we have a real emergency. I'm worried I won't be able to rely on either of them when it counts the most. That's the kind of thing I worry about. Me, I'm just a dedicated public servant. My job is being a professional firefighter. But some of these guys—Brewster, Renaldi, Lyons, Jacobs . . ." Slayton lowered his head and shook it in apparent dejection.

"Who's Jacobs?"

"Oh, he's the other captain. Jacobs and Renaldi are ranked just below Brewster, the chief. Jacobs hasn't stepped up much either. I hear he's the one who put Lyons up to chasing Renaldi's wife. I'm telling you, since Chief Wyatt's been gone, the entire department has lacked serious leadership. Renaldi's the problem. Brewster's totally incompetent and doesn't represent the interests of the town at all. Not when he allows all these shenanigans to go on during his watch and not when he tosses a wealthy taxpayer who's been wronged by one of the men out on his ear. If it were me, I'd give those two their walking papers immediately, and I'd keep my eye on Jacobs and Lyons."

"They may have to go too, if things are as bad as you say they are, Bill."

Slayton shrugged. "Do what you have to do. You're the Chairman of the Board of Selectmen now."

"Thank you for bringing this to my attention, Lieutenant."

"Just trying to do my job, sir," Slayton said with modest humility."

*   *   *

"Chief, HH here."

"Hi, Horace, to what do I owe the pleasure of this phone call this evening?"

"This is not pleasurable," Humphreys said in a very dissatisfied voice. "It seems your man, Renaldi, has had my client arrested for threatening to kill him. This is not very good at all, Pete. I told you to take care of Renaldi."

Even in the confines of his own home, Brewster hung his head when he heard those words. He was in a very compromised position. With financial debt mounting from his son's difficulties, he could ill afford losing his job over Dominic Renaldi. Already a puppet on a string to Humphreys and the selectmen, all the chief of the fire department could muster was, "I'm sorry, Horace."

"Sam will be arraigned tomorrow morning. These are very serious charges that may ruin the doctor, Pete. Can you imagine how it must feel to be ruined, Chief?"

"That fucking asshole, Renaldi!" said a pissed-off Brewster as he placated Humphreys, the master of Coventry's universe.

"That's right, Pete.

Having helped the chief out in the past, HH knew he had him by the short hairs.

"How is your son doing, Chief?" he asked as an unspoken reminder of where help had come from.

"He's got me in debt up to my eyeballs."

"Any luck selling your house yet?"

"A lot of lookers but no offers as of yet."

"Well, my client would like to make this unfortunate incident up to you, Chief. You know, for putting you in the middle. Why don't the three of us have dinner tomorrow night? Let's make it in the North End." To which Humphreys burst out laughing. "Yeah, the North End!" Humphreys laughed long and hard over the notion of orchestrating a plan to ruin Dominic Renaldi from a restaurant in the Italian neighborhood of Boston's North End. Ego at its finest!

"Call my office tomorrow, and we'll set up a time for dinner. Oh, and, Pete, bring all of your financials and information about your house too. Sam Temple's very good with numbers, and he always has young doctors looking for real estate. Do you know what I mean, Chief?"

"Yeah, I know what you mean," said a dejected Pete Brewster, knowing he had just become a victim of Coventry's ego and arrogance.

Chapter 26

Cromwell District Court. They say that everyone wants their day in court, but no one really ever wants to *be* in court. Certainly not defendants, rarely even their accusers. Lawyers make money in it, but all—lawyers, plaintiffs, and defendants—say they prefer to negotiate in the less formal setting of a conference room. Judges prefer it this way too; it helps defer the load of a backed up and overburdened judicial system. Besides, the courtroom in the courthouse is a contentious place anyway, and judges get paid the same whether they hear twelve cases or two.

Add to the list of unhappy participants, three particular people who sat in Cromwell District Court on this Wednesday morning—Sam and Liz Temple and their attorney—were all Coventry residents who knew full well that the Cromwell District Court was run by Judge James Muldoon, also a Coventry resident. Most assuredly, the Coventry grapevine would feast on fine caviar in coming weeks. Sam had been arrested the day before and released on personal recognizance. Threats, harassment, words not usually associated with a fine, refined gentleman such as himself. Perhaps malpractice or tax evasion and bankruptcy. People like Dr. Sam Temple were associated with actions like that a lot. But these charges were so detrimental to his pristine image that it could ruin his fine reputation.

"We can't be seen with Sam Temple," women would tell their husbands at the charity parties.

A humiliated Sam Temple sat with his arms folded across his chest, his jaw set in a hard grimace, and his glistening eyes stared straight ahead, seething in fury. Dr. Temple's attorney, Horace Humphreys—the former Chairman of the Board of Selectmen and family friend—sat between Sam and his wife. Only rarely did Sam turn his head to face his wife, whom he dragged into court as partial punishment for getting him in this mess in the first place. Surely, it wasn't Sam Temple's fault he had threatened "to put a bullet in his head." Liz sat solemnly, trying to get as comfortable as possible on the hard wooden bench as she stared at the floor, wishing she could squeeze into one of its cracks. She hung her head, played with her bracelets and rings. She tried not to look at either man. But neither man paid her much attention. Liz was terrified. Four hours on a cold wooden bench. Sam Temple leaned across his attorney and angrily told Liz, "I will get your loser friend for this, and you will pay a heavy price too!"

Humphreys uncrossed his arms and applied his hand to his client's chest and quietly said as he gently pushed Sam back into his own space, "Relax, Sam, I'll get you out of this mess. Don't worry. I helped Jim get his appointment to the bench several years ago. We'll be fine in his courtroom."

For hours, they sat mortified with all the other criminals, druggies, and assorted wrongdoers. Surely, Sam Temple was above all these riffraff. He was livid. Finally, the Clerk called the defendant forward. "Docket number 3858937866, Renaldi v. Temple." Sam Temple, accompanied by his lawyer, rose to hear the charges.

Humphreys may have helped Jim Muldoon get his judgeship, but Muldoon showed he had earned it. After perusing the official paperwork, Judge Muldoon spoke briefly yet judicially, "I cannot hear this case and must recuse myself from it. I will have to send it across the hall." Understanding the system, Judge Muldoon instructed his clerk to "deliver this case across the hall and have Judge Feeney move it to be heard next."

Out of the courtroom and across the hall, they walked. This was not the stage anyone of the three was accustomed to, and they were very uncomfortable. Sam Temple walked with his head down. Liz seemed to have lost her swagger, and Horace Humphreys was still the good shepherd leading his flock with pursed, then puckish lips as if to say, "He may be the a judge, but I am HH."

With Judge Feeney's clerk having just received the case, he called out, "Docket number 3858937866, *Renaldi v. Temple*." Judge Joanne Feeney took a few minutes to diligently review the paperwork she had just received from her clerk. "These are very serious charges," said the judge while stating the obvious. She then looked straight at Sam Temple and asked, "Do you understand the charges, which have been filed against you, Dr. Temple?"

"Yes, I do, ma'am." How humbling to have to submit to a female judicator.

With his response, Humphreys leaned toward his client and briefly whispered something. Temple looked agitated.

"And how do you plead?"

"Not guilty. Your . . . Your Honor." Sam Temple could barely address her properly.

"The clerk will set a trial date for sometime next month."

Sam Temple was beside himself. HH quickly muzzled his client before he could so much as utter a sound as the three walked out of the courthouse humiliated.

"I thought you told me you'd get me out of these charges. What am I paying you good money for?" the good doctor angrily asked his $500-an-hour mouthpiece.

"Relax, Sam, I'll negotiate with the plaintiff and get this taken care of."

A shaken Sam Temple looked at his wife with hatred and forcefully said, "You and lover boy will pay a heavy price for what you've done to me."

* * *

"Mr. Renaldi, this is Horace Humphreys, I represent Dr. Samuel Temple," Humphreys spoke professionally.

"Hello, Horace, nice to speak to you again," I said, taking great delight in knowing I was once again up against this egotistical man. Not that I was interested in doing so, but I just wasn't afraid of him—ever.

"We would like if you would consider discussing a possible settlement of this situation with my client so that we can all get on with our lives and not have to go through the rigors of a trial."

"Mr. Humphreys, I assure you I don't want this man to go to trial. All I want is for him to stop his incessant harassment and to guarantee he won't harm my family."

"We could sit down and iron that out before trial. In return, you'll drop the charges, am I correct?"

"I will as long you meet my stipulations."

"I think we can come to some agreement. Why don't you come to my office in Boston for a meeting."

"No, Mr. Humphreys, I'm not the one who will be inconvenienced here. Why don't you come out to meet me."

"Fine. How about the firehouse tonight?"

"Not a good place to meet. How about the library at 4:00 p.m.? I'll see you then."

"I don't think I can make it at that hour."

"Mr. Humphreys, you don't have a choice, and neither does your client. I'll see you then, or I'll see you in court."

After having hung up with Humphreys, I called Dennis to let him know what was happening.

"Hi, Dennis."

"So a trial date's been set for next month, huh?"

"Yeah, how'd you know?"

"Our prosecuting detective, Ken Macus, has been keeping me informed. He likes you, Dom. He says you've got guts for standing up to these men like you do. It makes all of us little guys feel good, my friend."

"Fuck these guys, Dennis. It's my turn to show ego and arrogance toward them. A little taste of their own medicine would be perfect. In the end, I'll probably go down, but I won't go down without a fight."

"Have you thought about hiring an attorney, Dom?"

I thought for a moment. *Good idea, but who would pay for it? With Ruth not working and me having to keep up two, albeit modest, households, money was tight.* "I can't even hire one for my divorce, Dennis. Certainly, I can't afford one for this. I don't even have a steady income right now."

"What do you mean by that?"

"Brewster suspended me for two months."

"Geezus. I'm sorry to hear that. Are you sure you know what you're doing?"

"Well, I know I have a meeting with Humphreys at the library at 4:00 p.m."

"Horace Humphreys, what for?"

"Seems he's representing his good friend, Dr. Temple."

"You hot shit, Dominic! Let me know what happens."

"Stay tuned, it ought to be fun."

* * *

A few hours later, my cell phone rang, and I didn't recognize the number. Nervously, I said, "Hello."

"Hi, it's me."

Liz's voice, even as distraught as it sounded, was unmistakable music to my ears. Suddenly, my heart began pounding, and I had a lump in my throat. I had not heard this sweet voice in over two weeks. "Hey, how are you calling me?"

"Pay phone. Do you know how hard it is to find one of these anymore? They've gone the way of the dodo bird. There's one in Sheridan's Pharmacy way in the back corner. If this place ever goes out of business, I'm screwed."

"How are you, Liz?"

"Dumb question. *Terrible* doesn't begin to describe the torture, Dom. I need to be in your arms, Dominic."

"And I need you in my arms, Liz. I'm sorry. It's all my fault."

"Well, some of it. I mean, we both decided to get involved. You can't take all the blame. But this thing with the arrest and the courts."

"What was I to do? That's what I'm really sorry about. But your husband is crazy. He's obsessed. I just want him to stop and leave my family and me alone. Do you know I've been suspended?"

"What?"

"Yeah. Brewster suspended me. Your husband threatens me, and *I* get suspended for two months. Go figure." With a laugh, I followed up with, "But then again, I did give him some shit. I thought I was going to get fired."

"I'm sorry. What are you doing for money?"

"This and that. I'll get by. The chief's being kind to me and not stopping my health insurance, so that's a relief for my family. I just have to pay the whole premium out of my own pocket."

I could hear the sound of sniffles and crying as Liz said, "I'm sorry, Dominic."

"No, I'm sorry, Liz. This whole thing is sorry."

"Are you sorry you ever met me?"

"No, how could I ever feel that way, Liz? You lifted me up when I was down."

"It would make sense if you did though."

"You and I never made sense from the get-go, but who cares? All that is water over the dam now. You know I'm no longer living with Ruth. We'll probably be starting divorce proceedings any day now."

"Wow. How do you feel about that?"

"Actually, kind of relieved. It's for the best. I just worry about the kids. What about you?"

"The opposite or something like that. Sam has me caged up like an animal at the zoo. I can't even go to the bathroom without permission!"

"So he's taken you back."

"Dom, I'm not a person to him. I'm a possession. You stole something of his. He's not going to just surrender me to you. He'd sooner kill me than do that."

"If he ever hurts you . . ."

"Don't talk that way. That's just the sort of thing he wants you to say, wants you to do. Dom, I'm not saying this to make you feel worse, but this legal thing—that was the last straw. Sam's a madman now possessed. No one's ever stood up to him like this before, and I admire you for doing that. You've knocked him off his pedestal. No one has ever been able to do that. Not even at the hospital or in business—nowhere. He's a bully in a passive-aggressive way. It's odd. He's not the biggest guy in the world, but he has this way about him, he's fearless. He intimidates everyone. You remember how he had you begging that he not tell Ruth?"

"But he had already done it."

"That's what I mean. He's a brilliant man. He thinks all this stuff out. I used to admire it, but now I see what it's like to be on the receiving end of it, and it's scary. He's going to get you, Dom. Just be forewarned. He's going to get you back for this, and then he's going to get me back too."

"But he's already ruined me, told my kids, my in-laws, my folks, got me suspended from my job—"

"It's still not enough, Dom. That was the last thing he said to me. It's still not enough. Watch yourself and be careful."

"You too. I worry about you. I love you."

"Dom, I can't survive without you, I need you so badly. I have a plan where we can communicate. You'll be receiving something from a post office box in Trowbridge." The phone then clicked off.

Chapter 27

Spring came to New England with its requisite warmth and rebirth of flowers and trees and sunshine that no longer simply reflected off the piles of snow. They say it elevates the human spirit as well. This was not the case for me. Crammed into a studio apartment, no longer employed, no wife nor lover, I was truly an island unto myself.

Nothing was more depressing than sitting in my cramped quarters. It fit one person, and there isn't even the ability to alter one's environment by moving to another room. Actually, sometimes I'd stare out the front window and turn around and stare out the rear window. Worst of all, I didn't have the day-to-day interactions with my children. Like a prison cell, the view always remained the same from the lone chair set in front of the TV. Including the bathroom with shower stall and vanity, there was 218 square feet of space. I didn't even have a table to eat meals. I had a stove, sink, refrigerator, and dishwasher in this made-over, single-car, attached garage space. Trying to maintain my humor, I did chuckle every time I removed a good shirt from the one-foot-wide broom closet that I turned into my clothes closet.

This is my fault. I will suck it up. I will make it work.

With my cell phone rarely ringing, I sat, day after day, listening to the deafening sound of my ears ringing as a torturous reminder that I alone was the one who deserved to be suspended for my own actions. Even Sam Temple no longer buzzed in my ear.

With trepidation, I represented myself against one of Boston's most powerful attorneys. With no money, I had no choice. Over the next few weeks, I continued to meet with Humphreys. The first meeting at the library went well, and it gave me the feeling I was on the right track, but I was on the lookout for danger. Humphreys was a ruthless man. Dealing with his like, you had best beware. He was eager to get his client off the hook, and I was eager to put Sam Temple behind me.

All I wanted was Dr. Temple to stop his campaign of abuse and harassment, and Temple's lawyer agreed. He codified it in a settlement agreement. Humphreys didn't become a $500-per-hour attorney by luck. He knew what he was doing. Humphreys' assistant called informing me the papers were ready to be signed, but "unfortunately, Mr. Humphreys can't be here, and he's hoping you'll be able to come to his Boston office to sign the necessary paperwork." I'd dealt with this power and ego long enough to know that it was time to give a little without losing a thing. I acquiesced to meeting in the city. Besides, it would be a far better view than the one I had from my new digs. The trap was set.

Parking my truck at the Riverside T stop in the western suburbs, I rode the Green Line into the city. Fenway Park, the Museum of Science, Boston Garden, and Faneuil Hall, all easily accessible by the T. But today's trip took me into the heart of the city, into the true inner workings of power, ego, and greed. Where men placated others with insincere handshakes and deceitful promises all in the name of gaining supremacy through the almighty dollar. The gentry I loathed so deeply, not over their money, but for the arrogance that came with it.

Government Center, City Hall Plaza, Post Office Square, and State Street, all high-rent districts in any city where the wheels turned and the spoils of power greased their axis. Walk into any office and take a whiff. I did just that on the top floor of the pretentious life insurance building, and I smelled a rat. Of course, Horace Humphreys' office was on Boston's prime real estate and had the finest view of the waterfront from anywhere in the city. I would have expected nothing less.

"Hello, may I help you?" asked the very professional secretary, who directed me to his executive assistant.

With a pleasant smile on my face, I greeted the assistant, "Hello, I'm Dominic Renaldi."

"Hello, Mr. Renaldi, I've been expecting you. Here are the necessary papers Mr. Humphreys asked me to give to you. Mr. Humphreys is sorry he can't be here to give them to you personally."

"Thank you. I'm sure he is. Is there a place I can review them?"

"There's no need for that, Mr. Renaldi, they're just as you asked for. I typed them myself," she said with a well-practiced smile. "Just sign the documents, and I'll be sure Mr. Humphreys gets them," she added, smiling yet again.

Ahh, the four-star general's lieutenant knew her lines well. With my own smile, I said, "I'd prefer to review them before I leave, just in case there's a misunderstanding of sorts."

The slightly perturbed assistant silently pointed to a conference room. Indeed, I knew I had to review this document if I wanted to leave with the cheese, and the trap still set.

Within five minutes, I returned to her desk. "It seems that, quite by accident, I'm sure," I said with an insincere smile on my face, "he's left out the section where Dr. Temple will no longer harass me or my family."

Now the not-so-pleasant woman said without a smile, "I typed the document just as I was instructed."

"I'm sure you did. But I think I need to speak to Mr. Humphreys."

"He's not available," said the frustrated assistant.

"Ya, know what I think?" I asked as I leaned slightly toward her and spoke softly. "I think he's in his office right behind that door." I pointed in the direction of what appeared to be his office, guarded by a grand mahogany door. "And I think it's in his client's best interest for him to become available."

With a frustrated huff seemingly to mean, "This is not what I expected," Humphreys' faithful foot soldier insisted, "Mr. Humphreys is not available."

Now standing erect, I said firmly, "Well then, would you please deliver a message to Mr. Humphreys when he is available," I countered with raised eyebrows as I leaned forward. "I'm not signing this unacceptable document. I'll see him in court tomorrow morning. Have a nice day." I turned and walked out. I was bold, I was brash, and I was scared shitless thinking I was entering a fight I didn't want to enter, but I held my ground.

The elevator came to rest in the lobby, and I exited for the Government Center T stop with a copy of the documents in hand and a smile on my face. As I munched on the freshly popped popcorn, I silently waited for the next D train destined for Riverside. Knowing I didn't want to go home to a drab one-room bunker, I jumped off the train and exited a few stops up at Copley Square. Up Boylston Street, I walked with no particular place to go. Suddenly, I found myself staring at engine 33 and ladder 15's house—such a beautiful old firehouse.

I reflected back. *June 17, 1972, I was a rookie attending the fire academy. Boston had a fire in the Vendome Hotel just a few blocks down the street. During the overhaul phase of operations, there was a sudden building collapse, ladder 15 was buried in the rubble, and nine firefighters lost their lives. On that day, eight more were injured, eight women widowed, twenty-five children lost their fathers; a shocked city mourned before the sympathetic eyes of the entire nation.* The tragic incident had a profound impact on me. It made me realize how dangerous the job could be, how brave real firefighters are. I vowed to reflect their bravery, and over my career as a firefighter, I tried to emulate them.

Down the side of the firehouse I walked. One street over, I turned right on Newbury Street and headed toward the Common. Aimlessly walking. I was lost in thought. My mind flashed from heroic firefighters to the backside of Slayton running from a fire and cherry bombs exploding at my feet. From my family to Liz Temple and finally to Sam Temple putting a bullet in my head. Suddenly, I found myself standing on a bridge and watching the swans swimming in the lagoon. "Geezus, I don't even remember crossing Arlington Street and entering the Public Gardens," I said out loud. I needed to find a place to sit down and relax. I needed to focus.

I went across Charles Street and on into Boston Common. Nestling myself into a wind-protected but sunny spot, I basked in the sun and deliberated over this proposal set forth by Sam Temple's mouthpiece. It was pretty simple; Horace Humphreys had done what any good lawyer would've done. He wrote a document favorable to his client in hopes the uneducated loser wouldn't understand what he was signing. I put the papers away knowing that I'd either be hearing from Humphreys shortly, or I'd be in court soon. Sitting back to relax even more, I stared at the State House atop of Beacon Hill, its golden dome glistening brilliantly in the sunshine. It was peaceful. I closed my eyes in contemplation, the warmth of the sun felt good on my face.

With startling affect, suddenly, something jolted me upright. It was my cell phone. "Hello."

"Dominic, Horace Humphreys here."

"Hello, Horace, I've been expecting your call."

"Dominic, I'm sorry for the confusion in the document. My assistant made an unacceptable mistake."

"Yes, I'm sure it was the assistant's fault," I said with disdain.

"Can I meet you somewhere this evening with the corrected documents?"

"You're in luck, Mr. Humphreys, I'm just three T stops away. How about if I come back to your office?"

"I'll make time for you, see you then."

Across the Common, past South Meetinghouse, and down Tremont Street, I walked toward Government Center. Within fifteen minutes, I was back in Humphreys' office where I was face to face with the foot soldier whom I knew was the scapegoat for this scheme.

"Go right in, Mr. Humphreys is expecting you, Mr. Renaldi."

Looking straight into her eyes, I said with a sincere smile, "Thank you very much."

Like the NBC peacock, Humphreys plumed his feathers and strutted his stuff while extending a handshake. "Lieutenant, it is lieutenant, or have they gotten smart enough to promote you to captain?"

"Don't placate me, Humphreys, this paperwork had best be correct, or your man goes to court."

"I think you'll find it all in order," he said quite businesslike.

Their end run having failed, they delivered. "You can also take my word for it, my client will stay away from you as long as you stay away from his wife."

Humphreys and I shook hands, and I left. As I rode the elevator down, I couldn't help but to smile as I thought, *Yum yum, Sharp Cheddar!*

I signed off on the document, and the next morning, they were delivered to the court. The charges against Sam Temple dropped.

Indeed, there were no longer any Temples in my life. For several weeks later, I kept calling Ruth and asked whether she had gotten any calls or contacts of any sort from him. She said no. So too her parents and anyone else. Sam Temple had apparently blown off his steam and gone back into whatever hole he had crawled out of. At least, long enough to develop a new game plan.

The other Temple was what was making my heart ache. Sometimes, I would stare at my cell phone or at my pager, waiting for either to make a jolting noise that would bring a smile to my face. It rarely happened, and when it did, it was never Liz. Where was she? How was she? Did she still have feelings for me, or was it over? Was she trying to repair her relationship with her husband, or did I still have a chance with her? Such an irony: I was now a free man, yet instead of being able to be with the woman I loved, I was simply alone and unable to speak to her.

One day, a Hallmark card came in the mail. It caught me by surprise. Few people had my new address, and there was no major holiday on the horizon. I opened it and hundreds of tiny glittery hearts fell out. I laughed out loud knowing this could be but one person. Then I remembered what a special lady had said to me about receiving something in the mail. Brushing aside the mess, I read the card; its message was profound.

Liz wrote, "You know how much music stirs my soul, so I'm going to use lyrics to best describe my love for you and what you truly have meant to me." She then penned the lyrics to "You Light Up My Life." She went on to say, "My favorite line is, 'You give me hope to carry on.'" Liz concluded her message with another line from the song. "It can't be wrong when it feels so right." The card was signed Wildflower and had 456838, 4812, 6969 and the cryptic instruction "look at the return address."

I turned back to the envelope, and there was a post office box in Trowbridge as the point of origin. Liz had taken out a post office box. With my landlord not wanting me to receive mail at the house, I did the same. *Would it become our new secret way of communicating?* I stared long and hard at the card. *Or was it a trick? Was it some sort of treachery of Sam Temple's?* What little trust I had was long gone. I stuffed it in my pocket and began to ponder the situation.

In the quiet confines of my spartan abode, I brought the card back out again and stared at it. Yes, the signature was Liz's. I'd seen it enough times. This was definitely Liz's handwriting. Still, I agonized about the repercussions as well as what it all meant. Was this just a nice kiss-off, a final period at the end of the personal sentence between Liz Temple and me? No, for then, there wouldn't be the issue of the return address. A post office box in Trowbridge. That would work. It wouldn't be as convenient as a phone call. Certainly not as immediate as our old pager system we developed. Like a starving fish, I took the bait and ran hard.

Regarding the eternal and broad-stroked differences between men and women, I was not satisfied to simply know that Liz still cared enough about me to send a nice card. I wanted answers and direction. For I was not ready to close this chapter of my life no matter how erratic and dangerous it might seem. I was used to putting my life on the line. Sam Temple was just another fire to put out, and Liz was the innocent victim, pinned in the corner of a room filling with noxious smoke. I had to get to her. I had to save her.

Over time, my relationship with Ruth had dwindled to less than communicative; but with Liz, I felt inspired, I felt a need to send romantic cards to her, and the words fell right off the pen. Inside the card, I wrote, "I miss you so much. Life without you is like solitary confinement. Not holding you in my arms is like a humming bird without its nectar. I cannot survive." I copied the mailing address from the red Hallmark envelope I'd gotten from Liz and mailed my card to her, praying it would reach the right hands. We each now had mailboxes to send correspondence to.

The next day, I received another card. It gave no indication of Liz having received mine yet, but it was a nice card—a funny, cute card—and it definitely showed her innermost feelings coming out. This time, she penned the lyrics to "Wind Beneath My Wings."

I could feel my pulse begin to return to life; I was beginning to feel alive again. Every day, I went to the post office box in hopes of finding more words from my distant and invisible source. Some days there were none, only for me to return to solitude. I was near depression. On other days, through the little window of the box, I'd see an envelope and be so excited I couldn't even get the combo right. I'd read and re-read her cards, trying to determine the sorts of meanings archeologists and scholars try to gather from ancient religious relics. She was being purposefully vague as to her motivation. It was driving me crazy.

Finally, on the third day, Liz responded to my first card. "Oh, Dom, I miss you so. Thank you for your card. This is a safe way for us to communicate. Sam has me caged up like a prisoner. He even fired our nanny so I'd have to take care of the children myself. Don't laugh. It's just a ploy to tie me up so I'd have no time to myself and for you. He has spies everywhere. People check in on me constantly. I want to see you, but I don't know how."

I went back to the card shop near home. If this was how it would be, so be it.

"My schedule is very open. I can be wherever you want me to be, whenever you want me to be there. There has to be a way we can see each other. I'm dying to see you again. 456838 4812. XOXOXO."

This continued for months. It was particularly helpful for me during my suspension. At least I had something to look forward to throughout that dismal time. Each day, a card would come; each day, I'd buy one of my own and respond. Liz seemed to really like these greeting cards with the opportunity to write only short messages inside, and so I kept it up.

One day, however, I received a small package from Liz. Inside was a CD containing the song "Because You Loved Me." Liz often listened to this CD because "it reminds me of what you truly do mean to me." Then she quoted the song, "'I am everything I am today because you loved me,' Dominic. And you will always hold a very special place in my heart. So, please, listen to this CD often and think of me when you do. 'You stood by me and I stood tall. I had your love, I had it all.'"

These lyrics Liz was penning may not have been her words, but they had a profound affect on me. They made me realize what I really did mean to her, and in my heart, I knew she meant twice as much to me.

In this particular package, there was also a folded piece of heavy paper with a very distinctive lip gloss kiss impressed upon it, and I immediately recognized the color as my favorite. Kissing the paper, I could taste her delicious lips.

After any one of our encounters, Liz would reapply her lip gloss, and I would always kiss her again, to which Liz would always jest about me removing her gloss.

"You know how much I love the taste of your lips, Liz," I'd told her.

With that shining smile, she replied, "Why do you think I wear it?"

Liz was now sending me kisses with those wonderful lyrics. Boy, this woman was something special. I kept every card Liz sent to me.

Due back to work in just a few weeks, I knew right where I wanted this kiss to be. Still, I pressed Liz for a meeting as well as more information as to what was going on between her and her husband.

Liz was sending more cards with more thoughts. "Anyone who's found out about the affair found out from him, Dominic. Ironic, huh? You'd think he'd be embarrassed that his wife stepped out on him. But he's doing it to play the victim and paint me as a whore. He's holding the boys over my head as leverage. He's telling everyone I'm an unfit mother, Dom."

Judging from the apparent tear-dropped stains on the card, Liz had broken down and cried as she penned the last few words. "I can't see you, Dom. If I do, I'll lose my children."

"You won't lose your children, Liz," I wrote back. "You're too good a mother, and the court system will see through his intent. Trust me on that, Liz, please trust me on that."

In another missive, she wrote, "He tells everyone we're trying a reconciliation. It's bullshit, but he's trying to represent himself to his crowd as having a 'human side.' He *has* no human side. He only wants me around for spite. He's punishing me, and he's punishing you. The whole point of his actions is to make sure I'm never happy again. That's what brings pleasure to him. That's how sick he is."

Feeling Liz's pain, my heart ached, and these messages were tearing me up inside. I felt so powerless. All I could do was continue to push Liz to stay strong and the best way for her to accomplish that was for her to figure out a way for us to see each other. I just knew it would help her gain some strength. As dangerous as it was, I thought it would help her to survive.

"He likes me to keep in shape, it's an ego thing for him, so he allows me to go to the pool at Holy Trinity College. He has a lot of connections there despite being Jewish. Money talks. He knows a lot of administrators from his cocktail party crowd, and he's donated to the college. That's one of the only times I can get out of the house without the kids. Maybe we can hook up in the parking lot like we used to."

I wrote back, "Oh yes, Liz. I'm well aware of your husband's connection at the college. I used to be able to walk that campus and be respectfully received everywhere, now I'm shunned and unwanted. My close connections are telling me they've heard I'm a threat to the girls. Where do you suppose that came from? We'll have to be very careful."

Chapter 28

I waited in my pickup truck in a parking deck at Holy Trinity College. After a few minutes, Liz's blond head made her appearance from around a corner. She was on foot, wrapped up in a camel-colored woolen coat protecting her against the still-nippy New England weather. Without an ounce of body fat on her, I could see why she was so susceptible to the cold. She carried neither a purse nor her gym bag, having left them both behind in her car, parked elsewhere.

My excitement rose. God, it seemed as if I hadn't seen her in years, not weeks. I was literally in physical pain, jonesing for her like a junkie. The moment she got in my truck, we mauled each other like deprived carnivores.

"Dom, Dom, wait! Not here. He could find us. Drive. Put some distance between this place and us."

"Okay." I was short of breath with anticipation. As I drove around with Liz directing me in strange circuitous routes seemingly leading nowhere across the countryside, we picked up right where we had left off. We held hands with fingers intertwined and touched each other as often as possible. "Where are you taking me?" I asked as I looked at her beautiful smile, so radiant and inviting.

"It's so nice to see you, Dom, we need to concentrate, though. He could be following us. I don't trust him at all."

"That's crazy, there's no one behind us."

"Here." Finally, Liz directed me behind a row of buildings in a nearly abandoned industrial park in Cromwell. "How the hell did you ever find this place, Liz?" I asked as I found a secluded spot to park.

"You know me, I do my homework," she said with her radiant smile, now more inviting than ever.

I did not speak but simply turned toward Liz, kissed her, and embraced her. This time, she returned my ardor. Soon, we were removing each other's clothing. "Don't take everything off. We can't, it's broad daylight. He could still find us," she insisted through zestful kisses.

We were well rehearsed at this, and she didn't have to remind me of the procedure. She was just scared to death. I could not find the words to argue as we became just naked enough to consummate our love. Despite Liz's shorter legs, she preferred being on top, quickly straddling me. As she slid down, she threw her head back, closed her eyes, and sighed in receptive desire. She was wet. I easily thrust upward, penetrating her deeply. Her eyes opened wide as I drove upward, picking her up off the seat as she trembled. Was it passion, or was it fear? I wondered. Still, I found it difficult to think or wonder at all. Soon we were there.

"Touch me, Dom, touch me . . . ohhhhh . . . myyyyy . . . God, don't stop, don't stop. Dominic, you feel good inside of me, so much warmth." Liz hugged me and said, "I've missed you so much." She remained on me, and I in her as we held each other in our arms for as long as we could.

Liz put her hands on her head and began shaking it side to side as she said with pleasure, "I've missed you soooooo much, I love you, Dom."

"Me too, Liz."

"You have to take me back right now. Right now." She began to whimper.

This was not the Liz Temple I knew; usually Liz loved to lie, sit, or stand intertwined in love when we were finished. Was this just a quickie, or was she really that scared? "Liz, why does it have to be this way? I don't care how much he thinks he owes you in payback. This is America. You have rights, and this is crazy. You have the right to be happy." The more I talked, the more Liz's whimpers turned to sobs.

As we continued talking, we began to readjust our clothing and put ourselves back together.

"Liz, please don't cry, you're making me sad." But still she cried.

"I can't escape. I just can't. He won't let go of me. He won't ever let go of me. He'd rather kill me first. It makes me so crazy, I might kill myself."

"No no. Hold it right there, Liz." I became quite ardent in response. "You can't be talking this way. Don't you see what he's trying to do? You're better off dead to him than him paying you millions in a divorce settlement. You can't talk this way at all. You have your children. They need you. What would they be like with him and not you? Liz, you've said it yourself many times over. He's breaking you down. You're just an investment to deal with. In this case, he's selling you short to make money."

This wasn't working; it only made her cry more. "I will not allow you to fall, Liz. I will not allow you to succumb to his will."

"Please, quickly, take me back. We have to go now," she pleaded insistently.

As much as I wanted to argue, I knew that I couldn't. I started the truck and headed back for the parking deck at Holy Trinity, parking again where I had waited for Liz before. Liz kept whipping her head around the entire time, looking, searching, like an escaped convict, certain that the marshals were hot on her trail. It was sickening to see her this way.

"I'm really scared for you, Liz. I've never seen you like this. You were cautious before, but this. No one should have the power to make anyone else feel this way."

Again, as I talked, her eyes darted from side to side, always on the lookout. A gray Nissan Altima moved steadily around the parking deck. Liz inhaled quickly.

The car slowed down as it cruised closer to us until finally it came to a complete halt.

Suddenly, Liz became petrified. "Shit, it's my husband! Oh my god, that's his receptionist's car," She whispered loudly to me. "Oh my god, oh my god. It's my husband."

Sam Temple approached my truck. "Hello, Liz," he shouted, an angry edge to his voice cutting through the near-empty garage.

"We're just talking," a defenseless Liz blurted out.

"Well, hello, Mr. Renaldi," snarled the doctor with a wry satisfied smile.

I too was defenseless. "You're a pain in the ass. Yeah know that, Temple?"

"Not here, Renaldi. How about the three of us go over there and talk?" He pointed the way with his finger. "Both of you get in my car," he demanded.

"I'm not getting into any car being driven by you, Temple."

"Dom. Just let me out and get out of here. This is only going to get worse," Liz pleaded.

"Not until I know you're going to be safe. I'll drive you to where he wants us to go." I pulled out and brought my truck alongside the Nissan that the good doctor was driving. "I want you to call me when you get home so I know he didn't hurt you."

"Dom, you know I can't call you anymore."

"This is different. I have to know you're safe. I'll get out of this truck right now and tell him I told you to do that."

"No, Dom, do not get out of the truck! He'll want to provoke you to throw punches at him, and it'll be the biggest mistake of your life. Go! I'll try to call you later."

I watched as Liz exited my truck, straightening herself up and throwing back her hair while attempting to restore her composure. I watched as she entered the Nissan where there was no overt movement, no thrashing about. I figured I'd stay there until they pulled away. After a few moments, they did, and so did I.

Bracing myself for the worst, I returned home and puttered around, opening a can of soup and turning the TV on low. I didn't actually watch anything, just mindlessly channel-surfed and waited for my cell phone to ring. And waited. And waited. Hours went by. Then more hours. Days passed, and still nothing. I paged Liz with no response from her. Finally, I called the Temple's home number. An automated message came on. "The number you are trying to reach is no longer in service." My heart sank.

I hung up the phone and closed my eyes.

A few weeks of lifeless existence went by with nothing from Liz. One day, I was in the coffee shop with the owner of Coventry Travel, a former schoolmate of mine. Mary knew Liz professionally, and she knew I knew Liz. As Mary lit up a cigarette, she said, "That Liz Temple is something, you wanna see what she did?"

Not letting on to anything, except perhaps she saw my heart pounding out of my chest, I simply said, "Sure."

Pulling out an expensive-looking announcement of some sorts, I began to read.

"Dr. Samuel Temple and Liz are pleased to give you our new phone number."

My mind was a sea of fog, and my heart was of no use to my circulatory system at the moment. I did, however, manage to barely memorize the number. "Well, this is Coventry, Mary. What would you expect from her?"

Fully entangled in this web of desire, I picked up my phone and brazenly called Liz's new phone number. I knew this was not a smart thing to do and was relieved that Liz herself answered. Playfully, I said, "You can run, but you can't hide." I meant it as a joke, but Liz sounded anything but humored.

"Dom, don't ever call me again. I mean it. Please don't ever call me again. I'm going to lose my children."

"I wanted to see how you were."

The phone clicked dead in my ear.

"That wasn't a good idea," I said out loud.

Two days later, a process server showed up at my door.

"Mr. Dominic Renaldi?"

"Yes," I said knowingly.

"I am serving these papers to you. Please sign here as acknowledgment of receipt of same."

I signed, then sat down in the lone chair and opened the large envelope.

* * *

The following week, I was back in Cromwell District Court. Being one for one in representing myself, I did so again. This time, Sam Temple was nowhere to be found. Ken Macus, Coventry's prosecuting detective, the one who likes me, made arrangements for this to be heard before the court magistrate. This would be a little more informal than before a judge in the main courtroom but just as binding. While Liz Temple and her attorney sat in the front hall, I sat opposite them, trying to get some sort of signal from Liz. There was none.

When our case was called, Detective Macus read off a litany of complaints that amounted to me harassing and menacing the Temple family and Liz in particular as she and her husband attempted to resuscitate their marriage. The "you can run, but you can't hide" phone call was played in court. The conversation had been tape-recorded. Out of context, it damned me to hell.

Inside my briefcase, I had carried every card that Liz had sent me, including their envelopes proving their dates. All the evidence I would need to sink her allegations. As I was lambasted from stem to stern, I considered using them as a defense of my actions but thought better of it. Instead, I sat quietly being verbally eviscerated by the magistrate as Liz hung her head unable to look at me. For her part, Liz said very little, only responding meekly in the affirmative to the magistrate's leading questions about whether or not she was trying to patch up her marriage to Dr. Samuel Temple.

In my defense, I thought and then offered nothing. It became apparent I was just going to get a slap on the wrist today. I bit my tongue and took the reprimand in hope this was just Liz being used by her husband to get even with me. I still had all the proof I needed to show mutual agreement for getting back together.

The culmination of this exercise was for the magistrate to slap me with a six-month stay away order, a type of legal restraint. If I kept my nose clean and did not disturb or contact Liz Temple in any way for the next six months, the issue would be wiped off my criminal record without prejudice.

"Do you understand these charges, and do you understand this order?"

"Yes, sir, I do."

"Then I expect never to see you again in this courtroom, is that clear?"

"Yes, sir."

With a disgusted look from the magistrate, it was over. As I stood to leave, Detective Macus looked my way and gave me a wink. I nodded back in appreciation, then hung my head low, afraid to make any more attempts at looking at Liz.

Sam Temple was set on breaking Liz and ruining me at all cost.

Chapter 29

The first day back to work as a professional firefighter, I met with Chief Brewster, at his request, in his office.

A new beginning, a fresh start. Perhaps we have both learned something, I thought as I sat opposite the chief, watching, as he made damned sure the paperclips were perfectly arranged in his desk tray.

"Slayton and Jacobs told me that, for the good of the department, I needed to fire you. The selectmen told me to put you in the corner, but several members of the department came to your aid. You do have friends around here, Dominic." Brewster continued, "I even spoke to retired Chief Wyatt. He's the one who saved your ass by telling me, 'Something doesn't add up here, Pete, aside from the affair, something is driving this problem, and you've got to address that issue whatever it may be.' I don't agree with his assessment, but I owe Chief Wyatt too, so you'll get another chance. As for a demotion, there isn't anybody to handle the fire alarm aspect of your job as well as you, so you'll stay as a lieutenant, but I'll be watching you carefully. Now get back to work and do your job to your capabilities, Lieutenant."

At this point in my career, and given how I felt emotionally, I really didn't give a shit what the chief had to say or did. No matter what it was, it would be weak and just plain aimed in the wrong direction. You could count on that. Knowing I should have been fired, not for the affair but for my disrespectful words to my chief, I tried sucking it up—I just listened to this ineffectual leader. It was just too difficult for me, though. Nothing had really changed during the months of my suspension.

"Oh, I'm sure you'll be watching me better than you've watched Slayton and Jacobs. I've always done my job to my capabilities, Chief. Others also need to step to the plate and do their jobs."

"How can they do their jobs when the assholes don't even show up for work? Nobody's even coming back to cover the ambulance anymore. If it weren't for you and the mechanic, we wouldn't be able run the damn station," the chief said in frustration.

"Chief, did you ever stop to think that's a huge red flag? You once told me you know what 'cause and effect' means, but if you really did know, you'd remove the very heavy negative ground that's draining this place of all its power. Then you'd reapply this heavy cable and allow the positive energy to flow."

I was on a roll and not ready to yield. "I'll tell you why you won't do that, because if you rewarded the deserving people around here, the chosen few wouldn't be rewarded. The members whom this town wants in power wouldn't be in power. This place has ruined more talent than it has ever developed. Why do you think nobody comes back to help on routine calls? With your policies in place, you've told fifteen firefighters they're not good enough around here. It's as if the military has taken fifteen big and powerful Titan missiles and set them in a field to rot away, their capabilities untapped and never to be utilized. So much power, so much strength wasted away. Who wants to play on a team like that, Chief?" To which, the chief walked out of his own office without uttering a word. I shook my head in both disbelief and disappointment.

During my suspension, I had tried to understand it all. Not the affair, that I understood, but how this fire department really worked. This place wasn't a cohesive team, only a place of deceit and backstabbing, where if you didn't go along with the devil you knew, you were going to burn in hell some other way. It was just plain better for one to stay away from this sick house. However, this being my professional career for thirty years, staying away was impossible for me.

I contemplated applying for a similar job in another town or in the private sector, but this place was my life, and I had too many vested interests here. Besides, the cloud of the suspension and ensuing legal action against me made me an unappealing candidate for any job in any sector. Emergency workers weren't typical political appointees, but we had the ability to embarrass those with political aspirations. And right now, I was "radioactive"—do not touch.

Immersing myself in my work would help get my mind off my personal life. There was a lot of backed-up fire alarm work, particularly in meeting with architects, engineers, and project managers from all the construction and rehab going on in town. It was a very busy time. Virtually at every meeting, I was greeted with, "How are you feeling, Lieutenant? What is up with that chief of yours, does he know anything?"

I often thought to myself, *Why was his weakness so obvious to outsiders, yet the town was so blind to it? Ahhh, I remember. "As long as he delivers the budget to us, we don't care how he runs his department."* Such sound judgment in municipal management.

"What do you mean 'how are you feeling'?" I asked of those present.

"The chief told us you were injured at a fire and would be out for two months."

I silently seethed, then stated, "Yeah, I've been injured all right."

* * *

To my utter astonishment, I received a card in the mail about two weeks after my court hearing. Liz sent one last card to me, which opened with, "I know we should end our relationship, and that is not easy for me to do. I have such deep feelings for you. I can't find it in me not to continue. Perhaps these lyrics will help you to understand." Liz wrote the Lyrics to "I Will Always Love You." She went on to say, "You have meant so much to me, I will think of you every day. Every time I have success, it will be with the image of your support in my mind. Every night I go to bed, I will hold you close to me."

Liz ended with a quote from the song, "Above all this, I wish you love."

I sat down in my chair, my head back and tears running down my cheek.

The next day, I closed the post office box. I never responded to her.

* * *

After I received her good-bye card, a persistent Liz called from a pay phone the day before my first station assignment after suspension. She sounded both nervous and shaken as she begged, "I know this is crazy for me to call, but please don't go back, Dominic. I'm very worried something bad is going to happen. I know my husband well, and he's hell bent on getting you at all cost. Please don't go back to work!" She was now crying.

"Jesus Christ, Liz. First, you take me to court, then you send me a good-bye card, and now you call me on the phone." I was scared, I was anxious, but I still had to tell her, "Liz, the words you penned were meaningful and beautiful to me. I will always love you too."

"You know how music stirs my soul, Dominic. I meant every one of those words."

Then I asked, "Was that court business you or your husband?"

"It was all Sam. He made me do it. I can't talk to you—ever. I have to go. Please I beg of you, don't go back to work, Dominic!"

"I have to go back to work. Firefighting is all I know how to do, and I have to support my family."

"You won't be able to support them if you're dead!"

"Hey, if I get killed on the job, at least they'll be taken care of."

"That's not funny."

"It wasn't meant to be funny, Liz, but the hell with everybody and everything too. I am a professional firefighter, that is all I know how to do. I have committed my life to getting my children through college without student loans, and I will not rest until that is accomplished. No matter what the cost to me personally. I got myself into this mess, and I'll get myself out."

"Not even if I ask you?" Liz said in a sultry and seductive voice.

"Liz, I love you very much, and I've always taken your words to heart but not on this matter. You just don't understand what it's like not to have anything. I've read many biographies, and in every one, there's a great-great-grandfather who was strong enough to stand his ground enabling the family roots to take hold, where a footing could be set and future growth started. All I want in life is to be that great-great-grandfather. The best course for this process to continue is to educate my children. If I can accomplish that much, I can rest in peace. I will prevail. I must prevail."

"Oh, Dom, I love you so much for your determination, but I hate you right now," and then she hung up the phone.

That would be the last time I ever heard from Liz Temple. It was over.

* * *

As if a rookie, I entered headquarters with consternation. Chief Brewster had transferred me again. My first order of business was to take that plump and tasty kiss Liz had sent to me and put it inside my helmet where I'd always have one lasting memory of her with me.

Much to my dismay, I was assigned to Captain Slayton's shift. Yes, Slayton had received a promotion. He immediately told me I was assigned to the desk permanently. Now stuck in another small singular room of my life, I didn't know what to expect. There were preparations for me, though. Some of Jacobs's disciples wore custom-designed T-shirts with a picture of a cartoon man with a fire hose between his legs and the headline "You can run, but you can't hide." In this perverse firehouse, there was even a picture drawn on the chalkboard—a stickman picture of S-1, the fire alarm truck, with its bucket extended in the air, and a firefighter standing there holding a gun to his head. The handwritten caption was, "So long ego, Dom."

Brewster walked in the front door and greeted me with "Welcome back, Dom."

"Thank you, Chief. It's nice to be back. You may be interested in looking at the chalkboard."

Several minutes passed when Brewster returned to the fire alarm office and pathetically said with an angry tone, "What the fuck am I supposed to do about it?"

"Believe me when I say I don't expect you to do anything about it, Chief. Sad but true. I see you did do something about Slayton."

"Don't start up again, Lieutenant! Captain Slayton deserved the promotion."

"Chief, I don't wish to start up again, but on what grounds does Slayton deserve anything in the fire service?

"What the fuck was I supposed to do, Renaldi?"

"What about Lyons, Chief? He did the same thing as I did. Did he get suspended?" Then very sarcastically, I said, "Maybe he got a promotion too."

"That was a personal matter, Lieutenant. Nothing was done to Lyons."

"Oh, what a surprise, Chief"

"It ain't the same, Dom." Brewster was furious. "What happens in this house is supposed to stay in this house. You fucked with a taxpayer, and then you did it again after you were warned to stay away. Lyons never went to court or got charged with anything."

"Yeah, well, that's only because I did keep it in the house. I didn't make the kind of fuss shithead Temple did."

"Regarding Lyons, I am hereby ordering you not to use him on fire alarm with you. I am afraid there may be bad blood, and I'm not sure what you may do next. Is that clear, Lieutenant?"

"Chief, I need someone on fire alarm with me. I can continue to work with Lyons. I'm man enough to understand my wife did what she did because of my shortcomings. How about Slayton, Jacobs, and Lyons, are they men enough to admit to anything? How about you, Chief, are you man enough to admit to anything?"

"That's how life works, Renaldi. Effective immediately, start training Paul Frieze on fire alarm. He's always been on your side. Now are you ready to come back and follow the rules around here, or do you want to just hand me your resignation right now? 'Cause if you're back, I don't want to hear another peep out of you so long as I am chief."

"I'm back, Chief, and I'll do my job better than most. But there are no rules around here, at least not for some. There are no boundaries to contain their actions, Chief. And you refuse to punish a few when they cross the line." Brewster just turned and walked out of his office.

Several uneventful weeks passed, Slayton proved he had complete control of Brewster and the entire firehouse. He and Jacobs were now feuding. All members were hissing, snarling cats ready to pounce on anyone, and morale was as low as it had ever been. Sick-time abuse clearly indicated everybody's unhappiness. Frieze was working out fine with me; he was willing to learn and eager enough to do the job. I continued to work hard both because there was a lot to do, and I also needed to make up for lost wages. But along with everyone else, I too had a very poor attitude going into work each day.

Boyles and Dunn were working at station 2 when they got an ambulance call in their district, which meant the full complement of on-duty personnel would be responding. Dunn was a good, tough firefighter whom I had beaten out for the lieutenant's job several years back. He had never gotten over that and had developed a bad attitude toward me over not getting promoted. He began to concentrate on his side business of installing septic systems. He even held meetings at station 2 with his clients. Dunn's men would walk into the station dragging all kinds of crap with them. He didn't care. The more repugnant he could make it, the better. Liz would often call him, "Mr. Repulsive," and right she was. He was powerful but fat, always dressed in sloppy disarray and was generally very shabby. He had a chip on his shoulder the size of a septic tank. Shit was a perfect business for him.

The radio tone went out for "one man to cover headquarters," the customary practice for an ambulance call, and so I called in. *One man, not two?* I thought to myself. "Someone must be hanging around." At time and a half with a two-hour minimum, it was a quick seventy-five bucks. When I arrived at the station, Dan Roberts, a dedicated firefighter who lives in Cromwell, happened to be at the station. He told me a box had just been struck for a kitchen fire at 27 Farnsworth Road.

Farnsworth Road was a mature neighborhood on the south side of town, which used to be part of the sprawling Farnsworth estate. The eight-foot-high stone pillars to the estate's original entrance still remained at the corner of Bridle Path and Farnsworth Road as a reminder of a grander era in history.

Dan and I responded from headquarters in E-1. Captain Jacobs was on the road in C-2 (the captain's vehicle) and was on the way. E-3 quickly made up and responded from the ambulance call and was still first in to the fire. The chief also responded.

E-3 signed off with fire showing from the rear of the building. Dunn pulled the truck into the very short driveway. This would be a mistake because the ladder couldn't fit where it had to go. Paul's an excellent firefighter and should have known better. But because of the prevailing bad attitude, he didn't care. Boyles advanced the attack line no further than the front entrance. He never did like entering burning buildings.

The house on fire was a modern, well-built two-and-a-half-storied structure with a sunroom to the rear and off the kitchen. The point of origin was the kitchen, and the fire extended into the sunroom where it had burned through a skylight. Unbeknownst to the men, the fire had extended, up the outside of the house and into the attic from under the eaves. This went unchecked for a long time—another huge mistake. One of the first things an officer does on arrival is to walk all around the building on fire, from the outside, sizing up what he's dealing with. This wasn't done. When our truck arrived, some off-duty men were dressing the hydrant and getting water to E-3. The chief instructed E-1's crew to mask up and advance a line to the second floor with another attack line from E-3. Dan and I, both eager and very good firefighters who had come on the job together, were happy to respond to the orders. Dan is one of the fifteen Titan missiles, who managed to "just sit there and keep your mouth shut." We donned our air-paks, Dan putting his on one arm at a time, which is a prescribed, but slower method. I dropped my SCBA (self-contained breathing apparatus) over my head, cinching the straps while quickly moving toward E-3. Perhaps from my athletic days, this was just my nature—always thinking, always advancing forward. Most felt I was just trying to ensure that I would be at the line ahead of Dan, therefore making me the nozzle man. Call it what you want, but time was always of the essence when dealing with too few men and dangerous fire. I was accomplishing two jobs at once, which allowed us to get inside faster to put the fire out. That was just my nature.

As I pulled the line off E-3, Dan called out to Dunn, "We'll let you know when to charge the line."

A good pump operator knows how many lines are being used from his piece, where they are going and who's on them. The positioning of E-3 in the driveway notwithstanding, Paul Dunn was a good pump operator.

Dan and I met Captain Jacobs at the top of the stairs, which were just inside the main entrance, making them an easy access. Something was strange: the fire had gone from the first floor and into the attic without ever touching the second floor. I wondered how the hell that happened. Surely this home wasn't of balloon frame construction. "Captain, where are the attic stairs?" I asked as Dan called for our line to be charged. The entire second floor was charged with thick smoke, and the heavily plastered walls were holding the heat like an oven.

"There are no stairs, Renaldi," the captain shot back.

I thought to myself, *This house is too big not to have attic stairs. Surely it would have at least a set of pull-down stairs.* Always getting in trouble for questioning my superiors, this time I kept my mouth shut about the stairs.

The captain directed Dan and me to a small scuttle hole in a closet off the master bedroom and said, "Here's the entrance to the attic."

As I looked into the attic through the twenty-four-by-twenty-four-inch scuttle, I could see several large plastic clothing storage bags hanging from metal frames and suggested to the captain, "There must be another entrance because those items are too big to fit up through the scuttle."

"We've looked but couldn't find another access. This is the only way up, Lieutenant. You just be quiet and listen to me, you asshole!" said an infuriated Jacobs.

Surely these small scuttles were the case in many smaller homes; mostly one-and-half-story ranch houses built in the fifties, but this house was just too big. Nonetheless, I thought to myself, *Okay, you're the captain*. A small pencil ladder was put in place for us to enter the attic via the scuttle. A pencil ladder is a small narrow ladder ten feet in length, which collapses together and is carried on all trucks for occasions such as this. It looks like a pencil when folded.

By now, Captain Slayton had showed up and stood next to the chief as if he was the assistant chief. Ladder 1 arrived with just one man, so Brewster told Slayton to take over as E-3's pump operator. Dunn could then help with laddering the building to effectively improve ventilation. A captain as pump operator? Yet again Slayton escapes danger. Meanwhile, Boyles just stood at the front door like the Pillsbury Doughboy aimlessly spraying water into the house. Now why not put Boyles as the pump operator and have Captain Slayton lead the attack on the fire?

Before ascending the small ladder, I asked my captain, "Is the roof opened yet?"

"L-1 is taking care of that as we speak."

It was imperative to cut a hole in the roof directly over the fire allowing all the superheated air and gasses to escape while creating a safer environment for us to enter.

As good a firefighter as Dan was, he wasn't very athletic. I knew he'd have a hard time getting up through the scuttle opening. Letting him go first, I finagled his SCBA through the opening, then literally pushed him up and through. After Dan squeezed through the small opening, I handed the line to him and quickly got myself into the attic. Dan allowed me to retake the nozzle and the lead. We were in a very small portion of the attic, and I knew there had to be a larger portion over the main body of the house, so I started to look around. To the right of the clothes racks, I approached a wall, which was made of ten-inch-wide boards. Over the years, these boards had shrunk leaving half-inch gaps between them. The smoke in our section of the attic was getting thick and heavy, which meant there was a tremendous amount of incomplete combustion somewhere. The air temperature was rising too, and we both realized this room was primed to erupt in a flashover or a backdraft any minute.

Peering through the gaps in the boards, I was astounded to see the entire larger portion of the attic glowing red, looking like a huge charcoal fire. Any and all combustible material in the attic was glowing red; it was as if I was looking into a lava pit.

"Dan, look at this."

"Look at what?"

"Between the cracks, Dan."

"Holy shit, Dom, this place is about to light up."

Immediately, we knew our fears of a flashover were very real. At the same time, I suddenly saw the complete picture in my mind as to what was happening and how the attic must have been set up. The main access to the main attic must be located down the hall on the second floor, a typical location for such an attic's pull-down access in this type of construction. It was simply missed when the crew was looking for it. There also had to be something connecting the portion of the attic we were in with the main portion of the attic. This access has to be behind the clothing racks. Where else could it be? Realizing time was suddenly of the essence, I quickly spun around and said to Dan, "Come with me, we don't have much time."

Forcefully, I pushed the clothing racks over and landed on top of them. Dan enjoyed the action as much as I did, so without as much as a blink of the eye, he scurried with me in perfect unison. Sure enough, behind the racks was a walkway passage to the main attic. "Fuck!" I exclaimed to Dan.

"You got that right, bro!" he exclaimed back. Funny how during this dangerous time, I remember seeing his curly handlebar mustache through his mask's face piece.

We both knew there was a better way into the attic, and now, we were caught in this small enclave with a scuttle hole too small to escape quickly if need be. It was too hot and smoky to walk, so Dan and I were down on the floor when suddenly, a ferocious wall of flames started to hurtle toward us. In the fire service, any firefighter who has experienced this knows he has just met the deadly "fiery fingers of hell."

I raised the line to hit the fire at the rafters. Opening the nozzle, our line went dead, so I shut it down. Under normal conditions, this should not have happened. As we were struggling inside, the chief was outside directing the overall operations, exactly what he should be doing, and Brewster, for all his faults, was very good at it. As he looked around, he noticed Slayton—E-3's pump operator—and yelled, "Renaldi's on the line in the attic."

Slayton told the chief, "Don't worry, I know what I'm doing."

The fiery fingers of hell took another leap toward Dan and me, this time a little closer. The line stiffened, and I opened the nozzle again. We lost the water for a second time as the fire beckoned even closer, seemingly yearning to take us over.

"What the fuck is happening?" I asked Dan.

With eyes the size of golf balls, he said, "I don't know, but it isn't good!" as he tried to reposition the line in hopes it may have been kinked.

I felt it in my bones something wasn't going right outside, and we were stuck in a hellish situation that was tense and enormously dangerous. I knew our best bet was to try to knock the fire down as getting through that scuttle from the topside would be nearly impossible. The line stiffened for the third time as the fire consumed the space over our heads. It's a sight I'll never forget. The colors were a brilliant orangish yellow and red, so purely defined in shape. It was as if the flames were speaking to us, "It's your time, and we're coming for you. You have defeated us too many times in the past, now it's our time to seek revenge on you."

Though this was an extremely dangerous situation, it was also such a magnificent sight to see. Picture the devil with horns and a pitchfork in hand, seductively imploring his victim to come closer in very slow motion by stretching his arm out in a fluid movement, then fanning each finger while encompassing the object of his desire. In a poetic way, he pulls his arm back with an evil, but satisfied, look on his face. "Your time is now," he might have said. Hell's kitchen had announced lunch was ready, and Dan Roberts and I were its feast.

Yet again, I opened the nozzle, and the line went dead. Three strikes, and you're out. I knew we were fucked, and death was knocking at the door, so I yelled to Dan, "Bail out!" Forget the slow motion, we were now in fast forward. Thinking Dan may have trouble getting through the scuttle while praying he didn't get stuck, I removed my SCBA but not my mask. I didn't want to get myself stuck in the scuttle with the entire attic now erupting in flames. When I knelt up to remove my SCBA, I could feel how hot it had suddenly gotten in the attic. I know I'm going to die in hell someday, and this may have been a vivid preview, but it wasn't going to happen on the job. Miraculously, Dan dove head first through the scuttle, sliding like shit through a tinhorn, and I fell through feet first, falling out of my mask with my SCBA and helmet remaining in the attic.

Dan and I landed on top of one another in a heap. As several men were pulling us out of the closet, I turned to Dan and laughingly said, "I've never seen you move so fast."

To which he laughingly replied, "Dominic Renaldi doesn't bail out. If he says to bail, something must be wrong, and I'm out of there fast!" We both laughed and patted each other, perhaps more in gratitude that we were still alive than in appreciation for what we had done.

Indeed, something had gone very wrong, and it should not have happened. The fire eventually burned a big-enough hole in the roof to vent itself, and several attack lines later, the fire was out.

Dan and I were ordered out of the building. As we rested outside, Barbara Pickens brought my helmet to me. It was a little more darkened and burned. She, too, looked tired and dirty after the battle. Reaching inside of its singed yellow, but sooty liner, I pulled out that special folded piece of paper and opened it up. With a smile on my face, I kissed the still-intact lip impression. I then returned it to the place so close to me.

Dan asked, "What's that?"

Silently shaking my head for a few seconds as Dan looked on, I muttered, "Something very special, Dan."

Several hours after the all-out, back at the firehouse, we were all standing around after the cleanup. All the engines were back in service, and all mutual aid companies had been released. It was decompression time, a time of good banter about a seemingly well-done job as good as banter got in Coventry these days. Slayton was there, not a smudge on his face, clean as usual. There were a lot of men in the station, some senior and some junior. Suddenly, the chief raised his voice; with everyone quieting, he said, "And you, Renaldi"—pausing as we looked at him, he seemed to change his course of thought—"you are one helluva firefighter."

I responded, "You know me, Chief, I stare fire in the face and spit at it." All the men yelled out as if we'd just scored a goal.

Someone laughed and said, "Fire talk, Lieutenant, I love it." It was as if I unintentionally sent a bolt of electricity through the firehouse.

Jacobs fumed, saying, "He's a fucking asshole. He's a loner, always freelancing."

An irritated Slayton turned to Jacobs and said, "We have to take this guy down. We have to try harder, Tommy!"

After everyone had left, I went to Brewster and asked, "What did you really want to say when you called out my name?"

"I worry about you not having the right support to fight fire the way they should be fought," and he hung his head.

On the evening news, there was a mere mention of "two Coventry firefighters narrowly escaped a fire today."

During the fire investigation, it was determined that the hole in the roof was too small, and it was in the wrong place to vent the fire properly. In addition, the springs to the main pull-down stairs burned off, allowing the assembly to fall open with a massive supply of air rushing in, giving the fire its final component to fuel a fireball of superheated energy, hence the flashover. It was further determined that human error, traced back to E-3's pump operator, was causing our line to shut down with frequency.

Human error or just a human knowing what he was doing?

I turned and looked at Chief Brewster. What was there to do? What could I do? How do you prove some guy on your own department was trying to kill another member while you fought a fire?

Chapter 30

"Dom?"

Liz Temple's was the last voice I ever expected to hear again on the other end of my phone.

"Why are you calling me? Are you fucking with my mind too?" I said sternly.

"I'm at the pharmacy again. I need your help."

Torn between anger and happiness that she called, I paused to collect my thoughts. Then, I said, "Yeah, I know the feeling. I could have used your help the day you took out a complaint against me in court and then lied through your teeth to blame it all on me."

"Dom, you know who was behind that. You handed yourself up to Sam on a silver platter when you called me."

"And now I'm handing myself up to the court on a silver platter by speaking to you. I'm not sure I do know who's behind anything anymore, Liz."

"Listen, he's killing me. I can't live this way. He's having me tailed everywhere I go. You can't imagine what it's like."

"So go to the police. Go to your friend over there, Liz. Surely you know how to go to the police for the assistance you need."

"You know Alan and I have been friends for years."

"And you know I've always been uncomfortable with that. I don't trust two-faced, pretty boys, Liz."

"Yes, he's handsome, but he's not two-faced."

"A cop who fences stolen jewelry isn't two-faced? Please!"

"He does not fence jewelry!"

At this point, I didn't even care what I said to her. "Oh please, Liz, I've lived in this town all my life and have worked here long enough to know what happens here. He gets off duty at 11:00 p.m., and his "friend" shows up with all types of discounted jewelry."

"Stop it, Dominic. He's not like that. Sam's tied up all our accounts. I can't get at anything. My name has been taken off of everything of value. He knows that money binds me to him. Now I'm worried he'll take all my jewelry, and I want to get it before he does. You know where I keep it, don't you?"

"Have your cop friend help you. I've seen his cruiser in your driveway enough."

"Dom, he's just a friend giving me personalized service."

"Oh yes, I'm sure it's very personalized!"

"Dom, you just don't understand. I'm shut off from anything financial, and I need money to survive."

"Poor little child. That's the last thing to look to me for. I couldn't give you money even if I didn't have a stay away order pinned to my ass. I'm broke. You'll just have to see how the real world lives, Liz."

"Do you remember where my jewelry is?"

"Yeah, your jewelry's in the master bedroom. So why can't you get it yourself. I mean, you do live there. Hey, Bard can even stand guard while you steal your own jewelry. How perfect. The cop, the cruiser in the driveway, and the theft."

"Get over it, Dom! I told you, my husband's tailing me. Private detectives 24/7. I've got to get out of here in a minute, or they'll get suspicious."

"So where do I come in?"

"All I want you to do is check to make sure the jewelry is still there, then leave. I know you know how to sneak into my house. You've done it before when we made love in the basement while Sam slept upstairs"—Liz paused, then laughed—"Boy, that was fun wasn't it, Dom?"

I laughed with her, then said, "It sure was. We had to be out of our minds for doing that, Liz." Then we laughed some more.

Are you working tomorrow?"

"No."

"Come by my house at noon, sneak in to check, and then get out fast."

I paused for a long time.

"Dom? Dom, are you still there?"

"Yeah," I said reluctantly, "I'm trying to figure you out, and I smell a rat!"

"Dom, there's nothing to figure. That day in the courtroom, didn't that show you everything? He's crazy. He humiliated me, and he humiliated you. You have to know I'd never do something like that to you. But he made me . . . with the kids and all."

"Dom, I'm no longer living at home. Sam has tortured me too much, and I fear for my life."

"Where are you living?"

"I'm not telling anyone. My attorney helped me find a condo to rent for six months while I look for a place."

"And you don't want me to come by?"

"I can't take the chance, Dominic. If he finds out, he'll torture me all the more. No telling what he might do."

"Torture you, Liz?"

"You don't know what I'm going through, Dominic. My husband is an angry, controlling man, who is seeking ruthless revenge."

"File a restraining order then."

"I already have."

For a few moments, I paused to comprehend all of the information Liz just shared with me. Then I inquired, "When am I supposed to pull this caper off?"

"Tomorrow at noon, Sam will be at work, the housekeeper won't be there, and I'll make sure the alarm is off."

Like the last two calls I'd received from Liz, the phone clicked dead in my ear. No good-bye to be heard.

Foolishly, the next day, I parked my truck on a side street, which had a dead end off it and backed up to some woods. Getting out of the truck, I cut through the woods on the well-worn path I had established over time, which lead directly to the rear of Liz's house. My instincts clearly told me something was wrong with this whole operation, but I just had to see where this intrigue would lead, so I altered the plans.

The Temple's five-bedroom house was cut into a small hill and had a walkout basement door under the large first floor deck, which had an electric roll-down awning to it. To cover the basic support framework of the deck, there was eight-foot-tall lattice, painted white, surrounding it at the basement level. There was also plantings and a few step-down stonewalls to finish off the sprawling back lawn, which ended with Liz's greenhouse, containing her precious wildflower garden.

Despite my nerves, the greenhouse made me chuckle a little. "Why do you need a greenhouse to grow wildflowers? The whole concept is that the flowers are . . . wild. I don't get it."

"You get the seedlings started in there. I start in the middle of the winter. It's an art."

Over time, the hothouse wildflowers became a joke between Liz and me, in a melancholy way, a metaphor for our relationship. Wildflowers, stuck inside a glass house, unable to escape, overlooking a real world that was just beyond our reach. I had even begun nicknaming her wildflower. She, in turn, said to me, "Now when I look at them, I think of you."

I was nervous and apprehensive as I stood there and contemplated why I was doing such a foolish thing for this irresistible woman. Suddenly, it dawned on me. *The longer I stand here, the more likely it will be that I get caught.* So I approached the rear basement door. This was more intense than any fire I'd ever been in. The key was in its usual location just above the latticed door. Whenever Liz had invited me in this way, the alarm was always off, but I really wasn't sure of that today.

Making sure to cover my hand with my shirttail whenever I opened a door, I slowly entered the basement. The housekeeper kept an immaculate house, and everyone was required to remove their shoes. For this reason and the fact that I wasn't about to leave a shoe impression on the plush carpeting for Alan Bard to miraculously discover, I removed my work boots and left them at the door. Cautiously, I climbed the stairs to the first floor. Once I was sure the house was clear, I tiptoed to the master bedroom, top of the stairs and turn right. I had done this dozens of times before, sometimes carrying Liz up the stairs as we kissed.

I went right to the drawer where the jewels had always been. Liz had shown them off to me one fun day, stringing glittering necklaces around her neck, letting them hang down her naked body. "I give a whole new meaning to the phrase *rich bitch*, don't I?" Those were the good times as we laughed and made love with Liz wearing the jewelry and I taking each piece in my mouth, then inserting it in Liz's mouth with my tongue. It was decadent.

I still was quite uneasy about doing this whole operation and continued to analyze why Liz was having me do it this way. Her logic had gaps in it you could drive a truck through. Trying not to leave any fingerprints, I opened the drawer. There was no jewelry.

"FUCK, *I've been set up."*

I closed the drawer and beat it out of the bedroom, down the stairs, around the corner, and down the basement stairs to my work boots. Surely, I thought, Sam Temple or Alan Bard would be around every corner or that the police were in the driveway. *I can't believe she set me up again,* I thought to myself as I quickly put my boots on. Taking a quick look outside and not seeing anyone, I, like a white-tailed deer on the run with its tail between its legs, raced through the woods to my truck and slowly drove away like nothing was wrong. I looked at my wristwatch—11:00 a.m. Who did they think they were screwing with?

As soon as I could gather my thoughts, I called my friend, Dennis, at the police station.

Ten minutes later, we were sitting in Dennis's cruiser in the cemetery behind the police station. I said, "That's exactly how it went down, Dennis."

"That was a pretty stupid thing to do, you jackass!"

"No shit, buddy! But I did do it, and now I'm telling you before you find out about this some other way."

"So there was no jewelry in the drawer?"

"None whatsoever."

"Where do you think it is?"

"I don't know. I don't know what's happening at all. Did Temple move it? Did he steal it? Did Liz steal it? I'm way too confused, Dennis. All I do know is that I did not steal the jewelry."

"Okay, Dominic, it's good you came to me beforehand. Let's sit on this and see what develops. I'll brief my chief. He's a good man, Dom, and he likes you too."

Two days later, Dennis called and told me a burglary was reported at the Temples' house, and $110,000 worth of jewelry was missing.

"You called that one, Dom. This is a real mess now. We dusted for prints, and Dr. Temple specifically insisted we try to match what we found against your prints. There were no fingerprints and no matches. Funny, because I expected I'd find some of yours even if they were old. But the place was pristine. Hell, we hardly even found any belonging to the doctor or his wife. Either the place was wiped clean, or they must have one hell of a housekeeper. We couldn't even find a speck of dust. And the surfaces are all flat and glossy. You'd think it would have been a piece of cake for us."

"Yeah, *funny* doesn't begin to describe it, Dennis."

The veteran police officer may have been my friend, but he was a professional police officer above all else. "You know something you're not telling me, Dominic?"

"Dennis, we've known each other for over forty years. Have you ever known me to lie to anyone in that time?"

"No, I haven't Dom. If I had to say anything, I'd say you're truthful to a fault, my friend."

"Yeah, I know. Thanks, buddy," I said with a strained chuckle as I looked down.

"Dennis, I want you to look me straight in the eye." With the both of us looking into each other's eyes, without so much as a blink, I said, "Dennis, I swear to you on my children's lives, I did not steal that jewelry."

"No, Dominic, I don't believe you did either. So outside of the good doctor trying to pin it on you, do you have any ideas who did it?"

"Well, surely you know you have to look at five people in this case."

"Why don't you go ahead and tell me who they are, Dominic."

"Sam Temple, Liz Temple, the housekeeper, me, and your very own Alan Bard." As soon as I mentioned Bard's name, Dennis dropped his head. "I know all about him, Dennis, and you do too!"

"Yes, I do, Dominic."

"Then why haven't you done anything about it?"

"It's the "thin blue line" thing, Dom. Ya know, don't rat out your fellow officers. It's something I don't like, but we all know it exists."

"I'm sorry, Dennis, but it's fucking hypocrisy at the highest levels, and it is destructive."

Dennis wanted to get off that subject and quickly started questioning me again. "Temple still has quite a hair across his ass for you. I think he mentioned your name fifty times. Had us looking for shoe prints too. But nothing, I think it's an inside job. But I thought I'd call you since he kept yakking you up."

"Of course, you have to suspect me, Dennis. I don't think you have to look any further than those five names, though."

"Dom, you're sounding mighty strange to me, buddy. You got something you want to get off your chest? I know you really cared for the lady."

"Yeah, Dennis, I did. But that was a lifetime ago."

"Knowing you the way I do, I'd a thought it would have taken you a helluva lot longer to get over it."

"I'll never get over her. I wish it could have gone on forever. We helped each other in so many ways. That's probably why I pulled this stupid stunt, but betrayal is a real kick in the ass, Dennis. Straightens a man right up no matter how much he likes a lady. This was the wake-up call for me, Dennis. I have always operated on three strikes, and you're out, ya know, cut your losses and run kinda thing."

"Yeah, I understand, buddy. I think it's best for you to do that right away!"

"I'm all done with Liz Temple, Dennis. She's shown me a very ugly side I've never seen before, but I do have a question for you."

"Shoot."

"Who reported this theft, and when was it reported?"

"The doctor called around twenty after twelve on Tuesday afternoon. Why?"

I snorted. "Dennis, faithfully every Tuesday morning, ten to twelve, Liz and I had reserved for us to be together at her house. I can say this without hesitation. Dr. Temple has never been in that house at that time of day on a Tuesday—*ever*. Liz instructed me to enter that house at noontime, but I had a very bad feeling, so I went an hour earlier. You can narrow that list of five names to a list of three: Sam Temple, Liz Temple, and Alan Bard!"

Chapter 31

Being a fireman in a small town is not all about fighting fires. There's a lot of downtime, and everyone finds different ways of dealing with it. There is also the nagging pinch from the local taxpayers regardless of how able they are to pay their tax bills. "What am I getting for my money?"

The Coventry Fire Department was often called upon to make use of the equipment they owned that could serve dual purposes. One of the most popular pieces of equipment was the bucket truck, a cherry picker that could assist in many a town activity. This truck, S-1, was under my supervision.

All town organizations found the truck useful. Sometimes, I'd perform a task while working fire alarm, thus getting paid for it. Usually, this work would be for other official town organizations, such as the school department. The chief would pay me out of his budget, therefore not draining the smaller fire alarm budget for this favor. I made good money throughout the year performing this work, and men were jealous of all the time and a half I was receiving.

Often, Jacobs and St. James would pressure the chief about my overtime, but Brewster knew full well what a valuable service I was providing, especially since the penny-pinching finance committee was on my side. How quickly men like St. James forgot we all had the same opportunity to get involved with fire alarm work years ago, but I was the only one who chose to pick up the ball and run with it. Everyone else went outside the department for other incomes. I even tried placating those who had complained by putting up a sign-up sheet for opportunity to do fire alarm work, where everyone picked up their paycheck on Thursdays. Occasionally, a few names appeared on the sign-up sheet, but Jacobs would quickly pressure them, and their names would be scratched out. Only Lyons's name was allowed to stay.

Being civic minded, I sometimes volunteered the use of the truck along with my time. However one wanted to view my work with the bucket truck, it was a very valuable PR tool for the fire department. Slayton and Jacobs did not like me receiving accolades for my work, especially Jacobs. "We don't need him or his truck," he said often.

Some of the volunteer organizations in the town would advertise their projects with banners hung across the road in the town center. I was very much in favor of these banners, so quaint, so small town America. It gave a nice New England flavor to the community; but it was clear to me a better job could be done in coordinating and putting up these banners in a less helter-skelter fashion. Several years back, when times were better, I was given permission from the Town Manager and my chief to speak to the utility company about finding an alternative way for accomplishing this banner business. Using any favor I had with BECO (Boston Edison Company), I was able to use the bucket truck to install steel cables from one of their utility poles cross the road and secure them to a large oak tree. Shortly after this was accomplished, the chief called me into his office and showed me a copy of a letter written to the Board of Selectmen, which was signed by seventeen town organizations. In short, the letter thanked the board and specifically mentioned me. In part, the letter said, "We owe Mr. Dominic Renaldi, of the fire department, a debt of gratitude for getting this accomplished."

As was customary, the letter was hung on the bulletin board in the firehouse. Despite how well we worked together in previous years, Jacobs still had a propensity to rant and rage when he saw S-1 and me missing. Jealousy? Who knew? But what he did know was, every time I was out doing something with that truck, I was getting kudos somewhere. For every banner clip I hung to a cable, I'd receive honks, hellos, and waves from a myriad of people. It truly was small town America. Despite the acknowledgments, these certainly were not glamour jobs: hanging street banners; raising window repairmen to fix public buildings, and electricians to work on field lights at the local gridiron/tennis courts. One project done every year was to clean out the town hall gutters after the leaves fell, not to mention the three inches of pigeon shit that came with it! How glamorous was that? But I did it all in good faith.

Despite the present tumultuous time, Chief Brewster, for the good of the town, continued to allow me to have carte blanche during hurricanes and blizzards. He knew damned well how valuable this truck was and how well it served the town under my supervision. I was allowed to handpick my men, usually Lyons and Dan Roberts made up the crew. This was the piece to be on if you wanted action. We were free to roam the entire town and respond to any and all calls, all at my discretion. I'd instruct the guys to load up the truck with skill saws, plastic, nails, chainsaws, fuel, and be ready to handle anything nature threw at the town. I always made sure they had their fire gear on board too. Usually, the truck was used to cut trees and branches in an effort to maintain open roadways from north to south, east to west all over town.

In addition, we were at the chief's beck and call. I recall one hurricane. The schools couldn't open until the power came back on, and the utility company refused to turn the power on until the broken pole outside the high school was replaced, or at least secured.

Boston Edison gave this pole a low priority on a list of a thousand things to do. It might be days before they got to it. At 0400 hours, the chief called for S-1 to meet him in front of the high school where he was standing by with a supervisor from Boston Edison. “Can you do anything to secure that pole, Lieutenant?” the chief asked as he pointed to the obvious pole in question.

“Piece of cake, Chief!”

As the chief looked on, the Boston Edison supervisor verified the power was off. I positioned the truck in just the right spot, then climbed into the bucket and extended the boom as I instructed Lyons, “Okay, now just back me in slowly” as we angled precariously for the back of the pole. Dan was outside the truck, always watching, observing for danger. He was a very cautious man and played an important role in all we did.

“GOOD!” was the loud and firm one-word instruction for Lyons to stop. By voice inflection, he’d know how quickly to stop, a signal well rehearsed many times before. Within a half hour, the pole was secured for however long it would take for BECO (Boston Edison Company) to replace it, and the school could open. With mission accomplished, I climbed down off the truck where I was greeted by the Edison supervisor, “Nice job Lieutenant. Before we go I have to ask you a question. How the hell did you ever get permission to string those cables across the Boston Post Road to hang banners? No town in metropolitan Boston has ever been give permission for that before.”

I just smiled and said, “This is Coventry, sir, they get what they want.” Brewster feebly watched the exchange.

All this was just part of what the fire department did for a community; it was just a part of what I did for the fire department. Still, I was looked upon as a hero of sorts in the community, and Jacobs seethed over it. Often, a picture of the bucket truck with me performing a task was on the front page of the *Town Crier*.

“He’s a fucking asshole. He should never have been doing that. He’s just a loner always freelancing,” Jacobs expounded. There was another storm, Jacobs was OIC (officer in charge), but Chief Brewster was there too. It was an icy, rainy, late winter storm. While on duty and in S-1, I came across an Edison electrical transformer burning on a pole just outside of the town center. I noted the lights were still on in several buildings in the area, and I called it in. Never in my years on the job have we not stood by, especially with the power still on, so I concluded with, “I’ll be standing by until Boston Edison arrives.”

A few minutes later I was informed by dispatch, “Edison has been notified, there is a one hour ETA” (estimated time of arrival).

I acknowledged, “message received.” The location of the transformer fire was at the entrance to a small, but busy parking lot, so I began using the fire alarm cones off S-1 to cordon off the immediate area. The potential for a wire coming down on a car, or worse, a pedestrian was great. Then I would direct traffic around the situation.

About ten minutes went by when Jacobs got on the radio, “Car two to S-1, you can return to quarters.”

I was surprised, but not shocked by the order. In Jacobs's eyes all that ever mattered was to get me out of the picture, no matter what the cost.

So I said, "Car two, the transformer and the pole are burning pretty good and the power is still on. This is a very dangerous condition here."

Jacobs pounced right on me over the radio, "I gave you an order Lieutenant. Now follow it out," he said angrily.

I shook my head and simply said, "Message received. S-1 is returning to quarters."

Jacobs would later tell his cronies, "We don't need him or his truck around here."

Brewster never overruled him on it, and a half hour later an electrical wire burned off the transformer and fell to the ground narrowly missing a few people. Those who saw me leave complained to the chief about it, and I took the hit for it.

* * *

Most male children fantasize about being a fireman. Few actually grow up to become one. Some firemen bring "the child in him" to work. Practical jokes were the norm. Despite how angry I got when my truck was egged and my ears damaged from an M-80 going off, many of the guys simply wrote it off as pranks and hijinks. After all, that's what they were being brainwashed into believing. Short-sheeting someone's bed? Now that's a practical joke. A few years before Barbara Pickens was hired by the fire department, the police hired Lisa Nichols, the first female police officer in Coventry. She was a good cop whom I supported in the same manner as I did Barbara.

I was sitting at the fire alarm desk one afternoon when, over the police scanner, I heard Lisa call in a wire down on Buckskin Drive. With difficulty, she tried describing which wire it was. "I don't know. It's small and black."

Recently built into the fire alarm console, we had a pager system and could page anyone programmed into it. Lisa was in the system, so I paged her to stop by headquarters. A few minutes later, she was standing in the lobby.

Briefly, I gave her the lowdown on how to identify wires on a utility pole. I began drawing a diagram for her on the back of an unused incident report form as I continued speaking to an interested student. "Telephone is the first wire from the bottom, sometimes there's more than one telephone cable. Then there's cable TV, usually three wires bundled together, one of which is silver in color. After that is the fire alarm cable, sometimes red, sometimes black. Look for the red terminal boxes on a lot of poles and think of *me*," I said jokingly. This was a serious learning exercise, and Lisa took it earnestly as she listened intently, knowing how important it was to her job and her safety; she was grasping it.

"This is where the real danger begins, Lisa. Perhaps my emphasis on the fire alarm wires would help set a dividing line of danger on the pole for her to remember.

The wire above fire alarm is the Edison secondary. The secondary wires carry electricity to the homes and most buildings in a community, usually 240 volts, that one can kill you. Above that, the very top wire is the Edison primary wire, and that will definitely kill you, Lisa! These wires carry huge voltage across the BECO system to feed the secondary wires—13,800 volts, Lisa. They can be singular wires across a long wooden arm, or it can be three wires grouped closely together but not touching."

Developing the diagram as I spoke, I abbreviated each wire with a capital letter that went something like this from the bottom up.

T telephone
T telephone
C cable TV
FA fire alarm
S Edison secondary
P Edison primary

"Whenever in doubt, Lisa, treat all wires as if they were alive and of primary voltage and never get close to them as they can energize the ground around them. It's quite simple, Lisa. From bottom to top, they get more dangerous. If you remember nothing more, please remember that much."

"I will. Thank you. Geez, I didn't know they were so organized or dangerous. Thank you very much, Dom. Others have always said you were a good instructor, now I see why. I'll have to come up with an acronym or some way to remember this."

Within a few days Lisa returned to the firehouse with a huge shit-eating grin on her face. "Lieutenant, I've figured out a way to remember the wire positions on a utility pole."

With that look on her face, all I could say was, "This ought to be good."

Lisa handed me a short note to read.

T time
T to
C see
FA Dom's
S small
P penis

All I could do was just sit there and laugh as Lisa joined in. I called for a few men to come read it. They too started cracking up.

This was absolutely hysterical, humor that will live in infamy in both departments. I wouldn't be surprised if, today, new recruits were told the story.

But there was malice and contempt behind too many other practical jokes, maybe worse. I had a temper, which was very much exploited, and had always felt that practical jokes of this type were, above all else, very impractical and very destructive—my ears were proof of that. In the back of my mind, I always felt a prank might be so destructive as to result in my death.

All of this played heavily on my mind whenever I went to get the fire alarm truck. Such was the case when Frieze and I went to get the bucket truck out of station 2 one summer's day. I was always apprehensive when I saw the truck; you just never knew what they might have done next. I'd often flash back to the loosened fuel pump leaking gas all over the hot engine, the time the front brake lines were loosened, and the time when there was water in the gas tank. These weren't practical jokes, and this is what infuriated me so much. That and Brewster's inability to do anything about it!

But I was still more within my own head about my status with the department, my status with my family, and my status with Liz. I'd been severely punished by all parties and was still treated as a pariah—the guy who had just served a sixty-day suspension and had come close to starting several fights, both physical and verbal, in the firehouse. "Hotheaded dago," was muttered behind my back as frequently as "what do you think about the Sox this year?"

My soon-to-be ex-wife, Ruth, was being seen around town with an older fellow whom we'd both known most of our lives. Funny. She had given the younger Ben Lyons a test-drive and now she was opting for a much older model, a decade or two older than me, and I had five years on her.

This didn't surprise me, nor did it throw me. Ruth had always struck me as the kind of woman who couldn't stand to live alone. A women's libber she was not. Ruth needed a man around the house and as much constant company as possible. She was looking for her grandfather, whom she loved so much. That's where I had let her down. Sitting next to her like two old folks in rocking chairs was something I wasn't quite ready for in my life, and so she had set out to find him. With a great deal of sorrow, I wished her nothing but love and happiness for the rest of her days.

I'd heard nothing more from Liz, nor did I wish too. Having finally come to the conclusion Liz had used me to her own advantage, I was no longer interested in being her puppet.

Dennis did keep me in the loop on the jewelry heist, but there wasn't much to tell. I already knew in my heart what had happened. Liz had set me up. What a coup that would have been had I fallen into the trap—jail time. Talk about ruining a man for good. Liz Temple turned out to be a conniving cutthroat, who had used me to collect $110,000 from her insurance company while having fenced the goods through her longtime friend at the police station for who knows how much more. I was sure of it. Either way, Sam Temple had won. Guys like him always win. Why was that? I considered myself an uncomplicated man, and perhaps, that was the problem. An uncomplicated man was easy prey for a person like Sam Temple who spent every waking minute planning his next scheme. Slayton was much the same way. Who but Slayton would have ever thought that you could become a ranked, powerful, and well-connected firefighter without ever really fighting a fire?

Sam had used Liz to get me, and Liz used me to get money. I was quite sure of all that as my depressed moods swept me along. The optimist in me thought she's being tortured—mentally and even, perhaps, physically—into taking the lead on some of these acts of revenge. What else made more sense? Why else would she turn so against me? I hadn't done anything to her but love her. To her I was "The Wind Beneath My Wings," where "I Will Always Love You," forever "My Heart Will Go On," and any other garbage she fed me. As it turned out, I was so blinded by the glare of her beautiful smile.

Either way, I tried to push images of Liz far to the back of my mind as much as possible, trying to amble through life day by day in an effort to resuscitate myself back to the man I once was. Times were not easy, and I had no one to blame but myself. I will go on, I must go on.

* * *

Our department worked an eight-day cycle, so we sometimes worked fire alarm on the weekends. It was a Sunday, just after lunch, and a banner advertising a free summer outdoor concert awaited Frieze and me. With the less traffic, Sundays were the best banner-hanging days. In fact, I had set up the permitting process to have the banners hanged from Sunday to Sunday for this very reason. At worst, there might be a slew of cars going to or from church services; there were five churches within a quarter mile of the center, three of which were within one hundred yards, but most of the drivers were more placid than during the week. Having picked up the banner at headquarters, Frieze and I drove the one hundred yards to where the banner would hang in the picturesque center of Coventry, right on Boston Post Road. Norman Rockwell could not have painted a more quintessential picture: The magnificent sunken with the town hall set on the other side of its lush green grass, the stone church with its high steeple and golden clock, the antique watering trough now filled with colorful flowers and maintained by the garden club, the stately brick library right out of Harvard University's architecture with walls of ivy, and the historic tavern with the adjoining barn now used as a reception hall for small quaint gatherings. The banner would hang just one utility pole down from the historic tavern toward the firehouse.

Mundanely, I climbed onto the heavy-duty rear bumper of S-1, up the steel step, and into the bucket to perform this task for the umpteenth time.

"So do I get to fly through the air today, eh, boss?" Frieze called out eagerly from the ground.

Looking down at Frieze from in the bucket, which was still at rest, I said in jest, "I sincerely hope not, buddy. Besides, it would take a Titan missile to get you off the ground!" We both laughed. Changing my mind, I said, "Yeah sure, cement head. This will be a good opportunity for you to gain more experience with the bucket usage. Good idea. Don't kill yourself or, worse yet, me." And I climbed out of the bucket. With confidence, Frieze climbed in.

The protocol is that the ground man worries about the traffic. With Paul's lack of experience in the bucket, I instructed him thoroughly in this very easy task and was very confident in his ability to carry it out. Paul had the basics and had good common sense. The banner hanging was easy enough, so I could let Paul be bucket man and, thereby, gain some valuable experience and confidence. “Up you go,” I shouted to him as I began watching on the traffic.

What a difference a year makes. The previous summer, Lyons had been my primary partner on projects like this; but he had broken a cardinal rule. You don’t screw the wife of another firefighter you had to depend on in life-or-death situations. In the military, you’d face a court martial for this. You leave that stuff outside.

Benny had been my protégé. Now Lyons hung with Slayton and Jacobs. He was their boy now. And I was persona non grata. I’d gone from being Chief Wyatt’s handpicked successor to the permanent doghouse. Had Liz Temple been worth it? I was having my doubts.

Frieze may not have been as experienced in the bucket as Lyons and certainly not as experienced as me, but he was a good kid and gave his very best effort at everything he did. To put a banner up, it was easiest if the truck was positioned in the middle of the road and traffic allowed to flow on either side. As intelligent as people of this town were, the ground man was always busy going from front to back of the cherry picker keeping cars moving in their lane. Why anyone would think they had to cross the yellow line to go around the truck was well beyond my comprehension, but some insisted on trying. I was kept busy on the ground.

Hanging the middle of the banner first, Paul would first move right and then left, attaching the top of the banner to the top cable first. Then he’d go straight across the bottom and attach the bottom clips to the bottom cable. It was really a simple operation that was best accomplished this way because of the wind, which always blew down the post road. In addition, while this installation was being done, the banner would hang down directly behind S-1, not into the travel lanes with the potential of getting snagged by a passing car or truck. This method was proven sound over time. Everything was moving quite smoothly.

Paul was about half done hanging the top of the banner, which would put him approximately twenty feet above the back of the truck. Occasionally, I would look up to make sure Paul was okay as I paid attention to the cars. Slowly, he maneuvered the upper boom’s lever, but nothing happened. I detected an unusual sound and turned to the truck. “What’s wrong?” I asked.

“Something’s not working right, Dom.” Paul moved the lever again—still nothing; but this time, he held the lever over.

As he did so, it all clicked in my head. Suddenly, I screamed, “NO! STOP!” But it was too late. From fifteen feet in front of the truck, I heard a loud snap and a twang echoing from within the boom. The bucket flipped upside down, and in a split second, Paul was being catapulted out of it. He tried grabbing anything he could, but it happened too fast, and he couldn’t stop his six-foot-two-inch, athletic body from falling downward, headfirst, into the back of the truck. It was over in seconds. He was doomed from the start; the back of the truck was all steel and had a rigidly welded step—made of jagged-edged, saw-toothed steel for nonskid purposes—attached to it for getting in and out of the bucket.

I was horrified. At first, I just wanted to puke; but in an instant, I was on the radio screaming for help for a badly injured and unconscious member. I didn't have to see Paul's body to know that much.

Chaos erupted in Coventry. Civilians strolling the streets converged on the scene. Cars stopped. Doctors in their Sunday best came out of the woodwork to assist us; they too knew it was futile. Men ran up the street from the firehouse.

"Get the life-flight helicopter in the air now!" I screamed over the truck radio before racing to Paul's body. He had hit the step on the way down and crushed his skull, his lifeless body landed on the ground behind the truck. It would be a blessing if he broke his neck, ending it quickly. I was performing CPR and mouth-to-mouth on Paul when the first firemen arrived. My mouth was covered in Paul's blood, and my hands had his brain matter on them from trying to tilt his head as I operated in shock mode, saying, "We can do this, we can save him." Everyone knew there was nothing we could do to save Paul's life, but I frantically tried in vain. Jacobs was a screaming maniac. Slayton, who had also appeared on the scene, remained silent in numbness from afar. Still, I kept up my ministrations. *Live, you big cement head, live.*

The fire ambulance arrived quickly, and Paul was expeditiously loaded into the back.

"I'm going too," I said.

"Are you hurt?"

"No, but he's my man, he's my responsibility," I said authoritatively as I pushed my way in.

"Dom, step away. Let them do their job. You're too shaken." It was Chief Brewster.

I watched as the ambulance drove away. Brewster made the righteous call for once. I was too shaken. Shock and numbness invaded my being.

"I know with every fiber of my body that should have been me. I should have been up there, not Frieze," I said to Brewster. "I hope you're happy now, you no-good, yellow-bellied, gutless, fucking idiot."

An engine arrived and closed down the street. Soon, the police were all over the place controlling the gathering crowd and cordoning off what was now a crime scene.

I was taken over to an embankment on the side of the street and sat by myself in solitude. How ironic. I leaned against the historic stone. *Gen. George Washington passed through here on his way toward driving the British out of Boston.* Someone handed me a wet towel to wipe myself off with. Finally, I looked up. It was an eerie sight. S-1's boom extended up in the air with no apparent usefulness, an empty bucket just setting up there, and the banner flapping in the wind. The truck was still running with all its warning lights and headlights on, which was customary when in use. The back of the truck was a sick sight, all splattered with Paul's blood and brain matter. Parts of his skull, with hair still attached, was embedded into the saw-toothed steel step. I felt very sick to my stomach.

My friend, Dennis, from the police found me after he had been informed that I had been part of the banner-hanging team. Dennis approached me stoically. He put his hand on my shoulder as a priest would his parishioner.

“That should have been me and not Paul. This was no accident, Dennis. It was meant for me, trust me when I tell you that, Dennis. Please I beg of you to believe me.”

“I know, pal. I know how you’re feeling. Don’t beat yourself up. Do you have any clue how or why this accident happened?”

“Dennis, this was no accident. Nothing could have caused this. It was too simple an operation with no obstacles in the way,” I continued muttering to myself, almost ignoring Dennis’s presence. “Did I train him well enough? Would this have happened if I were in the bucket?” My voice was just above a whisper.

“Stop it, stop it now. You got media coming around now. I can see the vans pulling up already. Just shut your mouth and don’t go giving out statements. You’re in no condition.”

I looked up at my policeman friend. “But I’m supposed to be in condition for anything. I’m not supposed to lose my head in an emergency.”

“And you didn’t lose your head, Dominic. No one has ever seen you lose your head in an emergency. What did you do the moment it happened?”

“I called it in, and I began first aid.”

“And that’s your job. That’s all there is to it. There’s nothing else you were supposed to do. There’s nothing else you’re supposed to do now. You didn’t drop the ball. Now stay here and allow yourself to be cared for. That’s part of your job too.”

“You don’t understand. He was my responsibility, Dennis. Why couldn’t it have been me instead? Paul didn’t deserve this! When will people start listening to me? What the hell will it take? Paul Frieze is gonna die, isn’t that enough for someone to start paying attention?”

Dennis stayed with me as he watched the scene unfolding before us. Brewster had called for the state police recon team, and they had just arrived and were beginning to take over.

“Dennis, listen to me, something isn’t right here. This should not have happened. That truck was in fine shape. The cable snapped. There’s no way that should have happened. I think it was tampered with. Make damn sure the state police know that.”

Dennis paused to gather his thoughts. “I don’t know whether to agree with you or not. Part of me thinks you’re paranoid. The other part of me thinks you’ve got every reason to be.”

Chapter 32

On my way back to the firehouse, I stopped at St. Joseph's Church. The church I was baptized in, had my first communion in, and was confirmed in. St. Joseph's is adjacent to the firehouse. Its priest had given Frieze his last rites in the ambulance. I was raised Catholic, but looked upon it as hypocritical, so it had been years since I was in church. I am, however, a strong believer in God. I removed my fire coat and knelt in a pew. With tears in my eyes, I prayed for Paul and his family, asking God, "Why did it have to be Paul? Why couldn't it have been me?"

I never got a reply.

By the time I got to the firehouse, Capt. Tom Jacobs was just beginning to gather everyone together as we waited for the news we feared was forthcoming.

"I just got off the phone with the chief. He's at the hospital. Paul Frieze has died."

The room fell silent. Jacobs's face betrayed nothing. These are the times when internalizing emotions begins. For some, it's much easier to do.

Jacobs was trying to act chiefly, but his true inner madness revealed itself, "Renaldi, you caused this. You are a fucking asshole!"

"This is Jack William, WBZ-TV News. We break into our regularly scheduled programming to bring you a developing story we are working on. Let's take it live to Dan Rea, who is on scene now."

"Thank you, Jack. This is Dan Rea reporting live from Coventry, where a very tragic accident has taken the life of a young firefighter. I've got to say, in my fifteen years of reporting, I've never seen such a gruesome sight just up the street from here at the firehouse."

More thoughtful members of the fire department, led by Dan Roberts, braved the cameras out front and lowered the firehouse flag to half-staff as the half dozen news cameras panned from the tragic scene one hundred yards up the post road to record this solemn event for the world to see.

“Let’s take it back, live, to Dan Rea,” said the steady news anchor. “Dan, can you give us any details of what has happened?”

“Yes, Jack. Apparently a firefighter was simply putting up a banner across the road, and somehow fell from the bucket to his death. His name has not yet been released, and we are still trying to piece the facts together here. Right now we are watching firefighters lower the flag here in front of the firehouse. We all know how closely knit a group firefighters are, it must be a very sober scene inside.”

If only these cameras could see into the inner workings of this department just beyond the brick walls, so unlike a real fire department made of real men and women. Unable to contain myself over Jacobs’s remarks, I suddenly bolted out of my chair and headed for Jacobs. “You’re the fucking asshole, Jacobs—you and Slayton. This was meant for me, and you two were behind it.”

I slammed into Jacobs, taking him down to the floor just as easily as I did the clothes racks on Farnsworth Road a short while back.

“You’re a no good fucking murderer. I should kill you! You’re the fucking asshole.” My wrath for Jacobs was so great it took four men to pull me off of the equally powerful Jacobs.

Jacobs climbed to his feet and came after me with equal rage as I was being restrained, pushing the entire pile of men into the wall. “See what your little civic duty just did? You just got a man killed. It would be one thing if we lost a guy working a fire. But losing a guy putting up some fucking stupid street banner?”

Both of us knew what had really happened. My rage was out of passion. His rage was out of cover-up defense.

Both of us were fighting, wrestling, punching, and kicking at one another. It didn’t last long as it took everyone in the firehouse to pull the two of us apart.

The Coventry Fire Department had shit the bed. Someone had the presence of mind to call for mutual aid from Cromwell; surely Coventry was in no position to handle anything at all. It was probably Dan Roberts.

While wiping his mouth with the back of his hand, Jacobs asked, “Any of you guys get that blood on you, you’ll have to go to the hospital too. Way to go, Renaldi. Thanks for sharing,” said an enraged but nervous Jacobs.

I raged one more time, “Fuck you, dickhead! You used to be a firefighter, now you’re just a murderer like your buddy, Slayton. I may have blood all over me, but you have guilt all over you. Who cut the cable? You? Slayton?” Men fought to hold me back. “Did the good doctor pay you to do this?” Finally subdued, I gave way to Dan and other members trying to help him.

Slayton was nowhere to be found. Gutless little Billy Slayton was hiding.

* * *

As soon as I walked into the hospital, the chief and several male orderlies greeted me. There was also a police presence in the hallway. “Lieutenant, you will have to be checked out in a private room, which you will not be allowed to leave. The door will be guarded.”

I stood shaking my head in disbelief. I had nothing left. I was running on empty. Adrenaline had even abandoned me. This must be a dream, a nightmare. *It's time to wake up. Please let me wake up.*

"Chief, I'm all done. Stop this madness. Stop this stupid, crazy, fucking madness. I can't handle this job anymore."

I began sobbing, "Paul Frieze is dead, Chief. I told you they'd stop at nothing, but you just wouldn't believe it. You wouldn't believe it 'cause you're a part of it, Brewster. I can feel it in my bones. You're a no-good fucking part of the chosen few. I was the only guy on your side, and you took me down. May you burn in hell, you no-good bastard!"

Brewster walked out, and I was left in the hands of the medical team, one of the same teams who had collaborated with me as I performed my firefighter duties. I was now on their watch list; they were ready to put me in restraints if need be.

* * *

Jacobs just stared at Slayton as he pulled out of the parking lot toward the hospital. "Jesus Christ, Bill. It's one thing to lie to me, it's another to treat me like a fool. They're going to check that truck, and they're going to see someone tampered with the cable. And who else would be fucking with Renaldi but you? The M-80? The egging of his truck? We're both going to jail over this. You're a fucking asshole!"

"Oh, and you're equating little Halloween pranks with murder? Yeah, that makes sense."

"Well then, if not you, who?"

Slayton smirked. "Oh, I see. You're drawing conclusions because you think I'm the only guy in this world who hates Dom Renaldi. I get it now."

"Slayton, who else has access to that truck? Who else would know who was going to use it when? Who else would know how to mess with it?"

"Well, I guess you have me tried *and* convicted. Funny, but that's not the way the system works, Chief."

"I ain't the chief, asshole. And I don't want to become chief with this kind of shit on my conscience."

"What's on your conscience, Tom? Did *you* cut the cable? I mean, you're the only one talking about such a thing. Maybe it *was* you."

"I can punch you in the side of the head right now while you're driving and kill us both, and I don't know that I'd mind that right about now. I'm out. Finished. I don't need Paul Frieze's blood on my hands."

"This ain't no joke, but you already got it all over you when you provoked Renaldi. As to the cable breaking, accuse me all you like. Bring it on. I didn't do it. It's going to be investigated. They can drag me in because people like you think I hate Renaldi, but that's all you've got."

Jacobs rode in silence, ruminating. "Was it the doctor?"

"Hmmm?"

"The doctor. The guy whose wife Renaldi was banging."

"How the fuck would I know? Besides, if it were, it would be pretty fucked up, don't you think? I mean, he killed an innocent man today. If that ever got traced back to him, he'd go to hell and jail at the same time, you know what I'm saying? He'd have more to lose than any of us. Think about it. Guys like us, we don't have much to begin with. But you take a doctor and pull his license, put him in jail with all these hardened criminal types. That'd be worse than the death penalty." Slayton smirked, then said, "And that would leave the door open for his wife to run around with Renaldi." Slayton followed up with his hideous laugh.

Jacobs didn't laugh but kept staring at Slayton, trying to figure him out, getting more confused and frightened by the minute. "You talked to the doctor, didn't you?"

"I've met the man. He knows me from around town. Why?" Slayton's small grin was confident, yet sinister. Never before had Jacobs been sincerely afraid of Slayton. But now he was.

"Well, we're here. I'll go park the car. Hope you didn't get any blood on my ride."

"It's already all over you. Thanks for the lift."

"Watch out for Renaldi. They may have to sedate him to keep him from charging you again. You really pissed him off, Jacobs. You have to watch how you talk to people sometimes. You say the wrong thing to the wrong guy at the wrong time, and you can really cause problems. Shit like that can come back to haunt you. I'll be there in a minute. I have a phone call to make," said Slayton as he reached for his cell phone.

Jacobs exited the car and headed into the emergency ward while Slayton parked the car, then took out his cell phone. "Hello, MetroWest Mercedes, this is Bill Slayton. Let's go forward with ordering the black CL600 we talked about. That's right, it will be in my name, and the bill will be paid for by someone else, an older, taller man with white hair. Cash, I believe."

* * *

I got home from the hospital just in time to turn on the eleven o'clock news. Just in time to see Dan Rea in front of our fire station. I sat there numbed, trying to watch; but when they showed S-1, I ran to the bathroom and puked!

After a cold shower, I sat in my chair and lifelessly stared into the quiet darkness until the sun came up.

There would be a funeral I'd have to muster for, a funeral I would not miss. To honor my man, the fine young man I was responsible for, I'd find the strength.

I tried to get answers from the firehouse, answers regarding Paul's arrangements, but it was as if I had the bubonic plague. No one would speak to me. I kept calling, and finally, Barbara answered and told me, "We've been ordered not to speak to you, Dom, I'm sorry."

"Thank you, Barbara, I'm glad someone has the balls to say something to me."

Finally, word came to me through an unusual source, one that I should have expected.

Beep beep beep beep beep beep. It was the fire radio. Three times it sounded, followed by the fire alarm operator speaking, "Signal 666 has been struck. It is with deep regret the chief of department announces the death of Firefighter Paul B. Frieze, who was killed in the line of duty."

Paul's wake would be Wednesday and Thursday, from 1400-1600 hours and 1900-2100 hours. The funeral would be on, Friday, at 1000 hours with mass at St. Joseph's at 1100 hours. The procession would then walk to the Maplewood Cemetery for interment. The same route we walked every Memorial Day in the same rinky-dink small town Memorial Day parade. A parade I marched in for several years wearing my Red Sox little league uniform. For the past 20 years I proudly marched in the parade wearing my firefighter's uniform.

This day would be anything but rinky-dink.

Tuesday evening, there was a knock at my door. It was a police officer, Bob Sullivan, from the Coventry Police Department. "Dominic, don't hurt the messenger. No one wanted to do this, some were too afraid, and others thought it to be wrong. The town ordered me to deliver this letter to you."

"Thanks, Bob. No. I know it's not you. Oh, so very well do I know it's not you." We shook hands, and he was gone. Opening the short two-paragraph letter, I sat and began reading it.

> You are hereby notified pursuant to Massachusetts General Laws Chapter 266 Section 120 that you are prohibited from participation in the wake and funeral of Firefighter Paul B. Frieze, of the Coventry Fire Department.
>
> Further, if found to be present at the above-mentioned services, you will be deemed a trespasser and will be arrested.
>
> Snidely Ryan
> Town Manager

I was banned from paying my respects to Paul Frieze. How low could they stoop?

Chapter 33

Feeling like months later, Wednesday afternoon finally arrived. I had wanted to send flowers but wasn't sure how they'd be received, if they'd be received. I had wanted to go to the funeral home but knew I absolutely couldn't. I felt a loss and sorrow deeper inside of me than I'd ever felt before. I felt as if my body wanted to explode; there was no relief valve. There was no work to tire my straining muscles, no Liz Temple to defuse me. My children didn't even call me. I was an island, an uninhabitable island.

Night after night, I sat in mournful solitude. Saddled with guilt and responsibility for Paul's death, I didn't want to eat, drink, or even shower. I must have looked like an alcoholic.

Friday morning, I set out with a plan. Knowing Coventry as well as I did, I would find a way to at least view the procession from afar. Staying under the radar, I borrowed my landlord's car and parked it up Townfaire Way, across the street from St. Joseph's Church; I was early enough not to be seen. In a while, I could drive out the back way, cut across the two-lane highway, and into the school properties where I could park and walk into the cemetery from the backside. This hypocritical town wasn't going to stop me from attending!

It was an awesome sight. Firefighters arrived by the busload—ten, fifteen, twenty, or more. The main road was shut down to traffic. Townspeople gathered to say good-bye to a fallen hero. Coventry Police, Cromwell, Trowbridge, MDC, state police. Boston fire's fife and bugle core was there, their bagpipes playing, amongst other somber songs "Amazing Grace" and "Danny Boy."

Pocket-sized, laminated copies of the Fireman's Prayer were handed out to all.

A Fireman's Prayer

When I am called to duty, God,
Whenever flames may rage;
Give me strength to save a life,
Whatever be its age.

Help me embrace a little child
Before it is too late
Or save an older person
From the horror of that fate.

Enable me to be alert
And hear the weakest shout,
And quickly and efficiently
To put the fire out.

I want to fill my calling
And to give the best in me
To guard my every neighbor
And protect his property.

And if, according to my fate,
I am to lose my life,
Please bless with your protecting hand
My children and my wife. (Author Unknown)

The Coventry and Cromwell ladder trucks were positioned opposite each other in front of the fire station, their aerial ladders extended over the road where they'd touch above the center of the street with an American flag hanging between them.

One hundred yards up the street there must have been one thousand bouquets of flowers left as a makeshift memorial at the tragic site of the accident a few days earlier; Coventry people showing their good side. How ironic the funeral procession would have to drive right over the spot where I did CPR on Paul.

By the time 1100 hours came, there must have been two thousand firefighters lining the street, four deep. Every news station in Boston was there. I so wanted to run right up to them and just blurt out, "Look into this travesty, I beg of you, look into this travesty!" Obviously, I knew better.

Then the hush fell over the crowd as engine 1 came into view while leading the procession down the post road. Its hose bed emptied of hose and now carrying the casket of a fallen warrior as six firefighters stood guard, three on each side of the casket.

In absolute, disgusting hypocrisy of a very sick and demented fire department, Capt. Tom Jacobs and Capt. Bill Slayton stood next to a hero's casket. So valiantly leading, so honorably serving.

I could almost hear that Coventry patron from back in the Double L Steak House, in Cromwell, saying, "Look at how close knit those firemen are. Isn't it wonderful?"

It was too hideous for me. I couldn't handle the hypocrisy any longer, and so I left.

* * *

A few days later I visited Paul's grave and said my good-bye. It was cold and misty. Fog swept through the cemetery. The atmosphere was peculiar, almost spooky. Standing over his final resting place, Paul and I seemed to spiritually connect briefly.

"Why did you have to convince me to let you go up in the bucket, you big cement head?"

A distant eerie voice, a spirit, spoke, "It wasn't your fault. It was just my time to go."

Startled, I looked around to see whose voice it was. Except for me, the cemetery was empty. Shocked and confused, I said, "Paul. Paul, is that you? I'm so sorry, Paul. This was meant for me not for you."

"I know it was meant for you, old man, that's why it's not your fault. That's why I'm not mad at you."

Excited over this out-of-body experience, I said in a rushed and confused voice, "Hey, Paul, I brought my apple strudel recipe, I thought you might like to have it."

"Thanks, buddy, but it's time for me to go. I'll see you in heaven someday, Lieutenant. Together, we can watch those bastards rot in hell."

As quickly as a baby comes to life in your hand, the voice came; and now, just as quickly as a child's life is snatched from your arms, the voice was gone forever.

Falling to the ground, I clutched the headstone and wept.

* * *

Having been out on sick time since the accident, I was ordered to meet with the chief. I sat before Chief Pete Brewster in his office.

Brewster stared down at some papers while straightening those paper clips on his desk. "Jacobs submitted his papers yesterday."

"Halleluiah! Now all we have to do is to get rid of Slayton."

"It seems the selectmen suggested to him that he leave as well. He's taking his accumulated vacation time, then he's history."

Suddenly, I did not have a very good feeling.

"I'm placing you on administrative leave, Lieutenant." Brewster couldn't even look up at me as he continued, "I have consulted with the Town Manager, in fact. This is his plan. He wanted me to do this."

"This is what he wants you to do? Of course, as chief of the department, you fought to send a member in need to rehabilitation of some sort, right, Chief? It's been a fucked-up year, and I did witness a friend, a member, fall to his death."

Brewster rubbed at his mouth and cheeks lethargically. "I have thirty days to clean up my business. Not completely my idea either. But with all the shenanigans going on in this house, then Frieze dying, it all just piled up. The selectmen pretty much gave me an ultimatum. They gave me a six-month umbrella package for being so faithful. I have enough time in to get the maximum, so that's a cue to go before they throw me out. I always wanted to be chief, and I got to for a while. That's all I ever really wanted."

"Good for you, Chief. Just hand them Renaldi on a silver platter, and they'll take good care of you. How courageous, Chief. Is that what the past few years has been all about?"

I got up and walked out without so much as a good-bye. Brewster didn't deserve one. *Damn*, I thought. *Brewster, Jacobs, Slayton, and I, now all gone, who the hell was left to run the department? Maybe they'd go outside the department for some new blood. Lord knows, it could use some.*

I'd been around long enough to know the administrative leave business was just a way for them to get one started out the door. They'd build their case from there. I was finished as a professional firefighter.

Too beaten down to fight any longer, I knew it was time for me to move on. Except for my children, I had already lost everything that ever mattered to me, even they didn't speak to me much anymore. All that was left was my freedom, and it simply wasn't worth it. For now, I'll just ride out this leave while collecting my base pay, 50 percent of what I was accustomed to bringing home. And while on administrative leave, it would be against regulations for me to work on the outside. Times would be very difficult.

I was already a marked man in town. No one wanted to be seen with me, talk to me, or associate with me. Department heads, whom I'd done so much for, walked the other way when they saw me coming. Townspeople ran scared, "We'll be looked down upon at the club, maybe even black balled."

Few on the Coventry Fire Department cared about me anymore; they wouldn't have Dominic Renaldi to kick around. All the new men coming on the job, no additional woman, were being told negative stories about me; the truth, now so distorted, never to be told, or believed.

I walked slowly over to my locker in the bunkroom and cleared out the last of my personal belongings—the pictures of my kids I'd collected over the years while chronicling their growth, a few mementos from school groups who had sent cute thank-you notes over the years, some department records, my commendations I'd received, and whatever else I shoved into my duffle bag. Barbara Pickens stood silently in the hall, a stream of tears running down her cheek. Too fearful to say a word to me, her eye contact expressed her feeling.

I then went to my locker on the apparatus floor to retrieve something still very special to me. How gracious of them to allow Dan Roberts to stand at my side as a silent reminder there were still a few damn good men on this department. Reaching into my helmet, I pulled out that folded piece of paper adorned by the lip-glossed kiss of Liz Temple. Wistfully, I stared at it until it became obvious. Kissing it good-bye, I then tore it up and threw it away. I was finished everywhere!

As I walked toward the exit, I took one final look up into the chief's window overlooking the apparatus floor. Brewster was standing there looking at me while on his cell phone. "Hello, Horace, Pete Brewster here," he said as if wracked in guilt as he watched me walk out.

"Well hello, ole pistol Pete. I presume you have some good news for me?" Humphreys' voice portrayed anticipated victory.

"Yeah, Mission accomplished." Brewster said in a shameful way.

"Well congratulations, Chief. I knew you had it in you." Ruining a man meant nothing to Horace Humphreys.

Brewster paused, then asked, "What about our doctor friend?"

"I just happen to have some good news for you, too, Pete. He's found an associate of his, a doctor friend, who wants to purchase your house for well above asking price, Pete. Will you accept the offer?" Horace Humphreys laughed a loud and egotistical laugh. Brewster hung his head in shame.

Exiting via the very unceremonious side door, well out of the view of others and of the CCTV cameras that kept a watchful eye over the apparatus floor from the fire alarm office, Dan embraced me in a manly hug as he said, "Lieutenant, Renaldi, you are the best goddamn firefighter I have ever known."

"Thanks, Dan, it's been my pleasure working with you. You are a damn good man too." We shook hands and I departed.

As I drove away from the firehouse, with my truck radio always set on the FM oldies station, Elvis came on singing.

And now the end is near
So I face the final curtain
My friend, I'll say it clear
I'll state my case of which I'm certain

I've lived a life that's full
I've traveled each and every highway
And more, much more than this
I did it my way

Regrets, I've had a few
But then again, too few to mention
I did what I had to do
And saw it through without exemption

I planned each charted course
Each careful step along the byway
Oh, and more, much more than this
I did it my way

Yes, there were times, I'm sure you knew
When I bit off more than I could chew
But through it all when there was doubt
I ate it up and spit it out
I faced it all and I stood tall
And did it my way

I've loved, I've laughed and cried
I've had my fill, my share of losing
And now as tears subside
I find it all so amusing
To think I did all that
And may I say, not in a shy way
Oh, no, no not me
I did it my way

For what is a man, what has he got
If not himself, then he has not
To say the words he truly feels
And not the words of one who kneels
The record shows I took the blows
And did it my way
The record shows I took the blows
And did it my way

Welcome to Coventry!

The End